For Claud[e]
lovely lad[y]
my special good
wishes!

Betsy Shaman

HOMESTEAD

An Epic Rich With Emotion In The Post Civil War South

By Betsy Bishop Thomas

georgia v. williams

ISBN: 0-942407-72-5

07 06 05 04 / 10 9 8 7 6 5 4 3 2

Photo of author by Ashley Baudoin
Illustrations by georgia williams

FATHER & SON

PUBLISHING, INC.

4909 N. Monroe Street
Tallahassee, Florida 32303
http://fatherson.com
800-741-2712

In memory of my paternal grandparents,

Victoria Jones Bishop, January 12, 1861 – April 18, 1941
And
Joseph Francis Bishop, August 31, 1849 – January 4, 1944.
They were the *real* homesteaders and taught me much.

And

My maternal grandparents, Melissa Gay Polk and
Robert Alexander Polk who were early settlers and did much
to make Santa Rosa County what it is today.

Also in memory of my parents,

Cles Polk Bishop, May 5, 1907 – September 1, 1978
And
Wade Hampton Bishop II,
September 26, 1900 – January 21, 1983,
who sacrificed much for me to obtain a journalism degree
from Florida State University.

Acknowledgments

To my special friends, Charlotte Neighbors, Judy Driver, Jane and Ballard Daniels, Dr. Christie Hunley, Katherine Wilkinson, Connie Emerson and my minister, Rev. James Ross, who read the manuscript of Homestead and offered valued comments, thank you very much.

A special thank you to my friend, Florence Stacy, who allowed me to read the book to her. We share a deep bond, because of her generosity.

My dear friend, Jean Rivard, not only read the book and encouraged me greatly, but helped in publicity and most of all, provided a gentle listening ear to me for hours during the writing process. Thanks so much.

My daughters, Paige Williams and Ashley Baudoin and their families, the lights of my life, have listened, read and encouraged me from the beginning, and I do love and appreciate you so! You believed in the book from the beginning and leaving you the Homestead legacy gave me my inspiration.

And ... from the very first page, my husband, E. Gordon Thomas III, has delighted in the writing process, given me infinite amounts of encouragement, proof read and cheered me on when it became difficult. You make my life happy and provide a wonderful climate in which to write. Thank you sincerely, my dear.

There have been many others who have shown excitement and interest in the book and caused me to feel the undertaking was worthwhile. You know who you are, and I deeply appreciate all of you.

No book would be possible without a publisher, and I am profoundly fortunate to have become associated with a fine man, A. Lance Coalson, my publisher, and his capable staff at Father & Son Publishing, Inc., in Tallahassee, Florida. Thank you sincerely for believing in me and in Homestead.

To God be all glory!

Special Acknowledgment:

As is often the case in any endeavor, there is one person who has spent countless hours in computer work, proofing, researching and offering helpful suggestions in each phase of writing this book. That person is Richard R. Weaver, my friend and very astute critic. He has attempted to teach me some of his vast computer skills, read each page tirelessly for errors, and is single-handedly responsible for putting it on a computer disk. My deepest appreciation to him.

To Barbara Gay Weaver, his wife and my dear and longtime friend, thank you for tolerating us while we worked for many hours. Your enthusiasm as you read each page was a wonderful encouragement to me. I am deeply grateful to both of you.

Contents

New Love

Nathan York had been plowing since before sun-up except for the few minutes about midday when he stopped under the big oak to eat his lunch. It consisted of two of Miss Mattie's big cathead biscuits; not much for a big man using up energy at the rate he was plowing in the hot sun, but he couldn't stop now to eat supper. He had plans, and time was fast slipping away.

As he pulled the mule into the barnyard, Nate slipped the bridle off, left the plow where he could start again the next morning and headed for the house. He threw the bridle over a peg in the shed as he hurriedly passed by. He could see that Mr. Mac had already thrown down hay for the mule and horse. There was feed in the trough and plenty of water in the old metal syrup kettle now being used as a watering trough.

The well, although only fifteen or sixteen feet deep, was on a good stream and always provided plenty of cool water. He stopped, drank long and hard, and blew the dust out of his nose onto a big, red handkerchief, which doubled at times as a mask against dust storms the wind kicked up. He was plowing a dry field with a heavy clay base, not at all easy work. Nate was tired but strong and ready to continue on with his evening plans.

As he drew a large bucket of the cool water, he unhooked the bucket from the rope, secured the rope and took the bucket into Miss Mattie's washhouse where he would take a bath. His mind was on the evening. He poured that bucket of water into a washtub, then went for another, and another until he had a tub full for his bath. The water was cold, but Nate didn't mind. He sank his parched body into it and began to scrub. Red clay dust was in his ears, his hair and virtually all over, turning the water a slight red as he bathed. It was getting late and Nate had to hurry. Mr. McDougald was letting him take the horse and buggy to the services. They usually started about dark.

Services were at the Tates' that quarter. Nate had not always attended when the circuit-riding Methodist preacher came through to conduct the church services, but there was a reason why he was intent on going tonight. He had spotted Melissa Tate at a gathering a few days before and liked what he saw. She was the oldest of the Tate girls, a small girl with blue eyes and long hair, which curled slightly around her face. Nate thought they were the bluest eyes he'd ever seen. He had not spoken to her, but he sure planned to tonight.

Nate finished his bath and pulled on an old pair of pants he kept in the wash shed for the purpose, then made his way over to his bunkhouse to dress in his best pants and shirt. He didn't have a suit, because blue serge was expensive, but he did have a good pair of shoes. When he finished dressing and combed his dark hair into place, he was a fine specimen of man. He had shaved that morning early, because Mr. Mac would expect him to work until sundown. He was a kind man, but he expected a full day's work for a day's pay, which Nate knew.

Once ready, he went to the barn where he hitched Sam, the horse, to the buggy and prepared to leave. The horse snorted and reared as he put the bridle on him. He had been in the lot all day and was ready for a run.

Mr. Mac appeared around the house just as Nate drove the buggy by on his way.

New Love

"Be careful, Nate," he called. "And say a prayer for us!"

"I will, Mr. Mac, and thanks for letting me have the horse and buggy," he answered.

Sam was rearing to go, so Nate let him have as much slack as he wanted to get into a good trot. It was a perfect evening as he started the horse down the lane from the McDougald homestead and headed toward the Tates'. A slight breeze was blowing which would keep the horse from getting too lathered. The sun, a huge, red ball, was just falling behind the trees and crickets were beginning to chirp. Now and then a frog could be heard in the pond at the end of the McDougald property as Sam started on down the narrow, little, sandy road. The road had two white ruts with a grassy mound in the middle. It was easy to follow even on a rather dark night. Nate gave Sam a lot of rein, leaving him to his thoughts, which of late had turned rather serious.

Nate, at thirty-three, had begun to realize he needed to make a move toward getting himself a wife and settling down. The government had made large tracts of land available recently for homestead, which Nate saw as his opportunity to acquire a place of his own. He knew that would be the only way. Nate's parents had been killed in what was described as an Indian "raid" when he was just fifteen in northern Alabama. Neighbors took his two younger sisters in to raise, but he was fifteen and considered to be a man in that day and age, capable of fending for himself. He was thankful to be six feet tall, muscular and able to do a good day's work that he found would get him by, but he could never save enough to buy a place of his own at that rate. He could not support his sisters, either, although he was devastated at having to give them up to strangers to raise. As time went by, he drifted on down to northwest Florida looking for jobs and found work with Mr. Tom McDougald and Miss Mattie. They had a bunkhouse of sorts where he could stay, although it had little heat in winter and little ventilation in summer. A potbellied stove provided what heat he had in winter.

Homestead

It was nearly dark as they pulled into the lane at the Tate home. Other horses and horses with buggies were tied here and there in the lane. He threw the reins over a picket in the fence as he hurried up the big steps and into the house. He was a little late for the church service. The small congregation was singing the first hymn. Lamplight illuminated the front room and people were fanning themselves with small cardboard fans cut from packing cartons, or whatever they could find, since it was a warm spring night.

People were on the porch trying to hear through the windows as the preacher began to preach, but Nate wanted to be inside where he could hopefully get a glimpse of Melissa Tate. He had to sit in the corner nearest the door, having arrived too late to get further into the room. His eyes had to adjust to the lamplight, but then he saw her sitting beside her mother in the second row of ladder-back chairs which had been brought from the kitchen or wherever they could be found about the house. She had on a pale blue dress, no doubt to match the blue of her eyes, although he couldn't see her face. Her hair was piled high on her head because of the warm evening. Little curls fell around her face, and he knew her cheeks were pink from the warmth in the room.

When the service was over, Nate realized he hardly knew what the sermon was about. His thoughts had been of the small girl, with the tiny waist, who looked like a doll in the soft glow of the lamplight. He had imagined touching her skin, her hair and encircling her waist with his large hands. Tremors ran through his body as he sat there trying ever so hard to pull his thoughts back to the sermon. He thought of how it would be to hold her in his arms, kiss the lips that had a slight fullness to them and cuddle her to him on a cold night. He thought of the loneliness he had felt since losing his parents and leaving his two little sisters with virtual strangers so long ago.

"Howdy," a voice said to him, drawing him back to the present. "Reckon you ain't been to a service before," the man next to him said. "Name's Rogers, Franklin Rogers. I live south of here about five miles."

Rogers was extending his hand when finally Nate thought of where he was and what the man was saying. He took Franklin Rogers' hand and shook it, all the while wanting to break away and seek out Melissa Tate before she disappeared into the back of the house.

"Nathan York," he said. "I live up the way. Work for Mr. McDougald."

"Glad to meet you," Rogers said. "You staying for the refreshments?"

"Yeah, I guess I am." He was edging away. "Glad to know you. Be seeing you around," he said to the friendly man.

Rogers appeared to be about his own age, but balding and rough in appearance. Nate was a work hand who did manual labor, but he had a certain refinement he had gotten from his mother. In her few short years on the earth, she had done a remarkable job bringing up her son and teaching him about the finer things of life such as manners and good behavior in company. He was, in effect, a gentleman. He was also quite handsome, although he was not aware of that fact, which added greatly to his charm.

Melissa Tate had no idea anyone had his eye on her. She was helping her mother serve lemonade when Nate entered the dining room and stood watching her. He loved the way she moved and especially the slight rise of her breast that showed just above the low neck of her dress. He was waiting for the nerve to go up to her and speak when she looked up and smiled at him. He began making his way over to the table where she would pour him a drink.

"Good evening, Miss Melissa," he said, finding his voice almost hoarse with nervousness. She was even lovelier up close, and his heart seemed to be beating right out of his chest. He felt sure she could see it beating! "You don't know me, but my name is Nathan York, and I work for Mr. McDougald up at the general store. I'm his farm hand." Nate knew he was talking too fast, but he wanted to get everything said before she turned away. He feared she would not be interested in him. "They call me Nate."

"Hello, Nathan York. Nate. I see that you already know my name." She smiled broadly revealing teeth so white they hardly appeared real. "Do you live at Mr. McDougald's?"

"Yes. I live in his bunkhouse. I help in the store when I'm not working the farm." He could hardly take his eyes off this lovely girl. Somehow he wanted her to know that he was not just a plow hand. Working in the store elevated him a bit, he thought, even though that was rare. Mr. Mac seemed to seldom leave the place. When he did, it was a welcome change for Nate to run the store — a lot better than plowing!

Nate knew he'd better arrange to see this young lady again before leaving for the evening. She kept very busy pouring lemonade and passing tea cakes to the guests while Nate sipped his drink and wolfed down as many cakes as he dared. He was ravenously hungry after working all day and not having supper.

Finally, Melissa managed to work her way back to the area where Nate stood. No doubt she had realized he'd hardly taken his eyes off her since entering the room. He was wondering how old she was; certainly not over sixteen. My, she was well developed, he kept thinking.

"Could I pour you another glass?" she was asking. Nate was glad the glasses were large.

"Yes, ma'am. Please." He extended his glass. Melissa's hand trembled a little as she poured "Ah, Miss Melissa. I was wondering if I could come calling on you one day? Like Sunday afternoon, maybe?"

"I would like that. Why don't you come to Sunday dinner?" Her eyes met his in a steady gaze.

"Yes. Sure. Yes, ah, what time?" he was stammering. This was more than he had hoped for, and he was not prepared for an invitation to Sunday dinner. "Uh, what time?" he managed to ask. He realized he was repeating himself in his eagerness. After being told to be there for Sunday dinner about the noon hour, Nate said goodnight and started for the buggy. He noticed others departing as he slipped the reins from over the fence picket and prepared to get into the buggy. He knew he needed to hurry along home because he had to work again the next day in the field, but he wanted to take his time going home and think about the future. Sam wanted to nip a blade or two of tender new grass in the middle of the road now and then, which Nate let him do. It was getting cooler, as spring nights do, so he pulled the buggy lap robe up around his shoulders and enjoyed the evening. The four miles home gave him plenty of time to think. All the homesteads were pretty far apart, so there were no houses between the Tates' and the McDougalds'. He was glad it had turned out to be a clear night so that he could go. The buggy would be little protection in a hard rain. As soon as he was out of sight of the house and danger of another traveler coming along, he stopped the buggy, got off and relieved himself, then hurried Sam along.

It was after midnight when he put Sam in the lot and returned to the bunkhouse for the rest of the night. Sleep came quickly in spite of his excitement and the ache he felt in his groin.

The Tate household settled down after the service when all the visitors had gone. Melissa and her younger sister, Mary, shared a bed in the little back shed room. It only took Mary a few deep breaths to fall asleep while Melissa lay wide-eyed in the cool darkness thinking. She liked Nathan York! He was big, strong and yet with a gentleness that women appreciate in a man. There were not many men living at the neighboring homesteads for some reason. It seemed most of their neighbors had girls, some of whom ended up old maids because there were not enough men to go around. Yes, Melissa was excited and looking forward to Sunday. She must not forget to tell her mother there would be an extra mouth to feed at the table for Sunday dinner.

Homestead

Tom McDougald and his wife, Mattie, were highly regarded among the homesteaders of the area. They had migrated down to the area from Georgia, where the McDougalds had been in the mercantile business for the past two generations. After Tom's father died, he took his share of the estate and managed to put up and stock his general store on his homestead in an area called Fox Hollow community. Tom and Matilda, who had always been called Mattie, had two daughters, both of marriage age, but both quite homely. Tom had really hoped Nate might be taken with one of the girls at least, but he suspected Nate had his eyes on the Tate girl. He had been mighty anxious to get down there for the church service. He couldn't picture a young feller like that riding four miles to hear a traveling preacher after the day he put in out in that field. He was one of the best workers Tom had ever had, and it would be good to have Callie or Pearl marry a man like that to help around the place. Tom made a mental note to mention to Nate that there might be a certain interest in the place awarded to a young man who would marry a McDougald girl. So far, Callie, who was twenty-seven, and Pearl, who was twenty-five, had had no suitors. He and Mattie were getting older, which caused him concern. If something should happen to him, what would the girls do? They would have the place with nobody to run it. Perhaps if he mentioned as much to the girls, they could put forth a little more effort in the direction of Nathan York; not that Pearl hadn't already been working in that direction.

At breakfast he asked, as Callie poured his second cup of strong, black coffee out of the mottled, blue percolator, "Have you made any eyes at Nate lately, daughter?"

"Daddy!" Callie exclaimed. "Why would you say a thing like that?" She was blushing from below the neck of her scooped-neck dress all the way to her scalp.

"Well, I just got to thinking last night. He took off from here in a mighty fast trot last night going down to the Tate's. You know they have a pretty little daughter getting about the right age to be getting married." He gave Callie a sidelong look as she sat down beside him at the table. "You girls had better be looking about. If anything happened to me or your mother, you might have to take over running the store and the farm. I'm already past the days of plowing all day."

"I get to run the store!" Pearl yelled from the pantry. "Callie can plow the farm!"

"I want to go to Mobile and train to be a nurse, Daddy. You know that," Callie said. "I will be twenty-eight in three more months. When are you going to let me go?"

"It's your ma, not me, who is the hang-up. Talk to her."

Mattie was just entering the kitchen in her dressing gown. She was still tired from cleaning house the day before. The girls helped, but it still wore her out.

"You are just going to keep on, aren't you Callie Mae?" She was about ready to give in. "Lord knows, there is not anything for you to do hereabouts, so I guess we might as well let you go."

Her mother had been hearing this plea from Callie for the last five years. She reckoned it was about time to help her along with the plan.

"Write to the Infirmary, and find out what we have to do to get you there," she said.

"Whee!" Callie shrieked. "Did you hear that little sister?"

"I heard," was all Pearl could say. What, she wondered, will become of me? I will sit right here in Fox Hollow and dry right up on the vine! But maybe not. Maybe not.

After the girls left the kitchen, Mattie turned to Tom with another matter that had been weighing heavily on her mind. "Tom, you know the Chavers children that lost their mama a few weeks ago?"

"Yes. I remember. Why? How does that concern us?" He knew perfectly well how it concerned them and what Mattie wanted to do about it.

"They have been staying around and about the community here lately with no real place to go. I was just thinking..." She paused.

"Yes, go on," he responded knowing also what was coming.

"I think we should adopt them. Just take them in and give them a good home. We can afford it, Tom. It's not like we can't."

"All right. If that's what you want. How old are they?"

Mattie was not sure of their exact ages, but she answered as best she could. "I think Rose is nine and Ben is five."

"We will do it", he answered, "But you had better talk to the girls about it and see how they feel. I don't want to be the one to tell them."

Mattie was a step ahead of him. "I already have, and they feel exactly as I do. We can afford to do that, and we should."

"Very well. We will look into it immediately."

Tom had known all along what Mattie wanted to do. She was a good woman. She had wanted to have more children, but after Pearl was born, they just never were able to have any more.

As Pearl looked out across the wide expanse of the farm, she could see the sun peeking up over the pines in the distance. Nate was sleeping mighty late this morning. Just about the time she finished that thought, he knocked on the outside kitchen door.

"Good morning, Nate," Pearl said as he entered for breakfast.

The others had left the kitchen to start their daily routine, leaving Pearl to serve Nate his breakfast. He looked sleepy and was still rubbing his eyes against the morning sunlight, which was streaming into the kitchen.

"Callie cooked this morning. We have sausage, eggs and biscuits." She was already pouring his coffee.

"You were out mighty late last night," she chided as he sat down at the end of the long table. Placing a plate laden with food in front of him, Pearl then sat right beside him despite the fact the rest of the table was empty.

"I went to the church service," was all he cared to answer.

"Yeah, church service. I know how religious you are, Nathan York!" Nate kept his head down, concentrating completely on his food.

Pearl bumped her shoulder into his. "You know there are things going on around here that could be mighty interesting if anyone wanted to notice them."

Nate had noticed all right. Pearl had big lips, too curly hair and a very large bosom. She was what he would call buxom and not at all to his liking. He preferred the more dainty kind of girl; a girl with a gentle nature, not a forward one. Pearl made up her mind to keep trying, even though it was clear he was not interested that morning. He made quick work of his food and excused himself from the table. "I'll be seeing you, Miss Pearl," he said as he hurried on to his job at hand. You sure will, Pearl was thinking.

Pearl had little interest in domestic things. She had many books that she had gotten at the Normal School in Creighton, where she and Callie went after they completed the six grades in the little country school for the homestead children. Pearl was just a wee bit lazy and preferred to read whenever possible.

Callie set right in writing to the Mobile Infirmary to find out about going there to become a nurse. Mattie began thinking about her clothes. She guessed she'd better go out to the store and get materials to start making her some new dresses. She had plenty, but she was going to want new ones. Mattie would worry about Callie in a big city like Mobile. She, herself, had only been there once with her parents, and she would be scared to death to be alone in that place. Hopefully, the Infirmary would have ladies to watch over the young ladies who were there in training. She was thinking about the house and how empty it would be without Callie. She was sometimes hard to get along with, but she was also the best cook and took a lot of burden off Mattie's shoulders in that respect. She sighed as she went about her work of the day.

Homestead

When Nate brought the mule and plow into the barn that afternoon as the sun was setting, he was too tired to take a bath, but he knew he had to. The dust had blown that day in the spring wind even more than usual. He had a fine coating of the red dust all over him and could feel dirt even in his shoes. He had drawn water for his bath and was just about to begin removing his clothes when he heard the creak of the washhouse door. Nate had not put the latch on the door, but that had never been necessary. Everyone on the place respected each other's privacy, but maybe someone didn't realize he had gone in to take his bath. As he whirled around in the late afternoon darkness of the windowless shed, he realized who it was. In the next second a soft, voluptuous body was against him and was grasping his hand.

"Miss Pearl!" he whispered hoarsely. Wondering if some of the family had seen her going into the shed, he struggled as arms went about his neck and she pressed her body to him. "Miss Pearl," he admonished, "you don't want to do this!"

He didn't want to embarrass her, but he certainly was not going to get into anything with his boss's daughter. He desperately needed a job and a place to stay. Nate was not very experienced in the world of women, but he knew enough to know that was not the way to go.

"Miss Pearl, I'm just covered in field dirt. I gotta get a bath. Please go. Please ma'am." He was imploring her not to go any further.

Pearl was not experienced either, but she knew she wanted Nathan York in the worst way; so badly that she took his hand and placed it between her breasts and began rubbing her leg against his. Nate felt things begin to happen that he couldn't control, and before he knew it, she was pulling her dress up and trying to force him back onto an old table used to sort clothes in the washroom. Nate was horrified and yet raw desire was welling up in him. He knew very shortly he would not be able to get off this runaway train.

"Stop it!" he commanded pushing her in his panic with one big thrust against the wall. She landed so hard it almost took her breath away, but it was effective. She gave a little shriek and rushed for the door. Nate slid the latch on the door into the catch and sank down on the table to get himself together before going ahead with his bath. He had never had such an encounter and hoped he never would again. Frightened and shocked, he prayed she would not tell her family anything about what had happened. He felt fairly certain she wouldn't. The shame would be on her if she told the truth, but what if she told it another way that she had gone to the washhouse and he had attacked her! Nate's heart was in his throat. It would be his word against hers. Please, God, he prayed, don't let that happen.

Pearl ran into the house. Her sister was in the kitchen preparing the evening meal when she burst through the door. "What on earth got in behind you?" she asked. Pearl continued on to her room without answering, leaving Callie to shake her head in wonder.

Nate dreaded going to supper, but he had to eat, which he did in nearly complete silence, then excused himself from the table and went to his quarters. He had clothes to wash, which he used as an excuse for his rapid departure from the table. Nobody seemed to think anything of it. Pearl had a headache and wasn't interested in supper.

Homestead

The Courting

Sunday was another lovely early spring day. Nate got out of bed early, shaved and went over to the main house for breakfast. He had been making himself scarce around there since his incident with Pearl. She was sullen around him on the few occasions they happened to be alone together, and he was as nervous as could be. He was thankful those meetings didn't occur often. The rest of the household didn't seem to notice.

The McDougalds were going into Creighton to church. It was a small town ten miles north which had the only Methodist church within eighty miles of Fox Hollow. It took a half day to get to town, so they always left early on Sunday morning in the buggy and sometimes stayed over with fellow church friends until Monday morning. Nate would take care of the rest of the stock, feeding the chickens, the mule and a couple of cows. He had to leave early also, and take the wagon since he would have only the mule to pull it; not quite as classy a way to travel as the buggy for sure. The wagon was much slower, and it was hard to keep Pete, the mule, from stopping to eat grass along the way. He plowed better than the horse, but when it came to pulling a wagon or buggy, he'd take the horse any day. Nate was looking forward to having his own horse. He hoped, when Mr. Mac paid him at the end of the month, to have enough to buy one. He had heard of a place down the way that might have a horse for sale. Someone had stopped at the store and mentioned it. Mr. Mac saw people all the time at the store, and he knew people for miles around. He had the only store in a ten-mile radius of Fox Hollow.

Melissa was up early, too. She helped get breakfast and straighten the house. The yard, which began where the lane ended, had white sand all over. There was not a blade of grass anywhere. If one grew, her mother quickly got the hoe and cut it down. Once a week, usually on Friday or Saturday, she would take her gallberry-brush broom and sweep the sandy yards clean of all leaves and trash. Sometimes Melissa helped her, or one of the other girls would make a pass at it, but Lily Tate was a perfectionist. She wanted her yards as clean as she could get them, not half swept as the younger girls would do.

The family and visitors tracked the white sand onto the porch and into the house as well, which necessitated sweeping everything thoroughly. This Melissa did cheerfully today. She had a lilt in her walk as she went about her chores. Someone had stepped in a spot of chicken manure, no doubt coming from the privy, and tracked it onto the porch, so Melissa got a dipper of water from the rain barrel, wet the spot and swished it away. Things had to look especially good this particular Sunday.

When Melissa heard the wagon coming, rattling along the sandy road, she dropped her embroidery and hurried out back to the privy. She would die before she would go after Nate got there. She had on her best voile dress. It was white with a pale blue flower pattern about the size of a fingernail scattered about and just tight enough to accentuate her tiny waist yet leave plenty of room for her breasts at the top. Melissa had gotten the curse the day before. Why did that have to happen just before a special day like this! For that matter, why did it have to happen at all?

The whole Tate family was on hand to meet and welcome Nate. He felt ill at ease as he secured the mule and wagon and entered the yard, but he felt exhilarated at the same time. Melissa was standing on the porch. He thought he had never seen anyone so beautiful. Her hair was down nearly to her waist. She had the creamy kind of complexion, and he was in love! He knew for sure he had never felt this way before. Of course, he had only called on two other girls before, neither of whom he was very taken with or wanted to marry.

Melissa made the introductions, then her family removed themselves one by one from the porch making excuses that they were fixing Sunday dinner.

"How are you today?" he asked.

"I am fine. Would you care to sit in the swing?" came her awkward reply." "I like to swing, don't you?" She led the way to the swing and sat down, holding the swing still as he sat.

"It is a mighty nice day." Nate wished he could think of something interesting to say. He knew what he wanted to say, but it was way too soon to say anything like that. They talked about the weather, his work in the field at Mr. Mac's, and her plans for the summer. She had gone as far as she could go in the school two miles from the house where all the children from the nearby homesteads went. It had six grades, all in one room, with one teacher. Melissa thought she would like to be a teacher, but where? There were no other schools, and the Catawba school had Miss Jessica Brown, who showed no signs of leaving.

Nate hated to tell her he could neither read nor write. He had no chance to attend school as a child, because his family moved too frequently with his father's work. Neither his mother nor his father could read or write; so they couldn't teach him. The plan had been for Nate to have some schooling as soon as they were able to settle down in north Alabama, but his parents were killed before that could happen.

Schools were few and far between, making it very difficult for children whose parents had to move often. Nate helped his mother from the time he was five as she tried to do what she could toward making a living. One year, he remembered painfully, they had been living near a potato farm where they picked up potatoes for the landowner after they were plowed up by a man with a mule. His father worked for the lumber company, cutting and loading timber on a flat car. As soon as one tract was cut, they moved to another area. Sometimes they had to transport the timber by wagons pulled with mules to the railroad and then load it onto flat cars. They moved sometimes once a month, most often to remote areas where there were no schools.

Thinking about it, Nate thought it better to go ahead and tell Melissa this rather than wait until later. She took the news without batting an eye. Few people were able to get any education, so it was not unusual. Times had been so hard that most people had to work instead of having the luxury of going to school.

Mary came out to tell them dinner was ready before too much time elapsed. They were both grateful for the interruption. Nate held Melissa's chair for her, a grace his mother had taught him, and one that impressed the young lady as well as her family. Everyone participated in the conversation, which helped greatly to get the couple through the next hour. Fried chicken, creamed potatoes, turnip greens and corn bread seemed like a banquet to Nate who had not eaten much in the past few days.

Mr. Tate asked him about his past. Nate explained about his family coming from Georgia to north Alabama where they had hoped to settle and stay. His father wanted to homestead and built a small cabin on the land. Before he could attend to getting the homestead process started, though, he and Nate's mother were killed, on their way from the nearest town where they had gone for supplies by marauding Indians. He told about how his sisters were taken in by neighbors who lived several miles away and how he had tried to stay on at the cabin, but had to go out eventually and look for work. He worked in several sawmills and made his way on down to northwest Florida, where he had heard homesteads were available.

The Courting

Mr. Tate allowed as how there were tracts of land still available. Nate explained that he had been saving his wages since coming to work for Mr. Mac and hoped to buy a horse this next payday.

"Tom McDougald is a fine man to work for, and Miss Mattie's a fine lady," Mr. Tate told Nate.

"Yes sir, he's been good to me. I plan to buy my tools and supplies from him when I get ready to build a house." Nate announced that as if he were going to start right away and wishing he could. It was not uncommon for a father-in-law to help his son or daughter and their mate get started, either. That was about the only way for young people to get a start in those days. Nate dared to hope.

Mr. Tate was a landman for the government, which meant he went about the area watching for timber poachers who stole timber off government land and reported them. He was gone sometimes for a week or two at a time and often had to go to Milton, where he testified in trials against poachers. It was not a job that made him popular with certain people, but it did pay reasonably well. It fed his family.

After dinner was over, Nate helped clear away the dishes, carrying them in to the kitchen table. The younger girls had the assignment of washing dishes today while Melissa had company. They didn't appear too happy over the task but got right to it. A big enamel pan on the wood stove held water and lye soap ready to clean the dishes. Mary washed while her sister dipped them in another pan of hot water to rinse them. The lye soap was certainly effective where sanitizing things was concerned, but it was also terribly hard on hands.

Melissa led the way back to the front porch where a cool breeze was blowing. Again they sat in the swing. The rest of the family found other things to do instead of sitting on the porch that day. Nate, wanting to pay her a compliment, said "Miss Melissa, you sure do have pretty blue eyes." Melissa blushed, as usual, hating herself for doing that, and murmured, "Thank you." He also wanted to tell her that her skin looked like cream, her teeth were very white, and that he wanted to squeeze her to pieces, but he decided that would have to be reserved for later.

As the afternoon wore on, it became much warmer, so Melissa suggested they walk down to the spring and get the lemonade that had been placed there earlier to cool. The Tates had a spring box. It was made of wood, about three feet by three feet square and built right up where the water came out of the hillside. It was ice cold and kept their milk, buttermilk, butter and other drinks cold and refreshing all summer. John Tate had built it. He made a lid heavy enough that an animal couldn't push it off and get into the box. The Tate girls loved to go to the spring. They often waded a while without their shoes, splashing each other and running in the shallow, cold water. There were some deep places perfect for taking a bath. It was almost routine to take baths there in the summer, but it was a little cool for that right now. Sometimes there were frosts in early April in northern Florida.

The spring was at the foot of a very steep hill. On the way down, Melissa's shiny, black patent shoes began to slip and Nate had to catch her. Perhaps he let his hand linger on her waist a little longer than was necessary. Finally, Melissa reached out her hand to him for assistance so that he held it the rest of the way down the hill. He had the greatest desire to pull her to him and kiss her hard on the lips, but he knew that would be highly premature. After they got to the bottom of the hill, Nate continued to hold her soft hand, which Melissa made no effort to take back from him.

There were birds everywhere chirping the news that spring had arrived. Somewhere nearby, a crow was cawing loudly, telling the rest of the bird population that strangers were in their midst. New growth filled the trees out where they had been bare from the cold. Near the edge of the spring a clump of wild honeysuckle was blooming. Their sweet smell, combined with the heavy smell of the bay blossoms, gave the entire area a perfumed quality. Pollen from the pines nearby had floated through the air and drifted into small banks along the foot of the hill and in the edge of the little stream. It formed bright yellow rivulets everywhere.

Nate kicked at a rotten log near the stream, causing crickets, bugs and a field mouse to run to the nearest cover of leaves nearby. Stately, old magnolias and tall, towering bay trees graced the creek bed area and the adjoining hillside. They preferred the wet areas, whereas the pines liked the high ground. They had long taproots that could find the water easily from the dry land.

As Melissa bent over to get the lemonade out of the box, a crayfish backed away from the box. She let out a little squeal that made Nate laugh. He could see the lace at the top of her camisole when she bent over and couldn't help but enjoy the lovely sight of her bosom bulging above her low-necked dress.

The couple enjoyed the activity and aliveness of the spring area. Nate leaned over almost too far to pick Melissa a bay blossom and nearly fell into the stream. She laughed at him then as he righted himself by catching onto a nearby branch. "That's poison, you know!" Melissa teased. Nate knew it wasn't. He put the tiny miniature magnolia into her hair and, again, almost kissed her, still thinking better of the idea.

"This would be a great place to make a swimming hole," he told her. "Did your dad ever think about digging it out?"

"No, I think he thought it would be too much work. Besides, he is not home long enough to do something like that." Melissa hated the idea that her father was gone as much as he was. Being a landman had a number of drawbacks. One was the inherent danger of the job.

"If we stand here any longer, this lemonade will be boiling," Nate told her. They both laughed at that idea and started back up the long, steep hill. Once again, Nate assisted by pulling Melissa along when the going got harder. She loved the feel of his strong hand even though it was rough from hard work.

Homestead

When they reached the house, Melissa told Nate to have a seat on the porch while she got glasses for the lemonade. He offered his assistance, which she declined. Melissa practically ran to the kitchen, set the jar down and flew to the privy. She would not excuse herself and go to the privy with a man around, so she hurried to keep him from realizing where she had gone.

Nate sat thinking about the serenity of the cool front porch, the pecan trees adjoining the yard and the long blooms on them. It looked as if there would be a bumper crop that fall. Now and then he swatted a hungry yellow fly who wanted to have lunch on his leg.

As the sun began to get lower in the sky, Nate told Melissa he must go. They went to find her mother so that he could thank her for the Sunday dinner. Lily Tate was piecing quilt scraps, one of her favorite things to do, and getting ready to put a quilt into the frame the next week for quilting. It was a great time when anyone in the vicinity got a quilt ready to quilt. The ladies would come from every homestead in the area to help quilt. It was one of the social events everyone looked forward to most. Lily, who was a perfectionist, though, hated for some of the ladies to quilt her quilts. They weren't careful enough, got in too big a hurry and made stitches entirely too long. When they left, Lily would spend hours taking out their stitches and replacing them with her tiny ones.

Melissa opened the door to the sitting room.

"Mama, Nathan would like to say good-bye."

Nate stuck his head in the door. "Good-bye, Mrs. Tate, and thank you for a most delicious dinner. I will be going now."

Lily looked up over her tiny, gold-rimmed spectacles. "Good-bye, Nathan. Come again," was her only reply.

As Nate walked to the edge of the porch, he took Melissa's hand again and kissed it. "Miss Melissa, I have enjoyed the afternoon greatly. Could I come again?"

"If you would care to, I'd like that. But first you have to stop calling me *Miss* Melissa." She gave him one of her smiles that made his heart leap.

It was nearly dark when Nate put up the wagon, gave the mule a bunch of hay and got to the main house for supper. When he entered the kitchen, there were two children sitting at the table, a girl about nine and a boy who looked to be about six. Tom McDougald pulled out a chair. "Here Nathan. Have a seat and meet our two new children. Our family is growing!" Nate was surprised to see the poor little things. The little girl didn't look up. She was intent on her food, as was the boy. They were frail children who looked as if they had not had a good meal in a month. Both children had dirty, stringy hair, and the boy needed a haircut something awful. Nate was puzzled, which must have shown on his face.

"They lost their Mamma and Daddy, so Mattie and I are going to adopt them. Have adopted them," Tom explained. "You remember the fire that burned the man and his wife to death about ten months ago over at Pollard? Well, that was their parents. The man got the children and went back in to try and get his wife, but the roof collapsed and they both burned to death," he explained graphically. Nate shuddered. He remembered all too well when his own parents were killed by the Indians, and he thought Mr. Mac could have been a little more tender. He studied the childen as he said, "Howdy, kids. My name's Nate. Glad to meet you." Neither child looked up. They were not exactly dirty, but their clothes were shabby and unkempt. He knew Miss Mattie would get them fixed up right away, though. He felt they were lucky children who had come to the right family.

Callie spoke up and told Nate the little girl's name was Rose and the boy's name was Ben. Pearl said nothing. Miss Mattie was busy hovering over them to be sure they had milk and plenty of food on their plates. Both ate a hearty meal in spite of their obvious discomfort at being in a new household. All this brought the sadness back into Nate's heart from leaving his own little sisters. At least they were both taken in by the same family. He had gone to see them several times before he got too far away. Having no money or transportation prevented him from seeing them often. He knew Jane would be about twenty-five now and Martha about twenty-three. He figured both had married if they had the opportunity and resolved once again to try to find them when he could afford it.

As the spring wore on and changed into summer, Nate made a number of trips to see Melissa. In fact, if he could get the horse and buggy or mule and wagon, he went, and now and then he walked the four miles on Sunday, which was his only day off, and if the weather was good.

At the store, Mr. Mac had heard of a man down the way who had a couple of fine horses he wanted to sell. He told Nate about it, knowing Nate was planning to buy one as soon as he could. "How much does he want?" was Nate's first question.

Mr. Mac hadn't found out the cost, but said one of his neighbors usually came to the store every other Tuesday to get supplies and he would ask the man's neighbor. Tuesday was the next day. Nate got excited. The idea that he might get his horse was a thrill. He could ride to see Melissa, and also ride her on the back, letting her hold on to him. He had his dad's saddle. That was one thing the Indians had not destroyed. His parents had been in the wagon with the horse pulling it. The saddle was left at home and escaped being taken, but the horse and wagon were never seen again. Nate had always doubted it was Indians who had killed his parents. He strongly felt it was white men. Others in the community had felt the same way by the nature of the killing. They were both shot in the back — not an Indian way of murdering someone. Besides, the Indians and white men had lived together peacefully for a number of years in that area. There had been no law anywhere, about making it impossible to track down the killers. It was just by the mercy of God that Nate and the girls had not been with their parents. They would have been killed, too, in all probability.

The Courting

The crop was pretty well laid by, and Nate was helping Mr. Mac in the store more now that late summer had come, making it possible to be there when the Jarvis fellow came in the next day to get his wagon load of supplies. Nate helped load sacks of flour, sugar, cans of lard and other staples. Mr. Mac told Mr. Jarvis Nate wanted to buy a horse. "Well, my neighbor, Paul Robinson, has a couple for sale. Why don't you go down and look 'em over?"

Nate got directions. He had never been that far south before, but Mr. Mac said he had and would take Nate down there in the buggy. If he got a horse, then he could ride back home. "Do you know how much he is asking?" Nate queried.

"About ten dollars a piece, I believe," Jarvis answered. Nate was more thrilled than ever! He had close to fifty dollars saved. He had been thinking horses cost more than that.

After Jarvis left, Mr. Mac told Nate he could get Callie or Pearl to keep the store the next day while they went down to look at the horse. Nate would put the saddle in the back of the buggy and they would set out early before it got too hot. Mr. Mac said he would get Mattie to make a couple of her big cathead biscuits with ham to eat at noon. It would take most of the day to get there and back with the buggy. The horse could rest and cool off while they looked at the Robinson horses. They always took along a feedbag for Pete at noon, too. He could drink at any or all of the small creeks they had to ford along the way.

It was a clear day, promising to be hot later on, when Nate and Mr. Mac set out for the Robinson homestead. Nate could hardly contain his excitement. If he got the horse, he would detour off by the Tates' to show Melissa. He also wanted to find out when John Tate was going to get home from his work with the government.

The two men talked as they rode along. Tom let Nate drive the buggy while he took it easy. It got hot as the day wore on and the sun was shining right in their faces because they were going right into it on their way south. Nate told Tom of his plans, that he wanted to marry Melissa but had no way to get a home until he got started on a homestead of his own. Tom listened intently, thinking as Nate talked. He well remembered striking out on his own and having help from his father's small estate. He knew the boy had to have help if he were going to be able to get a start.

"Tell you what, son. I will give you a day off soon so that you can go to Milton to the land office and see about getting started on a homestead," Mr. Mac told him. Milton was a tiny settlement about twenty-five miles south on the Black River. It had a small dock where skiffs and other boats docked to load and drop off supplies. People came from all over the country to trade, making it a likely place for a county seat, but that would come later. Florida had just become a state in 1845. Nate knew that would be a two or three day trip on a horse, so he would have to plan that ahead. The crop was finished, but there would be gathering time coming right up shortly. Corn had to be picked, velvet beans gathered and peanuts dug. Mr. Mac would get help in from neighboring families to pick the peanuts. Once dug, they had to be pulled off the small bush manually. That was drudgery, but it was easy for children who didn't have to stoop as far. It was backbreaking for grown-ups. He assumed the new McDougald children would help. They had settled in and were now feeling more sure of themselves and had become friendly. Nate talked to them as he was doing chores about the place. Ben especially liked Nate, following in his footsteps every chance he got. He loved to ride in the wagon when Nate hauled things about the place. They both had tans from spending so much time in the sun, giving them a healthy glow lately.

Nate hadn't gone so far as to say so, but Tom got the strong feeling that he wanted to propose to Melissa Tate soon. The horse was just step one. A horse was a necessity about a homestead. He could be used to move timber for building a cabin, planting a patch or whatever the need happened to be. Tom told Nate he would help by lending him tools until he could afford to buy his own. He assumed, rightly, that Nate would buy them from him at the store.

The horses were out in a nearby pasture when Nate and Tom got to the Robinson homestead. The men walked out, stepped over the low split-rail fence and Paul called the horses. They came at once. Nate had a handful of corn in his pocket, which he offered to each horse. One was black and white, the other solid black and sleek and shiny. It was love at first sight between him and the big black stallion.

"I want this one!" he announced to the men, who were watching and smiling. It was pretty obvious which horse he wanted from the start. "I am going to call him Dewey," Nate told the onlookers. Dewey was a year old and was mischievous and energetic — just what Nate wanted. He looked at Tom for approval, which he got with a vigorous nod. The price was discussed; ten dollars, just as Jarvis had said. Nate paid Pete Robinson and the two men started the trek back home, Nate detouring to the Tates' and Tom heading back to Fox Hollow. It was to be the beginning of a new life for Nate.

Homestead

Southern Infirmary
MOBILE - Alabama

Callie McDougald
Fox Hollow
c/o McDougald's Store
Catawba, Florida

A Dark Secret

One of Nate's responsibilities, which had evolved during his months at the McDougald homestead, was going to get the mail. He went once a week, if weather and work permitted, and everyone eagerly looked forward to the day. He had to go to the Gay homestead, where Mrs. Etta Gay was postmistress. It was five miles northwest of the McDougald property, a pretty good ride, but it would be a great trip now on Dewey. He threw the saddle on the horse, cinched him up and they were off. Dewey was spoiling for a ride.

At the Gay home, Nate pulled the mail from the little cubbyhole on the table in the hall where all the mail was stashed. Since he couldn't read, Mrs. Gay had shown him which cubbyhole was the McDougalds'. Nate, himself, did not expect any mail, but there were several pieces for the McDougalds. Mrs. Gay had looked it all over carefully, however. She learned all the goings on far and wide by looking over each piece of mail that was delivered by the carrier on horseback. He brought it from Creighton, the nearest post office, in a black leather saddlebag.

"Well, looks like Callie has something here from the Southern Infirmary in Mobile," Etta said to Nate. Nate was not inclined to tell her too much.

"Yes ma'am. She's been looking to get that. She wants to go there to nursing school," he told her. Etta was curious by nature, but she was especially curious about her neighbors' daughters. They were going to be old maids if somebody didn't come along pretty soon. She liked Pearl very well, but Callie was not one of her favorite people.

When Nate returned with the mail, there was great joy in the household for everyone but Pearl. He could see the sadness in her face as her sister jumped around and started planning with her mother for the clothes and other items she still needed to make. The needles would have to fly, because she was to leave on the twenty-sixth of September, which was coming right up. She had to be there five days before the classes would start to begin getting oriented and informed about the school, as well as the city.

Callie's leaving was coming at one of Nate's busiest times. It was time to gather the corn and velvet beans and, as it turned out, Mr. Mac had rheumatism in one knee badly. It was swollen twice its normal size. Naturally, it fell to Nate to get Callie to Creighton to the train. At breakfast the morning before, Mr. Mac had said to Pearl, "Daughter, why don't you ride over with Nate to take your sister to the train? I'm sure he would like some company on the long trip back." Nate almost swallowed a bite of sausage whole, but Pearl quickly declined, saying she had things she needed to get done that day. Little Rose spoke up, though, fast enough. "I'll go," she said eagerly. "Oh, can I go?" Miss Mattie was also quick to tell her that her math and spelling needed more attention before school began to catch her up with her class. She and her brother had missed a great deal of school when their parents died because of the shuttling around they were forced to do. Miss Mattie was a stickler for education and had seen to it her own girls went as far as they could in their area in school. Nate breathed a sigh of relief when he realized nobody would be going with him to take Callie. He subscribed to the old adage, "He who travels fastest travels alone."

A Dark Secret

The train was to leave Creighton at 1:00 in the afternoon; that would give them plenty of time to get there if they left early. Nate brought the horse and buggy around to the front porch, where he loaded all of Callie's belongings into the back of the buggy. Her mother had made a lunch for them to eat along the way, and Mr. Mac handed Nate his shotgun. "It's loaded," he said. "You never know when you might need this." Nate checked the lantern, also. It would be pretty nearly dark when he got home or maybe after dark. There was a slight delay while oil was added to the lantern, but they were off by six and Dewey was rearing to go. Nate chose to take Dewey, because he and that horse had a love affair going. They had become best friends since Nate purchased him.

They made it to Creighton with a short while to spare, so Nate tied Dewey up at the artesian well near the depot, where the horse could drink his fill of water. He also had a bag of feed for him that he put over his head while they waited. When they heard the train, Nate began taking Callie's baggage to the loading ramp. There were a few other people there seeing people off, but Tuesday was not a big traveling day, it appeared. She was terribly excited and had twittered all the way about leaving home, going to Mobile, nursing school which took six months, and what fun it was to be going on a new adventure.

Nate hugged Callie, told her to take care of herself and waited until the train pulled out of the station before leaving. They waved until she was out of sight. She looked mighty tiny and alone in that big train, he thought.

Dewey headed for home as if he had gone that way every day of his life, but Nate doubted he had ever been to Creighton. After all, the horse was only a year old. They made it to the river bridge before sundown, which was a relief to Nate. His only concern about the trip was that narrow wooden bridge over the Concord River. It was for one-lane traffic only, with no possibility whatever of two vehicles crossing at the same time. It was a high bridge, perhaps fifty feet in the center, and was all of two hundred feet long. When approaching it at night, a traveler had to call out into the darkness to be certain another traveler was not crossing. It had no guardrails at all making it a scary ride across even in broad daylight. Dewey had not flinched at the earlier crossing.

Nate pulled back on the reins, getting the horse under control as they started onto the old bridge. Then he began talking to him in a soothing voice while he pulled the little buggy over the bridge that at best was no more than twelve feet wide. With the horse's keen eyesight, Nate had no doubt he could have made it across the bridge even in darkness, but it was easier on Nate's nerves that they got across before dark.

They were a good four miles from home when darkness overtook them. Nate took the lantern off the hook on the buggy, reached into the watch pocket of his overalls for a match, and lit it, hanging it back on the hook. The light was welcome for Nate as it got darker and darker, but the horse didn't care at all. He had no trouble finding his way along the sandy road with the two ruts. Nate also reached into the back of the buggy, pulled the shotgun out and placed it beside him on the buggy seat.

A Dark Secret

The family had eaten when he got home and put the horse and buggy away, but Miss Mattie had supper saved in the warmer on the stove. They all gathered at the table again to hear of Callie's departure. "Was the train on time?" was Mr. Mac's question, while Miss Mattie wanted to know if Callie cried or looked sad. Pearl again said nothing. The children didn't seem to get the full importance of the event. Ben was such a quiet child that Nate worried about him. He seemed to have suffered more from the loss of their parents and all the moving about than Rose had.

Melissa was never far from Nate's mind that summer. He had ridden Dewey to see her as often as possible and, with the little Catawba School opening for the term in late September, he planned for them to attend several events there. The first one was the annual Box Supper. Each girl attending took a box supper. The boxes were decorated as beautifully as possible with flowers, ribbons, lace, paper or whatever they wanted to use. They would contain what was supposed to be a delicious dinner of fried chicken, fried steak, baked sweet or Irish potatoes, deviled eggs, potato salad; — any variety of foods suitable for a cold supper. The girls took them early, and when the men arrived, they had no idea who had made the boxed suppers. The idea was that each man would bid on the box he liked the looks of most. He would bid until he got a box and then eat supper with the girl who had made the box. Of course, Nate hoped to get Melissa's box, but there was no way to identify hers for sure, and if any girl told and was found out, she would be asked to leave the Box Supper immediately.

There were fifteen or twenty girls from neighboring homesteads who now attended or had attended Catawba School. There were fully as many men in attendance, if not more; some older, like Nate, who had come from some distance around to attend the supper and enjoy the company of some young lady. Lanterns had been hung from trees in the schoolyard that gave the area an ethereal look, and a beautiful harvest moon was coming up in the east as Nate rode up on Dewey. He knew very few people in the area, having been at Mr. Mac's hard at work most of his two years in the community. With each homestead a good four to five miles apart, at least, people of Nate's station in life had little time for socializing. A funeral now and then, or a church service once a quarter or often only every six months, were the main events for adults, unless they had friends they visited. Nate had no friends as such, and didn't know any of the people who had died.

He hitched Dewey to a low limb on an oak and searched the faces for Melissa. She had taken the buggy the two miles to the school. Nate would tie Dewey to the back of the buggy and drive her home when the affair was over at the school. He finally saw her coming out of the school building door and called to her, "Melissa!" She looked out into the faces and saw him. A huge smile broke over her face as she joined him in the crowd.

"The bidding is about to start," Melissa told Nate. "Pay close attention to the boxes and get a pretty one." was all she had time to say when the older gentleman in the black coat and string tie started the bidding holding up a large box. Nate thought it looked very pretty but had no idea whether he should bid or wait. Before he could decide it was sold for thirty cents. A little redheaded girl who could have hardly been fourteen was the girl who had made the box. It sold to an older man, a rather rough looking sort. Nate felt a little uneasy about the fact that the couples could eat anywhere together as long as they stayed within the rail fence of the schoolyard. There were some rather dark areas in that yard, especially behind the school.

The bidding continued and seven or eight boxes had sold. The prices being paid were good, because everyone knew the money was going to help pay the teacher's salary and buy books, a worthy cause, indeed.

All of a sudden, Melissa's box sold. "See you later," she whispered as she stepped up to meet the tall, rangy man who had bought her box. Nate watched, disappointed, when they stepped out of the main group and started toward the back of the building. There were bare board tables in the back with a couple of lanterns, but the main lights were in the front where most of the activities were being conducted. He decided he would bid on the next box and ask the girl if they could eat in the back also. He didn't like the situation at all, and he didn't know the man. He paid thirty-six cents for a box and the privilege of eating the food with a plump young woman whose name was Missy Rogers, Franklin's sister. Her family lived about three miles south of the school. Nate had met Franklin at the Tates' the night he met Melissa.

"Hello, I'm Nathan York," he said to her, somewhat distracted and without his heart in the meeting. "Do you mind eating at one of the tables in the back? Miss Rogers, I believe?" he asked. She readily agreed. Nate took the box and her elbow and guided her deftly around the building.

Missy, unaware of his interest in other things, started to chatter nervously about all sorts of things. She talked about the weather, the school, where he had come from, and everything she could think of while Nate was distracted by happenings at the table farthest back in the schoolyard, some fifty feet away. He tried his best to converse with her while plainly not interested until he suddenly saw the man with Melissa grab her in his arms and try to kiss her. Nate was up in a flash, striding rapidly toward their table. Melissa was pushing away with all her might, but he was too much for her. As he pressed his lips to hers, Nate caught him by the collar and pulled him backwards. The man was so off guard, he almost fell to the ground on his back, but then Nate got a good punch at his face and knocked him off the bench sideways on to the ground.

"Get up, Melissa!" he shouted. "We're leaving." Melissa was not hard to convince.

She grabbed her little purse from the table in front of her and was ready to go. Cal Little, whose name Melissa told him later on the way home, was too stunned to react. He just sat down and finished his supper. Nate escorted Missy back to the front of the school where he excused himself, handed her the box of food and then took Melissa to her buggy. They drove it over, tied Dewey on to the back and drove away, leaving several stunned people, including the chaperones, to wonder what had happened.

On the way home, the two talked over the situation. "Nathan, you didn't have to hit him so hard," Melissa told him.

"No use half doing a job. The nerve of that fellow, anyway." He put his arm around her shoulders and pulled her to him. "You are my girl, and nobody bothers my girl." The moon was lovely, casting just enough light for them to make out the sandy road with the grassy middle. The Tates' horse, Dixie, certainly didn't need any help to get them to Melissa's house, nor did she seem to mind stopping to nip grass when Nate told her to whoa at the big magnolia just below the Tates' house. Dewey nipped a few blades, too, while his master courted.

They sat for a few minutes looking through the thick trees at the half moon. Melissa was not expected home for a while, because the supper was not over at the school and would not be for another hour or more. She and Nate had, of late, been seizing every opportunity to be alone. When he visited at the Tate home, her family disappeared for long periods, but sometimes they would reappear unexpectedly, especially Mary and Liz, her younger sisters. Mary was fourteen and old enough to know better, but Liz at eleven was mischievous, and it was a lark for her to suddenly appear around the corner of the house and try to catch Nate and Melissa kissing or something!

It had cooled off after sundown, making the late September evening quite pleasant. Normally, on hot evenings clothes would stick to the body, the starch in them causing more wrinkles than ever. If a lady sat close to a gentleman, she had a mass of wrinkles in her dress on that side. It was a telltale sign, so Melissa made a special effort to get her skirt tail pulled smoothly across her lap before she melted into Nate's arms. He kissed her several times in rapid succession, all the while becoming more and more aroused. Melissa, too, felt desire mounting up in her like a warm ocean wave engulfing her. A few kisses was as far as things would go, however, and they both knew it. In 1881 young ladies knew when to stop. It was totally unacceptable to go beyond a simple kiss. Besides, Nate would think she was forward and wonder about her character if she kissed him too many times. Words were not necessary as they sat in the quiet evening with only a few crickets chirping here and there, Nate's arm tightly about her shoulders.

"Melissa, how old are you?" he asked finally, breaking the silence and drawing her thoughts back to reality.

"Sixteen and a half," she said simply. "Why?"

"Well, do you want to know how old I am?"

"I already know you are a good bit older than that." She knew he had lost his parents many years before when he was fifteen. She had done some simple math and figured him to be about thirty.

"I am thirty-three," he said flatly." "You realize I am seventeen years older than you. That's twice your age. Does that matter to you?"

"No, Nathan. It doesn't," she assured him. Her father was thirteen years older than her mother, not an uncommon thing in that day and time. Men waited late to get married. Women married early.

Nathan pulled this lovely tiny girl to him again gently, but nearly crushed her then as he hugged her so hard. Goodness! She fit into his arms so well. He wanted so much to propose to her right then and there, but he knew it was not the time yet. He must wait a little while longer. There were things to be done first. As he kissed her once more long and hard, they both knew they were deeply in love.

Nate took Melissa to the front steps, after they had backed the buggy into the shed and put the horse in the lot. Lily's gardenias were overpowering the whole area of the front yard with their heavy sweet smell. There was a bush on either side of the gate. Nate snapped one off and tucked it into Melissa's hair. On the steps, he pulled her to him once more. "I love you, Melissa Tate," he whispered ever so softly into her ear.

"I love you too, Nathan York," she whispered back. There was a lamp burning in the hall near the steps casting the dimmest light on the porch and steps where they stood. Nathan wanted to stand there forever in that perfect moment, holding this girl. He could just make out her pink cheeks, her white teeth and the curls, warm from the evening, outlining her face. Melissa felt she was going to burst with love for this tall, handsome man, so tough and strong, yet so gentle.

On the way home, Nate had a lot of time to think again. He had to map out plans in his mind since there were so many things to do. First, he needed to talk to Mr. Mac again about how to homestead his property. Mr. Mac homesteaded and would know how to get started. Then he had to talk to him about tools and equipment he would need to build a cabin. As soon as the cabin was built, he and Melissa could get married, but he had to talk to her father, also. John Tate was a sort of hard man to read, so Nate was not sure whether John really approved of him or not. After all, Melissa was his oldest daughter. Maybe he had higher expectations for a husband for her. With Nate's lack of education and having no parents to help him get a start in life, he was saving money as fast as he could, but at present didn't have much. He did have Dewey, though. Good old Dewey! His very first real purchase of any import in his life — he loved that horse!

Nate knew from what Melissa had told him that her parents had started with their homestead and a small cabin. As they were able to afford it, they started building the big house. The sawmill at the little settlement of Cobbtown could cut the timber on his property for the big house he and Melissa would build. Nate wanted it to be large enough for several children. Dewey would be necessary when he started cutting and moving logs for the cabin, but he had to invest in a wagon next. It would be needed for hauling lumber. Fortunately, wagons didn't cost too much. He hoped Mr. Mac could help him get one at a reduced cost through the store. It was his lucky day when he got the job working as Mr. Mac's farmhand.

After Nate arrived home and put Dewey away, he stood and looked at the moon again for a few seconds. He had really kissed Melissa tonight! She kissed him back, too. She had not held back and been prim and proper. He worried a bit that he was kissing her too much there in the buggy, but when she melded into his arms the way she did, he knew she wanted him as much as he wanted her. Yes, sir. Nate walked into the bunkhouse and prepared for bed a happy man. He had no way of knowing what consternation he would face tomorrow.

Day dawned clear and cooler the next morning. It was early to be gathering corn yet Nate wanted to get on with it. He had much to do, so that would be one more disagreeable job finished. He would get started with it that day and talk to Mr. Mac as soon as the opportunity presented itself. The only problem with starting before really cool weather was the problem of snakes. Nothing could spook a horse faster than a snake. Rattlers would run if given time, but when cornered or surprised, they would coil and strike before anyone could discern where they were exactly. The timber rattlers and diamondbacks were prevalent in the area, yet Nate felt it was worth the risk to go ahead with corn gathering. No telling when the first real cold snap would come to cause the snakes to hibernate for the winter.

At breakfast he told the McDougalds his plans. Mr. Mac thought it was a bit early. "Have you checked the velvet beans to see if they are dry enough to pick?"

Nate answered in the affirmative. "Yes sir, I looked at 'em last week. They're dry enough to come off the vines with no problem at all." Velvet beans were huge, probably six inches long, very tough and black. They were good food for cows in the winter, but even better for horses. Being as tough as they were, they would help keep the horses' teeth ground down so they would not have to be filed so often. The beans were usually planted among the stalks of corn so they would have somewhere to run. They would entwine themselves among the corn making it necessary to pull corn and beans usually at the same time. Nate would have huge galvanized washtubs for the beans, and the corn would go into the wagon bed. It would probably be a three or four day job, at least. He really needed someone to drive the wagon as he pulled, but that was not going to happen.

Little Ben started right in, wanting to go with Nate and ride in the wagon. "I'll be good and stay in the wagon," he begged. Nate knew about how long that would last before the six-year-old got tired, hot or sleepy and have to be brought to the house, but he gave in. He knew the child had little real joy in life, staying around the house all day with the women or at the store with Mr. Mac. He wanted to see everything and got into things badly.

"Tell you what, Ben," Nate said. "You can go, but you cannot get out of the wagon. I'd be askeered of snakes on the ground." Ben agreed to the terms. Nate told him to be ready in half an hour. "I have to get the mule hitched to the wagon, and I'll call you."

Nate went to the barn and hitched the mule to the wagon. He had decided not to use the horse. It sounded like more of a job for the mule. Ben was soon out there climbing into the wagon. Nate gave him a little boost, then they were off. He rode in the seat, feet not touching the floor of the wagon, proudly and like a man. They talked, with Ben asking the questions and Nate trying to come up with answers a boy his age would understand. Nate's exposure to children was limited. He had the two younger sisters whom he still missed after eighteen long years. He often thought of them. For three or four years he had tried to stay in the area so that they could visit, but his work had taken him further and further away. He had resolved to find them one day, however.

A Dark Secret

Maybe he and Melissa could go looking for them after they were married. It saddened Nate, also, that he could never visit his parents' graves. They were buried near the tiny cabin in which they had lived, under a huge red oak, but there was no marker so Nate wondered if he could even find the graves. The oak may have been cut down, the cabin torn down or burned, and the graves desecrated in all kinds of ways. Oh, well. He could not stop to think of that now. He had done the best he could at the time. Neighbors from miles and miles away had come to help with the burial. There were about nine or ten people there. Someone read a scripture, offered up a prayer and that was it. There were not even any coffins.

Ben had a wonderful morning until the sun got too hot. Nate wore a huge sun hat, but the small boy had no hat, so it was time for him to go to the house. They had been out in the field for about three hours. They had water in a fruit jar and they stopped so Ben could stand and pee off the end of the wagon, but Nate decided to take him to the house. Ben was so small and frail that Nate could carry him with little effort.

As they rounded the corner to the barn, Ben was looking back in the direction of the field, but Nate was looking straight into the barn, where to his shock and amazement, Mr. Mac stood with his left arm about little Rose and his right hand down in her drawers! Her skirt was up about her shoulders. The child had a horrified look on her face, which intensified at the sight of her brother and Mr. Nate. He could do nothing but cry, "Oh!" wheel around and leave the way he had come in, hoping that surely Ben didn't see what he had seen. Apparently, he didn't, or, if he did, he didn't say a word. Nate went behind the barn and to the house another way.

Instead of going straight back to the field where the mule was tied to a sassafras bush, Nate went to the bunkhouse to get hold of himself. He felt nauseated. He was shaking. But most of all, he didn't know what to do. He went over to the rough board shelf where he kept a galvanized bucket full of water with a dipper. He filled the wash pan on the shelf with the dipper and washed his face, drying it on the feedbag towel hanging nearby on a nail. What should he do? What could he do? As he sat there, he realized he could do nothing. He must have a job and a place to live. If he told anyone, they wouldn't believe it, and whom would he tell? He knew few people in the area, all of whom thought highly of the McDougalds. There was no law, no law enforcement. It would cause a terrible situation if Miss Mattie found out, not to mention the girls and what it would do to them. No, Nate decided. *I must never tell this to a soul.*

As he left the bunkhouse, he looked carefully to be sure neither Rose nor Mr. Mac was in sight before going out through the back lot to the field. Nate put every ounce of energy he had into the work in order to try to somehow purge his mind of what he had seen. He wondered, *has it happened before? Will it happen again, and has it happened to other little girls?* He hoped he would never know the answers to those questions.

Nate was not sure how he would ever face Rose or Mr. Mac again. He felt so sorry for the little girl. He knew little of sexual matters, but he knew what he had seen was very, very wrong. He also hated the feeling of revulsion he felt toward his boss. He knew this feeling would never go away and would forever ruin the high esteem he had always had for the man. Nate returned to the field with a heavy heart and a feeling that he should do something to help little Rose.

Trouble

October came and with it much cooler weather. In northwest Florida, there is a definite change of seasons. Fall brings deep maroon leaves of the black gum trees. Sumac turns red, gold and brown, and maples get a golden yellow. There is often a frost which kills all the tender green vegetation, but that sometimes waits until November or even December. The air is crisp and cool, taking with it the steamy humidity and fog everyone dreads. Native pines, many virgin and huge in size, give off pollen. It turns everything in its path yellow. It coats the porches, requiring sweeping every morning.

Melissa was completing her sweeping when her mother walked out onto the porch and started to work at the spinning wheel. She needed thread for quilting. It seemed to Melissa a good time to have a talk with her mother about something she had dreaded mentioning. Lily had avoided the same subject but knew it was going to come up soon.

"Mama?" Melissa said. "You know Nathan has been calling on me now for about six months."

"Yes?" was all Lily said. Melissa was thinking, hum, she isn't going to make this easy on me.

"Well, I've been thinking about what if he asks me to marry him? What will Daddy say?"

Homestead

Lily sat there for what seemed forever to Melissa who was dreading the answer. "I think he might agree for you to marry Nathan."

"Do you really? Even though he is a lot older than I am?" She was sure her mother knew Nathan was much older than she.

"How much older, Melissa?"

Melissa thought for a moment. There was no way to put it except just to put it! "Seventeen years, Mama."

Lily didn't flinch. She was starting to spin, and the conversation seemed over when she stopped, looked way off into the distance and finally said, "You know, you are my first born, and I will never be ready for you to leave home. I know it has to happen though, so I guess it may as well be with Nathan. He seems like a good man and he is a hard worker."

Melissa flew over, kissed her mother on the forehead and shouted, "Whee!" One hurdle was jumped. Her father was away at his job, so anything she might say to him, if anything, would have to wait another week, at least. In the meantime, Melissa would dream of the night they had parked the buggy in the moonlight on the way from the box supper and kissed so many times. She could remember the clean, mannish smell he had and how strong his arms were around her. She longed for those arms. She ached to see him. She also wondered about having babies, what it would feel like when you were in bed together and all the things she had never experienced. Most of all, she wanted to feel the pressure of having a part of him inside her. It was time to clean the privy now, however, and she decided she'd better get on with it. That should take the romance right out of her mind, she thought.

The privy was a few yards from the back porch. It was plain boards, just like the house, unpainted and very weathered. Inside there were three hole, two regular size and one small for little people. Below the holes, about three feet down, was a sandy area where the refuse fell. All the urine soaked into the sand, but the solid waste had to be scooped up with the shovel and buried in the field that ran right up to the privy in the back. Melissa went out to the washhouse and got the shovel from the shed in the back. She selected a spot, dug a hole in the soft field dirt, then began taking scoops out to bury it. The chore only took a few minutes, but the reward was great.

Mary and Liz were shelling peas on the back porch when Melissa got back to the house. They had picked the last batch before frost. It won't be long 'till cold weather, Melissa was thinking. She figured Nate would not come as often when it got cold. She wondered what he was doing at that moment and what he had in his mind where she was concerned.

The McDougald household was pretty much as it had been after Nate's encounter with Mr. Mac and Rose, but he was not at all the same. He dreaded each meal, ate as fast as he could without making eye contact with Mr. Mac and headed on back to his quarters or to do his chores. With the corn and beans gathered, there was little to do in the field. He would begin plowing later on in the year just to be ahead in the spring when planting time was coming near — that is, if he were still going to be there. He figured he'd better go ahead and talk to Mr. Mac about the homestead request so he could get started with that. It was late afternoon, and the children were playing in the back. Miss Mattie was sitting out in a cane-bottom chair under the pecan tree watching them while she tatted. She was making edging for pillowcases. Mr. Mac was just leaving the store for the night and heading that way. Nate waited to talk to him. It would be much easier with Miss Mattie and the children there than face-to-face alone.

Tom McDougald had been agonizing some on his own since Nate had walked in on him with Rose. He had tried to think of anything on earth that would justify what he was doing or explain it away. There was nothing... nothing. He thought of talking to Nate about it, but that would be too difficult. He just didn't have enough guts to bring the subject out into the open and talk about it. He realized Nate had been avoiding him as much as possible since that day.

"Mr. Mac," Nate said, "I wanted to talk to you about something." Tom froze. His insides curdled. His hands started getting clammy and shaking. What could Nate mean? Surely he wasn't going to bring it up right in front of Mattie and the children! What relief he felt when Nate said, "I want to ask you about homesteading. How do you go about it?"

"Oh, it's not hard at all. You can just write to the Land Patent office in Gainesville, Florida and apply," he answered with great relief. "Now that I think about it, there's no real need to go to Milton."

"But you see, I never learned to write," Nate told him in a flat tone.

"No matter, son, we can handle that. I don't write so well no more with my stiff fingers, but we can get Pearl to write the letter for you. Won't take long, and you oughta hear in a month or so." Nate would have rather died than get involved with Pearl writing the letter for him. There would be some degree of explanation necessary, but beggars can't be choosers he decided. "All right, sir, I'd appreciate that," he told Mr. Mac.

"I will talk to her at supper, or you can," Tom said.

Nate really didn't want to ask her himself, but, again decided he'd have to swallow his disdain and get it done. "Right, sir. I will." As he turned to go to his quarters to get washed up for supper, Rose and Ben came running up. Each had a kitten to show him. They were excited. Minnie, the gray tabby cat, had a litter and lived in the barn. She was the resident mouser, not too friendly, and the kittens were really skittish. The children were delighted to have caught one each, though. Nate looked at their kittens and noticed how sad Rose looked even in her delight at catching the kitten. She had a small little face, anyway, and she rarely smiled. Even her eyes were sad. She had what he called a hang-dog look. He wondered if Miss Mattie had noticed anything.

Trouble

He supposed she thought it was because of all Rose and Ben had been through.

Pearl gladly accepted the job of writing to the Land Patent office. She told Nate she would get the letter ready for him to sign right away. Nate then had to confess that he was illiterate. Pearl mentioned that maybe she could teach him, but Nate told her he'd have to wait until he had more time.

The next morning as Nate was feeding the animals, he kept hearing a dog yelp. The sound was coming from the back of the field that was really little more than a patch. It was thirteen acres but plenty for one man to keep up. Nate stopped and listened carefully. It sounded like a dog in distress. Ben was out in the yard with Nate, following him around while he fed the animals. Of course, when Nate started out to see about the dog, he wanted to go. Nate agreed, knowing full well it was probably not a good idea. The boy couldn't walk fast enough to keep up, so Nate would have to wait up for him. Then he got tired, but Nate urged him on because he could hear more clearly what he was sure was a dog. He was, no doubt, hung up somehow, and Nate hoped it wouldn't be a terrible sight since Ben was along. He listened carefully, deciding the sound was coming from a small thicket of trees due east of the house. They went that way with Ben dragging along. Briars sometimes cut into their overalls and branches slapped them in the face as the brush got thicker.

Nate began to whistle to the dog in a calling way, which caused the poor hapless animal to yelp all the louder. At last they found him, a hound with long ears and soulful eyes, his foot caught in a steel trap. Nate was enraged. Ben was horrified and began to cry. The dog beat his tail helplessly and whimpered all the louder.

"There, there," Nate said in a consoling way. "We'll get you out, boy." But he didn't know how he was going to do it. He had no tools, nothing. Steel traps were strong. "Ben, we'll have to go home and let me get something to open this trap with."

Ben was even more agonized at leaving the dog. "He'll think we are not going to help him!" he pled.

"We have to go. Don't worry, fella. We'll be back." He hurried Ben along as best he could and ended up carrying the child halfway home. Remember, he said to himself, and don't let him go again.

When they reached the house, Nate got a heavy crow bar to pry the trap open with and set out going back to where the dog waited. Ben didn't try to go that time. He'd had enough of the rough going for that day. When Nate arrived, he pried until the trap finally gave letting the foot free. It was terribly swollen and the dog was going to have a difficult time walking, so Nate decided to carry him. He was a good-sized dog, but Nate was a strong and big man. "Come on, fella," he said in a reassuring tone. "I will get you home."

When they arrived at the house, Nate got a pan with warm, salty water in it to soak the foot. Fortunately, the water in the warmer was still warm from breakfast. Salt water was used for everything from treating and soaking wounds to sore throats. A gargle of warm salt water would help a sore throat every time.

The whole family gathered about to demean whoever had put the trap out. It was considered a cruel thing to do, but trappers made their living from selling skins of animals they caught. Nate would have liked to get his hands on that so and so. The dog, who had quickly been named "Trouble", and seemed to be mighty grateful to have been rescued, licked Nate's hand when he put the foot into the water. The flesh would very likely rot out holes where the trap had cut into the flesh, but it would, no doubt, get well healing from the inside out. In any case, Nate had himself a dog. Animals heal quickly from wounds. They often lick their wounds, and were known to gnaw a foot, or even a leg, off to free themselves from a trap. Nate was glad Trouble didn't have to do that. He felt sure he would be able to run again soon.

November came. Frost came with it making it, necessary for the sweet potatoes to be dug and banked. Nate, with Ben along when he wasn't at school, started plowing up the rows. The little boy seemed to idolize the man and would work along side Nate any time he could, so he helped pick the potatoes up where they lay on top of the ground, placing them carefully into the wagon. Nate taught him not to bruise them. As soon as they would get a load, they would take them back to the house and place them in a little dugout near the smokehouse. When they were all gathered, Nate covered the pile with dirt, making a bank. It had a small opening in front he covered with a piece of tin. That way, Miss Mattie or Pearl could open it and get the potatoes out. The purpose of the bank was to protect the potatoes from freezing in very cold weather.

Ben was excited and wanted to have sweet potatoes for supper, so he ran to the house to ask Miss Mattie. Naturally, she said yes. Trouble was looking on approvingly, walking much better since his foot was healing nicely.

Every week, Nate went to the Gay's for the mail, always hoping to hear from the homestead request, while the McDougalds hoped to hear from Callie. Finally, the day came. He got there about mid-afternoon that particular week. Miss Etta was sweeping her yard and saw him coming way up the road. She dropped the broom and went for the pack of letters, which she handed over to him with excitement as soon as he rode up. "Here it is, Nate. Your letter's here!"

He could not contain his excitement. Ripping the envelope open, he asked her to read it to him.

Miss Etta read:

Dear Mr. York,

We are pleased to inform you that homestead tracts are available in the area around Catawba, Florida. You are required to live on the land for seven years, at which time you will be given a land grant.

Homestead

Select one hundred and sixty acres. Notify the Land
Patent office of the general location, and you will be
sent the description of the land.
We wish you good luck with your endeavor.

The letter was signed by the manager of the Land Patent
office. Nate could hardly wait to tell the McDougalds and especially Melissa. He turned Dewey around, thanking Miss Etta,
and headed happily for home. On the way, he made some pretty
definite plans.

Nate got back to the house to be greeted by a happy Trouble
who had wanted to go. His foot was not entirely healed, however,
and Nate couldn't take the dog on Dewey. He could only go in the
wagon or buggy. The McDougalds were happy, also, to hear from
Callie, who said she loved nursing school, had several good friends
now, and often got invited to have Sunday dinner with families
in the Mobile area who had daughters in her class. She planned
to come home for Christmas, asking if someone could meet her.
Classes would end on December nineteenth, allowing her to leave
on the twentieth. The train would get into Creighton at eleven in
the morning.

Miss Mattie set right in to write Callie back and tell her someone would definitely meet her. She would line Nate up if Mr. Mac
was not able to go. Nate thought that would be an ideal time to
go over to town on Dewey, buy a wagon and pull Callie and her
things home in it — that is, if Miss Callie would not mind being
driven in the wagon. It would not be as comfortable or fast as the
buggy, but they would have plenty of time to get home before too
late. The biggest problem could be the weather. Sometimes December days were cold and rainy, and the wagon had no top as
the buggy did. Well, he would try.

Everyone at the McDougald household seemed pleased
enough about the homestead letter but Pearl, who tried not to
show her fears: that Nate would homestead and marry Melissa

Trouble

Tate! Mr. Mac had about given up the idea of Nate ever wanting to marry one of his girls. Miss Mattie had never shown that she had given the idea of him as her son-in-law the first tiny bit of consideration. Ben and Rose wanted to know what that meant, a homestead? When Nate explained, they were full of questions. Would Mr. Nate be leaving and going to live at that new place? Would he ever come back to see them or would he work there anymore? He did all he could to reassure the children that he would always come back to the store and to visit and that he would always be their friend. Both children had a crestfallen look that made him feel awfully bad.

As luck would have it, the next day was Sunday when Nate would make his regularly scheduled visit to see Melissa. Saddling Dewey let the horse know they were going somewhere important. Otherwise, Nate would just ride him bareback if he were not going far. Just as he got the saddle on him and started to slip the bridle on, Dewey gave Nate a huge, wet sloppy nuzzle right on his jaw! "Dewey!" he yelled. "Bad boy!" He took out his red handkerchief and cleaned the slobber off as best he could, laughing at the mischievous big oaf.

Melissa would be ready and waiting in the swing for him unless it was too cool. He did his chores and left early so that he would be at her house as soon as Sunday dinner was over. The days were so short in December that he didn't want to waste a minute. Dewey trotted some along the way, but as they neared the house, he started into a full gallop. The four miles to the Tates' was nothing for him, as young and strong as he was.

Nobody was on the porch when Nate threw the reins over the gatepost and started up the steps, but suddenly the door burst open and Melissa appeared in a new green dress with her shawl around her shoulders. "Hello!" she greeted Nate. He looked about quickly to see how many onlookers there might be at hand and seeing none, he grabbed her, picked her completely up off the floor and kissed her soundly.

Homestead

Melissa scolded, "Nathan! Put me down this instant!", but all the while loving it. She couldn't get enough of being with that man, nor he with her.

Gosh, Nate was thinking, I've got to marry this girl fast.

She led him into the front room, or sitting room, as it was often called. Nobody was in there, either, which usually meant they could be really alone for a while. Nate took the letter out of the pocket of his great coat. It was warm by the fire; so he shed the coat, handing her the letter. While he warmed from the cold ride, she read the letter.

"Oh, Nathan!" was all she could say. "Oh, Nathan!" When she finished, she stood beside him for a minute, letting the meaning of it sink in. She had not known Nathan had written. Why didn't he tell her, or ask her to write the letter? Did he mean to surprise her this way for some reason? Surely he did. How soon would he start building his house? Who would he ask to share it with him? All kinds of things went through her mind before she returned to reality and the tall man now standing over her. Nate looked down at her wanting desperately to propose, but knowing full well he must speak to her father first. Instead, he took her in his arms again and kissed her slowly and sensuously on her lovely pink lips. After that they sat beside each other on the settee in front of the wonderful oak fire, holding hands but wanting to do much more. They talked until late afternoon, when Nate knew he must head for home. Melissa felt satisfied about most of her questions except the burning one, and she knew she would just have to be patient for that. Her father was gone at that time, anyway, so Nate couldn't ask for her hand in marriage even if he wanted to. Oh, how she hoped he wanted to!

One thing she and Nate had decided was that he would talk to her father about helping him select the homestead site. John knew the area probably better than anyone in the region. He knew every homesteader personally, knew how to get help in building, and most of them were in his debt in some way or another. The fact that Melissa felt confident he would help Nate and guide him, was a great comfort to him. Had Nate's parents lived, things would have been entirely different for him. Through the misfortune of losing his parents, he had never gone to school, had nothing to start out with, and nobody to lean on or take his bride to live with until he could get a start in the world. That is what couples traditionally did: stayed with one set of parents or the other until they could build a cabin and get a few furnishings. He hoped Miss Lily would be able to share some furnishings with them, seeing as how she had a house full of good furniture. He felt sure she would. John had long had a good enough salary from the government to help them build and furnish their home. Few of the homesteaders had that kind of income. They had to dig and pick a living out of the new ground they would clear and cultivate, selling any surplus to the nearest store for a few extra dollars. It was a primitive area still with few luxuries, although the cities, and even the towns in the South, were developing culturally and materially, finally.

The Civil War had only been over a few short years. Whereas many areas in the South were devastated, the northwest Florida area was virtually untouched. Pensacola had seen fighting but not the immediate area where the homesteads were located. It seemed to be an area time had forgotten: completely rural and undeveloped. Nate was too young for the Civil War. He knew Miss Lily's three younger brothers, barely teenagers all of them, had gone and that they were killed in the Battle of Chicamauga in Tennessee. He was not sure about Mr. Mac or Mr. Tate, whether they had gone to the war or not, but he thought not. He had no idea why not. Most people looked upon the war with such distaste that they hardly wanted to mention it. People were trying to get beyond the horror and misery of it. Nate knew little of the reason for the war, or of the history of it, except that his family had no slaves and, in fact, were more or less slaves themselves. Any one who couldn't read or write, had no family wealth or position, or, for that matter, no family, had to slave for a living. Nate knew nothing but deprivation and hard work. He prayed he could do well for his family and himself in the future.

Proposal of Marriage

The next few days went rapidly while Nate waited for John Tate to get back home. He started plowing the field to be ready for planting in the early spring. There were only thirteen acres, but it was still quite a job for one man who had most of the other chores to do about the McDougald place. Miss Mattie had become unable to milk the cow recently. She had such rheumatism in her hands and fingers that it hurt terribly to milk. Pearl had begged her father not to make her do it, so it fell to Nate. The cow had to be milked morning and afternoon, and on time, too, because her bag would get so full that it would become fevered and the milk could not be used. Nate had to be sure when she came from the pasture that she went right into the cow lot, because if she ate the bitter weeds in the back open lot, her milk would taste bitter, also. Cows loved the tender green plants with the yellow flowers, making it hard to get them to go into the lot in the spring. The calf would be waiting to nurse. The cow's bag would be full, which meant the calf had to be tied and then pulled away as soon as he nursed long enough to bring the milk down lest he drink all of it.

So, in general, milking and dealing with a cow and calf was a time-consuming and rather pesky task. It was just one more thing for Nate to do. After he would milk all the family needed for its use, he would then untie the calf and let it back in to finish getting the rest of the milk. After that, the calf had to again be pulled, and sometimes almost dragged, from the lot where the cow was since he would nurse in the night and drain all the milk before morning. Nate really hated that whole process. He could hardly wait until he could see himself clear to leave his job with Mr. Mac.

Often Minnie and her now large teenage-sized kittens would come out from the barn during the milking process. Nate would take an udder and aim it at Minnie or a kitten and send a long stream of milk into the mouth of the waiting cat. Rose and Ben loved to watch that happen. They would climb up onto the old wooden cow lot fence by putting their toes between the cracks and shriek with delight when the milk would hit its mark. The children seemed to be growing lately, Nate thought. He was happy to see that. He had not seen any further indication of impropriety on the part of Mr. Mac, but Nate knew there were plenty of times when he was not around when something could have happened.

Plowing gave Nate plenty of thinking time. He went over his plans every day several times. He wished so much that he could see Melissa more and talk things over with her. He had longed to tell someone about Mr. Mac and the situation with Rose, but there was no one with whom he could share that heavy burden. Certainly not Melissa now. Someday, perhaps.

In the evenings, after all of Nate's chores were done, he had a project he was working on. Since Christmas was coming right up, he had begun work on a small trinket box for Melissa. He would sit by the pot-bellied stove and carve on the little box he had put together from scraps in the shed with Mr. Mac's tools. It took up a few hours each dark evening with Trouble by his side, looking adoringly at his master. He had become Nate's slave, knowing the man had saved him from a horrible fate. He seemed to know what a lucky dog he was.

Proposal of Marriage

In the meantime, while Nate carved on the box, Melissa was sitting by the big fireplace at her house, knitting. She was making wool socks for Nate with a great deal of help from Lily. Mary and Liz had to study and work arithmetic, often with help from their older sister. Lily had some education, but Melissa's was more recent. She was a whiz in arithmetic, spelling and reading, but had about given up the idea of becoming a teacher. There appeared to be no chance of the Catawba teacher leaving any time soon. Melissa wished she would get married and leave the area.

Lily's latest project was making a braided rug. She had an idea it would be needed by Melissa and Nate before too long; so it was not a bit too soon to start on it. She took all the worn out stockings, saved from the entire family, braided them and then sewed them together either in an oval or round rug. The rug was coming together well. Melissa had no idea it was for her, but she did have a hope chest. Her father had made one for each of the girls as they started growing into womanhood. It was a custom since times were hard, and it was necessary to help girls get things together for their homes ahead of time. Most furnishings were homemade, including the furniture. Melissa had made a few things, such as pillowcases, with her mother's help. She was not a seamstress yet, but she was learning. She was hoping they could go up to McDougald's store soon where she would select the material for a wedding dress. If only Nate would get around to popping the question!

November brought more cloudy, overcast weather. It was great for Nate where the plowing was concerned; a lot better than the hot months. He had the field about ready for planting when spring arrived. Whether he was working for Mr. Mac or not, he had gotten that much done. It was a Sunday, he was off and figured Mr. Tate was probably home by now. He had planned to go down to see Melissa when he would talk with her father, if the opportunity presented itself.

Homestead

Trouble was determined to go along. Nate was taking Dewey, so he let him go, feeling it might present a problem. The dog trotted along beside Nate and the horse just fine for the first mile or so, but then the temptation to run off into the woods became too strong. It was winter; so there was no risk of snakes. It just took time for Nate to get him to come along. Melissa had never seen the dog, so Nate really wanted them to meet. He assumed he would be her dog, too, one day. She understood how much the dog meant to Nate after he had saved Trouble's life. She understood, also, that he provided a great deal of company for Nate.

Finally, Nate had to stop, get off Dewey and tie the rope he carried on his saddle around Trouble's neck so that he could pull the dog along. "You really are trouble, you know, buddy." Trouble got the picture. He ran along behind the horse from then on with no hanging back.

Melissa and Trouble met. She gave him a hug, and pulling his ears up, held them straight above his head. "They are almost long enough to tie in a knot, aren't they?" she said to Nate. They went up the steps and sat in the swing. "My Dad is home," Melissa said gleefully, knowing Nate wanted to talk to him about the homestead. She had no idea what else Nate might want to speak to him about.

After visiting with Melissa for a few minutes, Nate went to look for her father. He found John out at the smokehouse. There was a little shed roof in front of the smokehouse where he had tools. One thing was a workbench with an iron form of a shoe on which he would place a shoe to repair it. Sometimes the brads that held the sole would come out. John was quite adept at hammering more brads into the sole so that the shoe could be worn a while longer. That was what Nate found him doing. "Hello," he called as Nate walked out from the porch to join him. John extended his hand, and the two men shook hands.

"I'm glad to see you made it home. That trip was pretty long," Nate said.

Proposal of Marriage

"Yep. I had to go to court in Milton this time. We have a nasty case against one of the big lumber companies. They insist on cutting timber belonging to the government. I had to testify. Caught a bunch of log men right in the act of cutting virgin pines, a whole tract of them," John told Nate. Then he confided to Nate another fact. "I haven't told the family this. Worries Lily enough for me to be in this work, but the lumber company was hopping mad about the deal. Even made a few threats."

"I hate to hear that," Nate told him. If there is anything I can do to help you, let me know." John nodded, then dropped the subject. He knew Nate had something on his mind. Melissa had already told him about the homestead. What Nate said next caught him a little off guard, however.

"Mr. Tate," Nate began. "You know I have been calling on your daughter for a good while now, and I would like to have your permission to marry Melissa." There! He had said it!

John sucked in a big gulp of air and let it out slowly. He reckoned he knew Nate must have had something like this in mind, but Melissa had only just turned seventeen, and seemed so young to him. He wanted his girls to marry good men, but just not too young. Of course, he and Lily were married when she was just shy of seventeen.

"Well, son," he finally said. Nate had been looking at the sky, the trees, the smokehouse, anything in sight, thinking John would never answer. "I reckon I knew you wuz coming around here with something like that in mind. I don't suppose any man is ever ready to let go of his daughter, especially the first one, but I admire you as a person. You are a hard worker. You seem to have your head on straight, and if you love Melissa, I guess I have to give you my blessings."

Nate was almost overcome with emotion. He grabbed John's hand and shook it again hard. "Thank you sir," he said, fighting not to cry. "I do love her very much, and, if she will have me, I intend to ask her right away. One more thing I wanted to talk to you about," he said. John was thinking, here it comes, what I expected all the while.

"I have permission from the land office in Gainesville to homestead, and I need some help in that direction," he told John.

"I reckon you know more about that than anybody around."

"Yep, I am pretty up on that all right. I will be glad to help you, son. Let me finish this shoe. Then we can talk."

Nate joined Melissa in the front room by the fire. She was doing some handwork, and put it down as he entered the room. "What did Daddy say?" she asked.

"He said he would be glad to help. He's coming in as soon as he gets finished with the shoe he's working on." Nate was beaming. Melissa couldn't help but notice, thinking it was the homestead he was so happy about. He was really trying to decide how and when he wanted to propose.

When John got inside, he and Nate mapped out the plan for deciding which tract of land he should settle on. They arranged for Nate to come down during the week ahead while John was still at home. They would ride together through the woods, find markers for other homesteads and map out where Nate's would be. For now, the other topic would remain between the two men who were fast forming a bond. John certainly recognized that if anything should happen to him, his women would be left without anyone to help them in any way. In effect, he needed Nate about as much as Nate needed him. It was a time when people had to depend on each other. Neighbors helped neighbors. A man's word was his bond, and heaven help a man who couldn't be trusted.

The moon was already up when Nate left for the McDougalds' that night. Lily had insisted that he stay for supper, for which he was mighty grateful. He knew his supper would be on the stove at the Macs', and maybe kept warm by the hot water in the stove warmer, or maybe not. It would depend on whether or not they had cooked or eaten leftovers. As Nate rode along on Dewey, half pulling and half dragging Trouble, he enjoyed the moonlight. He was glad it was full and gave plenty of light. Nate had a bit of concern about riding in the night since his parents were killed when he was so young. It had left a mark on him. For that reason, he always stuck his dad's rifle into the saddle when he left the bunkhouse. Ever since President Jackson had moved the Indians out of the area, they were not a great threat. Now and then a renegade Indian was known to have been seen, and some did live in the area peacefully, but Nate worried more about white men who were up to no good.

He had decided to wait until his plans were a little firmer before telling Mr. Mac he was leaving his employ. The old man already knew it would be happening sooner or later.

The next Sunday was a bright, beautiful, late November day. The air was clean and crisp just after a little rainstorm had come through. Nate left early to go down to Melissa's, this time leaving Trouble behind. The dog howled a few minutes until Nate and Dewey got out of sight, tugging at the rope that tied him to a fig tree. He had water and shade; so Nate wasn't worried about him. He just hated not to take the poor dog that loved to go so much. Mr. Mac watched Nate ride off. "You want me to untie him when you get far enough away?" he asked Nate.

"Yes, sir. That will be fine," Nate answered. He knew Mr. Mac would have to wait a couple of hours. Trouble could track them with no problem even then, but maybe he wouldn't.

When Nate got to the Tate's, he said his greetings to the family. Then he teased Liz about her long braids and said, "Hello, Miss Mary," to Mary, who was these days looking mighty grown-up and attractive. He knew she would have suitors pretty soon herself. Liz was not as pretty as her sisters, but she had a certain spunkiness that would probably carry her along well.

"Melissa, would you like to go for a ride, if your dad will let us borrow his buggy?" he asked, knowing full well she would jump at the chance of getting away from the house for a while. Privacy was hard to come by there with everyone milling about. "It sure is a pretty day," he told her as they climbed into the buggy that her father, of course, let them borrow. Nate thought it was the most beautiful day he had ever seen in his entire life!

Dewey trotted along with the buggy behind him as though he were pulling a chariot of gold. He held his head high, tail back over the dashboard of the buggy in a regal manner. It wasn't often he had a chance to pull a buggy. Nate drove down the lane and onto the road that led toward the school.

When they reached the big magnolia where they had parked the buggy after the box supper, Nate stopped the buggy, got down and reached up to help Melissa down, also. She felt so light when he put his hands about her waist and helped her to the ground. Then, as if all in one motion, he took her into his arms and began to kiss her soundly. Melissa kissed Nate back as if she had waited all her life for that moment. They stood in each other's arms, as if they were one, for the longest time, both hearts beating as one. Nate knew this woman was to be his bride, his partner, his joy for the rest of his life.

"Melissa?" he said.

"Yes, Nathan," she whispered, not really wanting to talk. She just wanted to feel his strength, his warmth and his tenderness, in this very spot, their spot, forever.

"Melissa," he went on. "Will you marry me?" Melissa was dazed. She had somehow expected this to be different. She had not thought of it as being in such a lovely place as this spot had become for her. She thought it would probably happen in the swing at the house. She felt a little faint. Oh, I can't pass out now, she was thinking. I must savor every second of this time. "Nate! Oh, Nathan," was all she could say. He tipped her chin up, brushed a tear from her cheek and began kissing her again, holding her so tightly she had trouble breathing. Melissa didn't want this moment to ever end.

"Well?" he finally asked. "You haven't answered me?"

"I can't speak. I am too overcome to talk, Nathan. But, yes I will marry you. When?"

Proposal of Marriage

"Soon, my darling. Soon. I do love you so. It must be soon," He told her.

"I love you, Nathan. I love you so very much. I want to be your wife. I want to be with you forever."

As the afternoon wore on, the two of them sat in the buggy and talked as fast and hard as they could. They planned for the cabin, the wedding, and Melissa's thoughts were racing along to her trousseau and the things she would need for it. There were so many things to discuss — they had to leave some for next time. They had not talked about children, but it was understood couples would want children if it were possible to have them. Melissa said she would like to be married in April since it is such a pretty month in that area. Not too hot. Not too cool. Nate thought that was a perfect month, also, so that was agreed upon. He felt he could have the cabin built by then and many other things done that were essential to survival in an area that remote.

The afternoon shadows were beginning to lengthen as the couple returned to the house to tell Melissa's family the news. From then on, they would be considered a couple by the community. As soon as the announcement was made, it would be "Nate and Melissa" when anyone referred to them.

Mary and Liz both hugged Nate when they were told on the front porch. Their mother was cooking supper, so they walked on back toward the kitchen. Melissa was yelling "Mama!" as they went.

"In here, Melissa," she called back, knowing something was up. Lily took a dish towel, lifted the eye of the wood stove out with the key and prepared to place the tall, black wrought iron pot down into the coals that would cook the chicken for dumplings she was going to make. She almost dropped the pot when Melissa gleefully announced,

"Mama, Nate has asked me to marry him!"

"Well, now," Lily said, somewhat embarrassed. She was a shy lady who usually spoke when spoken to, and had little more to say. "I guess I will be mighty proud to have you in the family, Nate. I could use a son." That was it. She had welcomed him in a manner of speaking, and nothing more need be said.

Melissa was jubilant. She was hopping about looking for her father. Both of the sisters were excited. Mary wasn't sure what her sister's leaving home would do for her — probably mean a lot more work. Liz, now twelve, was only concerned with the excitement of the moment. John had been feeding the stock. As he came from the lot, Melissa met him to tell him the news, too. John looked mildly amused since he had known for a week this was going to happen. He congratulated Nate, shook his hand, and then Nate had to start for home. The cow would have to be milked by lantern light as it was.

A Homestead Found

The first part of December brought a cold snap and time to do many things in preparation for real winter. Butchering hogs was not anyone's favorite thing to do, but a necessity. The lard was used for storing meat in cans so that it would keep throughout the warm months. Meat was placed in large five gallon cans and lard poured around it. No part of the meat was wasted, and it had to be done in cold weather so that the meat would not spoil.

Everyone at the McDougald house had a task to do, even Pearl, who detested the butchering season. She had been somewhat sullen each time she and Nate encountered each other, but she had no choice but to participate. Hearing of Nate's and Melissa's betrothal had not made her any more pleasant toward him. She would have to work around him for the next two or three days, however. Mr. Mac and Miss Mattie, on the other hand, had taken the news pretty well. They had given up on the idea of marrying either Callie or Pearl off to him, but their mixed emotions came into play at the idea of losing Nate as a hand about the place. Miss Mattie's rheumatism in her hands and shoulders had grown increasingly worse with cooler weather, and Mr. Mac had to run the store. That might leave the little farm unattended unless he could find a sharecropper. He planned to ask Nate if he would farm it on halves. He figured he would need the income.

There was frost everywhere when Nate went out to feed the stock and milk. Minnie and her kittens were on hand for their dish of milk after a few streams were sent in their direction. They had to catch the rest of their food, usually, in the barn. Sometimes there were a few scraps of food for them, but with Minnie's teaching the kittens had learned well. Even in the nearby woods, and under piles of lumber and firewood, there were field mice for them. But hog killing day would provide many tasty tidbits for them as well as Trouble. It would also provide welcome fresh meat for the McDougalds and a good many neighbors who would gather to help in exchange for fresh meat. It was the custom to go and help neighbors. Then you were given roasts, sausage meat and cuts to take home. The men shot the hogs and dragged them to the scaffold to remove the insides, after which the women would begin the process of cutting up meat for sausage, bacon and ham. All fat was thrown into the wash pots, which were used for boiling clothes clean on wash days, but used for boiling fat into lard on hog killing days.

These were days of hard work, standing for long periods of time and getting terribly dirty, but they were also times for everyone to catch up on news and gossip. It was as much a social occasion as a work time. The McDougalds' two near neighbor families came to help. All the children were in school until late afternoon and thus missed the most unpleasant part: the actual shooting of the pigs with the rifle. Nate was given that task since he was an excellent shot and would make quick work of that part. He didn't relish that job, either, but it had to be done. Nate was not even much of a hunter, but in the spring and summer months, the only fresh meat was an unlucky squirrel or rabbit. Quail was another favorite, and sometimes doves, which were usually made into a pie. It was a matter of survival that things had to be killed.

A Homestead Found

The Sewards and Griffins from nearby arrived early. In about an hour, the first hog was hanging from the scaffold. It was a post placed well into the ground with two heavy cross bars forming an x where one animal could be hung on each enabling four men to work at a time. Mr. Mac acted more or less as the supervisor, running back and forth to the store as people came by to trade. Miss Mattie had to decide how much seasoning she wanted in her sausage, which she did to perfection. Everyone said she had the best sausage anywhere around. But first, there were the intestines to be cleaned. That was done by turning them inside out. The women would take a spoon to start the turning process and by pushing it into the end of one of the long tubes, they could start it turning. They were emptied and then thrown into a pot of boiling water, which further cleaned them and readied them for stuffing with sausage meat. The long strings of sausage were then hung on specially made poles over the rafters in the smoke house, where hickory smoke would further season and preserve them to perfection. It was a process that often took several weeks, depending on how much they were smoked during the day.

Matt Seward, one of the neighbors, was working along beside Nate. "I hear you're goin' to tie the knot with that little Tate girl you been seein'," he said as they worked.

"Yeah, next spring," Nate answered. He was a man of such few words that one had to pull every bit of information out of him.

Matt went on, "Well, when you get ready to build the cabin on your land, you can count on us to help." He liked this tall, quiet man. They had had little dealings except at the store, but Nate liked him, too. "Thanks. I appreciate that. I expect to start by the first of the year."

"Be a good idea to do it in cold weather. While the crops are laid by. That way you can be ready to plant a garden at least in the early spring. You won't get a crop made the first year. Too much new ground to clear, but you can plant your garden early. Ought to have all the vegetables you can use in that new ground," Matt explained.

Homestead

Of course, Nate knew all that, but the homestead was a favorite topic with him. He and Matt talked on about the plans. They were about the same ages, although Matt had been married for years and had three children.

Word was spreading about the impending marriage. All the ladies, except Pearl, were chattering away with Miss Mattie about how they could help Melissa with her trousseau. Miss Mattie had access to the store and would give her pots or pans, she said. Others were saving goose feathers for pillows and mattresses, so they would share them. A big bag of feathers was a cherished gift. They lasted virtually forever and were a true prize. When everyone came together, as they did for weddings and funerals, it was an easy matter to outfit a bride and groom with the things they needed. Melissa knew this, but Nate had not experienced as much of that sort of generosity as she had. He had no real concept of what people would actually do.

When the children arrived from school, even Ben and Rose had jobs to do. "Mr. Nate, can I turn the meat grinder?" Ben asked after he had changed into his play clothes.

"Sure, Ben. That job is made for you," Nate told him. Then, of course, Rose wanted to help. Before the meat was all ground and fed through the little, metal tube part of the grinder, right into the casings made from the intestines, both children had turned the grinder until their hearts were content! Nate figured they would all sleep well that night. The process could not all be completed in one day, so everything was secured from a possible roving animal in the night so that work could resume the next day in a hurry. Nate had promised to help John with his hog butchering, too, but that would be a lot more fun. He and Melissa would get to spend a couple of long days together albeit not the most romantic ones Nate hoped they would ever spend. John had told Nate they would stake out his land claim next, before any hogs were butchered, however. "What about the weather?" Nate had asked.

"Don't worry about that. We will have plenty of cold weather. Besides, the hogs will appreciate having a few more days to live," was John's reply. Nate hated so to shoot the poor old harmless things. He welcomed the reprieve, too. They looked at him so trustingly as he drew a bead on them with the rifle. He was glad it was very quick.

The day came for walking the land. Melissa did want so to go, but she had no horse, and it would be too much to have her ride behind Nate all day. They would be going into rough woods. "That is no place for you, my pretty little girl," John told her. "You will see it soon enough. Nate can show you where it is on the plat when we decide."

Mr. Mac gave Nate time off to search out the homestead property. Most of the main chores were done. Corn and beans were in the crib, the land was plowed for planting, and they could manage without Nate a couple of days. "You go do whatever you need to do," he told Nate.

On the sixth of December, Nate left home before daylight. His excitement could hardly be contained. Dewey undoubtedly knew something was up. He had a lot of energy that cold morning and was ready to go. Horse and rider arrived at the Tates' just after sunup. Miss Lily had coffee made and a big pot of grits cooking. She gave Nate a bowl filled to the brim and swimming with fresh butter. "My goodness, Miss Lily, you sure do make good grits," he said in the way of thanking her for the breakfast.

"If you and John would get the butchering done, you could have sausage with those grits," she said, teasing Nate. She had a dry sense of humor most people didn't recognize. Nate could tell by the twinkle in her blue eyes that she was teasing in her way, though.

The two men stuck their rifles into their saddles. John threw Nate a bedroll. "Just in case we don't get back." Miss Lily had also packed food, big biscuits with butter and jelly. "This may taste mighty good about the noon hour," John told his future son-in-law.

Homestead

They rode due east for an hour or so, both lost in their own thoughts and not talking. Finally, John broke the silence. "Now, son. This land is unclaimed. It joins mine and the Rogers homestead sandwiched right between. If you like this tract, it is available. If not, we can ride further. My advice to you would be to get as near neighbors as you conveniently can. Neighbors can be mighty helpful if they are the right neighbors, and the Rogers are the best."

The land was as it had been for hundreds, perhaps thousands, of years. As Nate looked at it, he wanted to laugh, and he wanted to cry. He thought he had never seen anything, short of Melissa, so beautiful in his life. The thought that it could one day be his was almost too much to take in. Settling this land would be the culmination of years of hoping, dreaming and waiting for him.

They stopped the horses and tied them to a small oak. Both men dismounted, with Nate gazing in wonder and awe at the virgin timber, mostly pines, which had never been cut. There were pines that were probably two feet thick. They had taken at least two hundred years to grow, he figured. John had intended to show this piece of land to Nate all along, but had said nothing. He wanted to surprise him, which he did. Nate had no idea what pieces were available and was ever so pleased that it was as close to the Tates' as it was. It would be good for Melissa to have her mother near, especially when the babies came along. A girl needs her mother at those times.

The big trees made a whirring sound as the brisk, cold air blew through them. It seemed to Nate the most peaceful place on earth. It would be a wonderful place to live and raise a family. John explained that the school was just south of the property about a mile, not too far for little ones to walk. They had ridden about four miles east to the farther-most side of the hundred sixty-acre tract. It was rough riding, but there was a slight trail, evidently made by cattle and the men who worked for the turpentine company which ran a turpentine still a few miles southeast of there. The next parcel over was undeveloped too, since the Rogers home was on its eastern edge. They had been able to start a small patch of a farm was all.

As John and Nate made their way through dense briars, brush and tall grass, they surveyed the land for a home-site. A small clearing appeared to be the right place where the least effort would be required for building the cabin, outhouses and a garden.

"Now, son," John began. "I would start with a lot and barn or corn crib. You know you will have to have a place for some livestock. You're gonna need to pen your stock up." Nate was wondering *what stock?* He had Dewey, but John had plans. He had a brood sow already picked out for Nate and his daughter. Then the cow had just had a female calf back in the fall — just what they would need for milk. She ought to be ready for breeding in the late spring or summer. As soon as the calf was born, she would have milk aplenty.—"You see, a crib is a necessity for storing anything you grow. We can build it out of small poles that you and I can cut and haul. Then when the neighbors come to help build the cabin, you'll have the crib all done," John continued. He was every bit as excited as Nate. "Let's get started right away." John didn't know why he felt such a sense of urgency. He was just a man who, faced with a task, wanted to get it done.

Nate was thinking about working on for Mr. Mac, as he had proposed recently, and farming his small field on halves. He told Nate he could sell his half right there in the store, if he wanted him to. Nate told him he surely did, except for enough corn and beans to use for feed. "You know, Mr. Mac wants me to work on for him on halves, which I think I can do by working about two days a week in the field. I've got it about ready to plant when the weather is right. I could spend two days there and the rest of the time here on the land," Nate told John.

"That is a good plan, Nate. You will need a little income for things requiring money." John was thinking this fellow is going to be a good manager and take mighty good care of my daughter. It was a great relief to him to have another man coming into the family who would have the family's interest at heart.

Homestead

While at the clearing, they paced off the area where the cabin could go, and then marked off an area for the lot and crib. Nate told his father-in-law-to-be that he would like for Melissa to see the area and help decide where she wanted these buildings placed. John thought that was also an excellent idea. "Lily and the younger girls will have a fit if they don't get to come along. What do you say we bring the whole family over here Sunday afternoon?" Nate readily agreed. It would be tough going for them, but they could follow the cow trail and manage. They were used to rough going. John told Nate they could take the horses and let the women take turns riding.

Nate was reluctant to leave the beautiful place. He drew the fresh, cold air into his lungs, looked long and hard at the land, as if not to forget one thing about it, and followed John down the tiny trail made through the tall wiregrass and bushes. "Well, there's one more thing I haven't told you about this property," John was telling Nate when he dragged his mind back to reality.

"What?" Nate asked, ready to hear all of it.

"There is a branch about an eighth of a mile from where we picked the home site." He looked at Nate to see his reaction. "The branch is another fork of the spring that heads up right down the hill from my house where the spring box is."

"Wonderful!" Nate began immediately thinking how handy the water source could be, especially until they got a well dug. It could provide enough water to keep them going. "That is wonderful! I have been thinking how we are going to get a well."

"You'll just have to wait until we can get hold of a well digger. They come through every now and then." It took a little special know-how to dig a good well. No use not doing it right. A well was a lifetime thing; a highly essential part of every home.

Nate also wanted the cabin to have a small shed room for privacy. He wanted his bride to have a place to retreat to dress or bathe or for whatever she needed it. Such a room was sometimes called a pouting room that a lady could take herself off to if she got mad with her husband. Nate didn't see much of that happening, but it was also a place to put the chamber pot they would have to use until a privy could be built.

While Nate and John were concentrating on cabin building and homesteading, the women were busy planning for the wedding and furnishings for the cabin. Lily went over a number of items she intended to give Melissa. She had to keep in mind some things she would retain for the other two girls, but Melissa and Nate could get their own things one day, and perhaps give back things for Mary and Liz to use.

"Mama, I want you to root me a cutting of each of your roses and some gardenias," Melissa told Lily one day.

"I am already ahead of you there. I put cuttings of everything under jars last summer. They should be rooted by now." Lily was one to think ahead. That was the way out in the wilderness where you couldn't run out and buy everything you wanted. She placed the cuttings in the soft ground, on the north side of the house and turned a fruit jar down over them. It was a sure way to root anything.

John had brought in an almanac for the new year on his most recent trip. It had a calendar from which Melissa had chosen the fourteenth of April for a wedding day. She wanted to wear a long sleeved, high-necked dress, and she hated the hot, damp weather summer would bring. Besides, they needed to get the wedding over with so they could be working at clearing new ground during the summer months. Nate intended to make a garden so that she would have beans to dry, seeds to save for the following year, and they could take full advantage of the growing season.

As Sunday approached, Melissa's excitement increased. She wanted to talk to Nate about the circuit-riding preacher. The Tates were a deeply religious family, so she wanted to have the preacher marry them. She knew Mr. Mac at the store was a notary public, but somehow that was not in accordance with her desires. The preacher had to be notified way in advance so that he could arrange his travels to include an area if there was to be a wedding. Nate's religious teachings had been neglected, along with all his other education, but his basic desire was to be a good man and do the right thing. He immediately agreed that Melissa's father should send word to the preacher for the fourteenth of April as their wedding day. If he couldn't come for some reason, then the wedding date would be changed. Four months notice was probably enough, John had said.

Nate arrived early, a s was his usual habit, and the family set out to go to the property. Everyone did well on the journey except Liz, who complained that she had a blister on her foot from her shoe. That entitled her to ride Dixie most. When they arrived at the small clearing, Melissa let out a squeal of pure delight! "This is the greatest!" she exclaimed, dashing about, suggesting places for this and that. Her father and Nate showed her their broken branches that marked the cabin site and places for other buildings. She loved each one and quickly stamped her approval on each, just as Nate had thought she would. She was a happy type person who took joy out of almost anything. Nate admired that quality in her greatly.

Lily, Mary and Liz took turns riding Dewey, but Melissa didn't need to ride. She bounced along with all the energy in the world needing nothing to keep her going but her own excitement. Plans were made for the three Tate ladies to drive up to Mr. Mac's store the following week, in the buggy, to look at material. They planned to get wedding dress material and a few other pieces for unmentionables. Luckily, Lily was an expert with a needle. She made such small stitches that the other ladies around could hardly see them. Being famous for her quilting, she had made many quilts, some of which she would give her daughters when they married. They were made from scraps of every dress she or the girls had ever had, plus some from John's shirts and old pants. When pants wore too thin to patch, they still had good spots of fabric that could be made into quilt scraps. Worsted wool made heavy cover, which was handy on very cold nights in homes and cabins depending solely on fireplaces for heat. When the fire went out in the night, cover had better be heavy.

Stormy Homecoming

Matt Seward lived about a quarter of a mile from McDougald's Store right on the road to Creighton, which was nothing but a well-traveled pair of ruts with a grassy hump in the middle. He and his family were generous and kind people who helped out in all situations, so it was characteristic of him to offer to help Nate with building the cabin. Nate was working in the store just before Christmas when Matt came in. "Have you started on that cabin, yet?" he asked, teasing Nate.

"No, but we did stake out the area and decided where to put it." Nate was eager to talk about the cabin.

"Well, I tell you what," Matt continued, "I have my crop laid by, my hogs butchered, and I don't have much to do from now till the first of the year. What do you say we get started? I can go with you to see about getting the logs cut," he offered. "I have a team, you know, that can pull those logs. I have a good crosscut saw, too."

Now Nate was really getting excited! "All right. I'm ready. My intended's dad is home right now, too, and he was planning to help me."

The two men went ahead planning the time. It would be the day after Christmas. That was only a week away. Nate had already worked it out with Mr. Mac to go to Creighton and get Callie when she came in on the train on the twentieth. At that time he planned to buy his wagon and bring her home in it. He would ride Dewey over to town so that he could pull the wagon back. They planned to take Dewey and the wagon and Matt's team, as well as his big saw and tools. Nate had few tools, but could use Mr. Mac's.

Before Nate left for Creighton, the weather turned foul. It rained and got colder by the minute. For a while, it looked as if he might have to take the buggy. It had a top. Of course, the rain still could blow right into their faces if it were coming from the south, the way they'd be heading on the way back. Miss Mattie packed him a lunch because he was leaving early and would be ravenous before the train arrived at 11:40. Dewey was, as usual, rearing to go. He was devilish and loved to nuzzle Nate with his wet nose. Nate always reacted with a "Dewey!" admonishment, which the horse seemed to understand and love. He surely did it over and over.

They made it in to Creighton early enough for Nate to buy the wagon before the train was due. He hitched Dewey to the post outside the store called Creighton Buggy Works. Inside he talked to a man who showed him what they had and he made a selection. It was a good looking-wagon with red wheels and tooling on the back of the seat which made it a little fancier than the usual wagon. He paid for it while a couple of other employees in the store pushed the wagon out of the back of the showroom and readied it for hitching Dewey up to it. Dewey watched, snorting a time or two, just to let Nate know he understood they finally had a wagon in which to move their belongings about: his saddle, Nate's rifle, a few clothes and things he had acquired since moving to Mr. Mac's.

Callie was the first person off the train. She looked thinner than Nate remembered and altogether better looking. Her hair was up in a new style, like the city girls were wearing, he guessed.

Stormy Homecoming

He loaded her things into the new wagon. "Oh, look at this!" she said excitedly. "Did my dad just get a new wagon?"

"No. I just got a new wagon," Nate said proudly. "I just bought it. In fact, Dewey thinks he bought it." Nate started Dewey out of town. He trotted along proudly, apparently feeling quite stylish himself.

The weather held for about an hour, then the sky darkened and began to look fierce. Nate grew concerned about lightning. It appeared a long way off, but you could never tell. He had heavy coats for them, just in case. As they progressed, the storm came closer. Finally, the wind picked up and the rain began. Callie grew alarmed. Dewey was hesitating, but kept going on as Nate coaxed him. He especially didn't like the lightning. The skies were so dark it could have been midnight, but there was nothing to do but continue on. There were no houses or barns anywhere near. It was three or four miles to the next house. Nate knew they couldn't get under a tree, because of the lightning, but thought it might be better than being out in the open. The next worry was they still had the river to cross. He feared he couldn't get the horse to go over that bridge in the wind. He thought it would be a quick storm that would pass in a hurry since it was so intense.

For lack of a better plan, Nate decided to stop the wagon, unhitch Dewey and pull him up as close as he could, then he and Callie got under the wagon. Nate held tightly to the reins in case Dewey decided to bolt. They sat on the wet, soggy ground but were sheltered a bit by the wagon bed. Callie was getting cold as she got wetter. Nate knew they would have to do something fast, because the temperature was dropping rapidly. It could be freezing by nightfall, although it was only about noon at the time they left Creighton. They had been about two miles, he judged.

As the rain pelted down, Nate covered Callie the best he could with his own body, hoping to keep her partially dry. All the while Dewey was snorting and rearing. Nate knew he must keep him from bolting. If that horse got loose, no telling when he would find him. He kept trying to soothe Dewey and Callie. "Just a little longer, Callie," he told her. "Just a little longer. It will be over soon. Storms like this usually don't last long. They blow themselves out pretty fast." Callie was sobbing softly. She was worried about her valise and other bags up in the wagon.

"What about my things?" she sobbed.

That stuff was the least of Nate's worries. "It'll be all right. Nothing up there that won't dry on a sunny day." With that came the thought of what he could do. As soon as the storm was over, he could have Callie change to dry clothes; at least a dry dress and undergarments. Surely the leather valise would keep her things dry! He would have to see about that as soon as the weather broke.

It seemed to Nate the storm must have lasted about an hour when the wind started calming a bit. Lightning had struck something nearby. They heard the report and saw a huge flash. Fortunately, Nate had the reins on Dewey tightly in his hand. "Steady, boy. Steady," he kept saying to the horse. As soon as the worst was over, Nate planned to move on. He knew they must make as much time as possible before dark when it would get much colder. Although they couldn't see the sun, it was up there warming the earth a little. "Callie?" he said, "I think, as soon as this slacks a little more, that you'd better change your clothes and try to dry up a bit. I fear this storm is bringing colder air behind it."

"Where will I change? There isn't any place!" Callie cried.

"You'll just have to use the back of the wagon. I won't look," he told the soggy girl. "Much!" he added, hoping to tease her a little and lighten things up. It didn't have the desired affect. She cried all the harder.

After the thunder and lightning stopped, the wind also died down, but the rain slowed to a drizzle and showed no signs of stopping, maybe for a day or two, so Nate decided they must push on. He got Callie to crawl out from under the wagon, and while he hitched Dewey back up to the wagon, he told her to try to find something dry in her valise to put on. She whimpered that everything would be soaked. Her own coat she had worn on the train was wet, as was the great coat Nate had brought along for her in case of just such a situation. His great coat was also soaked. They weighed a ton when they were wet, and he wondered just how long it would take them to dry out.

"Well, look in your valise and see what you can find. Get under things, too."

"Nathan York!" Callie admonished him.

"Look, Callie. This is no time to go getting shy. We are in a mess, and we have got to get out of it." Nathan was cold himself, and getting in no mood to put up with a sniveling woman. "Now look for something to put on!" Callie looked. She found things dry, except a spot or two, got out a warm dress, petticoat and step-ins, and prepared to change.

"They'll all just get wet again! There's no use doing this."

"Do it, anyway," Nate commanded. He felt it would help to have the under things dry even though their coats were wet. "And hurry. I'll turn around."

Callie stripped to the skin behind the wagon, which actually offered no privacy at all, and did as Nate had said. It took only a minute to dress, then she had to put the wet coat on over her almost dry clothes. It felt a little better, though. The drizzle was light at the moment, so Nate hoped she could stay a little drier than she had been. He was cold, too, but used to it. The times Nate had been soaked to the skin and freezing were too numerous to count. When he traveled about on foot, before ending up at the McDougald's, he was often wet and cold, with no place to sleep. He had carried matches in a tobacco tin, so he could make a fire and dry out his clothes, or at least warm them up, along with his bed roll, so that he could sleep a few hours. He had matches in the tin in his overall pocket now, but he thought they needed to make the time, if possible. The first homestead was about five miles away, Nate judged. If nothing else, he could leave Callie and the wagon there, ride Dewey on in, and go back for her and the wagon the next day.

Homestead

With Callie changed and Dewey hitched, they started on. The rain continued to drizzle, just enough to be cold and miserable. If only the sun would come out, it would dry them and warm them up. Callie's tears began then to turn to anger. "If you hadn't had to buy this wagon and had brought my daddy's buggy, Nathan, we wouldn't be in this fix," she accused.

"Well, there's where you are wrong, Miss McDougald," he flared right back. "Surely you don't think that little ole buggy would have protected us. You couldn't even get under it."

Callie began to cry again. She fussed, then cried. Nate knew she was just feeling frustrated and miserable, but heck, so was he!

They got to the bridge. Nate surveyed the situation, sizing it up. There must have been some heavy rain up in Alabama, because the river was swelling fast. It was red with clay and mud. Limbs were floating along with the swift current and along its banks he could see little streams of water running into the river from its banks here and there from the downpour they'd just had. The bridge looked undamaged from all he could see. It was high enough that there would be no problem if the river rose unless it damaged the pilings in the riverbed. Dewey seemed calmer, but he was still apprehensive.

"Looks like it is safe to cross," Nate said to the unhappy young lady in the wagon. "We can be home by good dark." She didn't look a bit happier. She was shivering, and Nate was getting more concerned about her. If she got the grip, he'd feel mighty bad.

As he urged the horse on, they crossed the bridge with no problem. Then he started him out at a good pace, trying to hurry as best he could. By the time they were nearing the next homestead, Nate realized he had to do something to get Callie dry and warm. He decided to stop there and leave her overnight. He knew she would not want to stay, being anxious to get home to see her family, as they were anxious to see her, but it was not worth the risk. "I am going to stop at the McDaniel place, Callie, and see if you can stay the night with them. It is getting colder, and you will be sick if we don't get you warmed up pretty soon."

"Oh, no," she protested. "I want to go home!"

"I know you do, but you are shivering. You could get the grip and be really sick."

"But what about you? What are you going to do?" she finally asked, thinking about him for the first time instead of herself.

"I will leave the wagon and ride Dewey on home. I will come back for you the first thing in the morning or as soon as the weather clears."

"But what if it doesn't clear tomorrow? I could miss being home for Christmas!" Callie was distressed and disappointed. She had gifts for everyone, including Nate, which she had bought in Mobile. Nate was thinking about what if it didn't clear so he could get her home and go to see Melissa on Christmas Day. He had a vested interest in getting Miss Callie McDougald home.

Although Nate didn't know the McDaniels well, he had seen them at the store, and Callie knew them. He threw the reins over the gatepost and took the wide steps two at the time. An old dog lying on the porch looked up and thumped his tail on the wide board floor, as if to say "Welcome." Nate knocked loudly on the doorframe and called out "Hello!" It took a minute, but Mrs. McDaniel peered out the window and seeing Callie shivering in the wagon, opened the door. She said certainly the girl could stay the night with her. At that time she was alone, anyway. He husband and son were on a trip to the mill to get corn ground and pick up some lumber. She didn't expect them home till the next day.

Nate got Callie unloaded and left her, telling her to get good and dry and asked Mrs. McDaniel to fix her a hot drink. "I'll put her to bed with a hot brick to her feet!" the lady told him. He explained that he would be back as soon as the weather cleared. Leaving Callie to tell her hostess the whole story, Nate unhitched Dewey and threw the saddle on the big horse, to ride the rest of the way home, leaving his new wagon sidetracked for the time being. All he took was his rifle out of the wagon.

The McDougald family had grown more than a little concerned after the weather turned bad so quickly. Nobody had anticipated that. Nate thought Miss Mattie was going to faint when she realized he was alone. "It's all right!" he quickly told them. "I left Callie at the McDaniels'. I will go back for her as soon as the rain stops." He recounted the events of the day, not leaving out the part about his new wagon, for sure, and they settled down for the evening. "I sure appreciate you looking after our girl, Nate," Mr. Mac said. Nate was not sure they were home-free still. He was concerned about her being sick from getting so wet and cold. He thought better of saying anything about that, however, and said goodnight. He needed to see about his dog and get some dry clothes on. Dewey was pleased with a big bunch of hay and some feed in the trough. He had a warm barn where he would spend the night.

Nate was greeted by a happy Trouble. He was glad he had not taken the dog. A fire in his potbellied stove and dry clothes made Nate feel a lot better. He had some dry beef and corn bread with a glass of buttermilk for supper and went right to bed.

As luck would have it, morning came with bright sun making the world look clean and fresh. After breakfast, Nate saddled Dewey and headed out to get Callie. He had no thought for how he would find her. Mrs. McDaniel met him with a worried look. "She's got a fever and chills," she told Nate. "I am afeered she ought not to travel."

Callie had other ideas, though. She had dressed and was preparing to leave. Nate felt her forehead and was greatly concerned. But he could see she was determined to go, so he went ahead and loaded her and her things into the buggy, which he had brought this time. Making arrangements to leave the wagon a while longer, he hurried Callie along home. She was coughing and felt terrible. "You'll get home and feel better soon," he said, trying to comfort the sick girl. Callie was not talking much. Her throat hurt. Her eyes were watering, and Nate diagnosed her problem as a nasty old cold. Mrs. McDaniel had dried her clothes by the fire all night; so she was dry and warm. That was the best Nate could do for the time being. Miss Mattie would have something from the store for her to take.

It was Christmas Eve, and when the pair arrived, there was both joy and concern at the McDougalds. Nate's concern was his new wagon parked under a pecan tree up the road about four miles. He did so want Melissa to see it, but that would have to wait.

Homestead

House Raising

Building the lot for the horse, cow and some pigs went smoothly and quickly. Nate was amazed at the expert way his friend and future father-in-law worked. They had experience, which he didn't have, and he was ever so grateful to both of them.

John started Nate digging holes for fence posts with the posthole diggers while he and Matt began cutting trees the size needed for the fence. They knew how to use a crosscut saw! Nate took delight in every tree that was felled, and worked all the faster, because of it. John had bought a load of wide boards to put at the bottom of the fence to keep pigs in. They would root right under pine logs. The boards were on his wagon, so he and Nate offloaded them so the wagon would be free for hauling poles. Dewey was hitched to Nate's wagon and put to use, also.

When noon came, the holes were dug, enough poles were cut, and within two hours, a fence was starting to take shape. They ate their lunches Lily had packed and got right back to work. Nate set the poles by putting them into the ground and closing up the holes. The other two men continued cutting poles, this time larger for the crib. The fence would be finished that day, but the crib would have to wait until the next day.

Homestead

Once Nate got the posts set, John and Matt helped him nail the poles on to make the fence bars. The one great thing about pine poles was their resistance to termites, a pest that had to be dealt with in the warm, moist climate of the south. The log cabin would be built of the same pine logs, rich in rosin, and termite resistant. They would chink the cracks between the logs with rosin that could be bought at the turpentine still three or four miles away. Tin on the roofs of all the buildings would be fire-proof and longwearing. It had been decided that Matt and Nate would go to the lumberyard in Creighton and haul the load of tin with Matt's team.

When the men got back to John's, Melissa met them, eyes dancing with interest and excitement. She wanted to know the particulars of the entire process, but Matt and Nate had to get on, so John took the responsibility of bringing her up on every move they had made. While John and Matt were planning ahead, Nate had a chance to steal a quick, wet kiss in the hall out of sight.

The men would work the next day from early morning until late evening on the corncrib. It began to take shape, but would require a lot more work. Nate had to work in the store a couple of days during that time because Mr. Mac's rheumatism was really bad in his knee, making it difficult to stand for long hours. Pearl could run the store, but she couldn't unload heavy feed, flour, salt and sugar bags. Her dad would sit out there and direct, which Pearl and Nate had just as soon he wouldn't do, while Nate un-loaded what the jobbers would bring in with their teams and wagons. They would be loaded with supplies needed in the store. It was the only store nearer than Creighton, so people had no choice but to trade there. Then on the thirteenth Nate and Matt would take Callie back to the train and get the load of tin. It seemed to be a good plan, but Nate was not sure Callie would hear of going on the wagon. If not, he would have to drive her in the buggy and let Matt bring up the rear in the wagon.

House Raising

"Callie, will you agree to ride in the wagon to the train?" Nate timidly asked her at breakfast the next morning.

She must have felt rather ashamed of her behavior on the way home, because she agreed without hesitation, to Nate's surprise. "Yes, I will be glad to," came the reply. Again, Ben and Rose chimed in, wanting to go, and Nate sorely hated not to take the children. They had so little chance to go anywhere and see things, but there was no way he could do it that time.

"Kids," he said,

"I can't take you this time. You would have to ride home on a huge load of tin, but I promise you, I will take you to Creighton one day very soon when the weather gets warmer and we don't have to haul anything." He had decided right then to have Melissa go along with him and the kids on a day trip to Creighton. That would work on one of the longer days in the spring. They were appeased and went on about their playing, satisfied. Nate needed to buy some clothes, anyway, and figured Melissa and the children could do something while he did his shopping. He needed a suit for the wedding, for one thing.

When Nate and Callie stopped to pick up Matt, his children and wife came out to talk. Nate had only seen them at the store. He didn't actually know Martha Seward, Matt's wife, or the children. They were cute, talkative kids with a lot of sparkle and personality. Nate liked them right off. He made a mental note to buy peppermint candy for them and Rose and Ben to bring back.

Callie sat between Matt and Nate in the wagon seat for the long ride. It would be nearly train time when they got to the depot, so they had to rush along. It was a little crowded, but she was a good sport about that. She had changed her attitude completely, Nate decided. He thought she might have come to the realization that he had done his best to manage the situation on the ride home.

Matt asked the first question after riding in silence for a few minutes. "So, how is the training going?"

"Just fine. I finish at the end of March," Callie replied proudly.

"Hey, good. Then what?" Matt continued.

"Well, I hope to stay in Mobile and find a job." The reply surprised Nate. He wondered if her parents were aware of that decision.

"You like it that much down there?" It was Nate who asked that question.

"Yes, I do. I love the city. It has so many things to do. There are always places to go and interesting things to see. It's terribly dull here at home." Matt was nodding his head. He had been to Mobile many times, whereas Nate had never been there. Nate had only been to Montgomery, Alabama, and only once. He liked the country and woods. Cities intimidated him.

Matt and Callie talked on about trivial things as Nate drove the team. They had left Dewey in his lot and parked the wagon since he had two horses and a big wagon sufficient for the heavy load of tin. Nate rode along in silence, his mind on a thousand things, mostly Melissa and the cabin.

As soon as Callie was on the train, the men drove to the hardware store for the tin. It took a chunk out of Nate's savings, but it was one of the biggest purchases he would have to make. Most of the other needs were growing right on the property. Tin was a great investment because of its durability, as well as the deterrent against fire. Woods fires were often set by lightning or someone's carelessness and were one of the greatest fears the homesteaders had. They had huge bells outside their homes to ring for help to alert neighbors, if there were any close by, because fire, accident, illnesses and injury were prevalent. It was the main way to summon help, and it was to be one of the first things Nate would need to invest in. Mr. Mac had some on hand. All he had to do was put up a post and hang the bell on it.

On the way home, Nate talked and Matt listened. He told Matt a few things about his parents, his sisters and his childhood, enough that Matt got the picture of Nate's unfortunate lack of education and opportunities, but he definitely was a man of few words. Matt determined to help this man in as many ways as he could, because he genuinely liked Nate York and could see what a fine man he truly was.

Martha had supper ready when they got back to Matt's, and she insisted Nate stay. He welcomed the opportunity to be a part of the little family's supper hour. She had cooked sweet potatoes that were so sweet they had almost candied. She had pork chops and turnip greens with cornbread. Nate thought he had never tasted such wonderful food.

"Thank you, ma'am, for the supper," he told her. "I am afraid I made a pig out of myself."

Martha had enjoyed watching him eat and said as much. "You and Melissa must come to see us whenever you can after you get caught up with all the work, and I want to come the day you get all the neighbors together to put up the cabin!" She had a certain excitement in her voice that Nate liked. She was a cheerful person, much like Melissa. He thought they would always be good friends.

"That will be pretty soon. We are making progress," Matt told her.

Nate pulled one of the little brown bags out of his pocket after supper, with the stick candy in it, and the children were elated. The main kind of candy they got was peanut brittle, which their mother made, unless they went to Creighton to see Matt's parents. Then Grandpa Seward took them to the Mercantile, and they got taffy. There was another bag in Nate's pocket for Rose and Ben.

When Nate started to leave, the three Seward children lined up at the door of the big house, which Matt had already built. They wanted to say thank you for the candy. Bonnie, seven and the oldest, said, "Thank you, Mr. Nate, for the candy. It is delicious." Then came Sissy, six, and little Matthew, just three. They tried to say the same thing Bonnie had said. Nate was struck with the children's manners and good looks. They looked most like their mother, who was a real beauty. She had very dark hair, straight and done in a bun at the nape of her neck. Her eyes were black and shiny, just like her hair. He figured she had some Indian blood, and he figured correctly. Her cheekbones were high, and her skin a lovely olive.

"You come back anytime, Nate," Martha said as he left.

By the first week of January, the three men had the crib built, the lot fenced and were ready to put up the cabin. Plans were made, and John had notified all the community of homesteaders. The women would attend with baskets of food, making a picnic at noon. They chose a day when the children were at school so that they would not be in the way. Only the little ones went, some toddlers and other babes in arms. One woman would watch the three or four children while the others hoed the grass and weeds that had not already been beaten down by the men working, because there would be a danger of snakes in grass and weeds. Nate had plowed new ground for a small, but adequate, garden for the two of them, so other women put out collard plants, and sowed a row of turnip seeds, which would come up right away and be ready by the time they moved into the cabin.

There were seven families represented at the site where the cabin was to go. Franklin Rogers came with his wife. He was the man Nate had met at the Tates' the night he met Melissa. "I really appreciate your willingness to help out," Nate told Franklin.

"Glad to do it. You know, you will be our closest neighbors. Our property joins on the south," he replied. "Have you met my wife? This here is Nate York, sugar," he told her. "Nate, my wife, Grace."

"Howdy, Miss Grace. I am mighty proud to make your acquaintance. I suppose you know Melissa, my intended?" Grace said, yes, that she had known Melissa since they were cutting teeth.

"Our families have known each other since they came here to homestead, and Melissa and I were in the same grade at school."

Melissa came up about that time, and the two began to talk about the wedding. Nate was able to escape at that point.

Melissa and Grace were sort of best friends. They had shared many secrets as they were growing up, so Melissa decided to ask Grace a few personal questions. There were things she could not ask her mother, and her mother was not about to tell her those things. Mothers were too embarrassed to talk to their daughters about private things.

"Grace, come over here. I want to talk to you," Melissa said. They huddled together, not obvious at all, and Melissa said, "Tell me how to keep from getting in the family way till we are married a while. I don't want to have a baby right off."

"Well, the only way I know is to have him pull out. Do you know what I mean?" Melissa was nodding her head "yes." "But that doesn't always work. You just have to hope and pray. Now once you have a baby, they say you won't get that way again as long as you nurse, but that sure didn't work in Martha's case. You can look at her three and tell that! She was married to Matt exactly nine months when Bonnie was born, and then along came Sissy a year later."

Melissa was all ears until Franklin came over to ask Grace something and broke up the conversation. As soon as he left, Grace started up again with her advice. "Now, you know one thing that will for sure work? Kick Nate out of the bed when he mentions doing it!"

"Shucks, Grace, after I've waited all this time? Not likely!" Melissa, a healthy, red-blooded girl, had no such intentions. Now that she was promised, she was considered one of the group of married and almost married young women, so she would be included in the "talk" from now on.

While the young women talked about babies and such, the older ladies were gossiping a bit. Lily had very little to say, because she was not a gossip, but when it came to listening, she did that as well as the next person. Clara Rogers was not one to tell untruths or hurtful things about anyone. She did enjoy a juicy bit of talk, too, though, so when Mozelle Weeks started to tell them what she had just heard, they listened intently. Mozelle lived some distance away near another homestead belonging to the Smiths. "Do you know what happened the other day?"

They nodded that they didn't know. "Jack was coming home from the sawmill and stopped by the Smiths' just to see Clayton for a few minutes about something, and who do you think was there?" They shook their heads again that they didn't know. "Well, he went up to the door and knocked. Nobody came to the door, so he waited a minute and knocked again. And that's when he heard it." The other ladies were most attentive by now.

Clara spoke up, "Well, for goodness sakes, Mozelle, do go on and tell us!" Her curiosity was getting the better of her fast.

Mozelle continued, relishing every word of her story, "So after the third knock, he hears the back door kind of slam, and when he looked, who do you think he saw leaving the Smith's house?" Everyone was by then totally exasperated with Mozelle, and growing more curious by the moment.

"Who, Mozelle, who?" Clara asked. "Tell it!"

"It was none other than Jeff Taylor!" Mozelle said, feeling quite satisfied with her big news. The others gasped and looked shocked when all the while they knew very well that Jeff Taylor had a reputation of being a ladies' man and calling on any woman who would allow it, be she married, single or whatever. He was a good-looking devil, a real scoundrel and, for that matter, the others had heard a tale or two on Mozelle Weeks.

When the day ended, the cabin was floored, logs were in place and the tin roof was on. Nate was the happiest man alive, and Melissa the happiest woman. She didn't feel she had gotten a lot of help from Grace on the other matter, but she would talk to her again about that later. They both thanked the friends for coming. John stood with Lily as everyone was leaving and thanked all of them, too. It was incredible what a group of men like that could

House Raising

do when they all got together. Now Nate and John would chink the spaces between the poles with rosin, which they would get the next day at the turpentine still, and as soon as the doors and windows were in, it would be ready for its new owners. It was twelve by eighteen feet, not counting the tiny shed room they put on, at Nate's request, for Melissa mostly. For the time being, the fireplace was a gaping hole in the wall covered over with tin. It would be built as soon as they could get a bricklayer to do it. John knew someone he could get.

Melissa would cook in the fireplace until they could afford a stove. She knew how to do that. Many nights at home, they didn't heat up the kitchen stove because it was too cold or too hot in there. They could make up corn meal with salt and water, heat a skillet in the fire and make lacy cornbread by pouring the watery mixture into the hot grease. It would run all over the pan and cook to a crispy golden brown with lacy edges. It was a favorite at the Tate house. A pot of field peas with white meat and a couple of green peppers made a wonderful meal. Melissa was already a good enough cook. She wanted to wait and buy a real stove like her mother's when they got one.

Homestead

Planning the Future

The weeks were going by rapidly. Spring had come for real in March. The wind blew a gale every day, but trees were putting out new growth, plants were coming up, including the weeds, and some flowers, like the bridal wreath, daffodils and some of Lily's roses were blooming. It looked as if there would be plenty of flowers for the wedding if a late cold snap didn't come and ruin all of them. Melissa hoped desperately that wouldn't happen. She decided to have the wedding outdoors in her mother's flower garden if the weather turned out to be good.

John had built Lily a rose trellis some years earlier. It was covered with a lovely running rose in a wedding pink, which should be in full bloom by April fourteenth. That was a Sunday, which Lily said would be the best day to have the wedding. So many more people could come on Sunday. They stopped work on the Lord's Day, but no other time. There was too much work to do and not enough hands to do it. John had sent word to the Circuit Rider and got word back that he could be counted on to be there. Melissa was pleased about that especially. She loved Reverend Lock, which would make it a happier occasion with him performing the ceremony. Her dress was complete; her hope chest full to the brim, and she was ready to start her new life with the man she adored.

ꞌHomestead

Nate still had a few things to do. He planned a trip to Creighton to take all the children; Rose, Ben and Matt's three. They would have to go in the wagon, starting out very early in the morning in order to have much time in town. Melissa would go to help with the children, but Martha decided since little Matthew was only three and still had to have naps that he'd better not go. He also had accidents now and then even though he was out of diapers. The children were thrilled, especially Rose and Ben. Nate wasn't sure they had ever been to a town. Martha was also invited, but declined, saying she had yard work to do.

Melissa drove her daddy's buggy as far as McDougald's, and then they decided everyone could get into the buggy which would go a lot faster and be much more comfortable. The children were wide-eyed when they reached the Concord and started to cross the bridge. Nate got out and checked things over before crossing, then they moved carefully across the narrow, high bridge. "The old Concord is low today," Matt told Melissa.

"No rain lately," she answered. "It will wait until the wedding and then pour for days."

"No," Nate told her. "It will be pretty weather." He had plans she didn't know anything about, which included good weather. He had talked to Matt, who suggested an overnight at the hotel in Creighton for their wedding night. He had taken Martha there. The hotel owner arranged some niceties for them, and it was a lot better than spending the night with your in-laws or in your brand-new cabin where things might be missing that you would end up needing. Nate had asked Matt about a few other things he was not sure about, man-to-man. "How should I, you know, start out, Matt?"

"Well, you should wait down in the hotel lobby for a little while to give her time to get undressed and into her nightgown. Then you go upstairs and knock on the door. She will say "come in" — if you are lucky and she doesn't change her mind," he teased.

"Oh, come on," Nate said. He was serious. If Melissa knew

little about sex, he knew less. He had seen the cows and pigs mating, but he didn't think he wanted to copy any of them!

Matt continued, "Then you undress."

"Right in front of her?" Nate asked thinking about that for a moment.

"Well, of course, unless you want to do it with your clothes on! You have to take them off at some point, pal. The sooner the better, I'd say." Matt was laughing and getting a big kick out of the conversation while Nate struggled with the idea of baring himself even to Melissa. He was modest to a fault and always had been. He hadn't been around girls since his little sisters, and they were small when he saw them last — almost babies.

"Matt?" he continued. "You know this is the first time for me and for her."

"I know, buddy, but all you have to do is what you feel like, and believe me, you'll feel like it when you see her in that nightgown!" Matt spoke with such assurance that it helped Nate a little. "Just go ahead and don't worry. Do what comes natural. You will be surprised at how well things go."

"Nate, what are you thinking?" Melissa asked, noticing that he was deep in thought, and bringing him back to the moment.

"Oh, nothing much — just things at the cabin." He was almost blushing.

"Yeah, the cabin, my foot," Melissa chided. She was devilish and loved to tease. Nate was holding her hand under the lap robe and she had been feeling tremors since the journey started. The children were riding behind them, nestled down under another robe since it was still early spring and chilly. It was windy, too, making some cover necessary. Just to see his reaction, she laid her hand over on his leg. Nate was having the same tremors.

"If you ever want to get to Creighton, Miss Tate, I suggest you stop that! Oh, no, on second thought, don't stop!" They planned some more and enjoyed each other, totally absorbed in themselves while the children played silly games and had a wonderful time in the back of the buggy.

In Creighton, Nate went to the Mill Store to look for work clothes. He needed tough denim as well as high boots for the woods. Then, he went to Johnson and Hart, where he bought a blue serge suit, tie and white shirt complete with socks to match. Then, he got new union suits; his underwear had been long handles, and was a little worse for the wear.

Melissa took the children to see the depot, the artesian well and the fishpond. Rose and Ben had never seen an artesian well. It was a great curiosity to them. Bonnie and Sissy were helping play hostess because, as they proudly told the other two, their grandparents lived in Creighton. "Does the water keep coming forever and ever?" Ben wanted to know.

"Well, I don't know about forever and ever, but it has been doing this for a very long time," Melissa told the curious child. She wondered herself what caused the well. She had just never gotten around to asking anyone.

Nate joined them back at the wagon. Dewey had drunk his fill of water at the well that ran out of a rusty, old pipe into a sort of trough. He had the usual devilish look in his eyes and was ready to move on. Nate picked each of the children up, put them into the back of the buggy and, after assisting Melissa, climbed in and started Dewey down to The Sundry Shoppe, where they would all have a cool drink and their choice of flavors in stick candy. Ben was smiling so broadly the spaces where his front teeth had been looked like craters. Rose seemed happy enough, but she was a quiet child, even at a time when everyone was having great fun. That worried Nate. He did long to talk to Matt about the situation with Mr. Mac and Rose, but felt he still didn't know Matt quite that well.

"Did you finish your shopping?" Melissa inquired.

"Sure did," was all Nate said. Will I ever get this man to talk to me, she was wondering. He certainly is a silent one.

Planning the Future

Martha and Matt had invited Melissa to spend the night with them since it would be nearly dark when they reached their house. She had gratefully accepted, so Nate put her and the children out there before going on home to take Rose and Ben. Ben was asleep by the time they reached the house, so Nate carried him in to supper.

The next day Nate drove Melissa home with Dixie pulling the buggy and Dewey tied on behind. Her father and Nate had been cutting a road through the rough woods to their cabin so that it was able to accommodate a buggy or wagon now. "Do you want to ride down to the place?" Nate asked after they had unloaded her things from the buggy. "We could go before I unhitch the horse."

Melissa was always ready to go to the cabin. She couldn't get enough of looking at the area, the corn crib, the fences they had finished and the cabin. It needed the windows, fireplace and doors still, but that would be getting finished later in the month. It was mid-March, just a month until the wedding.

As the couple rode along, Nate put his arm around her shoulders. She snuggled up to him, enjoying his presence, his smell, his very being. She loved his voice, his masculine features and the tiny bit of gray hair she could see creeping into the dark brown. He was a handsome man, and Melissa couldn't help thinking that they should have beautiful children. "Nathan, have you thought about children?" she blurted. She hadn't had time ever before to ask him that. Their time together was always so busy and frequently without privacy.

"Oh, yes. I have, and I want a bunch. You know I love children, don't you?" He looked down at her. "I want them all to be girls just like their mother with the bluest eyes in the world."

Melissa laughed. "No!" she said. "I want them all to be boys just like their father, strong and rugged and handsome." At that point, Nate pulled the buggy over, took her in his arms and kissed her a long, lusty kiss, feeling his passion rising as he did so. He could see the slight rise of her lovely breasts as they pushed up above her dress just a little when he looked down at her. Realizing what he was thinking, Melissa took his hand and placed it on her breast, then dissolved back into his arms. They sat for a few minutes like that before Nate decided they had better move along.

"It still gets dark pretty early. I guess we'd better get going," he said. Melissa straightened her hair and adjusted her dress as they moved further into the woods toward what would soon be home.

"Only thirty-two days, Nate. And by this time on the fourteenth of April, I will be Mrs. Nathan York!"

"I know, and I will have a wife." He longed to tell her about the plans to go to the hotel in Creighton for the wedding night, but that must remain a secret. Since he didn't have a buggy, he had talked to John about using his. John thought that was a great idea and sanctioned it completely. He would keep the secret. Nobody would know where the young couple was going for their wedding night.

Since Nate and Matt had become best friends and quite close, he had asked Matt to stand up with him. Matt was deeply touched and honored. "Why, I'd be mighty pleased to, Buddy," he told Nate. Little Matt would carry the ring, and Ben a cross while Rose, Bonnie and Sissy would carry baskets of flower petals and scatter them all over the ground. Melissa's sister, Mary, would be her maid of honor and Liz an attendant, also. Everyone would wear Sunday best. Even Lily had made herself a new frock for the occasion. She still looked very much like she did the day she married Melissa's father, the same small figure and dark hair, despite the hard work and hardships a woman must endure on a homestead.

Melissa planned for the preacher and Nate to stand under the rose trellis. Her mother's big pots of fern would be placed on either side of the trellis, which was serving as the focal point. Her father would escort her out the side door, across the white, sandy yard and up to the trellis and her waiting groom.

Lily and John had issued invitations days in advance, because word of mouth took awhile. There would probably be some forty or fifty people at the ceremony, as was usually the case at weddings, one of the main social events of the day. It was customary to invite everyone near and far in the homestead community.

When Nate got home that night, he went on over to supper. The household was in an uproar. "Mama and Papa just got a letter from Callie," Pearl told him. "Matt went to the post office and brought the mail for everyone."

"Is something wrong?" Nate asked with growing concern.

"Oh, yeah, something's wrong. Callie's not coming home after she finishes training in two weeks! She's staying in Mobile to work." Pearl didn't seem to care one way or the other particularly, except that her parents were in a foul mood. Miss Mattie looked as if she had sat on a nettle, and Mr. Mac sat eating without saying a word. The children looked confused. They hardly knew Callie and wondered what all the fuss was about. Nate had known since she left what her intentions were, but it certainly wasn't up to him to tell the McDougalds. He could hardly blame the girl. There was nothing for her to do in Fox Hollow, population about fifteen. Eligible men were nonexistent; there was no work for a nurse, so what did they really expect?

"I'm sure she will be fine, and there is surely more there for a nurse to do than here at home," was all he could offer.

Melissa had a birthday two weeks before the wedding. Nate had a small pin for a lapel he had bought for her at the store, but he also had another surprise. He selected one of Minnie's cutest kittens, a little girl, and, getting a piece of ribbon from Miss Mattie, tied it around her neck. The kittens were four months old, very playful and terribly cute. On the way to the Tates', he put the kitten under his coat to keep her warm and feeling secure. She seemed a little nervous at first, but with his cooing and rubbing her, she settled down for the ride. The Tates, for some reason, didn't have a cat, but he knew Melissa loved all little animals, and especially cats.

She was waiting in the swing when he got there and joined him at the gate as he tied Dewey to the gatepost. "Hi!" she greeted him. Nate bent to kiss her all the while trying to keep the kitten from poking its head out and spoiling the secret, but a "Mew!" gave her away. "Nathan! What have you got under your coat?" She was excited and demanded to see right that minute. Taking the small, furry animal, she stroked her and let her climb up the front of her dress and try to get under her arm.

"Look! Isn't she beautiful? It is a 'she' isn't it?" And being the inquisitive soul she was, Melissa turned the kitten over and checked her little bottom to see what she was. "It is a girl! I thought so. She looks like a girl, and look at her little button eyes. I'm going to call her Buttons!" She bounced on up the steps with Buttons and went to show her mother and the girls. John was out on the range working for a couple of weeks so that he could check his territory and be home for the wedding. Lily was somewhat amused by the kitten, but the younger girls loved her. They set off to find a suitable basket to use as a bed for her.

Melissa called out to them, "Look for a sandbox, too, girls." Buttons would share the room with Melissa and Mary for the next two weeks until the wedding, when she would move to yet another new home with her new owners.

As they sat in the swing, Melissa chattered on about all the plans for the wedding. Her mother had decided what they would serve the guests, where tables would be placed, where the chairs would be set up and on and on. Nate told her to plan to have her bags packed, leaving her to think they were going to the cabin. Her father and Nate would take most of her things down there the day before, and Nate would also move in that week. That would make him nearer and more accessible to help before the wedding.

John and Nate would also move the cow, three or four pigs and Dewey to their new home that week. The cow would be having her calf later in the spring, so for the time being, Lily would supply them with milk. They didn't have the well dug yet, either, so Nate secured a couple of barrels which he would put on the wagon to take down to the branch for fresh water. They would boil drinking water after it sat in the barrels for a day or two, but it would be just fine for bathing, putting out a fire, if one should start, and such.

In the cabin, Nate built a bed with boards, stationary, and with a space underneath for storage. They would place a mattress on this board frame — not the utmost in comfort, but adequate. There would be little space for storage. Every inch of space would count. Nails were placed on the wall to hang clothes on, what weren't placed in wooden boxes under the bed. Lily had given them a dresser to use until they got one.

Nate nailed together a small table about four feet by four where Melissa would cook and they would eat. They had two straight chairs with cowhide bottoms, which would do just fine until they could afford more. Then they would take the wagon, go to Creighton and buy some nicer ones. Neither of them was going to have much time for sitting for a long time, anyway. There was still too much work to do. Melissa had to get her yard planted, while Nate had to plant the garden and start clearing the patch. Trees would be cut down, moved out of the area by chaining them and having the horse pull them out. The stumps were usually burned out. Sometimes the area was burned off, but there had to be several people present to prevent the fire getting out of hand.

Homestead

Holy Matrimony

On the day before the wedding, The Reverend Lock arrived early in the afternoon. He had church business he had wanted to take care of, besides performing the wedding ceremony, so he had a chance to talk with John and Nate. What he wanted to do was build a church, and he needed help from the leading citizens of the homestead community. Nate assured him that he would help as soon as the wedding was over and he got his garden planted. He had to grow feed for the cow, horse and pigs, although the rest of the farmland would not be ready for planting for a very long time. Trees had to be cut, stumps burned out, bushes and debris cleared out, and, in general, it would take months, even years, to get the whole acreage under cultivation.

Lily cooked one of her famous hens for dinner, made cornbread dressing, green beans, sweet potatoes and pecan pie. Nate was invited to stay, of course, and the family talked excitedly about the coming event the next day. Nate and Melissa said goodnight early, knowing they had a full day on Sunday. Each had a few things yet to do as well. As he kissed her for the last time before their wedding day, he whispered, "Tomorrow, you will be my wife, Mrs. Nathan Hamilton York."

Melissa whispered back, "And I can't wait!"

Homestead

On the way home, he thought of his parents, his sisters, whom he planned to find as soon as possible, and the fact that he had no family. There would not be one person at the wedding related to him. Melissa had only her immediate family. The rest of her parents' families were left behind some years before in South Carolina. They had been unable to keep in contact after a while, because their parents had died, and there was little way to keep up with other relatives. Nate was glad he had new friends now, and that he would now have a family. He had spent many lonely years fending totally for himself. He had longed for a companion.

Since the minister had to have a room, that night Liz had to sleep with Mary and Melissa. They were whispering, long after she should have been asleep, about wedding nights and honeymoons that prompted Liz to ask, "What is a honeymoom?" She was all ears, wanting to know everything that was going on.

"Be quiet, and go to sleep," Melissa told her. "Anyway, it's not honeymoom. It's honey*moon*. Now, go to sleep." But Liz kept wiggling and squirming between them.

"Be still, too, you are worse than a wiggle worm," Mary scolded.

"Well, what is it? Are you going to a honey*moon* with Nate?" she wanted to know of Melissa. She would not be satisfied until Melissa feebly explained it to her. Melissa's information on honeymoons was somewhat limited. At the tender age of seventeen she had had little chance to find out about such things.

"Now, be quiet. The minister is right in the next room. He'll hear you." But they doubted that he would when loud snores attested to the fact that he wouldn't hear anything. They also doubted they would get much sleep that night, either.

Melissa awoke at five in the morning on her wedding day. She wondered if Nate were awake yet and what he was thinking about. The first thing she did was pull back the curtain in her room to see what the weather was like. Although it was not yet daylight, she could see a few stars shining still and knew it was clear. Knowing she needed to go back to sleep, she knew sleep would not come. There were too many things going around in her head.

Everything was done, including the house being clean. Fresh flowers were cut and placed everywhere, and her mother would be up shortly getting breakfast. All Melissa had to do was get a bath, dress and fix her hair. She had decided to use bridal wreath, gardenias and the wedding pink sprays of running roses in her bouquet. It would be tied with a blue ribbon to match her eyes. Nate loved her blue eyes and commented about them often.

Chairs were on the porch ready to be placed before the altar, leaving a space like an aisle for her to walk through on her father's arm. One of the Daugette boys played the violin and had agreed to play before the ceremony and for her to walk to the trellis, if he stayed sober long enough. Melissa wasn't counting on Harry Daugette, though. She knew they might not have any music.

As soon as the ceremony was over, everyone would go to the back porch for lemonade and teacakes. Lily had made dozens with real butter and they would melt in your mouth. Everything was planned with a contingency of rain in mind so that the ceremony could be held on the front porch with the food being on the back porch. Tables were set up out there with cut flowers everywhere.

Lily, John and the girls had their Sunday best clothes laid out already, neatly pressed, and Melissa's dress was hanging on a peg in her room. It had a full skirt that made her tiny waist look even smaller.

As daylight came, Nate fed and watered the cow, pigs and Dewey. "Old boy," he said to the horse, "pretty soon you're going to have a new mistress, and she'll be giving us both orders. You hear that?" Dewey looked as if he clearly understood. He rolled his eyes so that the whites could be seen and got his devilish look. "You be ready by about three o'clock, Dewey, because you have to pull me and my new wife off on our wedding trip. I want you to step lively." He groomed the horse and for his trouble got another of Dewey's famous wet kisses with his big horse lips. "Stop it, you old nag!" Nate told him. Dewey neighed as if to have the last word.

Nate had his new suit ready. He shaved, being careful not to cut himself, but he noticed a slight tremor in his hand as he started shaving. He had heated water in the newly built fireplace with a kettle that hung on a swinging rod above the fire. It was a little cool that morning — just cool enough for a small fire to feel good. By the time for the ceremony, it should be perfect temperature with no humidity. The humidity was what everyone in the area dreaded. It could make a moderate day seem hot.

Nate was supposed to be at the Tates' by ten-thirty. The wedding would start promptly at eleven, and with the refreshments, visits with the guests and loading the buggy with Melissa's stuff, they should be out of there by two o'clock at the latest, maybe three, but he hoped not since they had to go all the way to Creighton. He would have to hurry Melissa along if she got caught up in the visiting. That might not be easy since she still didn't know they were going to Creighton. He planned to tell her as soon as they got to the road that led to their cabin. That would be when she would start wondering where they were going.

The Reverend Lock was a kind man, tall, with thick gray hair and crinkles around his eyes when he smiled, which he did frequently. He wore a black suit, white shirt and black string tie, looking the part of a minister. He ate a large breakfast, cooked by Lily, and then enjoyed a stroll when he said he had a habit of meditating each morning. John, in the meantime, was busy setting the chairs up in the yard, getting cloths on the tables and, in general, being accessible to the lady of the house who was calling the shots. She had to stop sharply at ten and dress so that she could help Melissa put on her finishing touches. The younger girls were dressed early, but Liz had to be cautioned several times not to get into something and get dirty.

Melissa's dress was a cream satin with a low neckline. It was simple, but with an ankle length skirt which, with three crinolines underneath, stood out in a full circle. Lily had made a Juliet cap of lace for her dark hair, which she had up in a knot under the cap. Tiny curls framed her face, giving her an angelic look. Her cheeks, flushed from excitement, needed no extra color. She wore white slippers that her mother had been married in, carried a handkerchief edged in lace that had belonged to her maternal grandmother, and the blue ribbon she tied her bouquet with completed the 'something blue'. Early that morning, Melissa had gathered her flowers. She used bridal wreath, which cascaded down in the bouquet. The roses were in lovely clusters, giving it color, while the gardenias gave it a fragrance that could be detected as she walked past the guests.

The wisteria had climbed all through a dogwood tree near the trellis and hung in lovely purple clusters all about mixed in with the white dogwood blooms. On the trellis, the roses bloomed in profusion near the centerpiece in the yard, the trellis. It was a lovely sight on a lovely spring day — a perfect day, and by far the happiest day in Nate's, or Melissa's, life. Her mother had placed a potted fern on either side of the trellis. The trees overhead let in just enough sunlight to illuminate that whole area of the yard, giving it an ethereal appearance. Of course, Lily had the yard swept perfectly clean, leaving the sand gleaming white.

At exactly eleven o'clock Melissa walked out of the south door of the house on the arm of her father. Lily had gone out and taken a chair on the front row earlier. The children looked adorable, each doing his or her assigned task. Little Matt had a pillow without the ring on it, because he was so small, everyone feared he would drop it or lose it, but Ben carried his cross proudly. The girls dropped flower petals all over the white yard. Liz went next, with Mary following. Both carried small bouquets. John had a rather somber look on his face, and Lily wiped a tear now and then as the ceremony progressed. Nate was standing stiffly, Matt beside him, in their appointed places beside the minister and encircled by flowers. Nate looked happy, if a little uncomfortable and awkward. The violinist had made it, apparently sober, and was playing his very best for the occasion.

Most of the neighbors for miles around were in attendance. All heads were turned to see the lovely bride. Most of the young ladies present were looking at the dress; most of the young men were looking at the bride. All agreed Melissa was radiant and lovely.

Reverend Lock cleared his throat and began: "Dearly beloved, we are gathered together in the sight of God and of each other to bind this couple in the state of holy matrimony." Melissa's mind was wandering at that point. She was thinking, as she had done so many, many times in the past months: Mrs. Nathan York, Mrs. Nate York, Mrs. Nathan Hamilton York. Suddenly she heard the minister saying, "Who giveth this woman to be married to this man?" And then she heard her father saying, "I do." He sat down as Nate moved to stand beside her, taking her hand in his big, strong one. Her joy could not be described. As the minister continued with the service, he explained that whom God had joined together, no man should put asunder. Then came the part where he asked each of them: "Nathan Hamilton York, do you take Melissa to be your lawfully wedded wife?" Nate answered, "I do," feeling this was happening to someone else.

Then came the words: "Melissa Marie Tate, do you take Nathan to be your lawfully wedded husband?" She managed to say "I do," also. Next he asked Nate for the ring which Melissa had forgotten about! In fact, she had wondered earlier whether she would even have a ring. Nate had not mentioned it, and she would never have been so presumptive as to ask. He reached into his pocket, pulled out a lovely, wide, gold band and placed it on her finger. She could hear her mother sniffing just behind her.

"I now pronounce you man and wife. Nathan, you may kiss your bride," Reverend Lock was saying, and suddenly Nate was kissing her full on the mouth for the first time in front of people! Melissa was enchanted and wished these moments could last forever — moments when she was the star of the show, all eyes first upon the blushing bride, then on the happy couple.

They turned to face the guests and everyone applauded as they walked to the back porch, where the refreshments awaited. Melissa had, for the first time, a chance to really look at Nate and how very handsome he was in his blue suit. He had put a gardenia in his lapel and the gray in his hair was glistening silver. He's going to be gray very early, Melissa thought, as she poured lemonade into a glass for him. "It seems I've done this for you before, doesn't it?" she asked. Nate laughed, remembering the night they had met.

The neighbors began congratulating the radiant couple as they stood at the end of the porch with John and Lily. "My, you two do look happy," Mozelle Weeks said as she greeted them. "Now, the next thing we'll be doing is giving you a baby shower, Melissa," she added in parting. Poor Mrs. Weeks, Melissa was thinking as she blushed a deeper shade of red. She never has known what to say or when to keep her mouth shut.

Mrs. Clara Rogers was next in line and had obviously heard what Mozelle said. "Don't pay any attention to her. She's just a nosey, old busybody," she said. "Never did know how to mind her own business!"

Martha Seward and Grace Rogers hugged Melissa and shook Nate's hand, both telling him what a lovely bride he had. Nate was beaming. Oh, Melissa was thinking, he is so handsome. Missy Rogers seemed to agree. She bustled up to them, barely acknowledged Melissa, and shook Nate's hand warmly, all the while smiling and cooing up at him. Melissa wondered if she had forgotten the night Nate left her holding her box at the box supper when he knocked the whey out of Cal Little and rescued her from him? Missy didn't seem to be holding a grudge. She was glad when someone else was edging Missy out of the way in order to greet them. Missy had practically drooled on Nate!

John, who was in Nate's confidence, along with Matt, was supposed to see to it that the newlyweds were rescued and sent on their way before too late since they had such a long trip ahead of them they would arrive just at dark as it was. John had placed the lantern on the buggy and Nate stuck his dad's rifle under the seat just for security, but he wanted to arrive in Creighton by dark just the same. He looked around a time or two, noticing that Matt seemed to have disappeared. Everyone was talking to them, however, so he forgot about his absence. Perhaps, he thought, he'd gone to pay Reverend Lock the money Nate gave him for the purpose. John kept looking at his pocket watch. He wanted to be sure he didn't fail at his job.

Soon Lily handed Melissa a small basket with a jar of lemonade and a big batch of teacakes in it for the ride, knowing they had not had a chance for even a sip of anything. She knew Nate would be hungry, for sure. That man could eat his weight in her teacakes. "Honey," she said to her daughter, "It's about time you two left, your father says." Lily also knew where they were going, thanks to John. Since Melissa didn't know, however, she didn't understand the hurry.

"Everyone has been by to speak to us, Mrs. York. Let's get out of here!" Nate told her. She didn't protest any further. They went over and thanked Reverend Lock, Melissa kissed her parents and little sisters, thanking them too. Nate shook hands with Lily and John and kissed the girls. "Be good girls, and we'll see you soon," he said as Mary and Liz began to cry. "Don't worry, girls. We'll be just across the woods. You will see Melissa nearly every day." That was little consolation to them, however. They felt they were losing a sister, but Melissa had figured Mary would be happy to have the room all to herself.

As Nate and Melissa called "good-bye" to the guests and walked to the front gate where the buggy was parked waiting, Nate spotted Matt, Franklin Rogers and several of the other young men. They were grinning from ear to ear, having just finished tying a huge collection of old shoes and other junk items to the back of the buggy, all of which would rattle, clank and jingle as they started off up the road. There was a big sign painted on a side from a wooden box which read "Just Married" in big, white letters hanging from the back of the buggy, also. Then, just to be *sure* they couldn't get that off, they painted it in whitewash on the back of the black buggy. Nate and Melissa began to laugh. "You're supposed to be my friends!" he said to the men who were getting a huge kick out of what they had done. Melissa's face took on an even deeper crimson hue, if that were possible.

Leaving their guests to continue having a good time, Nate helped his bride into the buggy. He climbed in, took the reins and said to Dewey, "Get up!" They waved as far as they could see anyone. Some of the little children ran after the buggy for a short distance, waving and calling "good-bye." As they drove out of sight of her home for seventeen years, Melissa began to cry. Her perplexed new husband was concerned. "My dearest, what is the matter? Have I already upset you?"

"No," she sobbed. "I'm just so happy, Nathan. I am so happy."

"Yes, I can see that you are," the poor man said, and they both began to laugh.

Surely enough, and just as Nate suspected, when they got to the road which turned toward their cabin, Melissa looked at him questioningly because he didn't turn. "We aren't going home?" she asked.

"No, we are going on a honeymoon, Mrs. York. Just you wait and see," was all he told her.

The trip was delightful as they talked on and on about the wedding, friends who came and what everyone had said. It took Melissa's mind off the rest of the night for a time, but her thoughts kept returning to the wedding night, wondering and wondering about how it was going to be. She had no idea Nate was wondering the same thing.

Gaslights were being lit in Creighton as they were getting into the small town, which had the railroad running right down the middle. It was one main street, lined with stores, and behind them were livery stables, feed stores, blacksmith shops, a house of ill repute or two, unidentified, of course, and all the service-type businesses. Melissa had never been into most of those places. Her father always let her mother and the three girls out on Main Street while he attended to other business on the back streets. One day, she would ask Nate about some of those places. She had heard whispers among the girls, but they were not sure, either what some of them were.

Hotel Creighton was on Main Street, as one would expect. Nate drove up to the door, and a bellman assisted Melissa to the curb with a knowing look on his face. Seeing her wedding dress, he knew this had to be Mr. and Mrs. York, whom he had been told to expect. Nate had taken the junk off the back of the buggy, along with the sign, so he asked the bellman to wash the "Just Married" whitewash off the back.

Neither she nor Nate had ever spent the night in a hotel, so this was to be a new experience for them. Nate joined his bride and, taking her arm, led her into the hotel lobby as the bellman led Dewey down the alley and to the livery stable in back of the hotel. Melissa was beginning to enjoy herself and Nate had already been having a great time. They knew they were going to enjoy staying in a hotel and also being Mr. and Mrs. York. Since Melissa had been teaching Nate reading, writing and spelling in the months prior to the wedding, he could now sign their names on the hotel register, and thus Mr. and Mrs. York were registered guests at the Hotel Creighton. They were shown to their room by another employee. The door was unlocked, and their bags set inside. After the man left, Melissa looked up at Nate and said, "I could get used to this!"

After washing their hands in the huge washbowl provided, they went down to supper in the dining room. It was a very nice meal of roast pork and all the trimmings. "Is this what some people refer to as dinner?" she asked.

"It must be," Nate told her. "I've never had anything but supper." They had linen napkins, a linen tablecloth and real silver on the table. It was a far cry from what Nate was used to, and Melissa had never eaten with real silver. Nate was starved, but she was still too keyed up to eat very much, so she let him finish her dinner. They walked about the hotel a bit before he escorted her upstairs. Nate thought that would help ease the tension. Reaching their room, number two twenty-four, he unlocked the door and she started in.

"Wait!" he said, and, picking her up, carried her over the threshold. As he set her down, he said, "Now I am going back down to the lobby for a few minutes. You go ahead and get ready for bed. Take your time. I will be a few minutes."

Melissa opened her little valise, took out her soft, white night-gown her mother had made for this very night, and began getting out of her wedding gown. After she had dressed for bed, she took the pins out of her long hair and let it fall to her waist. She was standing at the vanity brushing it when Nate knocked at the door. In a voice with a slight quiver in it, she told him to enter.

Nate was stunned at the lovely picture before his eyes, that of his bride, the woman of his dreams standing before him in the soft gas light. He sucked in his breath and let it out slowly. "My beautiful one," he said. "I have never seen anything so lovely." At that moment he understood what Matt had said about all his inhibitions leaving him, and it was then that she came to him. As he enfolded her in his arms, he had the presence of mind to turn out the gas lamp.

In the morning, the Yorks awoke still in each other's arms. After they had dressed and gone down to the dining room for breakfast, they walked down Main Street, drinking in the wonderful spring air and enjoying the fact that they were one, for now, for always. What God hath joined together, let no man put asunder. Their hearts were glad and they could hardly contain their joy.

Homestead

Bonnie's Accident

Dewey hauled the little buggy home on Monday afternoon, and Melissa and Nate were jolted back to reality, and the world they knew, when they turned off the main road and started down the new, beaten out ruts in the road to their home. Nate had only spent five nights there — hardly enough time to make it seem like home. He had kept everything in order, just as Melissa and Grace Rogers had left it after their cleaning and decorating day a few Saturdays before.

Trouble and Buttons were staying at the Tates' while the Yorks were gone. Nate wanted them to get acquainted slowly before being thrown together in the small, cramped space they would call home at the cabin. For the time being, Buttons fuzzed up twice her tiny size and hissed at the hapless dog that only wanted to sniff her and perhaps lick her ears a little. She had to be kept inside, while he was allowed to have the run of the yard. There were many dangers lurking out in the big world: snakes to bite Trouble, and even a huge owl could carry off a kitten the size of Buttons. Owls caught chickens, carrying them away high into the air and off to their nests to feed their young.

When the owners got to their new home, they found a hungry cow, pig and chickens. The sow was about to have her pigs at any moment, and the cow's calf was due within days. One of the finest gifts a homesteading couple could be given was livestock about to give birth. That meant food: milk, eggs and bacon, all right in one pen.

It was not customary to send gifts before the wedding with times being hard, no place to shop conveniently, and little money with which to purchase new items. Instead, often the couple would be given useful or essential items and goods which they would need for their everyday lives, and they were frequently used things that could be spared by their owners. This was about to happen to Melissa and Nate. He had carried his bride over the threshold of the cabin, one last vestige of the honeymoon, before plunging into life as it really was with hardships, long hours and toil, when they heard the rattle of wagons and buggies. The neighbors were coming to give them a Pounding.

"I'd better run feed and water the animals, Melissa," Nate called. "You go ahead and get your things put away before everyone gets here!" A Pounding was like a shower. People would be bringing a pound of all kinds of things: meal, flour, sugar, salt, grease and oil, bacon, sausage, ham, seed corn and peanuts for planting, plus skillets, pots, eating utensils, dish cloths, wash rags, pillow cases, maybe a quilt or two, and any kind of vessel they could part with, because they could be used to hold things. Containers were always useful for something. Poundings were also an excuse for the neighbors to see your new home, thus it served two purposes. That was one reason Melissa and Grace had cleaned and decorated before the wedding.

The first to reach the cabin were Melissa's parents and sisters. They had to use the wagon since Melissa and Nate had their buggy, but Trouble sat happily in the back, barking as loudly as he could when he heard Nate call out "Hello!" Buttons had a more secure spot, under Liz's wrap. It was a little cool still, so she enjoyed being in a warm, dark spot where she felt safe. The two of them would be together from then on in close proximity so they would have to start accepting each other.

Bonnie's Accident

Melissa ran out to hug her family as Nate came from the lot to shake hands with her parents and hug the girls. It was a novelty to them still, to have Nate in the family. They had little exposure to men other than their father. It might be nice to have a "brother."

The Tates had the wagon loaded. There was barely room for the girls and Trouble in the back with quilts, pots, pans, linens, jars for canning, and enough staple groceries to last them for awhile. Lily had already given Melissa a load of things, including the rooted shrubs and flowers she and Martha Seward planted early in the cabin-building process. Most of them had lived, because they were planted in late winter, and with the warm April sun, most had begun to put out new growth.

Shortly, the whole Rogers family arrived, including Clara and Carl, Franklin's parents, who were known to the community as Aunt Clara and Uncle Carl. They, too, had brought several "pounds" of things, among them two bed sheets that were badly needed items. They were not as plentiful as they might have been. They were often torn up in a hurry to be used as cloths in the birth of a baby or in injury or illness. Nobody had enough sheets, but Melissa was on her way with the help of her mother and people like Aunt Clara. The Sewards got there right behind the Rogers with several useful gifts. "My goodness," Melissa told each family as she hugged and thanked them profusely, "you folks have brought so much, Nate and I won't have to work all summer! We can just sit in the shade and fan ourselves!"

Mr. Mac and Miss Mattie didn't go, but they sent Pearl with Rose and Ben and a load of things in the back of the buggy from the store. There was a lantern, because no family could have too many. One had to be lighted every time anyone went outside at night. They were made to withstand the hardest wind without going out, whereas a lamp would go out in the wind. Mr. Mac had sent a pound of nails, two long-handled frying pans for cooking over the fire in the open fireplace, which would be the only way the Yorks could cook until they could afford a stove. Then it would have to be hauled in by a team from Creighton. There was an iron kettle for placing in the fireplace coals to heat water for baths. The list went on. Nate greeted Pearl and helped her down out of the buggy. "Hello, Nathan," she said simply. "It is good to see you. We have been missing you terribly at the house. It seems lonely at mealtime, especially."

"Oh, Pearl. I thought you and Miss Mattie would be ever so glad not to have to cook for me anymore."

"Not so, and the children have been lost without Mr. Nate," she added. The two of them quickly confirmed that by converging on him, with both trying to get hugs at the same time. When Ben's turn came, he jumped into Nate's arms locking his legs around Nate's legs.

"Hello, pardner. I'm sure glad to see you kids," he said as he led them in to see Melissa. There was no room inside for the crowd that had begun to gather, so the men began getting into little groups to talk while the women spread a large cloth on the grass and sat down to continue conversations they had no doubt begun the day before at the wedding. Lily had brought more teacakes and lemonade, all left over from the wedding. She wanted to get rid of all of it, she said. As others from the area came, that wasn't hard to do. The ladies asked if she had gotten the sand out of her house yet, and all wanted to tell her and Melissa what a lovely wedding it had been.

Aunt Clara said she hoped Missy would get married in the spring when the flowers were all in bloom. "I declare, Lily, you have the prettiest yard of anyone in Catawba." Lily was thinking she just hoped Missy would get married at all. She was a chatterbox, and all the men talked about how she never shut up. Missy was not in attendance, which Melissa noticed. She was wondering why she would miss a chance to drool over Nate!

The women "oohed" and "aahed" over the cabin, the beautiful setting in which it had been built and the good job Melissa had already done on the yard. Mozelle Weeks said she had her mother's talent for making a pretty yard. The men complimented Nate on what he had already accomplished with the corncrib, fencing and the huge garden. Things were coming up rapidly with the warm spring sun. Uncle Carl said, "You sure got a good stand of corn, son. Looks like you'll have enough vegetables for the summer for you all and the stock." Nate got more offers of help when the time came to build a barn with stalls for the animals. That was next on the agenda, because when winter came in the next eight months or so, they'd need warm places to stay.

The next morning, the cabin was shrouded in ground fog so thick you couldn't see the corncrib, which was typical at that time of year. The heavy moisture clung to trees, bushes and plants of all kinds, so that when the sun came out the whole world glistened as if set with trillions of diamonds. Melissa got out of bed, opened the shutter window and closed it again. Without the glass windows, she couldn't leave them open and let the fog in, so she lit the kerosene lamp instead. It illuminated the room enough that she could see to fix breakfast. Nate was already up, dressed and, she presumed, out feeding the stock. Trouble had gone out, too, but Buttons was balled tightly on their bed. Melissa tickled her tummy causing her to wake up and stretch as far as she could. Then she promptly balled back up and went back to sleep.

Nate came in from doing the chores to the smell of bacon cooking. As soon as Melissa finished cooking the bacon, she broke two eggs into the bacon grease sizzling over the open fire in the fireplace. She had already made a hoecake out of flour, salt and water, which was sitting in the pan staying warm on the hearth. It was nice and brown and looked inviting. Coffee bubbled in the pot in the edge of the fire coals. Nate was not aware Melissa knew how to cook. He knew she helped her mother, but she had evidently learned a few things along the way. Shortly, they were able to sit down to breakfast at their kitchen table in front of the fireplace for their first meal in the cabin together. Melissa suggested they start their first meal at home with a blessing, which she said, realizing Nate probably didn't know one.

Later that week, Nate knew he would have to go up and work a couple of days at Mr. Mac's. He hated to leave Melissa alone there in the woods, so he suggested she come along and either stay with her mother that day or visit with Martha Seward. "I'll think about it," Melissa said, not committing.

"You don't have a great deal to do here," Nate told her. "Plan on going. I really want you nearby when I'm working." So it was decided she would go to Martha's one day and to her mother's the next. Feeling they both could use her help, she would sort of pay back for some of the help they had given her.

On Thursday, Nate drove Melissa to her mother's on his way to Mr. Mac's. Lily and the girls were happy to see her, assuring her she would have plenty to do there that day while Nate was gone. It was only two miles to the cabin from the Tates', but she would be totally isolated there while Nate was at the McDougalds'.

Nate kissed her good-bye and hurried on so that he would have a full day to work. As it turned out, Pearl was expecting a team to come in that day with a long wagon loaded with supplies, so Nate worked all day unloading and helping move things about in the store. He had gone outside for something when he heard the Sewards' dinner bell ringing the distress ring, three rings, then three more. Grabbing Mr. Mac's rifle from behind the counter, Nate started to run as fast as he could. It was slow going across newly ploughed ground until he could reach the main road, then he picked up speed. As he rounded the corner of the field fence, he could begin to hear sounds. Getting closer, he could tell it was screams. They were coming from Matt's house all right, and as he got nearer, it was clear it was a child. Not sure what he would find, he was glad he had taken the rifle, but it was the last thing he needed, as it turned out.

Nate bolted through the gate, up the steps and began calling for Martha, all the while listening to the blood curdling screams.

Bonnie's Accident

"In here. Help me. Oh, please help me," she was saying over and over. Nate ran to the north room that the family used as a bedroom. Little Matt and Sissy were screaming, but he soon determined it was Bonnie who was hurt. Martha was standing over her as she lay on the bed writhing in pain and continuing to scream. Her mother was smearing lard on what appeared to be terrible burns.

"Martha, what happened?" Nate asked, taking over the job of applying the lard.

"I washed this morning, and the wash pot still had scalding water in it. Oh, God, Nate she fell against the pot. They were playing, and she tripped. The fire coals partly burned her, and the hot water partly burned her when the pot tipped over!" Martha was sobbing so hard she could hardly talk.

"Oh, God, what will we do?" She was partially in shock, and Nate felt sure little Bonnie was also. He knew to cover someone when they are in shock, so he asked for a light spread. Martha handed it to him from the quilt press across the room.

"I think we'd better keep her warm. It is still a little cool, and she could go into deep shock," Nate explained. He surely didn't know what else to do, but told Martha he would go to Creighton for a doctor. Meanwhile, he ran to the edge of the porch and rang the distress bell again. Just at that moment, he saw Pearl coming. She had grabbed Dewey where he was hitched outside the store and was riding as fast as she dared sidesaddle. Good, Nate thought, now I can ride Dewey to Creighton for the doctor. He told Pearl what had happened as fast as he could. "Go stay with Martha and the children. I am going after Dr. Haygood. I will be back as fast as I can." He had no idea where Matt was, but he would have gone for the doctor in any case. The screaming continued as Pearl made her way in her long skirts up the tall steps and into the room of the injured child. She felt faint when she saw the burns. Soot from the wash pot had come off on her skin and would probably heal up in the wounds, but getting it out would be agony — too painful to be worth it. It would just have to stay unless the doctor knew some way to clean the wounds without too much pain.

Nate rode Dewey as hard as he dared. He knew if the horse dropped dead, he would never make it to Creighton, so felt it better to pace him. Dewey seemed to understand the urgency. He made a gallant run, and when they reached the McDaniels', Nate decided to see if he could borrow their horse and change out. He could pick Dewey back up on the return trip. As luck would have it, Mrs. McDaniel was again at home, twice helping Nate out of a jam. He explained the situation and, with her permission, changed the saddle from Dewey to the fresh horse, then sped on his way.

Dr. Haygood was in his office, but he was ill with influenza, and had a town full of sick people — some near death. He told Nate his actual presence would do no more good than what they had already done, but was able to give him a sedative powder which would help to ease some of Bonnie's pain. He also told Nate they should keep clean loose dressings on the burned areas that were worst and let the others heal in the open air. Nate took the powder and was on his way — again as fast as he dared make the horse go. Arriving at the McDaniels', he quickly changed the saddle over again and started on the five or six mile trip the rest of the way.

Back at the Sewards', Nate gave Pearl the powder so that she could mix a dose. Martha was in no condition to do much of anything, but little Bonnie had quieted somewhat. Nate decided to ask where Matt was, and Martha said he had gone to the gristmill to get corn ground into meal. He had to pick up some more lumber on the way home, but she expected him in by supper. Nate knew there was no point in his trying to find Matt, but prayed he would not tarry this time. At the thought of Matt getting home and seeing what had happened, Martha started to sob again. "Nate, what will he do? He will hate me for letting this happen to Bonnie. And I had just told the kids to stay away from the washpot, but they were running and playing and she just forgot."

"Now, now, Martha," Nate said, trying to comfort the grieving woman. "You are a wonderful mother, and this could have happened to anyone. Please don't torment yourself this way. Bonnie's wounds will heal." He wished he believed that as much as he tried to make her believe it.

Since Pearl was attending to Bonnie's needs and Nate felt somewhat out of place in the house, he decided to go out and tend the livestock. He knew it would take Matt an hour, at least when he got home, so he could spare him that. He milked the cow, put the calf into another pen so that he wouldn't drink the milk in the night, and completed all the other chores he knew about. The team would still have to be fed once Matt arrived with it. At that point, Nate decided to ride out and meet Matt. He had to leave for home before too long, lest Melissa begin to worry about him.

Matt was just fording the creek when Nate first saw him coming. Matt spotted Nate about the same time, getting alarmed at once because he knew something was wrong. He cracked his whip at the team to hurry the horses along.

When Nate got in hollering distance of Matt, he told him to stop, take Dewey and ride on in home as fast as he could. "Bonnie has been scalded by the washpot!" he yelled.

"How bad is it, Nate?" Matt called back to him.

"It's pretty bad, Matt. She has just started quieting down. She has been screaming and crying since it happened about eleven o'clock this morning. I went to Creighton for Dr. Haygood, but he couldn't come. He sent powders to help the pain, which it has done. He had people with influenza all over town and also has it himself. He didn't want to give it to everybody out here." Nate took over the team with that and sent Matt on ahead on Dewey.

When Nate got to the house, it was just past sunset. He fed the horses and secured them for the night. Then he went in to see how the child was doing. She was asleep; so Matt crept out onto the porch with Nate.

"She will probably sleep now for hours with the powder. You head for home. We will be all right through the night," Matt told his friend.

"I will go home, get Melissa and be back in a short while. You and Martha will need to rest so you'll be able to help her when she wakes. We will stay up through the night with her," Nate said. Matt started to protest, but Nate told him that was the way it was going to be.

Melissa had already suspected there had been a problem when Nate wasn't back to the Tates' by dark. He had not taken a lantern, thinking he'd be home, but Dewey was sure-footed and steady. He knew the road better than Nate.

Once Nate explained the situation, Melissa grabbed her shawl, in case it got cool in the night, and was ready to go. Lily couldn't leave the girls, but told Melissa she would go the next day as soon as Melissa and Nate got home to sleep and be with the girls. Neighbors always helped out with the sick by sitting up at night, washing clothes, tending the livestock and cooking for the family. When the man of the family was ill, other men in the community would even work his field and do whatever had to be done at the time.

Dewey got a rest since Nate could take the Tates' horse, Sally, to pull the buggy. Melissa dreaded seeing poor little Bonnie. "Will she have bad scars, Nate?" she asked.

"Some, I'm sure," he told her. "The worst problem is the smudges of soot from the washpot and fire that got into the burns. The soot will just have to stay there unless they try to clean it out some way."

Melissa asked about her face. Matt told her one side of her face had a burn. He had not seen all the areas, but knew that much. "I would think they'd try to get the dirt and soot out of the one on her face at least. It will be terribly painful, too, and may make a worse scar. You don't know what to do. Which will be worse, the scar or the dirt healing up in the scar?"

When Melissa entered the room, she couldn't tell much by the lamplight, but the child was sleeping restlessly. She and Nate ushered the worried parents on out, telling them to get some sleep, because they would be sorely needed the next day or whenever Bonnie awoke. "We will let you know the minute she wakes up," Melissa told Martha.

Martha hugged her friend and said, "Oh, Melissa, how could I let this happen?" Melissa comforted her the best she could, knowing full well she would feel as guilty as Martha.

"Dear, some things just happen no matter how careful we are. You were busy, and children don't always do as they are told." They hugged each other, both crying, both knowing the child would have scars and being defaced might mean never having a boyfriend, let alone a husband. It was very important that a girl get married. Women were dependent on men to make a living. Otherwise, they had to live at home the rest of their lives and depend on their fathers. A homely girl didn't stand a chance. There were not enough men to go around anyway, and not being pretty was the surest way to be an old maid.

Bonnie slept, mercifully. It was about five in the morning when she began to stir. She could have another dose of her powder as soon as she asked for it or began to whimper. They would spread out the doses, not giving it until they had to. When she was completely awake, Melissa went to call her parents.

Taking Martha aside, Melissa told her she thought they should consider trying to clean the wounds on Bonnie's face, at least. Martha agreed, but didn't know how to begin.

"I would take lard, put it on the wound and then with a clean cloth try to get out as much of the soot as possible," Melissa suggested.

"The men will have to hold her," Martha said, more or less thinking aloud.

"I know it will be painful, but it really does need to be done before any more healing takes place. It will only get harder to clean. We can try anyway." It seemed to Melissa the only thing to do.

And so it was decided the two men would hold the little girl while her mother and Melissa tried to clean the wounds on her face. There was one on her temple and another on her cheek. Neither appeared to be too deep, mostly just scrapes. Martha explained to Bonnie what they were going to do.

"We will give you your powder first so it won't hurt too much," she told her. "Now, Bonnie, Mama wants you to be very brave and let us do this. Otherwise you will have bad scars with dirt in them. We can't let that happen to this pretty face, now can we?" But Bonnie began to cry, not being convinced she wanted anything done to add misery to her situation.

As Matt and Nate held the child, trying not to hurt any of the scalded places, the two women worked carefully to get out all the dirt, soot and ashes. Bonnie did remarkably well, and seemed to be in less pain generally that day than she had been the day before. Her mother soothed as they worked, telling her all along how she would still be a pretty girl and that the scars were not going to show much at all. It really did appear to be the truth as far as her face was concerned. She did have one badly injured foot and leg where she actually stepped into the fire and caused the pot to turn over. It would have deep scars.

"Infection is what we have to worry about now," Melissa said. "We need to keep these wounds lightly covered while they heal."

Martha, who had recovered from her shock and was back in control again, knew Melissa and Nate had to get some rest, too. "Now, you two go home, get some sleep, and we can manage from here on." She handed Melissa her shawl and began shooing them out the door.

"My mother is coming as soon as we get home and help out today. Nate and I will be back later this evening," Melissa said as she went down the steps. As they started down the lane in the buggy, they saw Pearl going across the field on her way to the Sewards.

Lily was ready to leave when they got to the house; so Nate changed out the horses hitched to the buggy and she set out. "I will be home by dark," she called as she drove down the road.

The days and nights were long with suffering for Bonnie, but she was healing. The places on her face looked amazingly good. The skin was wonderful in the way it would heal from scrapes, bruises and burns, and the neighbors were wonderful in the way they helped. Pearl was there at least a part of every day, while Melissa, Lily and other ladies in the area went over to do washing, cleaning and cooking for Martha. Nate had to get things done at his own place and Mr. Mac's, but he helped Matt with his farming where it was necessary, too. He worked long hours in order to get everything done that was required in a day. He and Melissa had many jobs to complete at their own new place, but they had to wait until the crisis was over for Matt and Martha.

It was fortunate that the hottest part of summer had not yet arrived. The heat and humidity of summer complicated everything, especially an illness or injury. Infection was a grave concern, as was keeping a recovering patient comfortably cool. Another month would mean the beginning of June and the heat. Temperatures could range up into the nineties and that would mean someone would have to fan the child continuously. A mosquito net had to be spread over the bed at all times, also, to keep flies and mosquitoes from adding to her misery. Fortunately, the burns healed in record time due to her youth and general good health.

By mid-summer, Bonnie was up and stirring about the house, requiring much less care and having much less pain. Martha was able to assume her housekeeping duties without neighbors' help, but Melissa still went over to lend a hand on a regular basis. Always when Nate worked at Mr. Mac's, she went to Martha's.

Homestead

The two women formed a bond that summer much like that of their husbands.

"You know," Martha said to Melissa one day late in August, "I don't think Bonnie is going to have such awful scars. Do you?"

Melissa had thought the same thing and said as much. "She is such a pretty little thing, and the scars on her face are just pink places now where the new skin has formed. I really don't believe they will be noticeable once they return to the natural skin color." Both women were thinking the same thing. The scars would not keep her from being of marriageable quality later on.

In "The Family Way"

The summer went rapidly, it seemed to Melissa and Nate. They had been working toward getting the barn started, but with Bonnie's injury and Melissa canning food for winter with her mother, they had done very little else around the cabin. Melissa was hard pressed to even keep the weeds down in the yard.

Nate had collected lumber, poles and tin for the barn. They planned to build it in October. The crops had been laid by, and his corn from the huge garden was stored in the crib. Melissa, with the help of Lily, had canned peas, corn, okra and tomatoes, blackberries and pears. They had gotten some of the vegetables from their garden and some from Lily's and John's. They had an abundance of pears that summer, which made wonderful salads and pies. It would be a few years before the Yorks would have pears, but they had loads of blackberries; so many, in fact, that Lily and the girls had gone to Melissa's to pick them.

Melissa had begun limiting her visits to the Sewards to once a week earlier in the summer, but it was her day to go with Nate. She wasn't feeling particularly good that morning, but knew Martha would be disappointed if she didn't go. They took the buggy from John's so that the ride would be smoother, getting there at eight that morning. Nate left her at the Sewards and hurried on to Mr. Mac's to start to work.

As usual, the two women were happy to see each other and started right out in deep conversation, catching each other up on the week's happenings. Suddenly Melissa said, "Martha, how do you know if you are going to have a baby?"

Martha was taken aback and thrilled at the same time that Melissa might think she was in the family way.

"Well," she said, "You start out by missing the curse first off. Then you usually get sick at least every morning. Why? Are you…did you…have you missed?"

Melissa answered, "Yes! To both. I am so sick right now I could throw up my shoe soles."

Martha was so thrilled she could hardly contain herself. "When did you miss?"

"This is the second time. I should have started last month on the fourteenth and I didn't. Now here it is the eighteenth, and I still haven't started!"

"Well, let's see. You would be about six weeks which means the baby would be born about…November, December…." She counted until she got to June and said, "June. That's it! Somewhere in June."

"At least it will be the winter months when I am the biggest and I won't have to be canning and working in the yard and garden. Nate's going to have a fit!"

"Oh," Martha said, "you haven't told him yet then?"

"No. I wanted to wait and talk to you. I thought there might be something else that is causing me to be sick."

"That is very unlikely, my dear. You sound like you are in the family way to me!" her friend assured her.

Nate and Melissa were in bed with the light out when Melissa finally got up her courage and decided to tell Nate the news. "Nathan, have you noticed anything lately?"

"Like what?" he asked, sounding puzzled.

"You know. Have you missed anything?"

In "The Family Way"

More puzzled, Nate said, "What? I can't think of anything." Melissa was trying to get around having to come right out and say it, and he wasn't helping one bit.

"You know what happens every month? Well, haven't you realized it didn't happen this month or last?"

Nate sat bolt upright in bed and said, "What are you telling me? Are we-going-to-have-a-baby?"

"Yes!" She barely got the words out of her mouth when Nate grabbed her and started to hug her as hard as he dared." "Hey! Hold on! You are going to cause me to lose it before I get started!" Melissa yelled.

"Gosh, sweetheart. I've been so busy I hadn't realized you haven't had your monthlies! How long have you known?" he wanted to know.

"I talked to Martha today and she assured me I am going to have a baby. That is the reason I have been feeling sick every morning lately."

Nate couldn't have been more thrilled. They talked until late into the night about the baby, what it would be, how they would tell everyone and when. They decided only to tell the Tates for a few weeks, just in case something happened, as was often the case, especially with first babies.

Melissa, shy as she was, couldn't decide how to go about breaking the news to her parents and the girls. She thought it a good idea to tell all of them at once, but how? Nate suggested they tell them all at a family dinner, which suited her just fine. "But what will we *say*?" she wanted to know.

"We'll just tell them they are going to be grandparents in June!" Nate said simply.

"You tell them." Melissa pulled the cover up completely over her head and said, "I don't want to tell them!" Nate laughed at her and hugged her some more.

"Why don't you want to tell them, sweetheart? There is nothing wrong with being in the family way."

"Except that, well, you know," she giggled.

"Melissa! You think they don't already know?"

So it was decided that on their very next visit to her parents' for Sunday dinner, Nate would make the announcement. "But what if they don't have us up there soon for dinner?" Melissa worried.

"Then we'll have them down here," Nate offered.

"Of course, never mind the fact that we don't even have enough plates and forks! Just like a man not to think about the necessities. So, Mr. Smarty, what do you plan for us to eat on?"

"We'll tell them to bring their own," he said simply.

Melissa couldn't get to sleep that night, knowing full well the next day was going to be a big one. The neighbors were coming a little after sun-up the next morning to start the barn. Melissa would be expected to keep up conversation with the ladies who came along and help run after their children, cooing and oohing over each one. She wondered how she could possibly do that and be tossing up her breakfast all at the same time out in the back yard. Truthfully, right at that moment, she didn't even want to look at a child! The thoughts of having a baby scared the life out of her, and she dreaded the very idea of the actual birth process. In her seventeen and a half years, she had never even been near a birthing scene and had absolutely no idea what it entailed. Martha, dear Martha, would be her mentor. Not her Mother, whom she adored, because girls somehow just didn't discuss such matters with their mothers. Not having an older sister, Martha filled that slot in her life.

The barn building took a lot longer and was a much bigger job than the crib. It had to have stalls for the cow, calf and horse. It also had to have a place for corn, hay and other storage, including a wagon, buggy and tools. The ladies not only came, but they brought food for a picnic lunch, which everyone spread together. Being one of the social events of the year, everyone tried to bring their best recipes and show off their cooking abilities. Then the exchange of recipes began after the picnic when everyone wanted to know how everyone else made dishes. The gossip session also began with Eva Carpenter telling someone some news that brought about all the ladies wanting to get in on the secret. Of course, Eva was dying to tell it, but rather than be thought the gossip she really was, she insisted that her confidant tell the tale.

So it fell to Sara Helms to spread the word. "Well, Eva said last week that Tommy Cox and Wilbur Henry," lowering her voice so that everyone had to huddle around to hear, "got caught in an unnatural act!" Every lady gasped. Melissa looked at Martha quizzically, and Martha looked back at her with the same expression. Neither girl had ever heard of such a thing, but it sounded like the older ladies knew what it concerned.

"My word!" Miss Estelle cried. "What are they going to do about it?" She looked horrified, as did all the rest of the group.

Someone else said, "Who caught them?" and then someone else managed to utter a few words of dismay.

"We don't know what, if anything, is going to be done," Eva said.

"My husband says sometimes people get run out of the community for things like that!"

Each one again sucked in her breath, letting it our audibly. The fact that these young boys, in their late teens, could be run out of the community stunned all the ladies in the group. What must their parents think?

Someone asked where this happened and Eva did know that. "It was down by the branch south of the school," she said. Then, thinking about what she had done in telling this horrendous thing, she decided it would be a good idea to enlist everyone's silence. "Now ya'll don't go telling this, please. Jake would kill me if he knew I told it!" she said, as if all those women were going to keep that bit of news a secret.

Melissa could hardly wait to ask Martha what she knew about what they were talking about. As everyone began to gather their picnic items, she finally got her chance. "Martha! What was Miss Eva talking about? Do you know?"

Martha declared that she didn't, but said Melissa could rest assured she'd find out from Matt the minute she got him home and got the opportunity. Melissa was not sure she really wanted to ask Nate about it. They had never discussed things of that nature, so she decided to wait until her friend and confidant would be able to tell her about it at their next visit.

The barn was taking shape wonderfully by the time the neighbors left. The frame was up, the roof on and walls were almost finished. Nate would have to put in the partitions for the stalls, which he could do in his spare time, and John would help with the final touches when he was home for a spell.

As Lily and John left for the night, Lily said, "Come on up to our house for dinner tomorrow. I'll fry chicken." Nate's mouth began to water. Lily made the best fried chicken he had ever eaten, and he and Melissa exchanged glances. This would be the perfect time for telling! She felt it might be a bit much for her mother, though, after the day there at the picnic and protested weakly. Lily said that it wouldn't, however, and that they'd see them about noon the next day, Sunday.

"I'll be there early to help you, Mama," she said.

Martha Seward couldn't wait to get Matt to bed when they could have pillow talk. Right off the bat she asked about the two boys. Matt said, "Where did you hear that?" He was furious. His tone was such that Martha was startled. She had seldom seen Matt react in such a way about anything.

"I heard it today at the Yorks from one of the ladies. Why?"

Matt was stern. "Listen to me. I don't want to hear another word about that, and don't you be talking about it with anyone. Do you understand me?"

Martha was both hurt and surprised at his reaction, but she knew Matt well enough not to push the matter. "Yes, I understand," she answered contritely. She felt like a bad child who had just been chastised, but the matter was never brought up again in the Seward household. Matt turned over and went to sleep, leaving Martha to wonder what on earth two teenage boys could have done that would cause such a reaction from her husband.

When the Yorks and the Tates gathered around the dinner table the next day, everyone was served and had begun eating when Nate cleared his throat and said, "Well, how would you all like to be grandparents about next June?"

Lily almost dropped her fork. Having her daughter get married at such a tender age was one thing, but the idea of her having a child somehow had not even occurred to Lily. She knew the many problems that could occur in carrying a child and in birth, and she was just not ready for Melissa to go through any of that. She must have registered her shock on her face without meaning to, because Melissa was looking at her with a distressed look.

"Why, Mama. What is the matter?" she asked, becoming alarmed. This was certainly not the reaction she or Nate had expected. This was to be one of those joyous occasions when everyone concerned was excited and thrilled. John also had a serious look, but he recovered from the shock first and managed to say, "Gee, that is great," but not convincingly. "June, you say? Hum, that will be right after your eighteenth birthday, Melissa."

"Yes sir." She felt as if something were greatly amiss. "Mama, aren't you happy?" she asked Lily who still had not managed to say anything. Lily was thinking rapidly through the process and had reached the conclusion that what is done is done, and she might as well join in their excitement and make the most of it.

"Yes, I am happy, Melissa. I am very happy. I guess it's just a shock to realize your little girl is all grown up, married and starting a family of her own. Mothers never do seem to let go, I suppose." She was trying, but Lily knew she would have to work on coming to terms with this big news.

All this while Mary and Liz were gleeful, talking to each other in a side conversation, but quietly, because they sensed their parents' consternation. Neither of them had the faintest idea what childbirth was like, nor did they know how many young mothers died trying to deliver a too-large baby or through one of the other many complications of childbirth.

Lily and John assured the parents-to-be of their happiness over the idea of a grandchild and tried to make them understand their reluctance in not getting too excited right off. They explained that things can happen, and they would be terribly happy as time went on and everything went all right. Nate was not as put off by their reaction as Melissa was.

On the way back to the cabin, Melissa said, "Nate, they weren't a bit happy." She was hurt, obviously, and Nate could see that.

"Dearest, it is just that every set of parents hates to come to the realization that their daughter is a woman, married and just as your mother said, about to become a mother. It will be fine. Just you wait and see." Still, Melissa was not happy with their reaction. She had so looked forward to this time when she thought they would be the happiest people in the world. They would not tell anyone else for quite awhile.

Nate was ever so busy with the barn for a few days. Fall had arrived and winter would not be far behind. There would likely be a lot of rainfall during the early winter, and some of the weather could be pretty cold. He wanted stalls for the animals ready, just in case. He told Melissa he didn't want to lie down at night in a warm bed when the animals were out in the cold. That was Nate. Always thinking of other people and things. She thought he was one of the kindest people she had ever known.

The first of November and payday was there before they could believe it, and that was the target date for Melissa to get her stove. She was overjoyed at the prospect. Nate decided it should be a family affair picking the stove, so he told Melissa he wanted both of them to go into Creighton and look at the hardware. He said since she had to cook on it, she should have a chance to pick it out. Melissa was delighted. Then she had an idea.

"Nate, you know what a great time we had when we took the children to Creighton?" she asked.

"Yeah, that was fun. Would you like to do that again and take the children?" She said she would love doing that since they so seldom got to go anywhere.

With that, they decided to go on Saturday, three days away. They would go to Mr. Mac's for Nate to work and Melissa to have her regular visit with Martha on Friday. Then they'd tell the children about the trip so they could look forward to it. Bonnie was doing quite well now and would be able to go, too. Rose and Ben would be particularly happy. They had less opportunities than the Seward children with Mr. Mac and Miss Mattie being older. They just didn't go places as much. Mr. Mac's rheumatism was crippling him to the point that he did as little as possible. He depended on Pearl and Nate almost entirely to handle the store and farm. Miss Mattie, although a sweet and kind lady, was somewhat withdrawn of late. Nate had noticed she didn't seem to be quite herself the last few times he had seen her. And the poor children seemed starved for affection. Ben, particularly, latched on to Nate when he got there to work and hardly let go. Poor little Rose was shy and said very little, causing Nate to wonder how things were there for her. He still felt terribly guilty that he had never said anything about the situation he knew existed. Perhaps he should tell Melissa, and maybe Matt.

When they got to the Sewards', Nate let Melissa out and drove on across the way to the McDougalds'. He had picked up John's and Lily's buggy again to keep Melissa from jostling any more than she had to on the ride. He worried about her. She was such a small boned person, and he had already decided she would have the baby at the Infirmary in Creighton. He wanted her to have the very best of care possible. He tried all the time to keep her from over-exertion, but Melissa had a mind of her own and a lot of things she wanted to get done.

Homestead

Martha hugged Melissa and ushered her into the kitchen, where the stove was providing warmth. It was a rather cool day, and the coffeepot was still hot on the stove. As Martha poured each of them a tin of coffee, they launched into conversation about all the things that had happened to each of them that week. Melissa told her about her parents' reaction to her having a baby. Martha understood to a degree and explained to Melissa that when she had that child, if it turned out to be a girl, she would be feeling the same way in a few years. Melissa had not considered that. It made sense. They continued talking about various happenings. The barn was about finished, Melissa told Martha. She thanked her friend for coming to the picnic and for Matt's help.

"I don't think Nate could have built that barn by himself. He isn't really a carpenter, and so it was wonderful to have all the men come to help. Oh! And speaking of that, did you ever get to ask Matt about the thing with the two boys?" She could see Martha tense and begin to look distressed.

"Listen, Melissa. The strangest thing happened. That night, I asked Matt about that when we got to bed, and you wouldn't believe his reaction! I have seldom seen him so furious. He told me that I had no business knowing about that and said who told me, and I told him one of the ladies told me. Well, he said forget I had heard it and never mention it again and never tell that to a soul!"

"Really? What on earth could have caused him to have such feelings?" Melissa asked, half to herself and half to her friend. It really was a puzzle, indeed.

"Anyway, I think we'd better do as he said and forget about it, except I will not forget it. I will just not mention it again to him. I still want to know what it was about."

Melissa said, "I guess I could ask Nate, but I think he might tell me the same thing. He doesn't tell me about bad things he hears. He's kind of protective."

In "The Family Way"

With that, the two of them changed the subject and didn't speak of it again for a long, long time.

Saturday morning was cool. In fact, there was a light frost, Nate said as he sat down to an early breakfast with Melissa. It was just past daylight, and she had cooked their breakfast on the open fire, thinking it was probably the last time. That night they would have their new stove. It might take a day or two to get help to move it into the cabin, but it would at least be on the wagon ready to unload. They were cozy at their little table in front of the fire when Melissa got up to get more coffee. As she rose from the table and turned her back to him, Nate saw the bright red stain on the back of her dressing gown. At that moment, he also saw Melissa bend almost double and sink to the floor.

"Sweetheart!" he exclaimed. Reaching for her, he picked her up and carried her to the bed a few feet away. She was as white as the dressing gown and looked as though she were half unconscious. Nate had no idea what to do. The first thing he thought of was the bell and the distress rings. He ran to the edge of the front stoop and rang the bell three times furiously. Then he rang it three more times just hoping someone would hear. As early as it was, maybe the men would be out tending their stock at their barns. The Rogers, the Carpenters and Melissa's parents were the only neighbors who would be possibly able to hear. He hated to leave her to go anywhere for help. Creighton? No, that was too far and a rough trip, even in the buggy.

As Nate went back into the cabin, Melissa was trying to sit up. "What happened?" she asked, seeming puzzled about her condition.

"Sweetheart, stay in the bed. You are bleeding. I rang the bell for help, and I am going to have to go somewhere soon if somebody doesn't hear the bell and come."

"Oh, Nate. Don't leave me," she begged. "Am I losing the baby? I just can't! Oh, please, God, don't let me lose the baby."

"I don't know, sweetheart. Maybe not. I pray not." He had grabbed a heavy cloth to put under her and realized she was bleeding rather heavily. Not having a better solution, he went back to the door and rang the bell three more times. In a couple of seconds, he heard an answer at the Rogers place. Someone would be coming to help in a few minutes. If Grace came, she could stay with Melissa while he went for the doctor. If Franklin came, he'd send him and stay with Melissa himself.

Melissa was trying not to cry, but the pains were getting really strong. She gripped Nate's hand and held on through the bad ones. Thirty minutes passed and there was a knock at the door.

"Nate," Franklin called,

"What is the matter?" He was clearly distressed.

Nate went to the door and stepped outside. A few words of explanation and Franklin was ready to be on his way to Creighton for the doctor. Remembering they were supposed to take the children to town, Nate asked Franklin to stop at the Sewards and tell Martha what was happening. He told him to ask her to explain to her children and send word to Rose and Ben that they would have to go to town another day.

Franklin rode rapidly into the lane at the Sewards. Martha was sweeping the porch and realized immediately something was wrong. She met Franklin at the gate. "What is it?" she asked in distress.

Franklin explained the situation, told her about the children going to town another day and asked to borrow a fresh horse. As luck would have it, Matt had only one horse with him in the field and the other was in the lot. Franklin would trade that one out at the McLean's about half way. He could be in Creighton much faster that way.

Dr. Haygood was in his office. He peered up at Franklin over his half-glasses, realizing the urgency in the man's demeanor. "Yes, son? How can I help you?" he asked.

In "The Family Way"

Franklin explained the situation. Dr. Haygood listened intently and sympathetically, but began shaking his head. "You realize that if she is losing the baby, I won't be able to do a thing to stop it. In fact, if something is wrong, it is entirely best that she lose it now rather than have a child with something wrong."

"Yes sir, I know that, but I came as they asked me to. Can you go?"

"I will go," Dr. Haygood said. He started getting his bag and hat. Since it was a cool day, he took his great coat, just in case. Putting a card on the door that had a little clock on it, he moved the hands to read "Back at 8 AM", locked the door and started for the horse and buggy that stood near the door. "You go ahead on back. I will be slower than you, but I will be there as soon as I can."

"Thanks, Doc," Franklin said as he mounted his horse and started the long ride back.

Melissa was trying to get through the pains without screaming. She figured she was about two or two and a half months, maybe three, and thought if she could only get through this without losing the baby, she would be so happy. Nate was so good. He stayed right with her and tried to help her through the pains. Now and then he would go back and ring the bell in hopes Lily would hear it and come down to the cabin. He wished so much that he had told Franklin to run down that short way and tell her before going on to town.

About ten o'clock, Lily knocked at the door. She had finally been out to hang something on the clothesline and heard the bell. Leaving the girls at the house, she hitched Sally to the buggy and rushed down. Nate told her what was happening before letting her enter the room where her daughter was suffering one hard pain after another.

Lily went to her side and took her hand. "Hello, Mama," Melissa said between the pains.

"Hello, darling," was all Lily said. There was no need for words.

The two women understood the situation and their hearts were united at that moment as they had never been before.

It was late afternoon when Franklin returned from Creighton and told Nate the Doctor was on his way. "He should be here in another hour."

When Dr. Haygood got to the cabin, Melissa was resting and the pains had stopped. Lily took him aside and explained what had taken place. He then went over to Melissa and asked her some questions. He determined that she had aborted, but felt it was complete and that she should not have any infection or problems afterward. "Just keep her in bed for a few days, and she should be fine and ready to start over before long." He then explained to Melissa that this was most likely for the best and that she was very fortunate that it was complete. Anything remaining of the baby could cause infection that could be life- threatening. He left something for her to take that would help her sleep for several hours. Then he cautioned her again about staying in bed to help control the bleeding.

Melissa took little comfort in the fact that she had miscarried completely and that something might be wrong with the baby and it could be better that she lost it. She kept thinking, why couldn't she have her baby. Lily tried to comfort the best she could, realizing that Melissa would have to get through the pain of the loss before she could see that she was fortunate.

On his way out of the cabin, Dr. Haygood stopped to talk with Nate where he was waiting outside. "Son, be sure you don't get her pregnant again for at least three or four months. She needs that time to get her strength back, and I would like to see her in a month." Nate thanked the doctor and paid him from a roll of bills he had ready in his pocket.

Nate felt sad, but realized they could try again, and the most important thing was that Melissa was going to be all right.

Building the Church

With cooler weather came dry, clear days when the woods were like tinderboxes ready to burn with the least effort. Nate had remarked to Melissa that he needed to plow a fire line right away, but he had been reluctant to stay away from the house too long. She seemed so sad and he had been worried. She had little appetite and was losing weight. He could tell that she had been crying several times when he would come back into the cabin after being out for a while. Nothing he could say seemed to comfort her; so he decided to try another tactic.

"Sweetheart, would you like to go up to your mother's and stay for a few days? I need to be working outside a lot, and I don't want to leave you," he asked after he had made their breakfast one clear cool morning. She was sitting by the fire and had barely touched her bacon and hoecake.

"I guess I could," she said dispassionately. Nothing seemed to interest her, really.

"It would give me a chance to plow the fireline. You know woods fires are such a threat," Nate reminded her. "I also need to work up at the McDougalds', too."

"All right. I will go." Melissa was doing well physically. It was just her spirit that worried Nate. She seemed to have lost her zest for life and her will to do anything. Maybe she just needed more time. He hoped that would take care of the problem.

"You surely don't have to go unless you feel like it," he told her gently.

"I will be fine." With that, she got up and started slowly making preparations to go. It was obvious that her heart was not in it.

Lily and the girls welcomed Melissa when Nate drove her up in the wagon. She only took a few things, knowing that he could bring anything else she might need from the cabin, and she didn't expect to stay but a very few days.

"I will be up and spend the night with you, sweetheart," he told her as he left, kissing her good-bye. Mary and Liz understood that she was not going to be having the baby and they were sweet and attentive when they were not at school. Both girls chattered away about school, boys and all the things girls are interested in.

Mary started to tell about Miss Brown, the teacher, and how she had a boyfriend when Lily interrupted. "Now Mary, gossip isn't proper. You go finish getting ready for school."

After the girls left, Melissa asked her mother what Mary was going to tell about Jessica Brown.

"Never you mind," was all Lily would say." "It's nothing concerns us. The school board will handle it." Melissa wondered if it could be anything serious enough to get her dismissed. She secretly thought it would be wonderful if Miss Brown had to leave her job so she could try for it! But her sweeter nature took over and she knew she could not even think about such a thing again. Still, if that should happen, Melissa would certainly apply.

Nate began his heavy work by plowing the fire line through the rough woods. They were so thick with underbrush in places he had to make jogs around some areas, thinking all the while what a woods fire could do to the area. It had not burned in years, allowing the deep grass briars and tangle of bushes to get terribly thick. It would take three or four days to plow a wide enough line to deter fire from crossing it yet that he must do. It was the only protection from fire a place could have. Fortunately, John had his plowed. He simply could not afford to leave Lily and the children there alone so much without that protection. She had her rain barrel full of water, but that would only help with a small fire. Many houses had the kitchen separate from the main house because of the fire hazard, but John didn't build theirs that way. He reasoned that a fireplace caused as much fire hazard as the stove in the kitchen did, and he didn't want Lily off so far from the rest of the family when she was in the kitchen.

Nate was glad the weather was cooler when he started the hard plowing. Dewey was glad, too. He worked so hard for Nate that he got an extra handful of feed each night. "Dewey, you behave yourself now while I get ready to go up to the big house. Leave the pigs alone!" Every time Nate left that horse in the lot with the pigs, he'd bite a pig's tail off. Their tails were only skinny little ragged things, but Nate knew it hurt. He could hear one squeal now and then and surely enough, his tail would be gone. He finally had to start putting Dewey where he couldn't get to the pigs. In the cool weather, he was frisky and bad anyway, kicking up his back heels and bucking about the lot. Nate loved that horse, and Dewey loved Nate. Their bond had continued to grow as they worked long, hard hours together settling the place and making it a home.

As soon as he'd finished plowing the fire-line, Nate went to Mr. Mac's to work. Fire was not a problem from the woods standpoint there or at Matt's place. They had enough cleared area around both houses, big yards and lanes that it couldn't get in, so he would do other things about the place. Mr. Mac hardly got about at all anymore because of his knees, and Miss Mattie seemed to be failing. She was only in her late sixties, and Mr. Mac in his early seventies, but hard work had taken its toll on both of them. Pearl ran the store pretty much with him going out and sitting for her at times when she needed to get away to do something else. Nate felt rather sorry for her. Poor girl. She was homely, big boned and with a face that would stop an eight-day clock, and it seemed highly unlikely that she would ever find a husband. He could see that she was not only stuck with the store but most of the house duties, cooking, cleaning, etc., and the care of Ben and Rose as well.

When he rounded the last corner at the pond just down from the house, Nate heard the dinner bell ringing the three distress rings. He hurried on to the yard fence, where he tied Dewey as fast as he could, taking the steps three at the time. Pearl was at the door, having heard him coming onto the porch. "Nate, it's Mama. She fell, and I can't lift her up!" she called, hurrying into the kitchen area with Nate right behind her. Miss Mattie was in the floor beside the table, moaning as though in pain. Nate helped Pearl move her to the bedroom with Pearl taking her feet and him carrying her under the shoulder area. She was a good-sized woman and hard to lift.

They got Miss Mattie onto the bed and by that time Mr. Mac had hobbled back to the house the hundred yards or so from the store, obviously distressed, wanting to know what was the matter. Pearl explained and told her father to stay there with her while she went for a wet cloth to bathe her face. Miss Mattie started coming around a little as Pearl bathed her face with the cold cloth. Nate offered to go for the doctor, but Pearl told him Matt was going to Creighton anyway. He had just been to the store before she came to the house. She said, "He allowed as how he had to go to Creighton to see how his parents are doing. His father has been ill. They are all going, but if you would run over and tell them to send the doctor, I surely would appreciate it."

Nate started out immediately, catching the Sewards just as they drove hurriedly into the yard to see what was wrong. They had heard the bell while they were dressing to go to town. Nate told them what had happened. "Can we do anything?" Martha asked. Being told that everything was under control, they went on their way agreeing to send the doctor.

Before Nate had to leave that day, Dr. Haygood got there and checked Miss Mattie. Nobody had realized it, but she had lost some of the use of her right hand and her mouth was drawn to the side slightly. He told Pearl and Mr. Mac that Miss Mattie had had a light stroke. He said the only thing they could do was have her try to exercise her hand and limit her salt carefully. "Oh, she loves salt," Pearl told the doctor.

"Yes, so do I," Dr. Haygood lamented, "but I can't have very much. It runs the blood pressure up, and hers is probably high. That is about all we can do."

"Will she get the full use of her hand back Doctor?" Pearl inquired.

Dr. Haygood appeared skeptical and said he couldn't say for sure and that only time could tell.

Riding home on Dewey, Nate had time to reflect on the day, Miss Mattie's illness, and all the work Pearl had to do. He felt for her a great deal, but if he felt bad then, it was nothing compared to the way he would feel later. He wondered if Callie would come home to help and doubted that she would.

Melissa and Nate had taken Trouble and Buttons with them up to the Tates', and the cow could graze in the garden that no longer had vegetables but had gone to grass. The pigs rooted around for their living during the day and didn't have to be fed every day, so he could go home to the Tates' and have some of Miss Lily's good cooking. He was dreaming of that when he heard Trouble barking furiously. Now, I wonder what trouble that dog has gotten into this time, he thought. As he got to the picket fence of the yard, there was absolutely no doubt what he had gotten into: a skunk! The odor was like no other, and the women were holed up in the house with every window closed tightly. Not only was the air permeated totally with skunk musk, but so was Trouble! That dog would smell like a skunk until Christmas, was what Nate was thinking. Dewey snorted and reared, shying around the yard area where the poor, smelly critter was backing into the corner fearing for his life. If he had only known, Trouble was not going one step closer. He had already gotten himself into a mess of trouble as it was. Nate called the poor, wretched dog as soon as he put Dewey into the lot, and, of course, Trouble wanted to jump right into Nate's face.

"Stay down, boy," he yelled. Trouble apparently understood, because he tucked his tail between his legs and followed Nate to Miss Lily's chicken yard where he was shut up in a vacant chicken coop for the night. The skunk had sprayed a full dose of the musk on the hapless dog, probably before Trouble realized he had cornered it.

"Hello!" Nate called to the cloistered females, wondering if they were even going to let him in. The scent, fortunately, was far less odorous inside but they inquired as to whether Nate had been hit with the musk.

Assuring them he had not, he told them he'd take the dog to the branch and wash him thoroughly the next morning. It might not take the entire scent off, but he would be tolerable, at least. Meanwhile, the skunk had vacated the premises as fast as he could!

Being at her mother's had seemingly helped Melissa a great deal. She enjoyed her sisters and was a great help with their homework, plus she and Miss Lily had started another project, which Melissa would not discuss with Nate. He assumed it was something she was knitting for him for Christmas. He figured on making her a birdhouse for purple martins, which he had to get started on. He could make it in the barn by lantern light now that the barn was finished.

"I guess we can go home tomorrow night, Mama," Melissa said to Lily at supper.

"Don't rush. We love having you here, and you don't need to be down there by yourself any time. There is too much mischief going on in the community," Lily told her.

"What mischief, Mama?" asked Melissa curiously. "I never hear of any."

"Well, you just don't hear because Nathan works about the house and for the McDougalds instead of out in the county like your Dad does," she replied.

Then both Liz and Mary piped up wanting to know what mischief, but Lily was no gossip and would say no more. She was just glad Mary and Liz had to walk only a short way alone and could go the rest of the way to school with the Carpenter children. Later that evening, Melissa tried to find out what Mary knew about Miss Brown, but Mary said she didn't know anything except that something happened and Miss Brown was maybe going to get into trouble over it. Oh, well, Melissa was thinking. Maybe.

Back at the cabin, the Yorks sighed a sigh of relief. No matter how humble, there is no place like home. The cat and dog even seemed to feel more at ease, and Trouble was smelling better and no longer banished since his bath with lye soap in the cold water of the branch.

For the next few days Nate would work in the field that he was clearing. It was arduous work cutting trees and burning out the stumps, and then plowing it would be really tough. But it was beginning to shape up into a pretty fair-sized patch, which Nate would farm the next spring. Each year he would add a few acres until he had the whole one hundred and sixty acres under cultivation.

One late afternoon he called Melissa. "Sweetheart, come out to the woodpile."

"Whatever for?" Melissa questioned.

"Have you ever shot a rifle?" Nate asked, holding his father's rifle out to her. Melissa said she had shot her dad's a few times.

Homestead

"I want you to practice shooting awhile then." Nate went on to tell her that there would be times when he would have to be gone or even away from the house far enough that she couldn't call him or that he couldn't get there in time if she got into distress. "You know there are a few people, not many, but a few who mean you harm, and there are snakes, wild cats, mad dogs and all kinds of dangers that you might need to deal with. I just want you to be a good shot in case that comes about." He taught her how to load the rifle, how to hold it and how to shoot. Melissa tried three or four times and right off hit the wood chip he had placed on the woodpile as a target. Nate was pleased.

"Good! Good!" he told her. "You are a natural." Melissa was quite pleased at his reaction. "Now, we are going to keep this rifle right where it has been in the corner by the front door. If anyone comes here that you don't know, you go straight into the cabin, close and latch the door and stay until you find out what they want. Don't you come out until you are satisfied about who they are and what they want, you hear?"

Melissa wanted to know what he was going to do about having a firearm with him in the woods. "You are liable to be in more danger than I am."

"Your dad has two guns that never are used, so I am going to ask him when he gets home this time if I can borrow one until we can buy another."

There was another matter he and John had to tackle as soon as John returned from the trip he was presently on: getting a church built. They had already done the preliminaries by talking to the men of the area earlier and then again when the barn was being built, Nate talked to them again. They were all greatly interested and enthusiastic about having a church. "We should have done it long ago," one man said. Everyone else echoed his opinion. John was giving part of the land, while the Rogers family agreed to give adjoining land for the church and cemetery. They decided on a total of three acres. John was due in about a week. The Reverend Lock was also due. He would be on hand to give technical advice about the pulpit area, altar rail and so on.

The next time Nate went to Fox Hollow to work for Mr. Mac, Melissa went and offered to help out at the house for Pearl. With Miss Mattie unable to use her right hand for the most part, she was of little use in the kitchen or in cleaning, so Pearl gratefully accepted Melissa's offer. She did some wash, hung the clothes out to dry in the stiff, fall breeze, and used the wash water to scrub the kitchen and back porch. Then she swept the rest of the floors carefully, made the beds and dusted. When Pearl got back to the house for the noon meal, Melissa had it cooked. "I baked the sweet potatoes you had washed, cleaned and cooked the greens and fried the ham I found in the lard bucket. I hope that was all right," Melissa told her.

"All right!" Pearl exclaimed.

"That is wonderful! Oh, I am so hungry, and I thought I would have to cook when I got to the house. I left Daddy minding the store, but I declare, he can hardly get about on those knees. They are swollen double and so sore," Pearl confided to Melissa. She told her that Miss Mattie, who had been in the bed the entire time Melissa had been there, was not doing well and could do virtually nothing. She said Martha had sent supper over several times.

"With the kids, though, she can't get over often." Melissa told her she would come each time Nate went to work.

"I am mighty grateful, Melissa. I really am," Pearl told her. "We will have enough for supper, too." It was the custom to cook two meals at the time. When you cooked the noon meal, you cooked enough for supper.

Later in the afternoon, Pearl thought of the possibility of hiring Melissa to come the two days a week that Nate came to work. Maybe she could get her to do the washing, which was one of the most time-consuming tasks, and a little housework plus some cooking. It would be well worth the cost and it looked like she was going to have to get some help from somewhere. She was getting behind more every day with no let up in sight. That evening before they left for home, Pearl walked out into the back yard to thank Melissa. She hugged the younger woman and told her what a great help she had been. "Are you, by any chance, interested in working two days a week when Nate comes, Melissa? I can pay you the going wages."

Melissa looked quickly at Nate in a quizzical way. "What do you think, Nathan?"

He wasn't sure she was up to the work, but wanted her to make her own decision. "It's up to you," he told her.

"I had planned on coming back as often as I could, Pearl, anyway. You don't have to pay me," Melissa offered.

"Oh, no! I couldn't let you do that! Not on a regular basis. But it is settled then. You come for awhile, as long as you feel like it."

As the Yorks drove along home, Melissa told Nate she wanted to buy a buggy with her money. The month was about up since she lost the baby, so they would be having to go to Creighton very soon to have her see Dr. Haygood. They would take the children as promised, buy the stove, and look for a buggy. "It will take working for some little while to buy a buggy, sweetheart," Nate mentioned. Melissa told him they needed one so it was settled. It would be fun to shop for the buggy. If they could see what they cost, she would have a goal to work toward. The late afternoon and early evening was so pleasant for the two riding along in John's buggy. There were sounds along the way they both recognized from the woods. A cool breeze was blowing, causing the tall pines to make a whirring sound. Melissa thought she was the happiest she had been since she learned she was going to have the baby. Nate put his arm around her as Dewey trotted them home.

Callie McDougald was causing quite a stir in Mobile. She had begun work right after graduation as a special duty nurse. When members of well-to-do families became ill and wanted to be cared for in their own homes, Callie would stay with the family and nurse the patient. She made a name for herself immediately as a fine nurse and thus was sought after by many of the old Mobile families. It was choice work living in lovely homes where there were usually servants to prepare delightful meals, wash the nurse's clothes, clean her room and perform many other tasks she would have ordinarily had to do for herself besides working a shift in the infirmary. Callie made top wages, too. She would work for a family and pretty soon the word spread of her excellent care of the patient, and soon another family would send for her. Between cases, she and another nurse shared a small room in downtown Mobile. It cost them less by sharing.

Soon Callie opened a charge account at Cahill's, Mobile's finest department store. The clothes were the finest, and hats, shoes and purses were available, along with jewelry to compliment every outfit. Callie found that every outfit had to have shoes, hats, gloves and so on, to complete it. She was often invited out, after working for a family, to join them at a play, concert or some other social function, so she naturally needed outfits for those occasions. Dates were frequent with the young men in the families, and although Callie was not pretty, she had an arresting look, making it difficult for people to take their eyes off her. She was often asked out for an evening at the country club, causing the need for formal wear to present itself. Her life was shaping up just the way she wanted it to, and although she had heard about her mother from Pearl, she had no intention of going home to the sticks to live in Fox Hollow and take care of her aging parents. When she had the time, she would write home and tell Pearl, in so many words, that she couldn't leave her "profession" at this time. Not that Pearl had asked, but she could read the handwriting between the lines.

November was an overcast month with some rain and lots of humidity, for which northwest Florida is noted. The church building had gotten under way when John got home for ten days in October, and it was almost ready for services to be held there. Reverend Lock said he could be there every other Sunday at first, but that the Conference would assign a full time pastor when attendance warranted it. He estimated a membership of 60 to 70 in the beginning. John and Nate were hoping he was right.

The little church was quaint. It had windows with sashes and windowpanes, but because of hurricanes and storms near the gulf coast, it also had shutters on the outside that could be closed when the building was not in use. It would seat about a hundred people. While one crew was framing, putting on the roof and weatherboarding, another crew was building benches, a pulpit and making the altar rail and minister's chair. The weather boarding was of rough-hewn boards which were not going to be painted or white washed, so they would weather as the name seemed to imply. There was an area for a piano when, and if, they could ever afford one. The next problem was a pianist, but Reverend Lock solved that by saying he had married one. Surprise registered on everyone's face. Nobody had realized he was married. He was just Reverend Lock, the circuit-riding preacher.

Everyone was working as hard as possible, with any spare time available, to get the building finished for Christmas. It appeared that would be possible if the rain held up long enough.

Dr. Haygood had found Melissa to be as good as new after her miscarriage, and she had a brand-new stove for the cabin. They had a wonderful time on the November day when they went to Creighton and took the children. Rose and Ben had an especially good time, but Nate kept noticing how withdrawn Rose seemed to be. He wondered if Melissa had noticed anything.

Martha and Melissa had had little chance to visit since Melissa spent her time working for the McDougalds when she was there with Nate, but Martha expressed her regrets over Melissa losing the baby. She confided that she had the same experience between her two younger children and that she was sad for weeks afterward. The Yorks had stopped by for a short visit on their way home from a workday. Nate and Matt discussed the church. They would all be members. The congregation had decided to have a huge celebration when it opened, with dinner on the grounds and singing after the sermon on the first Sunday. That prompted little Sissy Seward to ask, "Why do we have to eat off the ground?"

Martha explained what it meant, telling the child everyone would be taking dinner to eat at the church.

On the following Wednesday, while Melissa was at the McDougalds' working, Pearl asked her if she would go out and work at the store for a while so that she could do some things at the house which required her attention. Melissa had been putting some hard candy in the glass display case out of a small barrel and had become somewhat engrossed, so that she failed to notice someone coming into the store. Suddenly, she felt eyes watching her. Looking up, she saw Eulon Fields standing there grinning at her. She had not seen the boy since they were in school together nearly two years earlier. Eulon was what the community called "not right." He had the mind of a four year old, and he was about twenty. He went to school for years and years, being retained in grade after grade and finally being allowed to stop school at the age of eighteen, because he could not learn. Eulon was said to be harmless, but Melissa didn't trust him because he stared and made her highly uncomfortable.

"Can I get something for you, Eulon?" she asked, anxious to get him served and out of the store. He just grunted "uh ah" and continued to stand there and stare, grinning. My word, Melissa was thinking, why doesn't Pearl come on back? Eulon had decayed teeth in the front that appeared to be about ready to fall out. His gums were puffy and red. She felt sure he had never brushed them. His hair had not been cut in weeks. It was matted with dirt, down below his ears and had been cut by his mother, most likely, the last time it was cut. Even though it was December and cool, the man had no shoes. His pants had holes the size of a quarter and were held on by a piece of rope run through the loops. The shirt he was wearing had sleeves nearly to his elbows and holes as big as those in his pants. He wore no jacket.

Getting a little more nervous, Melissa asked, "What do you want, Eulon?" He answered, "Nothin'."

He giggled a very silly giggle and continued to stand there and stare. Melissa went on about her business, all the while watching him out of one eye. She certainly didn't want to get cornered behind the counter by Eulon, although she thought Pearl would be back out in a short while. She encountered all sorts of people from week to week in the store. Melissa reckoned she could handle one situation without getting into a panic. Finally, he simply said' "bye" and wandered on out of the store. When Pearl returned, Melissa told her of the encounter.

"Oh, Eulon. Yes, he is harmless. He just likes to stare at girls. But I have a pistol right under the candy case in that drawer if you ever have to use it," Pearl told her. Melissa admired Pearl. She seemed to be a highly capable woman. How many ladies could run that store, keep the house going, care for ailing parents and get all the things done in a day that Pearl did? She thought it strange that Nate didn't seem to care much for her. Every time she brought up Pearl's name in a conversation, he changed the subject.

Christmas was going to be on Saturday that year, and the church was complete. On the last work day, while most of the children were still in school, the members in the homestead community went to help clean up around the new building. They picked up unused pieces of lumber, nails, little blocks of wood and other debris. Someone built a fire to burn some trash such as limbs, leaves and grass they had cut with the sling blades they had brought for the purpose. The grass was dead from the heavy frosts, and all the leaves had finally fallen from the trees surrounding the churchyard. It was a bleak time of year, but happiness abounded among the two dozen or so workers who attended that work session.

Reverend Lock called everyone together when they finished. "Brethren," he said, "Let's gather round and thank Almighty God for the completion of this new church built to His glory." He began a prayer that seemed to Melissa to last forever. Then he held a discussion about the dedication day, what it would entail and told them they would need to be thinking of people to be elected as deacons and stewards to serve as the governing body of the church. It was late in the afternoon when the meeting ended, and getting colder.

Nate and Melissa climbed into the wagon and started for home, pulling their great coats up snugly around them. Lily and the girls were following along behind in their buggy. John was out working the range, trying to finish before Christmas. The woods had an ethereal look. All the trees were bare except the towering pines, their trunks taking on a whitish hue, almost as if they had snow on them in the near darkness. It was a beautiful sight. They rode along to the Tates' calling back and forth to each other now and then. Lily told Nate and Melissa she had a pot of peas cooked and pork chops left from breakfast. She was going to build a fast fire in the stove to warm everything up and wanted them to stay for supper. "There's no use in you having to go home and cook," she offered. It sounded good to the Yorks, who gratefully accepted. The supper conversation was all about the new church and speculation as to who would make good deacons and stewards.

Homestead

Eulon

The McDougalds were hoping that Callie would come home for Christmas. As the time neared, no word came of her planning a visit, however. Nate and Melissa went to work a few days before the holiday to learn that Miss Mattie was not doing well again. She seemed somewhat confused and Pearl was worried. Having not had time to go for the mail in a number of days, Pearl asked Nate if he would ride up to Mrs. Gay's and get the mail. Perhaps Callie had written that she would be coming and it was late getting to them.

Etta Gay was cleaning the yard when Nate rode up. Tying Dewey to the fence post, he entered the yard, calling a greeting to Miss Etta. Her dog barked so loud they couldn't talk at first. He was a cur that made a great fuss but had never bitten anyone that Nate knew of. Just the same, he always kept an eye on the dog.

"Hello, Nate!" Etta was tired and needed a break, so she followed him on up onto the porch and sank into a cane-bottomed rocker. "Sit a spell, Nate, and rest a little while." She had worked up a sweat, although it was a cool day in December. She lifted her apron, fanning with it, and prepared herself for a lengthy conversation. Etta lived alone, having lost her husband a number of years before in some sort of accident. She was lonely, Nate knew, but she was also nosey to the point that he had to measure everything he told her, lest it get passed around the community as something he had said. As he talked, he studied her craggy face, the long, graying hair up in a knot at the back of her head, and the missing teeth very obvious when she smiled. He wondered for a fleeting moment if he and Melissa would look that way one day.

"Can't stay long, Miss Etta. I have a lot of work to do at the McDougalds' today."

Of course, Etta wanted to hear the news. She was hungry to know all the happenings in the community. "How is Mattie?" she asked. "Any better?"

"Not really," Nate told her. He went on to explain about her being confused, about Mr. Mac's knees, and said he thought he would end up having to have a wheelchair before long. Nate pulled the mail out of the cubbyhole on the table, glancing through to see if anything looked like a letter from Callie. Nothing did. He and Melissa never had mail, but she had taught him to read well enough to recognize it, if it ever came. They had spent some long evenings that winter working on his reading and writing and it was paying off.

"Looking for a letter from Callie? Don't hold your breath. That girl ain't coming back here any time soon," Etta told him. That was beginning to be obvious. She wanted to go on and on talking about people, but Nate had to move along.

"Take care, Miss Etta," he told her. "See you again soon."

"Come again," she called to his back as he and Dewey began their trot back to Fox Hollow. Dewey loved the cool days. He wanted to run full speed, but Nate wouldn't let him do that. They had to get home with Dewey pulling the wagon, this time loaded with feed and staple grocery items. Nate patted the horse and told him to hold up.

"You'll get your chance soon, boy. I'll let you run one day till your heart is content." He knew the trouble with Dewey was that he never knew when he had enough. He wanted to keep going and going.

Pearl scanned the mail, a catalog with seeds and one or two other junk pieces, with obvious disappointment. She had been hoping to hear back from Callie, at least. With the train running twice a day, how long could it take to get a letter back from Mobile 85 miles away?

December the twelfth was designated as dedication Sunday at the brand new Catawba Methodist Church. All the new members-to-be were up early, with the women preparing their dishes and getting ready to leave from the various areas where they all lived — some as far as eight and ten miles. It would require leaving early to be there for the eleven o'clock service. The workmen had built long board tables out of some of the leftover logs between two stately oaks. They would be used for the food. Benches had also been constructed for people to sit on shaded by other oaks, all of which were bare of leaves in the winter, but spring would bring heavy leaf growth and provide fine shade on hot days. The various ladies took tin plates and cups for their family members to fill up with food, including stainless-steel forks. The food would all be put out on the table. Then the people would go along, selecting whatever appealed to them, sharing what each other had brought. They all had their specialties. Lily was famous for her fried chicken while Mrs. Rogers was known for her chocolate cake. They were two of the first things to disappear.

The Reverend Lock began the service by asking everyone to stand and sing Amazing Grace, followed by a prayer in which he asked the Lord to bless the new church and let it be used to His glory. After the prayer, the sermon followed. Everything was going along quite well when Mr. Rufus Mathis came in late, causing a little stir, but the preacher continued. Mr. Mathis had tied his horse to a persimmon tree on the south side of the church and had sat by a window so he could watch him, because the horse had a habit of slipping his bridle off and getting loose. Mr.

Mathis, on the other hand, was known about the community to be extremely absent-minded, sometimes even starting out of the house without his pants on. So as the preacher was expounding away on the evils of sin with everyone paying rapt attention, the horse began working at the bridle, and just as he was about to slip it off, Mr. Mathis jumped right up and yelled, "Whoa!" as loud as he could. Some were startled out of their wits. The Reverend was annoyed, and the congregation broke up into uncontrolled laughter! Mr. Mathis, realizing what he had done, mumbled an apology as he hastily departed the church to try to stop his horse. The snickers continued periodically throughout the remainder of the service.

At the end of the service, the minister told the congregation that he would receive into the church any of those who had not joined when he had been visiting the area as a circuit rider. They sang another hymn, after which several people went up to the front and took the vows of the church: do you promise to be loyal to the Methodist church and uphold it with your prayers, presence, gifts and service, etc.? The dedication part of the service was a short statement giving the building to God to be used for the furtherance of His kingdom. Mr. Mathis had slipped quietly back into the back of the building before the dedication, obviously highly embarrassed.

In the afternoon, the children played games, ran races and had a wonderful time. They saw each other away from school infrequently, but that promised to change with regular services beginning. There would be Sunday school each church Sunday before the worship service. Melissa had been tapped as a teacher for the younger children. Grace Rogers would teach the older young people. John was to be a deacon; Nate and Matt, stewards. They would be the "hands-on" people who looked after the building and grounds, making decisions as to what repairs and changes needed to be made. John, as a deacon, would be more into the spiritual needs of the church. They were usually older men who were, hopefully, wiser, and could guide the church in its spiritual journey, along with the minister.

Mrs. Lock attended. She was a very pleasant lady with mouse-gray hair drawn up in a knot at the back of her neck. She wore a black dress, complimenting the Reverend's black suit and string tie. They looked the part of minister and wife. Everyone was in awe, because they knew she played the piano! Hopefully, one day, they could afford one after they caught up on cash from building the church.

When Nate and Melissa got back to the cabin, happy, tired and full of good food, they were greeted by a happy Trouble, barking his head off from his confinement in the cow lot designed to keep him from following the wagon. Nate took him as many places as he could. Sometimes he walked along beside Dewey; sometimes he rode in the wagon with Nate, or Nate and Melissa. Buttons was always content to sleep in a ball on their bed. She had water, food and her sandbox, so she was a self-contained cat. Melissa would pick her up from her balled position, love and squeeze her a little, then ball her and put her back where she found her. She was almost grown, making Nate begin to wonder about kittens.

"I expect to hear tomcats howling around here any day now," he told Melissa.

"No," Melissa said, "I don't want my baby having any kittens!"

"Uh huh. That must be the way your mother felt about you having a baby," Nate commented.

Christmas came and went. John was home, but it was cold, so everyone had to stay in except to do the chores. Nate and Melissa spent the day with her family. She had helped Lily with the cooking since she had her new stove and could bake. Nate had completed the purple martin house, which Melissa was crazy about, and she had made a beautiful sweater for him with a great deal of help from her mother. It was a quiet day, but it was to be a memorable one.

Homestead

On one of the trips to the McDougalds' in February, Nate was working in the field over on the side toward the Sewards'. He had just seen Matt, because he had brought his family to church the Sunday before, but Matt still tied up his horse and walked across the loose dirt Nate had just plowed to see him. Nate stopped his work, and leaned on his plow to talk with Matt. It was a cold day, but plowing in the sun made it warm enough to be tolerable and yet uncomfortable when one stopped to talk.

"Hey, man!" Nate yelled. "How you coming with *your* plowing?"

"Not too bad," Matt called back as he approached. "Say, I need to talk to you about something."

"Okay, shoot," Nate said wondering. Matt had a serious look on his face that Nate was not used to seeing.

"Do you know a young fellow named Eulon Fields?" Nate told his friend that he'd heard of the fellow but was not actually acquainted with him. "Why?" he inquired.

"Well, he's not right. He's got the mind of a small child but he has the body of a man, and he lives at home with his mother." Nate waited for Matt to go on. "They are about on starvation. The old lady manages to earn a few dollars washing for people down in the area where they live. Down near where you bought your horse. Anyway, people give them food and clothes, but the other night, I caught him peeping in our windows at the house, looking at Martha and the kids." Nate was beginning to get the picture.

Matt continued. "I had gone out to the barn after supper to close some stall doors and didn't have a lantern because the moon was shining. Apparently he didn't see me go out; so when I started back to the house, there he was peeping in the kitchen window."

"My goodness!" Nate exclaimed. "What did you do?"

"I walked up behind him while he was stretching his neck to see my wife and children, grabbed him by the shirt collar and scared the life out of him!" Matt got angry again just talking about it.

"And, did you let him go?" Nate was wondering what happened next and waited for Matt to finish the story, wondering all the while if he had been peeping in at Melissa.

"Yes, I let him go after I told him to get the heck away from my house and not to come back. I told him if I caught him there or at anyone else's house peeping again, I would take my shotgun to him!" Nate had no doubt at all that he meant that, too, just as he would do in the same situation.

"Anyway," Matt went on, "I have a feeling he has been doing that sort of thing all about the countryside. Probably spying on Pearl and Miss Mattie, and no telling who all down in his own neighborhood. I feel sorry for the fellow, but we can't have that going on, so what I want us to do, Nate, is go down and have a talk with his mother. We need to tell her to try to keep the boy at home, and if she can't, we have to take further steps."

"Sure thing! I don't want to hear of him peeping in at my wife. You know we have just put in our glass windows and some of them don't have any curtains. You wouldn't think you'd need them way down there in the woods like that." Nate was in total agreement on going down to the see the mother.

"Then it's settled. Suppose I get down your way Saturday morning and meet you where your little road comes into the main one? We will go down and have a talk with the old lady and the boy, too, if he is at home." Matt was happy that Nate agreed with him and had felt all along he would.

"Right. Seven o'clock all right with you? And I will take some meal, flour, sugar or whatever Melissa has she can spare. What else?" Matt replied that they needed clothes from what he could see. He said the boy was barefooted on that cold February night. People had very few clothes they could give away, because most hardly had enough for themselves, but Nate knew Melissa and her mother could get some things together.

On the way home, bundled against the cold, Melissa and Nate talked. They had a wool lap robe over their legs and their great coats on. Even Dewey had a blanket. Melissa and Nate were keeping each other warm.

As they rode along, Melissa remembered the episode with Eulon Fields at the store the last time they were there and decided to mention it to Nate. "A strange thing happened to me the other day while I was working alone in the store for Pearl," she told him. "Have you ever seen Eulon Fields?" she asked.

"No, but what happened?" he asked, with concern growing inside him as every minute passed. He had already been shaken by Matt's disclosure, and now Melissa was starting to tell him something else!

She related the occurrence to him telling him, also how poorly clothed Eulon was and how he didn't seem to want anything. That he just stood and grinned at her. She thought he might be hungry, but Nate wasn't buying that. He thought Eulon had something else in mind entirely. "Melissa!" Nathan said to her, and she knew he was upset because he never called her Melissa so formally. He always called her sweetheart. "Why on earth didn't you tell me about that?" he was practically yelling.

"Well, Nathan, don't yell. I just forgot about it. That's all. I really didn't think too much of it, because he just stood there a few minutes and then went away." Melissa had known Eulon most of her life; had gone to school with him even, and she never thought he meant to hurt her. Then Nate related what he was told by Matt and that they were going down to see him and his mother on Saturday.

"What are you going to do?" she asked Nate.

"That depends on what he does," Nate said. "We are prepared to do whatever it takes to keep him away from our families."

Melissa became alarmed, knowing Nate and his temper. She remembered with consternation when Nate had socked the man who tried to kiss her at the box supper and knocked him completely off the bench. She certainly wasn't going to let him unleash his wrath on poor Eulon Fields. "Now, Nathan, you listen to me. Eulon is harmless. I know he is, and you and Matt are going to have to go at this thing in just the right way," she began, but Nate interrupted her.

"No, you listen to me!" he said with his voice rising. "First, you don't tell me about how he came to the store and stood there staring at you, and then you try to stop me from doing something about it! What do you take me for?" He was getting mad, and then Melissa was getting mad, so there they were, riding down the road about as close as two people can get to each other, having their first argument with nowhere to storm off to. There was just nothing to do but settle the thing right then and there, it seemed.

"Nathan, I am warning you. If you and Matt start off to Mrs. Field's, I am coming right behind you. You *are not* going down there and upset that old lady. Why, she could have a heart attack and die right there, and you could knock Eulon over with a feather. He is so thin, pale and weak looking, I haven't been able to think about anything else since I saw him earlier in the week." At that point Nate tried to cut in, but Melissa hushed him and said, "It's my time to talk. We are both mad, and we have to fight fairly. It's my time to talk," she kept saying.

"Well, go ahead and talk!" Nate interjected. He gave Dewey a whack on his big broad behind and yelled, "Giddy up, Dewey, you old slow poke!" Melissa was rather tickled at him, even in her anger, so mad he was taking out his frustrations on the horse. Dewey just flicked his tail and kept right on at his same old pace.

"I am just trying to tell you that I don't believe, not for one minute do I believe, that poor ole Eulon is trying to *spy* on the ladies of this community. I have known that kid all my life, and he has never hurt anyone yet, and I do not want to think of you and Matthew going down there upsetting old Mrs. Fields and Eulon for no reason!"

"No reason?" Nate yelled back. "Are you saying you condone a man — he's not a boy — a man peeping in ladies' windows? I guess so since you didn't think it was necessary to even tell me."

Homestead

"I am telling you, Nathan, I *will* go with you unless I have your solemn word that you will proceed cautiously, see what is wrong there and then just quietly talk to them. If you can't promise that, I am going." Nate wasn't happy about the idea, but he did agree to do as she asked and promised to tell Matt exactly what he had promised and get his word on it, too. Then, and only then, was Melissa satisfied. She began to quiet down as did Nate, and the rest of the ride home was pleasant. In fact, it was very pleasant, and when they got home, he took her in his arms and told her that her good, common sense, sweet caring nature and good judgment were the things about her he loved most. He kissed her lovingly and told her she was absolutely right and he was sorry he yelled. Melissa apologized too.

Melissa got ready for bed, pulling her long-sleeved outing flannel gown over her head in the soft lamplight as Nate lay in bed watching. He always loved to watch her undress. Her arms, although slim and small-boned, were long and shapely. Her breasts were small but perfect. Her tiny waist and beautiful legs were never visible, except at bedtime, with dresses to the ankle. Nate often wondered why ladies didn't wear shorter dresses. Melissa took Buttons, who was balled up on her side of the bed, and placed her in a straight chair at the table. Of course, she would get cold and come back, but it would be all right later.

The firelight was flickering as Melissa got into bed. Nathan pulled her tightly to him and all the anger was forgotten. "I love you, my pretty one," he whispered. "I will always love you." Melissa answered with a long kiss and snuggled closer.

Saturday came, and Nate was preparing to leave. Melissa had dressed and said she wanted to go as far as her mother's with him and stay there until he came back. It would give her a chance to visit awhile. Nate was wondering if she really wanted to get hold of Matthew before they went to the Fields' and try to extract a promise from him, but he didn't say anything. As they neared the road where they could see Matthew waiting, Melissa gave Nate a long knowing look, as if to say "don't forget your promise," but she didn't say a word, either.

The ride to the Fields' home took about an hour. Nate and Matt talked about various things along the way, with Nate avoiding bringing up the subject at hand as long as he could. Matt knew where the road, no more than a trail, was to the little shack in the woods, so he led the way. It was a beautiful area. Old oaks lined the little road making it shady all along the way as well as cooler. Nate bunched his coat up a little against the stiff breeze that was blowing. He thought maybe nervousness made him cold. Finally, he got around to bringing up the situation to Matt. He related the circumstances of the argument to him, and Matt began to grin. "What is it?" Nate asked, puzzled.

"That's funny, because we had a similar discussion, and Martha said virtually the same thing. She told me under no circumstances to come down here like a storm and upset these people. She said there must be an explanation, but I dreaded telling you that maybe I had 'jumped the gun!' That is really funny." Both men were relieved that they had arrived at the same conclusion through their wives.

"So, I guess our little women serve a good purpose in our lives in helping us keep our lids on," Nate remarked, and Matt agreed heartily. They rode the few hundred yards more to the shack, talking happily. Nate was taking a pair of shoes for Eulon that were just brogans and had seen their best days, and he only hoped they would fit. Plus, he had a pair of overalls that he could spare, which were getting a little short and tight now that he was married to such a good cook. Matt had a shirt and an old denim jacket for him. Martha sent a dress. She knew Mrs. Fields and felt pretty sure it would fit. Melissa and Martha had both sacked up meal, flour and sugar, and Melissa fished a large slab of bacon out of the lard can she had in the cabin.

The shack was constructed of plain board, long ago weathered to a silvery gray. There were cracks between the board that a finger would fit through, and places that had rotted completely. It needed repairs terribly. The roof was tin and probably didn't leak, but Nate began thinking how some repairs needed to be made. It had one tiny window in the front with glass panes that were too dirty to see through. He knew Melissa would love to get hold of that place with a scrub broom and some soapy water. Matt knocked at the door. They waited for what seemed several minutes, but was only a minute in reality. Both men dreaded their mission.

Finally, the door creaked open to a small crack and a weak voice said, "Yes?"

Matt told the voice, obviously that of Mrs. Fields, who they were and that they needed to talk with her a few minutes. She slowly tugged at the old door until she got it open, with Matt helping push. It was about off its hinges completely.

After they had gained entrance into the small hut, there was no place to sit so they stood. She fell weakly into a straight, wood-bottomed chair nearby, gasping for breath. "I'm in bad shape. Heart, I think," she managed to say. "What brings you here to these woods?" was about all she could utter at once without a gasp.

"Well, Mrs. Fields, we needed to talk to you about Eulon a little bit," Matt said. "Is he about the place?" Mrs. Fields said he was not at home, that he was over at one of the neighbor's fields trying to dig up a few potatoes that were left in the fall when they were harvested. "What do you want with Eulon?"

Since Matt had done all the talking so far, Nate decided he needed to help with the job, so he spoke up. "Mrs. Fields, Matt here happened up on Eulon a few nights ago spying in his kitchen window at his wife and children." Nate was being as cautious as he possibly could in his delivery of this news to the poor lady.

"Spyin'? Lord, no! Eulon kain't spy. Why he kain't see no futher than his nose. The boy is nearly blind. I don't see how he gits about as well and goes as far as he does. He was jes' out looking for something to eat, and he probably didn't know whur the door wuz. I worry about that boy all the time. But we are about to starve, and he has to help out. I ain't able to do nothin'. We been eatin' potaters for weeks."

"And we brought you some food, Mrs. Fields." Both men spoke at once, handing over the things they had brought. They explained that there were shoes for Eulon and some clothes. They told her about the staple grocery items they had brought, and that they would bring some more soon. They told her how sorry they were for the misunderstanding and how dangerous it was for Eulon to be out at night looking in windows. Someone who didn't know about his plight might shoot him.

"Well, you know Eulon ain't right, and it don't do no good for me to tell him. Lord knows, I have tole him a many a time, but I'll tell him again." She sighed as though so world weary she could hardly go on. "He has been going to places begging, and I don't want him doin' that. I'd rather starve."

"No ma'am. We sure don't want you to starve, and we can see to it that doesn't happen," Matt said resolutely. "We will be back in a few days with more food. Is there anything else you badly need?"

"I reckin we need just about everything, so anything you can spare will be a Godsend. We shur do thank ye." As the men prepared to go, she heaved herself up out of the chair and went to the door of the small shack. They could see her ankles and feet were terribly swollen. She was barefoot, maybe because she had no shoes, but definitely they wouldn't fit if she did. She was not a large woman at all, but not being able to walk well made her seem large when she lumbered in her movements.

The two men discussed the dreadful state of affairs as they rode back, deciding what they could do and how they could help the Fields. For one thing, they had lumber or could get some cut, because both had trees and a sawmill not too far away. They had nails and rosin from the turpentine still. It would be a simple matter to fix up the hut and maybe even add on a small room since it was at present only one room. Nate suggested that it would give them a little more privacy. If they told the folks at church of the situation, people would bring food items to services, which could be dropped off as someone was passing by. If poor Eulon had enough to eat, maybe he would not need to look into windows. After all this seemed to have just started. No doubt he was going to ask for food or maybe try to slip in and steal some. In any case, they needed food desperately, and that was the problem. The community had never let anyone starve, and they were not about to do it now.

Neither Matt nor Nate spoke of their hasty judgment and narrowly averted disaster, but both resolved not to be so quick to judge again.

Nurse Callie

Spring in Mobile brought a great deal of rain and then flowers. The azaleas were beginning to pop open a little early because of the wonderfully warm weather, but all the old-timers were saying that a cool snap would ruin everything. Dogwoods were also showing a little white, which meant by Easter they would be in full bloom. The city would be a blaze of color in a few days. Every home had azaleas banking the sides of the homes and all through the gardens in the lovely lavender, pink and bright-pink colors, as well as white. It was a sight to see.

Callie McDougald felt she had the world by a string. Things were going her way. As soon as she would finish one case, she would have already been referred to another family, and so it was that lovely spring day when she was so happy. She was walking jauntily along on the way to the DeVille residence on South Avenue where she would care for the lady of the house. Mrs. DeVille had a spinal problem and was at present bedridden. According to her medical record, which Callie reviewed before taking the case, it was doubtful that she would survive, and at best, she would not be able to walk again. The ailment came about as a result of a high fever that had lasted for a number of days. Her doctors had diagnosed it as poliomyelitis. Not only did she have a severe weakness in her legs, but she also had a respiratory infection as well. She had been sent home from the Infirmary a few days before because she had demanded to go home to die.

Mr. DeVille, according to hospital talk, was quite wealthy and tried to give his wife everything she wanted. That included the privilege of dying in her own home. Callie didn't relish taking care of the dying, but what medical person does? She liked for her patients to live and dismiss her to another new family. That made life interesting, spread her fame as an excellent nurse and gave her new territory for husband-hunting. She rather dreaded this assignment, but as she rang the bell at 441 South Avenue, she drew herself up tall and straight and prepared herself for whatever was to come.

The maid opened the door in a black dress and starched white apron. She had on the customary little white lacy-looking cap to which Callie had become accustomed. It reminded her of her own white cap, not much difference and, when you got right down to it, their jobs were probably not too different. The maid cooks. The nurse cleans. The only difference was she cleaned people and waited on them. The main difference was that the maid worked for well people who could do some things for themselves. Callie had certainly found the seamy side of her profession — changing diapers for some of her patients who were incontinent. Wiping drool when their facial muscles were paralyzed. Feeding the ones who couldn't hold an eating utensil, and wiping their mouths. Oh, it had its drawbacks being a nurse, all right. She wondered at times how she had gotten herself into this "noble" profession. With any luck, though, she would get herself out soon enough. If her popularity continued in Mobile, it shouldn't take long.

"Good morning, Miss," the maid greeted her, stiffly. Callie was wondering, why so formal?

"Come this way, please," the maid said, and back over her shoulder as she led her down the red carpeted hallway, "My name is Mandy."

Nurse Callie

Callie attempted to be friendly. "Hello. I'm Callie," she called to the figure disappearing rapidly down the hall. Callie was almost in a trot trying to keep up with her. To herself she thought, why the hurry? She had no way of knowing that Mandy was the top of the heap there and was going to jealously guard her position. She had worked for the Mrs. for eighteen years, which meant she was fiercely loyal. This prissy young nurse need not expect any friendship out of her.

Mrs. DeVille was, indeed, very ill. She seemed oblivious to Callie, or anything else around her, and barely flickered her eyelids when Callie spoke to her.

"Mrs. DeVille, my name is Callie. I am going to be your nurse." Flicker. She took the limp, flaccid hand that lay outside the covers and said, "If you are understanding me, would you squeeze my hand, please?" Slight squeeze. "That's good," Callie said, overjoyed that the woman could at least respond in some measure to her questions. It helped tremendously in caring for someone if they could tell you anything at all, even that they hurt or were too hot, too cold, thirsty or hungry.

With that one fact established, Callie read the chart on the table at the foot of the bed. Then she surveyed the surroundings. This was obviously a room the couple had shared. There were remnants of a man having been using the room, such as a pipe resting in an ashtray across the room. There were two easy chairs with a table in between in the bay window. The ashtray was on that table along with several other items a man would normally use. Books lay about, indicating he had been there recently, and Mandy in cleaning had left them undisturbed.

Callie found herself wondering what the rest of the family looked like. She did several things about the room including feeling Mrs. DeVille's forehead for any signs of the fever's return. It had been gone long before she left the hospital but was still a threat. Checking the watch she wore around her neck, Callie could see it was noon, and she was getting hungry, so she decided to look for Mandy since her patient was not in need of her at the moment.

Going down the hall toward the kitchen, she ran right into Mandy. "Ah, I have a minute now for a bite if you have lunch ready," she said tentatively to the snippy little woman.

"Yes, come this way," was all Mandy said. "Sit here." She motioned her to the kitchen table. Oh, thought Callie. I am to be treated like hired help, which is, in effect, what I guess I am. Mandy set a serving of chicken pot pie in front of her with English peas and a glass of iced tea. Then she promptly left the kitchen, leaving Callie to eat alone. Well, Callie began thinking, maybe this assignment at least won't last long.

After she had had sufficient time to eat, Mandy reappeared and offered to take her to her room. Callie's small valise, with enough things for a short stay, after which she would go to her room and get more, was still sitting just inside the front door, where she had left it upon arrival. She picked it up and followed the maid up the tall stairs, which wound around as they got near the top. It really was a lovely house, probably built awhile before the war. Callie loved her room and thought that this assignment might not be so bad after all.

Nate was rushing around, getting ready to plant all the seeds. He had developed some plans he had not mentioned as yet to Melissa, and he was anxious to get things into the ground and growing. The warm sun would make them come up right away if it continued this way. By late March the chance of a freeze was minimal and worth the risk to take advantage of the long growing season. So, on a terribly windy day the last week of March, Nate began plowing his newly cleared new ground while Melissa went along behind dropping seeds. Whereas they had only had a patch the year before, they had several acres this year. It was just going to be very hard plowing it for the first time.

Melissa looked charming in her big bonnet made for the sun with a wide brim and puffing up in the back. Her mother said it would allow for air to circulate about her head. She made it for Melissa from her pattern. She had on her high-topped brogan shoes, an apron and long sleeves, so as not to get sunburned. She looked the part of the farmer's wife, Nate told her.

The planting went rapidly, considering Nate was using a huge plow he called a sodbuster to plow the virgin earth. The only people who could have tended that ground would have been the Indians hundreds of years before, because the trees Nate cut were probably two hundred or more years old. Some were waiting to go to mill as soon as he could get someone with a team to haul them. There they would be made into lumber suitable for use in the big house. It would be stored in his barn and John's. John only did minimal farming. He had about twelve acres where he grew feed mostly for the animals. His timber job kept him too busy to be a farmer, so that he had the room in his huge barn for the lumber. The big house was not a thing of the very near future. It would take money, time and supplies. When they actually got ready to build, John would give them some tall, straight timber to go along with what they already had for the lumber. It had to be a certain grade to use for a house.

When they got to the cabin each evening, Nate fed and secured the stock while Melissa prepared a meager supper. She had no time to make extras, so they often had hoecakes and butter with syrup from Mr. Crossley's sugar-cane mill. He made it so thick it would hardly run out of the can, and it made wonderful peanut brittle. Melissa had told Nate to plant enough peanuts for parching and making candy.

When everything was finished and it was bath time, Melissa prepared her little tub, which she kept in the shed room for her baths. Nate had rigged a sort of shower with a huge wooden barrel he brought from Mr. Mac's. Pearl gave it to him for the purpose. It had been used to ship dishes to the store. Nate put up four poles about six-feet-six inches high and mounted the barrel on top of them. He had put a stopper in the bottom somehow, to be removed at bath time, and he filled it from another barrel of water he brought from the branch, with help from Dewey. He had rigged up a set of skids, two by fours with light planks nailed across, that would slide easily when attached with a rope to Dewey's traces. They could bring the whole barrel full of water without spilling a drop! Dewey loved to go to the branch, besides, because he could always drink his fill of the cool branch water.

When Nate started out to his "shower," he tried to get Melissa to join him, but she refused. "No!" she told him. "Someone might come along! I am not going to take a bath right out in the yard for all to see."

Nate kept coaxing, though, telling her nobody would come there and besides it was dark. "You can have your dressing gown out here, and if someone comes, put it on."

"I might not hear them in time," she fretted. "Besides, it will be cold."

"No, it is not cold. It's warmer than yours, probably, from the sun," he coaxed his reluctant wife. Finally, he picked her up, pulled off her shoes, tossing them in the floor and took her out the door bodily, with her screeching all the way.

"Nathan York!" she yelled. "Put me down!" but Nate didn't obey.

"You will never know the joys of taking a shower in the evening shadows under a huge sycamore tree if I don't do this. Now, will you take off your clothes, or must I do that, too?" he said depositing her under the barrel. She started to run, but he caught her.

"Oh, no you don't," he said as he pulled her back under the barrel. Melissa gave up, laughing so hard she couldn't unbutton her camisole, so Nate gladly obliged, enjoying the whole situation to the fullest. And so Melissa had her first shower in the delightfully warm water of the wooden barrel as the crickets and frogs in the nearby marsh area chirped away. In the lot, the cow lowed. She was expecting her calf any minute, and Trouble was barking at some critter in the nearby woods. Melissa and Nate washed each other's backs, enjoying the feel of the water trickling slowly down their naked bodies. After they finished, he took the damask towel he had grabbed on the way out and dried her carefully with it. Then she dried him before they slid their feet into their homemade slippers and walked the few paces to the cabin, arm in arm, with the huge piece of damask wrapped about both of them.

That night, much later, Nate told Melissa about the plans he had. He had decided to go to north Alabama and try to find his sisters.

"Now that the cabin and barn are both built and most of ours and Mr. Mac's plowing is done for spring, I think I can take a week off without any problem. I want us to go up, make it a little holiday, and see if we can find them" Nate explained.

"Oh! Nate, that would be wonderful! I have sisters-in-law that I haven't seen yet." She was excited at the prospect, so they decided to go to Creighton, leave the wagon at the livery and catch the train for Guntersville on the Tennessee River. Nate remembered their place being not too far from there. He thought if he asked around there, he would surely be able to get some word on them. They planned to go at the end of the following week. John would be home to tend the stock, and the heifer would have had her calf by then. Nate couldn't go off and leave her until the calf had safely been born. Sometimes young heifers had to have help with their first calves.

Callie had taken her patient's pulse, fed her as much of her supper as she could swallow, which was very little, and was sitting quietly beside her when Marcus DeVille entered the room. Even in the dim light of the one lamp in the room, she could see that he was extremely handsome; not in a good-looking way, exactly, but in a rugged, strong and distinguished way. His graying hair had a slight wave. He was tall, probably at least six feet, and rather slender in build. Callie thought him very attractive.

"Hello, Miss McDougald, I believe?" he said hesitatingly.

"Hello. Just call me Callie, sir," she told her new employer.

"Fine, but you need not call me sir, either." He sat across the room so that he could further study this nurse who was attractive, also, in his opinion. He realized, finally, that he was actually there to see how his wife was and remembered to ask.

"She has been very quiet and unresponsive since I have been here. I did get her to take a few swallows of her dinner and she drank some warm tea," Callie told this unusual-looking man. She couldn't figure what it was about him that was different. Perhaps it was his bony, angular face? Or maybe his deep-set eyes. Were they brown or a dark blue?

"Did Mandy show you the house?" he inquired.

"No, sir. Not yet. Ah, no, not yet," she answered, remembering not to use the sir and correcting herself.

"I only arrived about ten, and I've been here with Mrs. DeVille continually except for a few minutes at lunch."

"My word! You must be totally exhausted! How like Mandy not to extend a hand of friendship. You will learn as you go along that she jealously guards her position here, and anyone who threatens it, well, woe be unto them." Rising, he gestured to her to follow him and, leading the way, he took her on a complete tour of the house, skipping the room Mandy used since she was in there with the door closed at the moment. When they were back to the front part of the house, he led her into the parlor. "Have a seat, Nurse Callie. We need to talk." Callie sank onto the velvet-covered settee, looking about as he talked. It was truly a lovely room. She wondered if his wife had decorated it or had a decorator. Someone with extremely good taste had done it. Marcus DeVille was saying something she was about to miss as her mind wandered.

"You do realize that my wife is very ill?" he said. "In fact, the doctors don't feel she will live, and while she is with us, I want to make her as comfortable as we possibly can, however, you are to be considered as well. I do not want you to work day and night. You must have rest; so I intend to have Mandy share the night duties with you. She can awaken you if Mrs. DeVille needs your care during the time you are sleeping."

"Oh, but Mandy may resent having to do that," she heard herself saying. Usually people had two nurses when they were wealthy and could afford it, but he said nothing about another nurse for the night.

"Never mind Mandy. She is very devoted to my wife, and I think you will find that she will do her shift without hesitation. Please call me if there is any significant change in my wife's condition. I suggest you take the first part of the night and call Mandy about midnight."

"Thank you, and I will certainly call you." With that, she arose and crossed the hall to her patient's room. Marcus watched her as she crossed the foyer and disappeared. Callie could feel those eyes on her back. She had decided what it was about him that seemed unusual. It was his deep-set, black eyes. French heritage, no doubt.

Apparently Mr. DeVille had told Mandy what was expected of her and she appeared at the sick room door just at midnight. Callie was very grateful and told the woman so, because she had gotten up early that morning to do laundry and prepare for her new assignment. She was tired and felt hungry again. "I'd like a bite to eat, if that is all right," she told the wily little woman who seemed to be suspicious of her every move. She certainly had not warmed up one bit. "Just look in the warmer on the stove. You will find the leftovers from dinner." That was all she had to offer.

Callie made her way down the long hall and back to the kitchen. It was really dark, and although she had a small lamp with her, it was hard to find the way in a strange house. Just as she rounded the corner into the kitchen, pleased to have at last found it, she bumped straight into Mr. DeVille.

"Oh!" she said, startled, and almost dropping the lamp. "I was coming in to get a bite to eat! I thought you were in bed hours ago."

"I was, but I don't sleep well these days. I thought a glass of milk might help. Come, let me help you." Taking the lamp, he set it in the middle of the kitchen table. "Now, let's see. I know very little about this kitchen, mind you, but I do know there is pound cake in the cupboard. How's that, or would you prefer something more substantial?" he asked.

"That will do nicely with a glass of that milk you were just having." She sank into a chair and let him get the cake, cut a piece, and then pour her milk. It felt wonderful to have someone waiting on her for a change. "This reminds me of home," she commented, feeling a bit nostalgic. She supposed she really should try to get home after this case was over. Her mother wasn't well, and she knew how those things sometimes went.

Marcus DeVille had pulled out a chair, also, and was sitting across the small table from her. "Tell me about home. Where is it?" he asked. Callie explained where home was and who was at home.

"How did you decide to become a nurse, Nurse Callie?" was his next question. She explained why she wanted to be a nurse: the need she had for caring for people, and how she had wanted to escape the country and try making a life for herself in the city. She also reminded him of the few professions for women in that day and age.

He listened intently, watching her as she ate her cake and drank the milk. "Is it all you thought it would be, this caring for people? And life in the city? Do you regret it?"

"Well," Callie measured her words carefully. "It is in most ways what I expected. I do love the city, but somehow, I thought all my patients would get well with enough intense care on my part, and they don't." Raising her eyes, she looked straight into his intense dark ones. What she saw puzzled her.

Nurse Callie

Melissa had packed and unpacked her small valise several times in trying to decide what to take to north Alabama. In the spring, it could be very cool or very hot. She wanted to dress nicely, but not overdress for the area. Having never been that far north, she hadn't a clue as to what it would be like there. Nate had told her to take some rough clothes for traveling out into the countryside looking for the sisters. He said one nice outfit would be plenty in case they went to church or to some other special event. But she took two, just in case.

The Tates agreed readily to care for the stock, including the heifer and her new baby calf, Tillie. Melissa always named things, and this was no exception. Since the calf was a girl, she thought Tillie was appropriate.

Leaving the wagon at the livery, they boarded the train early in the morning for the day- long trip. It was lovely weather, which they hoped would hold during the time they were searching for the sisters. Melissa made a lunch for the train, and they would stay at a boarding house Nate remembered, if it still existed.

Mr. Mac had given his blessings to Nate's venture. He even asked if they had money for the trip, which Nate assured him they had and told him they would return in a week.

The boarding house was very much there and busy, but there was a room for a couple. The first thing Nate did was ask the proprietor if he, by chance, remembered the Yorks who were killed about twenty years earlier, supposedly by renegade Indians. The man, a Mr. Curry, certainly did remember, he said. In fact, Mr. and Mrs. York had stopped to eat the noon meal at the boarding house the very day they were killed. He had no information on the girls or where they might be, but knew someone who would most likely know. He told Nate to contact the postmaster, offered his hand to Nate and told him he was very sorry about his parents and the tragedy. Nate looked at Melissa as if to say, "This may not be as hard as we thought."

Homestead

It was dark by the time they got to their room, and time for supper. They wanted to finish eating and get settled for the night as early as possible because they had left home before daylight in order to catch the train and both were tired. Nate went to sleep thinking of his sisters — small little things when he last had seen them — and wondered what they would look like all grown up and whether they would even know him or he them. He thought he could not wait until morning, but sleep overtook him along with exhaustion.

The Quest

The Yorks had left home on Sunday with plans to start inquiring on Monday morning bright and early. They were up, dressed and had finished breakfast by eight o'clock when the post office would probably be open.

Nate could remember only a few facts about the situation when he left his sisters. He knew the family that had taken them in. It was a Mr. and Mrs. Moore who had two children of their own: a boy about twelve named Calvin and a girl about Martha's age named Sarah. Jane was eight and Martha five when their parents were killed.

The family lived about six miles outside Guntersville, the best Nate could judge, and his parents, at the time of their deaths, had been staying a few miles farther south in a cabin belonging to the timber company for which his father had worked. It was more or less like camping.

They could only take a wagonload of belongings with them as they moved from place to place with their father's work cutting timber. It was not a good life, and the plans were to get some homestead property and try to settle, so the children could go to school and have a more stable life. They carried a few bed linens, cooking utensils, some bedding, and their clothes, which was about all the wagon could hold. Nate knew his father had been saving money for their home once he found homestead property, and he had always believed the money was taken when his parents were killed. He thought someone might have even known he had the money and thus had robbed him when they were killed. He wanted so much to track down the scum who had done that but had no way of getting any information. The area was practically lawless, anyway, and nobody bothered with drifters being killed.

Once he found his sisters, he hoped that he might soon tackle the job of finding the person or persons guilty of murdering his parents. He also knew the trail was growing colder and colder; yet crimes like that were hard to hide forever.

Nate told Melissa to wait at their room while he walked to the nearest livery stable and got a rig, but she insisted on walking with him. Once they got a horse and buggy, they inquired about the post office and started for it.

The postmaster was an older man, probably in his late sixties. He said he had lived in the area all his life and knew right where the Moores lived. They were in the same spot, he said. Mr. Moore had died, but his widow lived there just about eight miles from Guntersville. He was not sure about their children, other than that they were grown and gone. He had no information to offer as to where. Nate, of course, expected them to be grown and only hoped they had kept in touch with Mrs. Moore, if not stayed nearby. He got directions from the postmaster and he and Melissa began what they hoped would be the last leg of their quest.

The sun was shining brightly by the time they headed south. Melissa had asked for bread and meat sandwiches to take with them from the boarding house. They had a jar of water, and expected to return to the boarding house by night. "What do you plan to do, Nathan, if the girls have married and moved far away?" she asked as they hurried along.

"I want to find them, dear, no matter where they have gone, but we may not be able to complete the search today." At that

The Quest

time of year, the weather could suddenly turn cold after a quick rain and become very miserable. They both had their great coats and lap robes, just in case, but they couldn't afford to be caught after nightfall without shelter for the night.

The horse clopped along at a good pace. He was a big bay and well accustomed to pulling a buggy, but Nate missed Dewey. Man! He would love to be here pulling this buggy, Nate was thinking. Dewey had been a wonderful dray horse, and his dressage was such that he knew exactly what Nate wanted him to do, how to maneuver to pull a stump out of the ground or a small tree over

or haul a barrel of water up from the spring. Yep, he and Dewey were quite a pair, and he loved that horse!

The wind was cool, and the trees that were not evergreens were totally bare. One could see for miles and miles atop some of the little hills. They were the foothills of the Smoky Mountains and some were rather tall. Melissa had never seen hills this high. "Nathan, look yonder at the valley! What a beautiful sight!" she exclaimed. "I have never seen such hills." Nathan was amused at her excitement.

"Just wait until I take you one day on a real trip. We will go to see real mountains. They have some, you know, in Chattanooga up in Tennessee. My Dad told me about them and how the Yankees and Rebels had this big battle and so many of our soldiers were killed," Nate explained. "It took place on Lookout Mountain."

The Quest

Melissa knew about the battle from her history book. She told him some of the things she had read in history and they dreamed and planned for the day when they could board the train and go to such historical places.

As they neared a clearing Nate faintly remembered, his heartbeat quickened. He was nervous and his hands were clammy. It was hard to breathe, and he had a slight tremor in his hands as they drove down the lane and up to the house. It was a clapboard house, unpainted, but rather large, with huge trees in front and a well near the doorsteps. Nate decided to ask Mrs. Moore to let him water the horse. They hadn't crossed any streams, as would usually be the case on the way.

"Hello!" Nate called as he handed the reins to Melissa and stepped down from the buggy. "Anybody home?" Waiting a minute and hearing nothing, he called again, "Hello!"

In a moment, an older lady appeared on the large porch with a shotgun in her hands. "Who's that?" she asked, obviously not trusting people. She was squinting from the brightness of the noonday sun and, all the while, studying the face before her.

"Mrs. Moore?" Nate questioned, not at all sure who she was or whether this was the right place, for that matter. "I am looking for Mrs. Moore. I am Nathan York." A look came on her face of recognition and something akin to terror. Nate was puzzled. Perhaps she is afraid, he thought, being here alone, no doubt.

"Do you remember me? Are you Mrs. Moore?" he asked again.

"I am," she said. "What brings you here, Nathan?"

"I am looking for my sisters, Mrs. Moore." He moved closer, but tentatively, since she had still not put the shotgun down. Nate motioned to the gun.

"Could you lower that shotgun, please? I'd like to talk to you for a few minutes." Motioning to Melissa to come in, he continued talking to Mrs. Moore although she didn't appear receptive. Melissa threw the reins over the gatepost and entered the yard. Nate turned toward her. "Mrs. Moore, this is my wife, Melissa."

Homestead

"Howdy do?" Mrs. Moore said. She set the gun down against the wall and sat in a rocker next to it. "Sit down," she said. Melissa studied the woman's face etched with lines from hard work and a lot of sun. When she relaxed, the lines lessened and became white streaks where the sun hadn't reached. Melissa was thinking that she must have been pretty once before the years of toil, sun and hardship took their toll on her. Mrs. Moore smoothed out the apron she was wearing and studied it, looking down rather than at Nate. He knew she didn't want to talk, but he had come too far to stop now. Her feelings or not, he must get answers.

The Quest

"Can you tell me about my sisters? Where are they?"

"Well, Martha, God rest her soul, died from the fever when she was eight." She was holding her hands in her lap and twisting a corner of her apron. She was very nervous and not looking at her guests.

Melissa looked at Nate, who had sunken down to sit on the top step. His head was in his hands. She thought he was sobbing, but he raised his head and continued with his questions of Mrs. Moore. "And Jane? Where is Jane, Mrs. Moore? Is she alive and well? Please tell me about Jane," he implored. Melissa sat down beside Nate and took his hand.

Mrs. Moore looked up and across to the faraway hills. They were smoky like the mountains, hills she had looked across at most of her life, but somehow they no longer were the beautiful hills she had always loved. She knew, too, that things were not going to be the same any longer. The thing she had long dreaded had at last come to pass.

"Jane lives somewhere near Montgomery. I don't know where," she said, with a faraway look in her eyes.

"Well, doesn't she keep in touch? Don't you hear from her at all? Surely you must." It was Melissa who had asked that question.

"No, I haven't heard from her in a long time. She used to write now and then, but not any more. I reckon she got married and now she has a life of her own." Mrs. Moore clearly wanted to let the conversation end there, but Nate persisted.

"Did she have any friends who might know where she is? Was there anyone?"

"Nobody I know of," she answered vaguely.

"When did she leave here? How old was she? Did she have a boyfriend? Do you know whether she did get married or not?" The questions were tumbling out over each other.

Mrs. Moore finally looked up at the man she had dreaded talking to for years. "Jane was fifteen when she ran off from here.

She never did seem happy with us, and we later heard she was working as a cook in a log camp. That was the last we ever heard."

"And my little sister Martha. You said she died of the fever? When she was eight? Where is she buried, Mrs. Moore?"

"She is buried beside your mama and daddy. That was the best we could do. I go there from time to time and clean off the graves and put flowers." Mrs. Moore got that far away look again and seemed to be shutting down.

"Could you tell me how to get there, please? I don't remember." Nate waited while she collected her thoughts and told him the way.

"Mrs. Moore, I want to thank you for what you did for my sisters all those years, and I appreciate the information. My wife and I will be going now, but before we go, I understand Mr. Moore died, and I was wondering if you need anything?" Nate said.

"No. I thank you. I don't need anything." With that she turned and slowly walked down the hall and into the house.

Nate took Melissa's hand, led her to the buggy and helped her in. Once he was in and seated, he allowed himself a few moments of sadness before driving off toward the graves of his family. The site was back toward Guntersville, but off the road a way.

There were several cabins and a house or two along the road, new to the area where his parents and sister had been laid to rest. Melissa reached for his hand. "I am so sorry, Nathan," she said. "I had such high hopes they would both be alive, well and happy. I was hoping they were both married and with children of their own."

"Yes, well it was a lot to hope for after all these years, but I had the same hopes, yet fear, too."

They drove up to the wooded area, which was just as Mrs. Moore had described it would be. "Over there!" Nate said, jumping hastily down from the buggy. He took Melissa's hand, helped her down and then rushed to the big tree where the three graves waited. Kneeling down between his mother's and father's graves,

The Quest

Nate began to sob, and then he cried for all the times he had wanted to, for all the things he had wanted to do for them and all the times they had missed being together. He cried for the atrocity that had been committed against them which had gone unpunished, and for the little sisters he had been forced to leave with rank strangers, and most of all he cried for himself and the sadness he had carried all the many years. Then he took the big handkerchief that he carried out of his pocket and blew his nose. Melissa, who had been waiting patiently, took his hand and walked him back to the buggy. No words passed between them. No words were necessary. They were both lost in their own thoughts.

As they drove out to the little road from the wooded area where the graves were, they were surprised to meet another buggy that pulled out of the road and waited until they approached. A man who appeared to be in his forties nodded and indicated he wanted to talk. Nate stopped the horse and greeted the man.

"Hello, there. I'm James Green. I live near the Moore place and I heard in town you were in the area asking about your sisters."

"Nathan York, Mr. Green," Nate said, reaching across to shake the man's hand. "Do you know something about my sisters?"

"Yes, I do. I know where your older sister lives," he told the anxious couple.

"Oh, please. Tell me!" Nate was again full of hope after near despair.

"She lives just a few miles out of Guntersville. I can give you directions to the general area, but you will have to inquire when you get to that area." He told Nate all he could. At that point, Nate mentioned that they had just visited the graves of his parents and sister.

"My parents were killed by Indians, supposedly, and my little sister died of a fever. Did you know about that?" Nate was hoping for more information if the man had any, but he had no idea of the magnitude of the startling news Mr. Green would then deliver.

"It was more than likely the beatings old man Moore gave her that killed her than the fever," he told the horrified couple. Nate's mouth was wide open and Melissa looked as if she had seen a ghost.

"What!" Nate exclaimed. "Beatings? What on earth are you talking about, man? Are you sure?" He looked as if he were going to faint. Melissa reached for him putting her arms around him and holding him as tightly as she could.

"Yes, I am talking about beatings. You see, I worked for the Moores some, and he talked about that little one and how she would never settle down and behave. She was hard to control, he said. She couldn't seem to understand what the Moores were doing for her and her sister, and never gave up hoping her family would come back and get her. I have seen her with bruises all over. I'm sure sorry, Mr. York. There was nothing any of us could do."

"But surely there was something! Couldn't Mrs. Moore do something?" Nate implored.

"Oh, he beat her and their children, too. They couldn't do anything." Nate thanked Green and they drove on, but he knew he had to find Jane and confirm this awful news. Then he would confront Mrs. Moore once more. Oh, God, he thought, why did I leave them? Surely I could have found a way. I just thought they would be all right.

"Oh, my God, Melissa. I had no idea! How could that have happened? Oh, my God," he grieved.

Melissa did her best to comfort, but there was little she could say. "Nathan, you were doing the best you could. You were only a boy yourself and had no resources. Please darling, don't torture yourself."

The rest of the way to the boarding house they rode in silence, each lost in their own private thoughts, Melissa allowing Nate time to grieve.

Finding Jane

Mrs. Downing, Callie's landlady, was dusting in the living room when Callie went to collect more clothes and wash her soiled uniforms on Saturday morning. It was her first day off since starting at the DeVilles' the previous Monday. She spoke to Mrs. Downing, who immediately stopped dusting and propped up against the banister to the stairs Callie must climb up to the room she shared with the other nurse. She wanted to talk, but Callie knew she had very little time to waste and a great deal to do. "Is my roommate in?" she asked Mrs. Downing.

"I think so. Haven't seen her go out." Mrs. Downing loved to talk to the girls about their cases and get any tidbit of information she could about the gentry of Mobile, so Callie knew what was coming. Instead, though, *she* was the one to get the tidbits that day! Mrs. Downing continued. "You working for the DeVilles, are you?" she queried.

"Yes, ma'am. Mrs. DeVille has poliomyelitis, or so the doctors think. She isn't expected to live." With that, Callie hoped to get on up the stairs. Mrs. Downing wasn't to be deterred, however.

"You know, everybody in Mobile knows that she was the one with the money, and she got him from the other side of the tracks." She waited a moment for that to sink in with Callie, and then proceeded on with her story. "They say he was as poor as a church mouse till she married him and got him set up in the bank where her daddy had a big interest."

"Well, Mrs. Downing, I don't get into people's personal situations. I just care for the sick," Callie told her. She started up the stairs but only made it up a couple of steps.

"I've heard that they don't get along. Friend of mine used to do some sewing for her. Said she is something else to deal with. Tight and always complaining about what Nettie charged. One would think with all that money, she'd be a little more generous. Nettie's a widow. Lives off her earnings." Callie took another step.

"You be sure he pays you. All that money!" Callie actually escaped that time and found her roommate sound asleep. Wondering if she had just gotten off of a case, she tiptoed about the room so as not to wake her.

"Hi." Sara rolled over and squinted at Callie. "You don't need to worry. I was waking up." The two nurses talked a few minutes while Callie repacked her little bag for the next week, knowing she wouldn't be back to the room for at least a week in all probability. She gathered up her dirty uniforms and prepared to descend to the basement to wash. There were clean ones that also had to be ironed.

"Any mail?" she asked Sara.

"Oh, yes. Looks like you got a letter from home. I almost forgot," Sara said. Callie took the letter Sara offered, and it was from Pearl, all right. A little stab of guilt went through Callie as she thought of the situation at home with her parents, but she simply could not help that right now. She must get her career well under way and establish a name for herself as a nurse, then she could take a few days to go home and see how things were going.

When Callie returned to the DeVille home, she found her patient awake and Mandy feeding her soup. Mandy had a smug look on her face, which seemed to indicate that she felt she had affected a cure single-handedly! Callie really didn't like that woman. She figured she was probably a good fifteen years older than herself and her allegiance to "The Mrs." was unmistakable. Not that Callie cared. It just seemed a little strange. Here she was, the nurse, there to take care of Mrs. DeVille, and Mandy acted as if she were some intruder into the inner sanctum, trying to do some great harm.

As the days went by, Mrs. DeVille improved dramatically. She could sit for short periods in the bed with Callie moving her up and propping her with pillows. She still didn't say more than a few words, because of the respiratory problems, but she was definitely improved. Callie thought now she actually would live.

Mr. DeVille visited often with his wife, and when he entered the room, Callie would slip out and sit somewhere and read, leaving them alone. One evening as she started to the room to see if he had gone, she heard angry voices. The patient, who could talk more now, was speaking. "I don't like it!" Callie heard her say. "She's young and you two have a lot of time together."

Then Callie heard the husband's voice, so muffled she couldn't understand what he was saying, but he hurriedly left the room. Callie waited a few moments before going back into the room. She knew full well they had been talking about her.

The late spring evenings were delightfully cool and very long. With Mrs. DeVille feeling better and out of danger, Callie had some free time to sit on the porch and enjoy the sounds of the city, so different from those she had grown up with in the country. Marcus DeVille also enjoyed the porch and often joined her out there smoking his pipe and rocking in one of the chairs near the swing where Callie usually sat. She had been brooding over the little scene in the room when they were discussing her, but had not had the nerve to mention it. Marcus realized something was wrong, however, because of the way she avoided him. So he broached the subject.

"Nurse Callie," he said in his half-teasing way.

"I have noticed a definite attempt on your part lately to avoid me when at all possible. May I ask why?" Callie was stunned and caught completely off guard.

"Why, I don't know what you mean, Mr. DeVille," she protested.

"Oh, yes you do. Don't be coy with me. There is a difference in your demeanor. I know it," he persisted. Then, leaning forward in his chair, he reached for her hand. "Tell me. Is it my wife? Has she said something to you?"

"No! No, she hasn't. Nothing," Callie told him, but, thinking this might be her only opportunity to discuss the conversation she had heard, she decided to venture out. "Well, I did overhear, quite by accident, a discussion you and Mrs. DeVille were having about me, and I was somewhat disturbed by it. I didn't mean to. I was only..." but before she could finish, he interrupted.

"Look, my dear. You must not let anything she says disturb you. She sometimes imagines things that are not there, and I *do not* want you to concern yourself with it. You are doing a fine job here, and we are delighted to have you. Now, enough said. Right?"

"Right." Callie answered, happy to have that out in the open. But, he still had not turned loose her hand. Realizing that it was awkward for him to still be holding it, he gave a little squeeze and turned it loose.

Things were very difficult at the McDougald home for Pearl, making her wonder just how much longer she could manage both her parents, the house and the store. She knew Nate would take care of the farm, and when Melissa returned, she felt it would be bearable, but with her in north Alabama, she was about to founder.

The weather was getting hotter, Miss Mattie was less and less able to help herself even by turning over in the bed, and her father was now confined to a wheelchair all the time. His knees were terribly painful, swollen twice their normal size, and the medicine Dr. Haygood had given him was not doing any real good.

Finding Jane

Pearl knew the store was their livelihood. She couldn't close it. The people in the community depended on it totally, in some cases, for everything. It was quite a dilemma. When Nate and Melissa returned, she meant to see if Melissa could work every day of the week. If only Callie would come home.

After going to visit Mrs. Moore, Nate and Melissa got up early the next morning and started for the little settlement where Mr. Green at the cemetery had told him to go. It was a short trip to the area. Now, if Jane would just be there. When they came to the first house along the way, Nate stopped the horse, climbed down out of the buggy and went to the door, glancing around for dogs. The lady who came to the door was young, had lived there only a short time, and didn't know anything about Jane. She suggested the next neighbor who was an old-timer in the area, so Nate drove on.

Mrs. Stacy was at home, and Mrs. Stacy knew exactly who Nate was talking about. "Why, yes. She lives about two miles east of here. She's married, and they have two little children." Getting a few more specific directions, Nate hopped back into the buggy and off they went. Melissa could tell a decided difference in his mood.

Jane Jernigan went to the door of the small shotgun house, not suspecting a thing unusual. "Yes?" she said to the stranger before her, a little leery about opening the door too wide. Women were very vulnerable, because their menfolk were usually way out in the field somewhere, or even in the woods, leaving them prey to anyone who happened along.

"Jane? Sister Jane?" Nate said. "You don't recognize me. I am your big brother!" She gasped, then held her mouth open for a full five seconds before responding.

"Nathan! My brother, Nathan! Oh, no! I don't believe it. After all these years. I thought you were dead!" Then she began to sob. Nate reached for her and hugged her to him letting her cry tears of great joy as long as she needed to.

"Oh, my goodness. Look at me!" she finally said. "Do come in, and who might this pretty little thing be?" Melissa had gotten out of the buggy to go and stand beside the two happy people.

Nate recovered from his teary state and introduced the two. "This is my wife, Melissa, Jane. We have been married about a year."

"Well, you are lovely, my dear," Jane said as she reached to hug Melissa. The three of them went inside the small, but very neat, house to sit and catch up on nearly twenty years of happenings. Jane was still almost overcome with surprise and joy. She told Nate about her husband — a good man who had rescued her from the Moores and by whom she had the two tiny children who were staring wide-eyed at the visitors. They looked to be about eighteen months and three.

"Nate, you know about Martha?" As he nodded that he did, she continued, "Well, this is little Martha, named after the sister I lost, and this is Nathan, named after the brother I thought I had also lost. I did so want a boy and girl so I could name them after you and Martha." Nate wanted to ask about Martha and what had truly happened to her, but he thought better of asking right then and spoiling the magic of the wonderful moment. Melissa and Jane were starting to talk and get acquainted, so he let the two of them dominate the conversation while he rested and enjoyed the buttermilk Jane had poured for them.

The little shotgun house Jane and her husband had built was composed of three rooms. Nate looked around and admired the work his brother-in-law had done. Jane was a good housekeeper, too. It was spotless. He looked forward to meeting the man his sister appeared to be so happy with.

The visit was everything Nate had dreamed of, but dreaded, for nearly twenty years. He liked his brother-in-law immediately. Cal Jernigan was a fine man. It showed upon sight, and the two men formed a definite bond. Nate thanked him for the good treatment he had given Jane. They talked about their farm work since

Cal farmed, too, and it was time to leave much too soon. Even though Jane begged, Nate said they must get back to Guntersville and be prepared to leave the next day. He knew their work at home was calling, but he held the children, as did Melissa, and caught Jane and Cal up on everything he could think of from their lives after he last saw her.

"I never wanted to leave you children. I just had no other way," a tortured Nate told her with tears in his eyes. Finally, the time had come when he must ask about Mr. Moore and all that had happened to them.

Seeing the pain he had been through, Jane made a quick decision. "Nathan, it is true. He did beat us, but he beat his wife and children, too. Sometimes he was also good to us, but I don't think the occasional beatings are what killed Martha. She did have a fever. She got it right near Christmas the year she was seven, and died on Christmas Eve. Now, you must not grieve any more. What is done is done, so let's let bygones be bygones and enjoy our time together from now on out."

Nathan hugged her good-bye, promising to be back as soon as they could. "I have wanted to find you for so long. You all must come to visit us. Soon," he said as he and Melissa drove reluctantly away.

With that part of his life settled, Nate could now turn his attention to other things. The joy he felt as they went back to Guntersville to await the morning train was mixed with pain for his parents' and little sister's untimely deaths, but isn't life bittersweet, he thought.

On the way home from the train station in Creighton, Nate told Melissa he wanted to go back to see the Jernigans as soon as they could. Melissa, who had been keeping a secret for just the right time, however, said, "I don't think I will be doing much traveling for a few months, though, Nathan."

When the full impact of what she was saying hit him, Nate pulled Dewey to a stop, right in the middle of the road, took her in his arms and kissed her soundly. "Oh, Mrs. York. How happy you do make me! When?" Melissa wasn't sure herself. She had been caught completely off guard and was unable to calculate. She had waited months for this, almost despairing at times.

"I think it happened that first night you made me take a bath right out under the stars in the front yard, Nathan York! Shame on you. Taking advantage of a naked lady the way you did!" Yes, Nate thought, life is bittersweet, but this is nothing but sweet!

Pearl McDougald
Fox Hollow
Catawba, Florida

Callie McDougald
c/o Mrs. Margaret DeVille
Mobile, Alabama.

A Kiss in the Dark

Margaret Graybill DeVille had been dealt a hand of cards in life that had failed to make her happy. She grew up as the only daughter of one of Mobile's more prominent families. Her father was wealthy by the time he was thirty, having made his fortune in the shipping business out of the Port of Mobile. His father had left a sum at his death with which H. Cleveland Graybill had been able to buy a small fleet of ships and begin shipping naval stores from the turpentine stills of northwest Florida and South Alabama to all parts of the country. Her older brother, Jason, was interested in the business, so when their father died, Jason continued running the business, and the money kept pouring in.

Margaret was unattractive, which was the first drawback she had to deal with, and she was not a sweet-natured person naturally — a situation she could have controlled had she so desired. Since money does tend to make some people arrogant and hard to deal with however, Margaret chose to be that type instead of compensating for her lack of looks and being sweet. The second disappointment she had to deal with was the fact that when she rescued Marcus DeVille from the little house on the southside, she thought he would hop each time she said frog. Marcus, although not wealthy, was not a pushover type, however so he didn't do exactly what Margaret always wanted him to do.

Instead of working in the shipping business, as Margaret wanted him to, he tried several other things that he wanted to do, with little success. Finally, Jason was able to get him into the bank in which the Graybills were strong investors, where he did well in the job, got promotions and was happy — as happy as Margaret would let him be. She continually told him how much *more* money they could have if he would have worked in the business and how her brother had had to get him set up in the bank in the first place. She belittled his job with the bank, constantly wanted to know when he would get another promotion, and in general, made his life miserable. All of that, coupled with the fact that she could never conceive a child, made her miserable. Her mother had died before Mr. Graybill, so that left only Jason, who thought she was a pain in the neck and avoided her unless he just had to talk over business with her.

Aside from a few friends who were either just like her in temperament or were impressed by her money, Margaret had nobody except Mandy, who catered to her every whim.

Having been stricken with the dreadful paralysis was a terrible thing, but, whereas most people would struggle to get better and make the most of the misfortune, Margaret grew more and more bitter. She had some regular visitors who brought little gifts each visit, but usually stayed only a short time. Who wanted to listen to her maudlin complaints?

Callie made an assessment of Mrs. DeVille's situation for the doctor each week. It now looked as if she would not only live, but would only lose the use of her legs, thus making it possible for her to use a wheelchair and get about. Except that she refused to even try to roll the chair with her hands. She would cry, moan and pout each time they put her in it; therefore, Callie or Mandy had to roll her wherever she went. Mostly, she refused to even get into the chair when help was available. When Dr. Carpenter visited her at the house, he told her each time to start getting into the chair each day and moving about, but to no avail. Margaret would do nothing of the kind. She preferred to stay in the bed and seek the pity of any and all.

Mandy coddled. Callie did not. Mandy encouraged her to stay in the bed and be cared for, but Callie encouraged her to build up her strength by getting up and moving about all she could. Mandy was winning. Late one evening after Callie had "The Mrs.", as Mandy called her, all bathed and tucked in for the night, she went out to sit on the porch in the cool evening air. "The Mrs." didn't have to have a night shift anymore since she was no longer near death, so Callie had her late evenings free. She only had to check in on Mrs. DeVille before going up to bed.

Mr. DeVille had told her at dinner that he was going to a Masonic meeting, but she had dismissed it from her mind until she opened the door to the dark porch and started to step out bumping smack into him coming in the door. "Oh, sorry!" he said, catching Callie to prevent knocking her to the floor. "Gee, Nurse Callie, you took me by surprise!"

Callie was equally startled by being almost run over by a man in the darkness. She helped right herself, expecting to continue on to the swing. Instead, Mr. DeVille didn't let go of her arms right away. "Callie!" he whispered hoarsely in the darkness. "I have been wanting to do this ever since I first laid my eyes on you." With that, he tightened his arms around the astounded young woman and seeking her face, kissed her soundly on the lips.

"Mr. DeVille, please. Please," was all Callie could say. Trying to regain her composure, she proceeded on to the swing. Marcus took the chair nearest her, as was his usual custom. They had spent many evenings chatting there in the cool, but Callie had not realized he had any such thoughts. Now she realized why he looked at her the way he often did. He had insisted she join him at dinner each evening, which she usually did, apparently to Mandy's disgust. She was almost rude in fact. It did seem the poor man was hungry for conversation, because when he visited his wife, all she did was grouse about one thing or another.

"Callie, I'm sorry. I didn't mean to upset you, and I had no right to do a thing like that. It's just that you are everything I have not had. I love your bearing, your unique capability, your quiet calm and just everything about you. Can you forgive me?"

Still taken aback, Callie hardly knew what to say. She was flattered, on the one hand, and knew full well she shouldn't be on, the other. Callie had never had a man show such an interest in her. Things were happening inside her she hadn't experienced before, even though she had the normal desires any young woman would have. Things that she had no control over, try as she would to restrain herself.

"Yes, I can forgive you, but we mustn't. You are a married man with a sick wife. I am in your employ." Callie had been trained, she thought, to handle any situation that might arise, but her training did not include anything like this! She found that she had enjoyed the kiss, contraband though it was.

"My dear, there is something you need to know," Marcus said. "For many years, Margaret and I have been on very poor terms. We have seldom seen eye-to-eye on anything. She has been disappointed in me from the beginning of our marriage, and it has only made matters worse that she was stricken with this dreadful illness. She is, I am afraid, a very bitter woman."

"But you are still a married man, Mr. DeVille," Callie managed to mutter.

"Please call me Marcus. I insist."

"No. I cannot do that. I work for you. In fact, I must stop having dinner when you do and with you each evening, and I shall spend my evenings in my room from now on." Callie was resolute. She wanted to be loved, desperately, but she knew right from wrong, and an affair with Mr. DeVille would be very wrong.

"You will not stop having dinner with me, and you will not spend these long evenings in your hot room." He was equally adamant about that. "I will relent on the name, but not on the other."

Days flew by in the second year of Nate's and Melissa's marriage as they prepared themselves emotionally and mentally for the arrival of a baby. The Tates were again overjoyed at the prospect but cautiously so. Lily had never stopped making tiny things for a baby to wear, knowing that, sooner or later, they would have a baby. It paid to get a head start, especially when all the clothes had to be made. Melissa, although not doing heavy work now, was still helping Nate in the field dropping seeds, driving the wagon for gathering the crop and helping to throw corn into the crib. Nate, in turn, helped her with her heavier chores. They worked side-by-side most of the time except when she was up at her mother's canning or making preserves, or when she helped Pearl.

The McDougalds had come to depend on Melissa greatly as Miss Mattie's condition continued to deteriorate. That made Melissa dread having to quit working for Pearl. Poor thing. Melissa wondered how on earth she would manage. Nate could continue to go, but Melissa would not be able to for a month or more. She could leave the baby with Lily when she started back to work, except for nursing. That would make it impossible. Taking a tiny infant several miles twice a day in a buggy was also not possible, so Pearl would just have to make other arrangements. Melissa had already had to cut down the amount of heavy work she did for Pearl, so she worked more in the store and Pearl worked more at the house.

As spring faded into summer, Nate began to notice that Buttons was staying out a lot at night. If she came in at all, she wanted to get out again before bedtime. Then she wouldn't come when called as he and Melissa started to bed. One evening he remarked to the aloof cat, "Buttons, it just isn't ladylike for you to stay out all night. I think you should be in at a decent hour," but Buttons paid no heed. Each evening Melissa called and called, but no Buttons. In the daytime, the errant cat stayed balled on their bed in a tight ball. One night, Nate awoke to what he thought was a catfight outside the cabin. Jumping up, he ran to the door and called Buttons. He surely didn't want Melissa to hear the cats. It would alarm her unduly. Nate knew, of course, what was happening. When Buttons entered the door, her master upbraided her again for her scandalous behavior. "You are a disgrace, young lady," he told her.

Marcus DeVille was having trouble concentrating on his work at the bank. He had never had a problem before, but he had just discovered that he had never been in love before. Actually, he had never been enamored to the point of infatuation before. It was a completely new experience and all he thought about all day, every day. He could see Callie's face, her dark, slightly curly hair, which she wore in a bun at the nape of her neck so that her cap would fit nicely over it, and he could see her small, but beautifully pointed breasts beneath her uniform, just large enough, but not heavy enough, to be sagging. She was tall with narrow feet and tiny ankles. That was all he could see below her ankle-length skirt. She was not, at first glance, a beautiful woman, but she had an appeal that was becoming harder and harder for him to resist. How did one really describe Callie? Her appeal was not in looks alone, but in her very soul. Sometimes Marcus DeVille thought he would actually go mad if he could not have that woman!

Callie found herself in somewhat a similar situation. She was becoming increasingly more bored with Margaret DeVille's care. The woman would do nothing to help herself. She was dead weight when it was time to move her, making Callie's back ache more each day. She complained constantly to all who would listen. At times, she was rude to Callie and always demanding. Callie wanted to tell her what a drag she was and that she certainly didn't deserve Marcus. She even suggested to him that he could find a maid to help Mandy with his wife's care and dispense with nursing care, but he would not hear of it. It seemed a shame to waste skill on someone like her when so many others needed that skill. So she daydreamed more than usual, always thinking of the man she ate with, shared a house with and, in a manner of speaking, was "kept" by but whom she could not have in any way.

In late September, Miss Mattie had another stroke; this time severe, rendering her paralyzed completely and unable to speak coherently. She talked, rambling on about her mother, father and other people nobody even knew. She was very ill, making it necessary for someone to sit with her at all times, even at night. The fear was she would die in the night without anyone knowing it. Mr. Mac could take a turn now and then, but at his age, he couldn't stay up night after night. Pearl worried that he would collapse, also. Realizing the need, the neighbors came to their aid and took turns sitting with Miss Mattie as neighbors did in a time of need. Pearl thanked God for every one of them each day.

Matt and Martha Seward, being the closest neighbors, did a lion's share of the helping. Martha started helping with the undue amount of washing that was required, and Matt helped at the store when Nate and Melissa couldn't be there.

Finally, Pearl took a few minutes one day to write again to her sister and tell her the state of her mother's health. She explained to Callie that she was having to have help from the community and that she didn't see how their mother could last too much longer. Pearl didn't really know the nature of strokes, however, and the fact that patients can last an inordinate length of time despite the way things looked.

Callie went to her room on Saturday that late summer day to get fresh clothing and pick up her mail. She read the letter from Pearl, wondering if things were really that bad or if Pearl just wanted her to come home to relieve her. Again, she made a mental note to go home surely by Christmas. She just couldn't walk off from her work. She had a job to do whether it actually required a skilled nurse or not.

Homestead

Melissa was not able to calculate exactly when the baby was due, but thought it would be early January. She and Nate lay awake sometimes into the night thinking about names and trying to see what they could come up with that would be different but not too unusual. Nate didn't especially want to name a boy after himself, but liked the idea of having him named after his own father, if it were a boy. Melissa was ambivalent about names if it were a girl. Sometimes they talked over the progress they had made in the one and a half years they had been married. For one thing, Nate had learned to read from the Reader One Melissa borrowed from the school and was now way along in the third reader. He could also write and subtract and add very well. He was learning the multiplication tables so that she could start having him multiply and divide soon. He was delighted with his new abilities and very proud to no longer be completely illiterate.

As Melissa's belly began to swell, she also noticed that Buttons had a rather large one, too. Nate had said nothing to her about what he knew Miss Buttons to be up to, wanting it to be a surprise. Melissa was not as schooled in the things of nature as Nate was, having not had to deal with the more mundane things of life. So she failed to realize until Buttons was actually in labor that she, too, was in the family way!

The kittens arrived early one morning; three of them, all tabbies just like their mother. Nate had not yet gone to the field to work, thinking Buttons might need a little help. Melissa was beside herself when she discovered something strange was going on. First, Buttons began to cry and walk about the cabin. She finally found Melissa's gathering basket in the shed room and decided it would do. Nate went in and put an old scouring cloth in it for comfort, leaving the distraught cat to go about the birthing process. She seemed totally confused and puzzled about her strange condition, but soon a kitten appeared, then another and finally the third one. Nate knew they usually had more, like four or five, but thought, this being her first litter, three must be all. Melissa sat for hours and stared at the babies, so tiny and help-less. They managed to find where to nurse, though and all started feeding. Buttons was as proud as could be and purred like mad. They were hardly bigger than Nate's thumb, all with tightly closed eyes. "When will they have their eyes open?" Melissa wanted to know.

"Oh, in a couple of weeks," Nate told her. She marveled at the tiny creatures and thought of her own tiny child forming in her ever-growing middle.

Homestead

An Illicit Affair

It was a rainy and dark night. There was a terrible thunderstorm in the offing, with sharp lightning that always made Callie nervous. She had actually received a shock once, as a small child, while standing near a wire fence in lightning. So, as folks said, once burned, twice shy. She had been awakened by the loud thunder and was feeling cold from the dampness, so she went over to put her windows down. Next, she decided to get a light quilt from the hall linen closet.

Marcus was lying awake down the hall in his room, thinking, as usual, about the woman he so desired who was just two doors away. He had tossed and turned trying to decide what he was going to do about these feelings, which were getting the better of his self-restraint, when he heard Callie's door open. It had a squeak and needed oil, but if he put oil on it, he couldn't tell when she opened it. He knew that was a childish little thing, but it delighted him to have even *that* knowledge of her, and he wanted to know her in every way! He had become obsessed with Callie McDougald.

As Callie was fumbling in the dark to get the quilt, she heard another door open. Knowing full well who it was, she turned and started back across to her room. She was at her door when he caught up to her and took her in his arms. This time, Callie didn't resist at all. She couldn't. Every ounce of her resolve was gone, and, at that moment, she belonged totally to Marcus DeVille. He carried her into her room, laid her on the bed, and even though there was a terrible storm, Callie was oblivious to it. She was only conscious of the man who held her in his arms and did wonderful things to her! It was just as she had imagined a thousand times, only much, much more. She had never reckoned with the divine smell of a man so close to her, or the strength of his arms around her. She had not dreamed anything could be so wonderful, so completely marvelous.

One thing Marcus and Callie had not reckoned with was the proximity of Mandy to them in the house. As the days went by, they tried to restrain themselves and be totally discreet, but she had been watching and looking for something to happen. She could see the looks between the two of them and interpreted those looks to be guilt. She was not far from right. Callie was having an especially difficult time caring for Margaret DeVille and all the while carrying on a torrid affair with her husband, albeit not her intention ever to do so. She did sometimes feel that Margaret didn't deserve such a wonderful man when she was literally as mean as a snake.

John Tate had a few days at home at the end of the summer. Nate and Melissa were up at her parents' house a lot. It was a wonderful time for the family, knowing that Melissa's baby would be arriving soon after Christmas. They would be celebrating for more reasons than just the Christ child's birth this year. There were things going on at the church which the whole family enjoyed together, and one devastating one. It seemed that Franklin and Grace Rogers had gone to a barn dance at one of the nearby homesteads. They thought nothing of going, but someone reported it to the other deacons, and since Franklin was also a deacon, the board decided it was a highly inappropriate thing for them to have done. Thus, the decision was made that Grace and Franklin must apologize to the whole congregation or leave the church. They were given no other options.

Franklin's parents were incensed over the decision, as were Franklin and Grace themselves. They knew of things others had done which seemed much worse. Nate talked to Franklin. "We are sorry this has come to the point it has," he told Franklin. "Melissa and I don't agree with the board, and we are going to make our feelings known. I think John and Lily feel the same."

"Thanks, my friend, but we don't want you all to get into this mess. We have decided to leave the church because we just don't feel we have committed an unpardonable sin!" Franklin said.

Nate and John discussed it, and John said he thought they should register their feelings with the Board of Deacons, so the next week, they announced their feelings to the group after church when the deacons met.

Later the next week, one of the deacons rode up to John and Lily's to tell them if they were going to support the Rogers, they were as guilty as the Rogers were, so they were being given the same choices! John didn't waste a minute making the choice for all of them. They would leave the church — a decision the Board of Deacons had not counted on for one minute. Franklin's parents fell into the same category, making a little group which comprised a fair segment of the membership, and a group the church could ill afford to lose.

It would be several weeks before the deacons would begin to realize that John and Lily and Melissa and Nate were good paying members whose contributions were being sorely missed. It would only take a few more days for the decision to be reached to ask them all, the Rogers included, to rejoin, which they did immediately, and the whole ordeal was soon forgotten.

The fall was coming in with cool, sunny days. Leaves were changing in Mobile and falling all over the city lining the streets with color. Callie enjoyed the coolness, as did her "patient," who, being in the bed all the time, loved the dank cool sheets replac-

ing the damp hot ones she had endured all summer. She still refused to use the wheelchair. Callie was growing more and more frustrated with her, but was still able not to show it. Her guilt feelings were not helping, and she knew she had to do something, and soon. She adored Marcus, but her upbringing had taught her that fornication was a sin, not to mention with a married man! He seemed to feel little guilt, if any. Callie hated her weakness for this man. She was a very bright woman who fully understood what she and Marcus were doing.

One late night as Marcus was leaving Callie's room, he walked quietly into the hall, closing the door, which had long ago been greased to stop the squeak, and in the faint light from the window in the stairwell saw a dark figure hurriedly descending the stairs. He knew instantly, of course, who it was and what would now happen. Mandy had, no doubt, been sent up to spy. She had been waiting long, he knew, because he was with Callie for two to three hours. Walking over to the corner bedroom, he opened the door wider to find a telltale chair just inside the room. Well, he thought, this is it, the day I have been waiting for. Knowing he couldn't divorce an invalid wife without causing an awful stir in the community, he now felt he would have that chance. He wanted to marry Callie. Soon. He was madly in love with that woman. He would wait until morning to tell Callie but prepare her he must for the scene he was sure would be coming.

Melissa's pregnancy was progressing with no problems. Nate had been gathering the crop at their house and Mr. Mac's. Thankfully, it had been a good year. There was plenty for the winter of everything, which took the pressure off of him. He had worked at the McDougalds' for several days, taking Melissa to help Pearl as usual. At each visit, Rose and Ben were all over him, hugging and begging for attention. Nate still had an inner conflict going on because of what Mr. Mac had done to Rose. He feared that it had not stopped, because she was the most crest-fallen child he had ever seen. And he hated himself for his weakness in not being able to confront the man in order to be sure it didn't continue to happen. He still had not told Melissa, because she would insist that he talk to Mr. Mac. That would ruin his and her work situation — or maybe it wouldn't, given the way they needed help — but she would lose all respect for Nate, a situation he could not bear. In fact, he had never told a soul. If necessary, he would take the secret to his grave. He had no other choice, but he prayed for a successful resolution to his problem.

After Nate's work at Mr. Mac's for several days, he was trying to get caught up at home when a messenger came riding up to let the Yorks and Tates know that Eulon Fields had died. Nate was shocked. He knew Eulon was frail and had sugar, but somehow he had not thought it to be so serious. He and Matt had continued to take food down to him and Mrs. Fields as often as they could, as did others in the church.

"When is the funeral to be?" he asked the man who had come to tell them.

"We are not sure. They don't have anyone to make a coffin, and Mrs. Fields is too ill to deal with this. We don't think she will live much longer. They sure are poor." Nate told the man he would talk to his father-in-law and see if they could go and build a coffin. He had some lumber in the barn he could use.

"Just tell Mrs. Fields we will tend to it," he said as the man rode away to let other homesteaders know.

The next morning quite early, Nate kissed Melissa good-bye and told her he would be home as soon as he and her father got the coffin made. Then he rode off in the wagon with lumber for the job. John was waiting.

On the trip, the two men had a chance to talk. Nate had become increasingly fond of his father-in-law and John was feeling the same. He trusted this man who was his daughter's husband and the father of his coming grandchild. He also thanked God for sending him to their family.

"Nate, we never know when we are going to meet our Maker. In the work I am in, I certainly don't. I am going to court again in a few days to testify against a gang of poachers. They have made all kinds of threats that don't scare me, but I still have to take them seriously. These big lumber companies want timber any way they can get it, but they prefer not to pay for it."

"Have you told the sheriff about these threats, John?" he asked he older man.

"No, there is nothing anyone can do until they actually do it. Then you can never catch them, so it is useless. I just want you to know that if anything should happen to me, I know I can count on you to take care of the family. You are to have my tools and anything of mine you can use. I would want you to farm the patch and help Lily and the younger girls," he said.

"Of course, John. You know I would do all that, but you aren't seriously worried about these threats, are you? Surely they are just blowhards that don't have the nerve to hurt anyone." Nate was shocked. John sounded more serious than he had in the past when he had mentioned this kind of thing.

John, sensing Nate's alarm, changed his tune immediately and began to talk about something else, all the while assuring Nate he had just wanted to let him know all this just in case. They went along their way hurriedly so that they could put Mrs. Fields at rest about the coffin. Poor lady. Eulon was her only child and while more of a liability than an asset, he was company for her and kept her from being totally alone.

Nate and John pulled into the lane at her house about ten o'clock in the morning. It was cloudy and looked as if it would rain any minute, but they got the lumber unloaded quickly, set up some saw benches John had brought along to lay the lumber across and began work. Nate sawed, while John started nailing the pieces together. He had more skill than Nate did in that department. Besides, Nate had never made a coffin before.

Mrs. Fields had bathed Eulon and put his best clothes on him. His hair was combed nicely, probably for the first time ever, and she had shaved him, as well. At best, his clothes were shabby, but clean and decent. A neighbor from a couple of miles south of her shack had come over to sit with her, a Mrs. Johnson by name. Mrs. Johnson was doing what she could to clean up the little shack and comfort Mrs. Fields at the same time.

ᴴomestead

They had decided the funeral would be the next day at ten in the morning. Nate and John were to pass the word among the settlers along their way back home. It was a strange thing how fast word got around in the area.

When the men were finished, they took the coffin inside where Mrs. Fields had managed to clear a table for it to rest on. They placed it carefully, and tenderly picked up Eulon's now stiff form, putting it inside. His mother wanted the lid left off until just before the funeral, so they laid it to the side and prepared to leave.

"I shore do thank ye fer coming all this way and doin' this fer me," the poor lady said as they started for the wagon. "Hit's a fer piece down here, and I wanta ask ye to come tomorrie and help take my boy to his final restin' place." She was struggling to talk through her tears and with her huge swollen body looking, if anything, worse than when Nate had last taken food to her.

"Yes, we will be here, Mrs. Fields. Don't worry," John told her. It was obvious losing Eulon had cut deeply into this grieving woman. As he left, John pressed a coin into her rough and swollen hand.

On the way home, Nate and John talked about the coming baby, Melissa's health, which seemed excellent now, and their hopes for the future. Both dreamed of happy times together with the family growing and the younger girls getting married before too long.

Poor Eulon was laid to rest beside his father in the little cemetery up the road from the small shack. Mrs. Fields would be able to visit their graves often. Most of the community came out to the service conducted by a Baptist preacher from the tiny church two miles away. Overall, it was very nice, and Mrs. Fields seemed consoled when it was over. One thing could be said about the homestead community — the people surely supported each other.

Margaret's Revenge

At the DeVille residence the morning after Marcus saw the figure descending the stairs in the dark, he went down to see Margaret as usual before leaving for work. To his amazement, she was sitting up in bed, hair combed and a little rouge on her cheeks, looking almost happy. "Good morning, dear," he said, and leaning over, kissed her on the cheek, expecting the explosion he was sure would come.

"Good morning, Marcus. Are you ready for work?" she purred. She sounded pleasant.

"Yes, and you have a good day now. Let Nurse Callie get you up and help you to start getting some strength back. You know exercise is important." Marcus thought he'd better leave while things were calm. He knew it couldn't last. Surely Mandy knew what was going on and had reported to Margaret.

On the way to work, along a street he had walked for years, things looked different somehow. The fall leaves were lining the gutters in all colors. There was a cool north wind blowing, which signaled the coming of colder weather in the near future, and Marcus knew things were about to change. He could not ask for a divorce from an invalid wife, but if *she* got the divorce with good grounds, he would be free to marry Callie, the woman he loved more than he thought possible to love anyone. He adored her. To ask for a divorce would have caused a terrible stir in the community, and certainly what he had done would cause a stir, but it was not like desertion, exactly.

Marcus had not been happy with Margaret almost from the start of their marriage. Why, it was just at the last Christmas party while they were sitting around a table with a group of bank employees that she had belittled him in front of everyone. The conversation had to do with loans, and Marcus made a comment, to which Margaret promptly said, "What would *you* know about the loan department? You have been a teller all your life."

Marcus actually had thought she might have had her brother, Jason, arrange to keep him from getting recent promotions just to keep him in line and dependent upon her money for survival. He had been in line many times, but in the last couple of years, someone else always seemed to be promoted. If he had not liked the bank so much and felt there was really nothing else he had skills for, he'd have left long ago.

When Callie reported to "The Mrs." that morning, she also found a smiling Mrs. DeVille who immediately said she wanted to get into her chair. Callie gladly complied with her request by getting the wheelchair and helping her into it, somewhat puzzled by her patient's sudden desire to recuperate, but thinking all the while that it was about time! While Margaret was in her chair, Callie re-made her bed, straightened the room and then had breakfast. As she ate, Mandy stared at her from across the kitchen, where she was washing dishes. She is about as friendly as a cobra, Callie was thinking. She wanted to finish this job and go on to another, but she wanted Marcus to be there, too. What a dilemma. What a choice. There was no answer to this problem, but she had to find one. Things could not go on this way.

About nine that morning, Mandy left the house, Callie supposed, to go for groceries, as she did at least once a week. She went to the meat market around the corner almost every day and often did other errands for "The Mrs.," such as paying bills. Callie had rolled Margaret out onto the veranda so that she could enjoy the wonderful weather. Later in the morning, her best friend, Amanda Livingston, came for a visit. As usual, Callie went up to her room and left the two friends to visit alone.

"Oh, Callie," she heard Mrs. Livingston call in half an hour. "Mrs. DeVille is ready to go back to bed. Come and assist her." Her voice was curt and not at all the same as when she had arrived.

"I will be right there," Callie replied. She had turned into nothing more than a glorified servant here in this house who worked six, and sometimes seven, days a week, and it was getting old. Now, she supposed, she had to take orders from the patient's friends as well as from her. Mrs. DeVille had hardly been civil the entire stint of duty. Lately it had been worse. I wonder if she knows, Callie thought. Well, I can't say as I'd blame her for being nasty to her husband's paramour!

Since taking this case, Callie had more or less let her social life dwindle to nothingness. Mrs. DeVille had been so very ill right at first that she could not afford to take more than a day off, if even that. Sometimes she went to the boarding house, got fresh things, washed the dirty things, and left, going right back to the DeVilles'. Now she was feeling like a day off and a change of scene would do her good. In fact, she thought she was going to scream if she had to deal with that woman another hour! Saturday was two days away, and she would take the day off.

John Tate was enjoying his ten days off. He had planned to make the baby a cradle out in front of his smokehouse where he kept tools under the little shed. He was almost finished when Nate and Melissa arrived for supper. Lily had invited them several times while John was home so they could all be with him as much as possible. Melissa helped out by making bread and pie. When she got there that evening, John showed her the cradle he had not told her about. "Daddy!" she shrieked, "It is wonderful! I love it." With that, she threw her arms around his neck and gave him a wonderful, big hug. "Thank you, Pops. You are the very best daddy in the world." John beamed and enjoyed his family to the fullest that evening.

As they sat on the porch savoring the evening cool, they heard all about school from Mary and Liz. Mary was about to finish up at Catawba. She was now sixteen, and had a beau. Melissa inquired as to what her plans were when she finished. Mary said she would like to be a teacher, but until the one they had left Catawba, there was no chance. "We may hire another one at Catawba if the enrollment continues to pick up, though," John offered.

"Really, daddy?" He had gotten Mary's attention. "Do you think they would hire me?"

"Yes, but you will have to go to the Normal School over in Creighton and get your certificate."

"Oh, I will go! I will!" She was quite enthusiastic. Good, John was thinking. He was a school board member and was interested in having his girls get as much education as possible.

"Then I will have to work a little harder, I suppose, if my daughter is going to the Academy," he teased. It would require her to live in Creighton for a term, but that was not out of the question. Melissa was thinking that she had wanted to be a teacher, too, but it seemed impractical, given the area where they lived, and then Nate had come along, and now she was doing exactly what she wanted to do most!

On Friday morning, Callie announced that while Mr. DeVille would be home with "The Mrs." on Saturday, she would like to take the day off. Mrs. DeVille could not have been nicer. "Well, of course, my dear. You poor thing. You have hardly had a day off in months! You must take the day, go shopping or to a play or do something for yourself. I will be fine with Marcus and Mandy both here." I need to go to church, Callie was thinking, to get forgiveness for this sordid love affair I am having with your husband, but I will go shopping. That is just what I need! There is nothing like new clothes to lift the spirits, and she hadn't been shopping in weeks. In fact, she realized Marcus had never seen her in anything but a uniform! My word, he might not even like me in anything else. But, he likes me in nothing, she told herself.

The next day, Mrs. DeVille was still her most charming self. Marcus was in her room when Callie went down dressed in street wear. Mandy had fixed them a big breakfast, and they were eating together. She noticed he did a double take when she walked in with her brown, two-piece, fitted suit on which accentuated her tiny waist, small, firm breasts and complimented her skin tone. Her hair looked golden in the morning light, and she was wearing it down, tied in a ribbon at the back of her neck. Marcus thought she was beautiful, although, as beauty went, she was not considered beautiful. She just had a certain appeal.

Callie went to her favorite department store where she had an account, and bought several things. She knew she owed quite a sum there already from when she first got the account after graduation. She had needed so many things for her new life style, and goodness, things were high! But a few more couldn't make that much difference. She wanted a Panama hat desperately, because they were the rage, so she treated herself to one, expensive though it was.

Her roommate was there when she got to the room, and she had been thinking about telling her to find someone else to room with since she rarely left the DeVilles' anymore, but something made her decide against it. Her reasoning was that she just might get enough of that woman again and have to take a day away just as she had today. It did seem like an unnecessary expense, though.

John left on Monday morning for the county seat. He had breakfast with the family, including Nate and Melissa, and then headed out. It was a long ride, so he would not get there until nearly night, but Belle, the horse the government furnished him, was dependable, and he assured everyone he would be fine. Although Lily fixed him a lunch, he declined water, because there were creeks and branches all along the way where he and Belle would stop for water. He would appear for court the next day, then he would be back in the woods again, trying to control the poaching situation. Nate didn't say anything to the women, but he surely wished he could go along for protection.

The fifteenth of October was on Thursday after Callie's day off the Saturday before. Marcus went to work, collected his pay envelope, as usual, and opened it, preparing to deposit his check as he did every first and fifteenth of his life. This time, however, there was something else in the envelope. Pulling it out, Marcus recognized it immediately having seen dozens in his tenure with the bank. It was a severance slip that read: We, the officers of the bank, regret to inform you that your services are no longer needed. This is your final pay. Then another note had been added which was not usual. Pick up your personal effects and prepare to be out of the bank by noon.

Marcus was so stunned he almost fell to the floor. He had not dreamed of such a thing. He was prepared for Margaret's wrath, but this was beyond his wildest imagination! Literally staggering backward, he caught himself and slumped into his chair. His heart was pounding, his hands were wet and clammy, and he began to perspire profusely. Actually, he wondered if he were having a heart attack. Apparently, the rest of the bank personnel had been informed, because nobody came near his cubicle while he was trying to absorb what was happening. Looking around, he could see that everyone was quite busy. Everyone was avoiding eye contact, too.

As soon as he was able to pull himself together, Marcus began getting things out of his desk. He piled them on the top and then went to look for a bag, avoiding the rest of the staff. With everything bagged, and there weren't really many things to take, he went to the files, checked his balance with the latest addition, and wrote a check. He was preparing to cash it himself, as he had done thousands of times, when Ralph Jackson, the head cashier, jerked it from him and said, emphatically, "I will do that!" My word, Marcus thought, it would seem I am thought of as an embezzler or something. With every passing minute, he was seeing the picture more clearly. He understood what was happening: Margaret had somehow gotten in touch with Jason, who, being the dutiful brother he was, had gotten the bank to fire him and have him leave right then like a common criminal!

"That bastard!" Marcus said under his breath. "I ought to kill the son of a gun. After all the years I have given this bank, the very best years of my life. I ought to kill him." While gathering up his belongings and preparing to leave, only one person dared to go near him, his dear friend, Sam Crosson. He walked by Marcus and whispered, "I will see you soon, pal." Poor slobs. Marcus could see they were afraid to even *look* in his direction.

Practically staggering, Marcus made it across the street from the bank and to the park. He slumped down on a bench. The birds, mostly pigeons, were all over the place, but they held no charm for him this morning. He had sat many times, either at lunch or on the way home, looking at them feeding and sometimes had a bag of peanuts to shell for them. He tried to sort out just what must be going on so that he could be prepared, but with Margaret's devious mind, who could do that? Then he thought of Callie. Poor girl, she must be catching it. He supposed he'd better hurry on home and try to rescue her from the very door of hell.

Callie was unsuspecting. She had been doing her usual duties, those of a nursemaid. When she heard footsteps on the porch, they were those of someone walking with a purpose. The front door was open and the screen was jerked open and allowed to close with a loud bang! Then Marcus entered the room. Callie could see there was trouble in the air and prepared to leave the room, but Marcus motioned for her to stay. "You might as well hear this, Callie. Margaret, what in the hell have you been up to?" he yelled.

She bristled back at him. "I might ask you the same thing. The very idea of carrying on with this tramp right in *my* house, under *my* nose, with me an invalid! Oh, she needs to stay all right just long enough for me to tell her what I think of her, and then she is to get out of my house!"

Marcus said, "Margaret, for heaven's sake. Watch your mouth." But once she had unleashed her wrath, there was no stopping her. Callie just stood there, as Marcus did, and let her vent.

"You are nothing but white trash from the sticks. I never should have had you here in the first place. I should have asked the hospital to send someone with some breeding and culture, but I thought I should give you a chance. I had heard what a fine nurse you are. Well! If people only knew, and they will! You are just scum, so I want you out of here now. Pack your things and leave this morning." Margaret then turned to her husband and started again, "And as for you, I will deal with you in my own good time. She may be ignorant and not have any character, but you do know better. After all I have done for you."

"Wait, Callie," Marcus said when his wife stopped for breath. "I want you to hear this. Margaret, neither of us planned it or wanted it to happen, but we are very much in love, and I want a divorce. I want to marry Callie."

"I told you I will deal with you in my own good time, but for now, I want you out of here, too. I cannot stand the sight of either of you. It has been hell having to look at the two of you while I confirmed my suspicions. Now get out of my sight!"

Marcus took Callie by the arm and ushered her out to the porch. "Sit down, my dear. I am so dreadfully sorry about this. I had every intention of asking for a divorce, and I hoped you would marry me, but I never dreamed it would end like this."

"I know. I feared the worst when she found out, and I knew she would sooner or later, but I couldn't stop myself, knowing all the while what we have been doing was wrong." Callie looked into his eyes. She could see pain but misinterpreted the reason for the pain. She thought it was the situation with Margaret when, all the while, it was the job loss he was grieving over. He hadn't had time to tell her about that.

Marcus sat down in a chair and motioned for her to do the same. "Callie, when I got to the bank this morning, I was given my pay envelope with a severance notice inside." Callie caught her breath.

"No!" she said, "How could they?"

"Well, I am afraid my lovely wife was the cause of that. You see, her brother has great pull with the bank. They own a huge block of stock in the bank, and all it took was a word from him." Pride caused him to spare her the demeaning details, but what he had to tell her next pained him greatly, yet it must be told. "You see, she is the one with the money. I had nothing when I met and married her, so all these years she has been in control. I have managed to save a little money, which I have invested wisely, but the bulk of what we have has come from her family's business — the shipping business. They have friends in high places who will make things hard for me." Callie was getting the picture.

"I see," she said simply. Now things were beginning to make sense and what Mrs. Downing, her landlady, had said was now adding up.

"I intend to get a divorce, and although I had planned to ask you in a very romantic setting somewhere, I wanted to ask you to marry me, so I am asking you now, Callie. Will you marry me when this is all over?" She nodded in assent, too emotionally drained to say anything. Tears were near the surface, and she didn't want Margaret or Mandy to see her cry. Mandy, who had doubtless done the dirty work, was nowhere to be seen. She knew, of course, what was happening. She seldom missed anything. Callie had thought she was spying more than once on things that were going on.

After she got herself under control and the impact had begun to lessen, she said to Marcus, "Don't worry. I will marry you whenever you are free, and we can manage without that woman's money and power. I have a good profession, and so do you. We will make our own fortune."

Poor Callie, Marcus was thinking. She is so innocent of the ways of this world. She has no idea of the far-reaching effect this is going to have on me, and maybe her, too. For that matter, neither did he at that moment.

When they finished the conversation on the porch, Callie got up to go in and start packing. It would take several trips to get all the things she had brought over back to her room. Oh, that dreary room. She certainly hoped she would get a call soon from another family so that she wouldn't have to sit around there all day.

When her things were packed and ready, Marcus would not hear of her walking and taking things back to the room. "I will hire a driver to take you in a buggy," he said. No amount of protests did any good. The taxis were passing the house frequently, so he simply stepped to the street and hailed one.

Once back at the room, Callie allowed herself one good cry. Then she got ready and walked down to the hospital to check the Registry. She knew the lady, Mrs. De Paul, at the desk, having been there many times to get her assignments. "I am available now," she told the woman, a mousy-haired older lady who pursed her lips as she checked the Registry. She seemed less friendly than in past times, or was it just Callie's imagination?

Then curtly, she said, "I am afraid I have nothing for you today." With that she turned back to her work on the desk.

Callie was about as dejected as she could be. Her world seemed so great and now it was crumbling about her. She suddenly felt very afraid and alone. Marcus loved her; that much she now knew, but with his situation there would be no telling how long before they could get married. Her money was going to be depleted soon unless she got another job shortly. Of course, that would happen. It was just a matter of time with her reputation as a nurse until she would be working. Besides, a little rest would do her good.

The citizens of Mobile were of two types: the "haves" and the "have-nots." Marcus DeVille had been both, so it didn't take him long to decide which group he wanted to belong to. He began to think about his beginnings, the little house on the southside and the big house on South Avenue. He preferred the latter, but how was he going to have that and Callie? If Margaret would be fair, and she wouldn't, he could manage it. He still owned his parents' house, small though it was, and in a very poor neighborhood now. He had a small savings account at the bank that he closed. The money was now in his pocket and must be put in another bank shortly. He would start the next day looking for another job. Every banker in town knew of his abilities, so that shouldn't be too hard.

John finished his testimony in court on Thursday, got Belle out of the livery stable, and headed for the forest where he had not been in a few weeks. It was east of Milton in Yellow River swamp, a good thirty miles away. It would take John two hard days of riding to reach the area, so he would camp out that night, and for the next several nights while he patrolled. It was a rough life, but the pay was good, he got time off, and he was building up a small government pension. In five years, he could retire. Lily hated the job, but she understood that he had invested too much time to quit now.

The leaves in the branches and creeks were turning gold and crimson. Then out on the ridges where the timber was, the huge virgin pines were green and stately. They had shed their needles, already making a lovely brown carpet under each tree. As he rode the range, John enjoyed these scenes. He knew these woods for a forty-mile radius in all directions. They were his woods. This is where he belonged. Things looked all right as he went along, so he stopped for the night beside a small stream and built a fire to warm by. There was a slight nip in the air at night, but the days were still plenty warm. It was a clear night with stars everywhere. John enjoyed looking up at the sky and wondering about God and the world beyond. One thing for sure, he believed in God.

Each day in Mobile, Callie went to the hospital to see if there was any message at the Registry for her. Each day she was told there was nothing. It became embarrassing, so after a few days she just went every other day. She had heard nothing from Marcus either. That was most puzzling of all. He had indicated that he would be around to see her soon as she was leaving, but Marcus had problems of his own. He went in to talk to Margaret after Callie left.

"What a scene you made, Margaret. Couldn't you have saved some of our problems for us to discuss alone?" he asked. She was reading and barely looked up from the magazine she held. She had him right where she wanted him, and she was enjoying it immensely.

"You are the one who could have behaved differently. How do you think I feel, being an invalid and having a husband who is cheating on me right in my own house?" She gave him a sidelong glance and went back to her reading. He could see she was going to be as difficult as possible.

"Well, things might have been different, you know," he said to the magazine in front of her face. That got her attention.

"Oh, and how?"

"In all of our married years, you have treated me like a second-class citizen. I never should have married you in the first place, and I should have left you many years ago. You have treated me as though I married "up" to your level, never with respect, but I have taken it. Well, not anymore." He was emphatic. "I want a divorce. I will let you file to save face, but I want it and soon."

With that, Margaret laid her magazine aside and looked at

him with the most diabolical expression he had ever seen on anyone's face. "I *do not* want a divorce, and I *will not* file for one. You cannot get a divorce without my agreement, so you will get a divorce when hell freezes over!" Completely frustrated, Marcus left the room and slammed out of the house. He walked for three hours until the sun was going down and a cool breeze was coming in from off the bay. When he returned to his home for the past twenty-two years, his bags were sitting on the porch. "Damn that woman," he muttered under his breath. His only option was the hotel that night, so he walked around to the Battle House and got a room. It was a miserable night of tossing and turning and wanting Callie.

Homestead

Tragedy on the River

Nate had never joined a church. He was a believer, but his religious education had not progressed after his parents died. Churches were few and far between, making it especially hard to attend when someone was on the move hunting work as much as he had been. He had told Melissa he wanted to join and be baptized, so on the first Sunday of the month, when they had a regular service with Reverend Lock there, he went up during the invitation and joined. The minister asked the usual questions: do you promise to support the Methodist Church with your presence, your talents and your tithe, and so on? Nate said that he did, and after the service, he was asked to join the minister at the front door where everyone greeted him and welcomed him into the church as they left. Nate was very proud of his membership.

Nate told Melissa on the way home that he had pledged in his heart to live a new life with God first, then her and their family next. He was very happy. He said he felt he had been richly blessed and wanted God to know how much he appreciated all He had done for him. Melissa was especially delighted. She had talked to Nate many times about her religious beliefs. She had been taught that God was all-powerful, all-knowing and that He was able to do anything. That had been a great comfort to her many times — a real present help in time of trouble.

With the crops laid by and the gathering done, Nate began working around the cabin in earnest. He started early and worked until late, because the weather was good and there were things yet to be done, such as build on to the split rail-fence, enlarging it enough to encompass a small portion of the creek so the cow, pigs and Dewey could get to the water. That way they could be left in the patch to graze with plenty of water for three or four days if he had to be gone. He could put the calf in with its mother so it could nurse and keep her bag from getting so full it would spoil. He also built a washhouse for Melissa. It was attached to the cabin in back right beside the well. The cabin would provide a wall on one side; then he added two more sides that would knock most of the wind off of her in the cold weather and also provide a place for the baby to be out of the cold when it was moderate enough to have the baby out with her. She could take the cradle out, bundle the baby up and they could be close to each other.

Melissa spent some of those days at her mother's working on baby clothes and doing other sewing she needed to do. Lily helped her greatly once she got Liz and Mary's school clothes finished for the year. She was an expert seamstress. She also made all the covers they needed by quilting — an art Melissa had started to learn. Melissa had plenty of clothes for the time she was carrying the baby — clothes that could be adjusted for later on, also. Lily made them full in the waist with buttons on the sides where they could be let out or taken up as needed. Her tummy was swelling with each passing day so that the secret could no longer be kept. Nobody said anything, however, except Martha and Grace and one or two others of her friends. Pregnancy was just not talked about in social gatherings.

Another chore Nate had to complete was smoking the rats out of the barn. He had moved Buttons and the kittens out there several days before to catch rats, but there was such a population that she could not keep up, and the kittens were too little to help. He gathered up some very dry cow chips from the cow lot that had a lot of grass in them. Next, he placed them in an old lard can and set them on fire. The manure didn't readily burn but it smoked like mad, causing the rats and mice to desert the barn in bunches. Nate could shoot them with the rifle or hit them with the rake if there were too many for Buttons to catch. They would come back, but at least he cleared them out for a time, saving a little corn, peanuts and other grain. Rodents made a big dent in the winter store of seeds.

"You know what I think I'll do today," Nate told Melissa one morning. "I am going to the creek fishing. We haven't had fish in awhile." They loved the bream he caught so readily right down the hill at the little stream, not to mention how Nate loved catching them. He often hunted late in the afternoon, with John's shotgun, killing enough quail, doves or rabbits for them, and Lily and the girls when John was gone. Game was so plentiful that the woods would almost sustain them especially combined with what they grew. Sugar, flour and just a few other staples were all they had to buy.

Melissa said she was going to lie down for awhile with her feet up. Her ankles had begun to swell a little and backaches had become common. She was in her sixth month as best she could calculate, making her need for rest during the day greater.

Lily had spent most of the afternoon cleaning her yards. She was tired, so she sat down on the porch to rest and fan herself when she heard a horse rapidly approaching with hooves clopping loudly on the hard-packed dirt of the road. The rider was in a mighty hurry. Nobody rode like that unless there was an emergency! Her heart felt as if it literally stopped as a man rode up into the lane. She always feared a stranger, not knowing what his business was, so she glanced about for Liz and Mary. They were working on their school assignments on the back porch, but both had stopped to see what was going on as the rider brought the horse to a stop. He threw the reins over the fence post, took off his hat and approached the yard. "Mrs. Tate?" he asked.

Lily had become alarmed. "Yes?" she answered, fearing the worst. "I am Mrs. Tate."

"I am mighty sorry to be the bearer of bad news, but …

He paused as if dreading to tell her the rest.

"Go on! Please!" she begged. "Is it John? Is it my husband?"

"I am afraid so, ma'am." He hesitated again hating to tell this poor lady who seemed to be alone except for the two young daughters.

"Go on, sir. Please!"

"Well, Mr. Tate was found on the river, the Yellow River, with a bullet in his back." With that, Lily let out a little cry and collapsed, fainting dead away onto the porch floor. The girls, hearing what the man said, ran to their mother, both starting to sob, while the stranger grabbed a fan in the rocker next to her and began fanning her furiously. "Girls, get some water," he commanded. Mary jumped up and ran for the water bucket on the shelf at the end of the porch and raced back to her mother. The man poured the water in Lily's face, causing her to splutter and start coming to. As she did, the realization of what she had just been told began to sink in.

"John? Oh, John. How did it happen? Where?" was all she could ask in her agony.

"It was on the river, and he was found by some hunters. He was drifting in a canoe."

"When did it happen? Do you know when?" Lily managed.

"No, but it had been a few days."

"Oh!" she cried. The girls were clinging to her as if to assuage some of their pain and hurt.

"Can he be brought home? I want to arrange for him to come home," she pled.

The stranger didn't want to tell her the whole truth. "Do you have any other family around I can notify, Mrs. Tate? Perhaps if

Tragedy on the River

I could go and get someone for you?"

Mary finally was able to speak through her shock. "My sister and her husband live just two miles across the woods. You could go there and tell them." He looked quite relieved and said he would be back as soon as he could let them know.

Nate had no more than gotten to the fishing hole and begun to fish when the man arrived at the cabin. Melissa, being cautious, was afraid to answer the door; so she opened it a crack when she heard him call out "Hello! Anybody home?" She could hear an element of distress in the man's voice and knew it was no ordinary visit.

"Yes?" she answered through the crack.

The man, not realizing her delicate condition, told her straight out, "Ma'am, your daddy's met with foul play." The news hit her full force. It didn't take any time for it to sink in, at which time she began to scream. The poor stranger, not knowing what to do, just stood there. Then he saw the dinner bell. He walked over and began ringing it as hard as he could while Melissa tried to compose herself. "How?" was her first question. Wanting to avoid telling this poor girl the sad truth, he tried to change the subject temporarily.

"Is your husband at home?" he asked, knowing he wasn't or he would have shown himself by now. Melissa, realizing he was a stranger in the community, was still leery of letting him get too close or telling him too much. She knew Nate would hear the bell, so she stalled about telling him she was alone.

"Where did this happen? When did it happen?" she wanted facts in order to judge the validity of what he was telling her.

"We are not sure when it happened. He was found afloat on Yellow River yesterday." The news had traveled fast, because John Tate was a well-known man of note, and being a government man, it was big news that he had been killed, especially being shot in the back. The man went over and rang the bell again just as hard as before. Melissa realized he could not mean her any harm if he were ringing the bell to alert anyone in the area who might hear it. Nate was not that far away, so she knew he would be arriving any minute. Nate had heard the bell and was rushing as fast as he could up the hill to the cabin. When he got there, he saw Melissa was in an awful state and a strange man was standing there, hat in hand.

"Hello, sir," the man said. "I am Wilson McLean with the sheriff's office. I have had the sad duty to let your wife here and her mother up the way know that Mr. Tate has been killed." Nate didn't believe it. Shock took over his whole body and he felt as if he were going to faint, although he had never done that in his life. A mixture of grief and shock almost overwhelmed him. Not John! Of all people, not John, the man who had become a surrogate father to him. The man who had taught him so much, and upon whom he had come to rely so much. Then he thought of Lily and the girls.

"Melissa, we must go up to the big house to your mother. I'll get Dewey." He called a "thank you" back to the man as he ran for the barn. Dewey instinctively knew something was wrong. He could always sense trouble in Nate's voice and neighed loudly. Mr. McLean helped Melissa into the buggy as Nate brought it around, and told them he would follow. They went as fast as Nate dared in the little buggy with Melissa in her condition. Mr. McLean was right behind them on his horse. As soon as they entered the lane, they could hear crying. Melissa had quieted a little and begun to ask questions which Nate couldn't answer, but when she heard her mother and sisters crying, she started up again.

"Wait, sweetheart, until we get there. Just wait and Mr. Whatever-His-Name-Is will be able to tell us more, I am sure. He has come to tell us what he can."

Nate stopped the horse, looped the reins over the gatepost as he had always done and helped Melissa down. She ran to her mother, gathered her in her arms and the two women cried like babies while the man, Nate and the sisters stood by helplessly. Mary and Liz were having trouble getting it to sink in that their father was gone. Nate invited Mr. McLean to come up on the porch and have a seat. "Miss Lily, this man has more information, and I think we need to hear it. Go ahead, sir," he said to the poor messenger.

McLean looked as if he'd like to run somewhere and hide. It was clear and evident he did not relish his task of telling these people what had really happened to John Tate, but it was one of his duties at the sheriff's office. He looked at the ground, cleared his throat and finally, realizing the task was not going away, began to speak. Five pairs of eyes were boring holes into him wanting information. "Well, they found him yesterday. I got here as soon as I could. You see, John was shot from behind and set adrift in a canoe." He paused as if to let that sink in amid the shock and despair. Then continuing, he said, "It was about ten yesterday morning when two hunters were walking along the edge of the river and spied the canoe with what they thought was some kind of bag in it. When they got close, they could see it was a body." McLean looked terribly uncomfortable at having to tell them the next part, but Melissa asked him to please go on. She wanted to hear the details. "Perhaps, if I could talk to you alone?" he said, looking at Nate.

"No!" Melissa shouted. "I want to know what happened to my daddy!" Lily nodded her assent as well.

"We are stronger than you think, Mr. McLean," she said. "I am sorry I fainted a while ago, but I can take it. I must know what has happened to John." With that, he went ahead.

"Apparently, Mr. Tate had testified against some poachers who were working for the Callahan Lumber Company, and we figure some one of them did this. He was in court just the other day and, at that time, he told several people he knew they were out to get him. The sheriff is looking into this. We will find them. I know you are going to ask me about bringing the body home, but that won't be possible." Lily sucked in her breath and looked as if she were going to faint again. Melissa put her arms around her, and Liz and Mary looked as if they were finally getting the picture. Everyone was braced to hear why not.

"You see, this happened several days ago. Probably just after the trial, and the body was in bad shape when they found him. It was impossible to bring him home. They dug a hole on the riverbank and had to just dump the canoe. I sure am sorry, folks. I really am. John was a mighty fine man and a mighty good friend of mine." Nate was thinking about his parents and the situation when they died. No coffin. No real funeral. Nothing. Poor Melissa. Now he was worried about her losing this baby, but she appeared to be taking it better than her mother. He now shared something in common with Melissa; the pain of losing someone dear to you through tragedy. He hoped he could help her and be a comfort he didn't have when he lost his parents.

They talked on with Mr. McLean about the exact place of burial. Nate asked for the names of the two men who found the body. He wanted to contact them and thank them. He also wanted to go to the grave and needed to know from them where it was, but that would come later. Nate asked McLean if he would notify neighbors as he went along on the way back to Milton. He was happy to do so. He told Nate not to go into that area alone, though, when he got around to going. He said there could be more trouble and it would not be safe. He said the sheriff would send someone along with him. They thanked him for coming, and he left just as it was beginning to get dusk dark.

Nate decided he would have to take charge, because the women seemed unable to pull themselves together. "Listen now, there will be people here within an hour. The Rogers are going to come as soon as they hear. The Carpenters, everybody. We must get ourselves together and decide what we are going to do. We can't have a regular funeral, but what do you think about a memorial service at the church? I am sure Reverend Lock will be here as soon as he hears."

"I would like to have a service at the church. That is good," Lily said starting to cry again. She could only forget for a few moments, then the reality would set in again.

Melissa and the younger girls said they would like to have the service at the church, too. That way everyone could come. "Maybe it could be on Sunday after church," Nate suggested, and all agreed again. As the idea of being without John took hold in her mind, Lily was starting to think what on earth she would do without Nate. She could appreciate the fact that he was going to be a marvelous help to her and the girls now. She thanked God for him even amid her grief.

Nate's thoughts were of anger — even fury. He wanted to get his hands on the devils who had done this thing, and he vowed not to rest until he did. He began reliving the circumstances of his parents' murders. He had vowed the same thing then, but had become too engrossed in trying to make a living to do anything, but this would be different. John was a well-known, well-liked man who also had the government behind him. Perhaps he would not have to avenge John's death after all. Perhaps the government would take a hand. He was grieving and seething. It was hard for him to discern which emotion was strongest.

It was going to be a long, hard winter in Mobile unless something happened in a hurry, Callie decided. She had only worked two days on one case since being relieved of duty at the DeVilles'. Her money was running very low, and she had to do something fast. She had been able to see Marcus now and then, but not as much as she had hoped. He was getting his house worked on and getting settled there, which kept him busy, plus they had to see each other on the sly so as not to cause any more gossip than they already had. Mrs. Downing allowed them to sit in her parlor, and they were able to walk about the neighborhood at night, but that was all — a far cry from what they had been doing and wanted to do. So, Callie had reached a decision. The next time

Marcus came over, she would tell him. She had started packing. She was going home. She should have done that ages ago and never gotten mixed up with a patient's husband, a married man. She broke all the rules and she knew it. She had ruined her career, run up a large bill at the department store, failed her family in its time of need, and now she would have to suffer the consequences. She would tuck her tail and go home She would stay a while, help Pearl and then look for another job in another area — maybe Creighton.

Callie had wired her sister a cryptic message the week before saying, "Coming home. Can someone meet me?" When the messenger rode up with the telegram, Pearl read it, then turned around and wrote out a reply for him to take back with him which said, "Nobody to send. Hire a buggy." She had saved train fare, and that was about all, so she decided to leave the next day, Sunday.

When Marcus arrived that night for his visit, she told him the news. "I can't stay here another day, Marcus. I have no more money."

"Do you have train fare?"

"Yes, I have train fare, but I won't see you." Then she began to cry. The whole thing had finally caught up with her, and she sobbed from the depths of her soul. She had been brave, spunky, hopeful and encouraging to him as long as she could. She had kept up a front to Mrs. Downing, her roommate and everyone with whom she had come in contact, but she had reached the end of her tolerance. All her hopes had finally been dashed.

"Callie, darling. There, there. All is not lost. I am going to be coming up to see you, of course. Never fear, and we will have long walks in those woods of yours, days to lounge and enjoy each other's company, events to attend and time to spend together. I promise you that." But nothing he could say helped. Nothing could remove the fact she had made a complete fool of herself, disgraced herself and now she had to go home broke. She could hear her family now — well, maybe Pearl only. Her mother was very ill, and her father was in no condition to say much. His days of awareness were about over. He just sat mostly in his wheelchair beside his wife and moaned and groaned. Of course, the community would wonder, but let them. Nobody there had ever had the gumption to get out and better themselves.

After trying to quiet Callie, Marcus began telling her things he wanted her to remember. "Now, sweetheart, don't forget those wonderful nights we spent together. There will be more. I will be up to see you just as soon as I get moved into the house and settle in." How could Callie forget the wonderful nights? They were what got her into this fix to start with, but they were worth it! Her old spunk started to return as she dried her tears thinking about his first visit to Fox Hollow. There were things they could do all right.

"Come soon, please. I will be living for your visits. Promise me, Marc."

"I will, darling." They were standing on the porch at Mrs. Downing's in the shadows away from the gaslights on the street. He put his arms around her, pulled her to him and kissed her as he had never kissed her before. Callie could feel herself melting into those arms remembering why she had succumbed to his charms to start with when she never intended to.

"Oh, I *wish* there were some place we could go," he whispered.

"I know," Callie said. "My roommate is on duty for the entire weekend. We can go up to our room!"

"But Mrs. Downing. What if she saw us? That is too risky. Your reputation, Callie."

"My reputation! Why, Marc, what a silly thing to say! My reputation was ruined long ago by Margaret, and I have ceased to care. I just want you," she whispered. "I will lock the door just in case someone comes up." But nobody did. It was a glorious last fling designed to last for many weeks. When Marcus left, it was almost dawn. Callie would summon a rig and leave for the train in just three hours.

Homestead

The ride to the train station was nostalgic for the little country girl from Fox Hollow who had been so impressed with city life. She loved the huge old trees forming a tunnel across the streets. She loved the sounds of the city waking up to another day, a day she would not be enjoying there. If it were not for Margaret and her refusal to divorce Marc. What could she possibly hope to gain by not giving him a divorce? She had nothing to offer any longer but two useless legs. For that matter, she had, in Callie's opinion, very little to offer ever. What on earth had he seen in her — oh yeah, money, power and position. She supposed men were the same the world over. They all wanted all of that.

Memorial Service

As soon as the community heard about John's death, people started going over to see Lily and the family. They prepared food — enough food to feed an army — but it was all eaten, because the folks stayed for, what seemed to Lily, like days. It was really only the better part of three days. She was in such a state of shock and grief that the faces swam before her, offering condolences, help in any form, money or whatever she needed while all she needed was John back. The reality of it would not seem to take hold. Every thought she had was of him, of what he was going to do when he got home, of what they were going to do in the future, of John, John, John. Every waking moment, no matter who was there or what was happening, all she could think of was John. Her head knew he was gone, but her heart would not believe it. Part of the time, the weight on her chest was overwhelming. It hurt to breathe. Her head hurt from crying, and there were no more tears. Her eyes were almost swollen closed. One minute she would feel things were going to be all right, the next she felt she couldn't go on. She was no help to her children at that point. That would have to come later when she could somehow cope. She knew what John would want her to do, but the strength was not there.

Nate, although sorely grieved, mustered the strength to support Melissa. He was greatly concerned about her, but she held up and didn't have a bit of trouble with the pregnancy. She was angered beyond words. That, no doubt, helped her keep going. She wanted the men who killed her father to hang, and so did Nate. They vowed never to rest until those men were found. Nate intended to go to Milton shortly after the memorial service and talk to the sheriff. What he and Melissa did not know was that since John was a federal man, the murder would be investigated by other federal agents.

The church was packed for the service. After everyone was in and seated, Nate helped Lily and Melissa out of the buggy, along with the girls, who were in a daze. The congregation stood as they walked down the aisle and to the front pew. The choir sang "In the Sweet By and By," accompanied by Harry Daugette, who had played the violin for Melissa and Nate's wedding. The ladies sobbed, and Nate had to steel himself to keep from crying. Melissa kept thinking that her daddy would never see the baby, while Liz and Mary were thinking he'd never be able to give them away at their weddings. At least Melissa had had that.

The church was packed, with people even standing outside. It was the biggest service anyone in the whole area had ever seen, which made the Tate ladies very proud. Some of John's associates drove buggies or rode horses all the way out from Milton. One man rode Belle, the horse assigned to John for his work, so that when it was time to go out to the newly created cemetery and place a cross the family had bought with his name, date of birth and date of death on it, the man led Belle out to the site, without a rider, to signify a fallen rider. When they got out to the cemetery, the choir sang "When the Roll is Called Up Yonder, I'll Be There." Nate glanced around after the song, noticing there wasn't a dry eye among the whole group.

Reverend Lock, knowing John as well as he had, was able to eulogize him to the fullest. He told of John's faith, his dedication to his family, friends and the community, and how he had been instrumental in building the church. To the family he said, "There is no limit to the height you can reach in the spiritual realm, and I know John Tate has reached great heights. I would that you, too, could live in high places and never have to go down to the valley, but here on earth, we must have valleys. Yet we can live so that when our time comes to meet our Lord, we can reach great heights in the spiritual realm. John would want his family and friends to do that."

At the cemetery, Lily, the girls and Nate all helped move the cross into the hole that had already been dug for it. Then the deacons, of whom John had been a member, took turns putting shovels of dirt into the hole.

Reverend Lock closed by asking everyone to join in the Lord's Prayer. It was getting very late and cool by the time the service was over, but many people still followed the family back to the house, as was the custom, and helped finish the food which had been brought in.

Mozelle Weeks, Sara Helms, Clara Rogers, Eva Carpenter and several others of Lily's friends hugged her and told her they would be available if she needed anything at all. They said the hardest time would be after everyone left and she was alone. Lily would find that to be true.

Nate and Melissa stayed at Lily's the week following the service. Franklin Rogers cared for their animals while they were at Lily's. He was glad Nate had enlarged the patch so the stock could get water down at the stream.

Callie's return to Fox Hollow caused quite a stir in the homestead community. There was speculation about why she left Mobile, but Callie wasn't talking. She simply told her family she knew she was needed. Then when she saw the condition her mother was in, she *knew* that was the truth. Her guilt increased after realizing she had let her family down terribly by not getting there sooner. Well, she was home, and she would make up for it.

Mozelle Weeks, who had trouble keeping her mouth shut anyway, went to the store shortly after Callie got home, to get supplies. Pearl was behind the counter when she walked in. "I hear your sister finally got home," she said. "What happened in Mobile? Didn't she like the city?"

"Yes, she just came home to help," was all Pearl answered.

"Took her long enough," came the reply from Mozelle. Pearl gave her a "none of your business" look, filled the order and told her very curtly to come again. Pearl, irritated as she had been with Callie, certainly wasn't discussing her family affairs with Mozelle Weeks. Tactless old lady.

As Mozelle drove by the house on her way home, Callie happened to be hanging out sheets, so Mozelle got a whack at her, too. "Hello Callie. Welcome home. What brought you back?" she asked. Callie, knowing her as she did, just said hello, turned her back and went right on hanging out clothes. Mozelle took one parting shot as she drove off. "I thought you were getting quite a name for yourself down there in the big city!" Callie was thinking, yes, I surely did, and if you only knew! She told Pearl and her father about Marcus, but she told them only that he was separated from his wife, who wouldn't give him a divorce and not why or how that all came about. At least they wouldn't be expecting them to get married one day.

Nate mentioned to Melissa that Callie had come home. "I can't possibly work any longer for Pearl with mother needing me, so it is a good thing Callie came home," Melissa told Nate as they talked about things that were going on. Liz and Mary had gone back to school, leaving Lily alone during the day. Nate had to be working about the place, which would have left Melissa alone, so it was good to have the two women together. He would have double the work to do now with two places to keep up, so he couldn't continue at Mr. Mac's either. They had already told Pearl to begin looking for someone to tend the farm. Lily mentioned having Nate and Melissa move up to the big house, but neither wanted to do that. They felt with the baby coming it would be best if they had a place of their own. They told her they'd spend a lot of time up there anyway. Melissa had already helped Lily go through John's clothes, most of which she gave to Nate. They had been about the same size, and clothing was a thing nobody wasted.

As the days wore on after John's death, Lily became somewhat consoled, although still sad and lonely. Melissa and her sisters were adjusting, too, but she became aware that Nate had a strange attitude, especially about church. One Sunday morning he told her he would hitch the horse to the buggy for her, but that he didn't want to go. Somewhat puzzled, she tried to draw him out and discuss his strange behavior. Nate refused to talk about it, however. "Nathan, you have never refused to go to church before. What on earth is wrong, dear?" she asked. She was caught completely off guard.

"I just don't see any point in going to worship a God that takes away people we love," was all he would say, so Melissa drove the buggy up to her mother's and told her she didn't think she would go either. She felt Nate needed her. She was also finding it hard to sit through a service so soon after the memorial service. Being seven months pregnant didn't help, either. Lily and the girls were willing to forego church that Sunday, also. They decided to have a big Sunday dinner, instead, and sent Liz down to the cabin to get Nate. They had not talked about the particulars of John's death until that day, when they began talking about exactly what happened. Nate announced that he was planning to go to Milton and talk with the sheriff right away, which pleased the rest of the family greatly.

"We have to find out some more details," Nate told them. "I want to know exactly where he is buried, and later see if we can have the remains moved home."

"So do I," Lily agreed. Then the girls chimed in, echoing what Lily and Nate had said. Nobody would be content until John was home and the killers brought to justice. That was that, then. Nate would go to Milton the next week.

Homestead

The week after John's memorial service, Pearl talked with a stranger who came by the store looking for work.

"Name's Talbot, Hector Talbot, but everyone just calls me Heck. I am looking for work, ma'am." He was a nice enough looking man. Not handsome exactly, but strong, good features, and he was neat with reddish hair, a mustache and neatly trimmed beard. Pearl liked the man right off. She really needed someone and had put the word out in the community. Perhaps someone referred him to her.

"Did you hear that I needed someone, Mr. Talbot?" she asked.

"No, I just happened this way. I was on my way up to the area to see if I could work at the turpentine still and thought I'd stop by here first," the tall stranger said.

"I do need someone to tend the field, help me here at the store and do odd jobs about the place. I can't handle everything myself. My father is in a wheelchair, unable to work, and my mother has had a stroke."

"You didn't name anything I can't do. I am available right here and now," he told her. She explained how the teams came in with wagons loaded with heavy goods that he would need to unload. She told him about the acreage and how it was managed and so on.

So they settled on the pay, she showed him the makeshift bunkhouse, and they were in business. Nate had left the place spotless when he moved. All it needed was a little dusting and sweeping up. Heck had a few clothes in a bundle, and that was about all. Pearl wondered where he had come from that he had so little. He appeared to be about her same age. Surely he could have acquired more by now. Or maybe he only brought a small part of what he owned. Maybe the rest was elsewhere. She would inquire about him from passersby. Someone would know more about him, and he might volunteer more later. She only hoped he wasn't some kind of a crook. Everyone had been taught to be suspicious of strangers. They had heard about carpetbaggers, Yankees and all sorts of weird people.

Memorial Service

On the way to the bunkhouse, they encountered Callie, who was sitting on the back steps resting while supper cooked. She had taken over the cooking again, along with the care of her parents. When Pearl introduced Heck, he said, "I'm pleased to meet you, Miss Callie. I'm here to help with whatever I can."

"The first thing I have to request, Heck, is that you go and get the mail." She told him how to get to Mrs. Gay's and told him to ride Sam. "That horse will be so glad to get out of the lot for awhile. He may run all the way," she told him. "He hasn't been ridden since Nate York left."

"I will go first thing tomorrow."

Things were busy at the York-Tate houses. Hogs had to be killed on the first cool day. Once that was done and the bacon and sausage was hanging in the smokehouse, everyone could relax. Winter could come. Nate had gotten plenty of wood in for both places. He had to think double now. He kept thinking also of what John had said to him about being glad he was in the family in case John was not there anymore. John must have had a premonition, or did he outright know someone was planning to kill him? Nate had not told the family about his last conversation with John on the way to make Eulon's coffin. Oh, God, Nate kept thinking. Why on earth didn't I do something? Why didn't I draw him out more and try to see what he was really thinking? How could I have been so stupid? Had he told Miss Lily about his concerns? Surely not. She hated the job anyway, and would have probably insisted he quit it. Nate would eventually tell all of the women about what John had said, but he feared they would blame him for not saying something. Nate had that burden to carry now, along with the one regarding Rose. He must go to Milton right away.

Callie waited anxiously for Heck to return with the mail. She had waited so long to hear from Marcus. Maybe he had changed his mind and gone back to Margaret. Men did things like that, and the women took them back. In Margaret's condition, she would never find another man, so she would surely take Marcus back.

As Heck rounded the corner of the Sewards' field, she could hear the horse's hooves pounding on the hard surface of the road. He rode right up to the back door where Callie waited and handed over the mail. There it was! Right on top — the beautifully drawn letters of his handwriting to Miss Callie McDougald. Her long, slender fingers trembled as she tore the envelope open. It read:

> My Dearest Callie,
>
> My life has been dreary since you left, and I miss you more than you can imagine. I long to see you more with each passing day.
>
> I have only seen Margaret once, when I went over to pack some more of my things. I have almost finished with my house and soon can move everything. I will not need to see her again after that unless she agrees to a divorce. I am hoping against hope for that once she realizes I am not giving in to her this time. It should have ended long ago.
>
> I want you to remember, my darling, that I love you with all my heart, and am counting the days until I can go to visit you. You are my soul mate, the woman I have always loved in my dreams.
>
> If everything goes as planned, I should be able to leave here in two weeks for a visit with you. Expect me around the first of the month. I will go up on the train and hire a rig in Creighton. Until then,
>
> I love you, dearest.
> Yours forever,
> Marcus DeVille

Memorial Service

Callie nearly cried with relief that he had not gone back to Margaret and with joy that he truly planned to come to Fox Hollow. She decided she had better prepare Pearl and her father for the visit. She would tell them only what she had to, that his wife would not give him a divorce, so they couldn't get married, but intended to see each other as often as they could.

From the moment Pearl saw the tall man walk into the store, she was attracted to him. There was something about his bony face, deep-set eyes and tall frame that was interesting to her. It was a strong physical attraction Heck had felt also. They both knew they wanted this to develop. Heck thought of her as the most woman he had seen in awhile, her large breasts, small waist and height made her handsome although not actually pretty. Her long hair had some curl, which showed when she put it up, letting some strands fall about her face. He also admired her determination, what with her parents ill, the farm and store to run. She had her hands full. He was glad he could help. Heck saw Callie as aloof and not interested in anyone but herself. She also appeared quite unhappy. She was certainly interested in the letter she got from M. DeVille, whoever that was. He wondered what her story was.

Nate left early in the morning for Milton riding Dewey. It was not even daylight but only first light, as they say. It was a very long trip that would probably necessitate spending the night. He would let the horse rest, stay at the hotel and leave for home the next morning, if he had completed his business. Melissa was at Lily's, so he could stay two nights if need be. It was foggy at first, particularly in the bottoms, giving the earth an ethereal look. Nate felt forlorn and was not at all relishing the task before him, so the sun was a welcome sight coming up through the trees. He was approaching a small creek with thick swamp along its edges when suddenly a bobcat let out a loud scream. Dewey shied, reared straight up on his hind legs, and threw Nate, who was caught completely off guard, sprawling into the edge of the creek.

He was not hurt, but his clothes were wet and terribly muddy. Having figured he might have to stay overnight, he took a change of clothes. He quickly put them on right there in the edge of the creek. He was pleased with his careful planning. Dewey was still distressed and wanted to get out of the area. Nate calmed him the best he could, remounted, and they were on their way. The bobcat had apparently gone on wherever he was going, also.

The homestead community was in a stir of late over Missy Rogers getting married. The wedding was coming up the next weekend with everyone invited. It was to be at the church, but when Nate had told Melissa, she said she wasn't going.

"What?" Nate asked, completely puzzled.""Why, I didn't think wild horses could keep you from going to a wedding." He thought it might be her condition. She was getting pretty big, but she was really quite proud of being in the family way.

"I don't want to go and have Missy drool all over you like she always does, and I don't like that jarhead she is marrying any better than I do her!"

"Melissa York! She is getting married, for goodness sakes. She surely isn't interested in me. Never was. That was just your imagination all the time."

"No, it wasn't," Melissa said emphatically. Her very blue eyes were snapping, and her cheeks were flushed. Nate could see she was serious.

"Well, if you don't go, it will look odd. You will miss a good time, too." Then getting a little of the devil in him, he said,""I promise not to let her drool on me one bit, so there now. You can go."

Melissa seemed to have a lot of the devil in her that day when she countered with,""And I don't want to give her a present, either."

Lily was struggling to just keep going and had not made anything for Missy, either, as she usually would have done. They talked about the wedding while Melissa was staying up there.

Memorial Service

Lily said she doubted she would go. The matter continued to be unresolved for awhile longer until Nate got home from Milton.

At the McDougald residence, the ladies were talking about Missy and the wedding, too. Callie knew she couldn't leave her parents, but Pearl wanted to go. She had kept up on all the preparations since Missy and Miss Clara were in the store all the time buying material and other needed items for the wedding. But Callie thought little of the whole tacky deal. It paled in comparison to weddings in Mobile. She missed the lovely homes with china, crystal, Persian rugs, heavy drapes and beautiful furniture, mostly imported. Oh, well. Things might have been different.

Heck said he would be very happy to drive Pearl to the church for the wedding. Callie said she would stay home with their parents, and Pearl could close the store early. She closed at noon on Saturday, anyway.

Nate tied Dewey up to the hitching post beside the frame building where the sheriff had his quarters. There was a small jail that would hold three or four on a busy Saturday night after the logging and turpentine crowd got to town and drank for a few hours. There was usually a fight of some sort — the kind that blew over after the participants slept for a few hours behind bars. Two or three men were hanging out next door in the barber shop spitting tobacco juice out into the sandy street and swapping stories they had each heard dozens of times. They eyed Nate suspiciously, wondering where he had come from and why.

The steps into the office were rickety. All it would have taken to make them sturdier was several well-placed nails, but it never occurred to anyone to fix anything until it fell down completely. Sheriff Mills was looking over some papers on his desk.—"What can I do for you?" he asked as Nate sank wearily into a chair provided beside the dust-laden desk.

"My father-in-law, John Tate, was murdered a short time ago. I am here to find out as much as I can about it and see what you are doing to find who did it. My name is Nathan York."

The sheriff leaned back in his creaky chair and studied Nate, thinking he is certainly to the point.

"Well, son, you are in the wrong pew. That case is being investigated by the government agents. John was a federal man." Nate was getting up again as fast as he had sat. He crammed the broad-brimmed felt hat he had just removed back on his head and prepared to leave. But Sheriff Mills continued. "Darn shame about John. He was a fine man. I hope they catch the scoundrels that did that. Good luck."

Nate thanked him, asked directions to the Federal Land Office and went out the door. A couple of ruffians passed him on the street and gave him the once over, but Nate didn't even look their way. He was in a hurry to talk to someone who could tell him something.

Lily was in a hurry to hear something, also. She was not bearing up well under the strain. Melissa went down to the cabin for a few hours the next day to be sure Trouble and Buttons were all right and to feed them. She checked the other animals, too, then headed back to her mother's. Lily, in the meantime, had started looking for something to ease the tension when she thought of the elderberry wine of which she had quite a stock. She had made it and blackberry for years and used very little except in cakes and cooking now and then. It was stored in the pantry beside the kitchen. Finding a bottle, she had a small glass; then in a little while another and finally one more. After that, she went out to clean her yards, thinking the activity would also help to work off her worries.

The yard brooms were outside the main yard, standing up in a barrel that had no top or bottom. The fence separating the yard from the field area was low enough that Lily decided to step over it rather than going all the way around to the little gate. She lifted one leg over and then felt a little dizzy. Oh, she thought, it is from the wine. Maybe I had a little too much. She couldn't get the other leg over, so she padded down toward the gate, but a fence post separated her from the gate that she couldn't get around. Then she backed down the fence a little way thinking she could find a lower spot and get the other leg over, but that wouldn't work, either. She was literally and hopelessly straddling the fence. More than that, she was a little drunk. All the while she padded back and forth, hoping to get the other leg over before Melissa got back.

Melissa took the buggy and put it in the buggy house, then she led Dixie into the lot, took the bridle off and gave her a love smack on her broad backside. When she went into the house, her mother was nowhere in sight. Thinking she must have started supper, she wandered on down the hall looking as she went. Mary and Liz were still at school. Melissa was getting rather concerned when she suddenly saw her mother outside in the backyard walking up and down the fence. She ran out there to help yelling, "Mama, what are you trying to do?" as she went. Lily had a sneaky look on her face that Melissa understood when she got close enough to help her get the other leg over.

"Mama, for goodness sakes. You have been drinking!" she exclaimed. Never in her entire life had she ever seen her mother take a drink of anything. "What *is* going on?"

Lily hiccupped loudly not bothering to answer and explain herself. In fact, she looked rather defiant.

Then it occurred to Melissa that she had a pantry full of wine. "You'd better leave that stuff alone. I may not come along next time," she told her errant mother.

Homestead

Hired Help

Pearl got a new dress for Missy's wedding, something she hadn't done in ages. She was ready ahead of time, so she wandered outside in the back and sat in the swing, which hung from the big oak near Heck's quarters, to wait for him. It was cool enough for her to wear a shawl, but she was careful not to have it cover the cleavage of her ample bosoms. The dress accentuated her small waist, which was one of her better assets, along with her bust line. She had rouged her cheeks just enough to add a healthy glow, and her dress was lovely. It was a soft rose chosen especially because it complimented her complexion and made her dark hair look even darker. All in all, she was a striking woman. It paid to manage a store. She could at least have access to nice clothes when she needed them, and she needed them now if she ever had! She wondered what the community would be saying when she arrived at the church on Heck's arm.

"Well, Miss Pearl, you sure are a pretty sight this afternoon," Heck said, startling her out of her daydream.

"I am going to be mighty proud to escort you to the wedding." She stood, giving him a better look, and he didn't miss the cleavage. His eyes rested for just a flickering moment between her breasts, then moved over her entire body admiringly. Pearl felt little sensations going through her unlike any she had ever felt before. My word, she wondered, can this be what love is like?

When Heck brought the buggy around, he took her arm, lifted it slightly and helped her into the seat. Then he got in, sitting as close as he could to her. They rode that way the entire four or more miles to the church, both perfectly aware of the presence of the other. Pearl knew she needed to know more, much more, about Heck before falling hopelessly in love, yet somehow she had a wonderful sense of well being when she was in his presence.

They rode along for perhaps half a mile, each lost in his and her own thoughts. Finally, it was Heck who broke the silence. "I know you have a lot of questions to ask me, and I want to answer them, but first, I need to tell you something. I am not just a young sprout who wants to play the courting game. I am a grown man. I have been in the war. I was wounded at Shiloh, and I really don't feel I have any time to waste. Life is a serious and too short business for me to waste time. I am very attracted to you, and I would like to know if you feel the same about me?"

Pearl was taken aback, to say the least, but in such a wonderful way. What a perfectly divine man! As soon as she could get her balance, she began to formulate her answer. "I understand exactly what you are saying. It makes perfect sense to me, and I feel the same way you do. I do have some questions. You are right about that, but I am sure you can answer them to my satisfaction. I just want to know about your life. There is nothing to tell about mine except that I have lived in Fox Hollow all my life. I have not been anywhere to speak of, and I have been taking care of my parents and the store for the past couple of years pretty much alone. Now, please proceed."

As they drove along, he took her hand in his and began telling her how old he was (just a few years older than she) where he had come from and about his war experience. It was about as Pearl had suspected. Nothing out of the ordinary except that he had a small disability pension from the leg injury that he could live on if he had to. "I surely don't plan to live on that small check, but it will help to add it to what I earn. My folks are living back in Georgia, and I want to see them from time to time, but right now, I just want to see what I can do on my own."

After the wedding, they drove back home in the dark except for the lantern on the buggy. Just as they got to the pond south of the house, Heck stopped the buggy. He reached for the woman beside him who came into his arms as though she had waited all her life for that moment. As his mouth found hers in the darkness, he whispered, "Pearl McDougald, I have wanted to do this since I first laid eyes on you." He kissed her softly at first, then roughly, passionately and then his big hands began to roam over her entire body as though to acquaint himself with every inch of her. Pearl was overcome with passion. As Heck got down from the buggy, he lifted her, holding her around the waist, onto the ground.

The grass was as soft as a carpet at the spot where he first laid his coat and then gently laid Pearl on top of it. She was powerless to stop herself, knowing there could be dire consequences, and thinking all the while that she didn't care. She had heard of a place in Creighton where problems could be taken care of, and knew, in fact, of some young ladies who had used the services of that place. She would worry about that if and when it became necessary. For now, feeling his breath as he kissed her neck, then continued on down to her breasts and finally began to slip the dress off her shoulders, was heavenly. It was a though time stood still and nothing else mattered. Let this moment never end, she prayed. She had never made love before, and he was a wonderful teacher.

It was well after dark when Nate got back to Lily's after spending only one night in Milton. He had news, but not exactly what everyone hoped to hear. How could he tell the women that John's body was entirely too decomposed to move? There were no facilities for doing such a thing. How could he tell them the federal men had no idea who killed him? He could only say that they were looking into it and hoped one day someone would talk. There were rumors that Atlantic Land and Lumber Company had hired someone to get rid of him so the company could cut tracts of timber which were at that time off limits. The agents had nothing for certain at that time, however. They had taken information from Nate that John had given him during their last conversation about his fears and promised to notify the family of any developments. Melissa and Nate went on home that night, because they had things to do.

When they got into bed, they talked for a long time. Melissa cried because of her disappointment that nothing came of Nate's trip. "Something may come up later, sweetheart," Nate told her. "The agents were very hopeful." They were all upset that the body couldn't be moved home. How could Nate tell them nobody even knew exactly where it was buried? The men who found him afloat were not sure right where it was.

It was late in the night. Everyone was in bed when the squeaking started. It was always late when it started. Rose curled into a ball, but it didn't help. The squeaking came down the hall and into her room. She pretended to be asleep, but that didn't help either. She felt the cover being moved off of her; felt her legs getting cold. Then the cold moved up and all over her body as the cover was pulled off entirely, then it began. The hands. The rough hands that probed and hurt her. The smell was bad, too. There was always the smell of sweat and chewing tobacco. Never clean the way she smelled. The breathing was heavy. It got heavier and heavier. Rose wanted to die. She didn't know what die meant, but she wanted to do anything that would be better. Tomorrow, when it was daylight she would do something to make it better. She had to. She had to find a way to make the hurting stop. She wanted the squeaking to stop!

When the cow didn't get home at the usual time to be milked, there was some discussion at the McDougalds' about her being a

Hired Help

little thin from having another calf and about her age. She was not young anymore, so there was the possibility she was in a bog somewhere. They decided to wait until the next morning. Then they would start hunting. Morning came, but still no cow. Heck was going to look for her but needed Pearl to go and show him the way to the nearest bog. Callie said she would get breakfast while they went to look. They had to hurry so Pearl could get back and open the store.

The woods were showing the effects of one frost. It was a cool morning. Leaves were down covering the forest floor and pine straw made a carpet under every huge pine. They were down in the ravine just about to the bog when Pearl stumbled, almost falling. Heck grabbed for her. When he caught her, he pulled her to him. Then the kisses and caresses began. What a wonderfully soft and beautiful body she had. He wanted to devour her totally. Once again Pearl was helpless. Heck pulled her down on to a pine straw mat. She was ready for him instantly.

They knew they couldn't linger as they had done the first time, but there would be other opportunities.

The cow was in the bog. They couldn't get right up to her. It was too wet with mud three feet deep, which was going to require the horse, ropes and sacks to get her out. Heck felt he could manage it alone with the horse when he got back with the things he needed.

"Let's get back to the house. Now that I know where she is, I can bring the horse down here, and I think I can pull her out," Heck told Pearl. The cow made a humming sound. Not even a moo. She had tried to get out until she was completely exhausted and had given up. Her soulful eyes were pleading as Heck and Pearl made their way back up the hill and left her.

Pearl got the straw and twigs out of her hair and off of her clothes before going back to the house. Starting up the steep hill, Heck took her in his arms once more. "Pearl, I have thought of nothing but you since the day we went to the wedding. I am in love with you, and I want you all the time. I lie awake in the bunkhouse aching for you."

Pearl told him she felt the same way. "I can't concentrate at the store. I look forward to seeing you milking the cow or throwing hay to the horses. I am constantly looking out the window just to catch sight of you."

Heck said, "I think we should plan to get married and soon. We can't go on this way. You could have a child, and I don't want to bring disgrace to you. Will you marry me? Soon?"

Pearl's heart was pumping so hard she felt dizzy! Marry him! She hadn't really expected a proposal this quickly, but he was right. Anything could happen. Someone was bound to find out about their little trysts and then she would truly be disgraced. Mozelle Weeks would surely love to find out about her and Heck.

Hired Help

She would have every tongue in the whole community wagging. Besides, Pearl's conscience was bothering her something awful, too. She was doing something that was frowned upon terribly. Opportunity didn't always knock at all in Fox Hollow, and it might never knock for her again, so her answer was fast and sure. "Yes, I will marry you and soon."

"Wonderful! Then it is settled. You start making plans, and so will I!" Heck said as they hurried up the hill to the house. "We can talk more tonight. Go ahead and tell your family if you want to."

Pearl's mind was in a complete whirl. She had so many things to think about. Her parents. The store. Callie. What would they all say? What would everybody say? What kind of wedding should she have? Where? Should it be big, small, public or quiet? As they were nearing the house, her thoughts had come together enough for her to tell Heck, "Let's wait a little while until I have time to think before we tell anyone. If you don't mind? I'd like to think about plans first. Then we can tell everyone in the whole world. Oh, Heck, I am so happy!"

"Me, too. Now, you go on in and open the store. I will take care of the cow, and I'll see you later." He stole a quick kiss as they parted in the little grove of trees near the house.

Pearl literally bounced out to the store. She had never opened those doors so joyfully before. The sun was coming up, and a wagon was already approaching with someone coming to trade. Pearl was thinking, if only you knew what I know. It was, of all people, Mozelle Weeks for her monthly supply of staples. They chatted as Pearl filled her order, gleefully hopping from item to item in the store. Never had sugar, flour and meal been so beautiful. Even Mozelle looked beautiful in her flowered print dress with the high ruffled collar and shiny buttons and her hair knotted in a little ball at the nape of her neck. The wrinkles in her weathered, old face were beautiful. The knobby fingers of her arthritic hands were beautiful. Mozelle wanted to talk, too. She had come on her one outing of the month to the store, so she wanted to make the most of it. Gossip was what she thrived on, but Pearl had plans to make and thoughts to think and didn't want to bother with her that day.

"Anything else, Mrs. Weeks?" she asked when the last item seemed to have been added to the pile.

"No, I guess not. How's your mother?" Mozelle asked, as everyone did.

"About the same, thank you. She's just lying there."

"Your daddy about the same, too?"

"Yes ma'am. He gets about some in his wheelchair in the house. Just sits there by mother." Pearl told her. "Our cow's in a bog. Our hired hand has gone now to try to get her out. I'm expecting to have to close up and go help him if he can't get her out by himself."

"Oh, you have another hired hand? Who is it? When did you get him?" Mozelle's interest began to peak. "Nathan York had to quit when John died, huh?"

"Yes, and with Melissa expecting, he needed to be near her. She had to quit also." Pearl had now told her all she intended to tell for this round. "I had better run to the house, Mrs. Weeks, and see what is going on. You come back, though." With that, she turned and went out the back door toward the house, leaving Mozelle standing there with her mouth wide open.

Humph! Mozelle was thinking. She sure is in a big hurry. Oh, well. She could stop by Clara Rogers' on the way home. Maybe Clara knew the latest. Mozelle did wish they lived a little nearer the rest of the homesteaders. They were just so blooming far out.

Heck put the bridle on Sam, gathered up some rope, along with a couple of burlap corn sacks, and headed back down to the bog. His mind was racing, too. He was happier than he had ever dreamed of being. All the months in the cavalry during the war, he kept alive by daydreaming, and thinking of a good woman like Pearl to settle down with when it was over. Now, it was coming to pass. He could hardly believe it. The time in the hospital with the leg injury, which had been so awful, was now a thing of the past and was being overshadowed at last by his joy. He could forget it. As he approached the poor cow, she made her little humming sound again. He supposed that was her way of showing happiness at his return, if cows were ever happy. Maybe contented was a better word. "All right, girl. We're going to get you out. Just be patient a little longer," he told the poor animal. He had to be careful not to get himself into the bog, also. Throwing the rope, he managed to hold to a nearby tree with one hand, get the rope around her neck and under her front legs with the other hand, since it was her back legs mostly that had sunk down into the mire. He secured it carefully, tied it to the traces and told the horse to "Git up!"

Sam gave a pretty good tug, and Susie was free! She was a muddy sight, but that was not Heck's concern. Sometimes a cow would not be able to stand or walk after spending a number of hours in a bog like that, but she seemed to be all right. A few more tugs got her moving and with Heck to nudge her along, she walked well. They took the longer way home around the steep little hill so that she would have a better shot at getting there. If need be, Heck would put the rope around her and let Sam pull a little along. That didn't have to happen; however, the next morning would tell the tale. She might not be able to get up after lying down in the night. That's where the burlap corn sacks would come in. If she couldn't get up the next morning, they would work one of the bags under her stomach and pull it out on the other side. Then they would take the ends of the bag and give her a lift.

Pearl met him at the lot gate when his little entourage made it in. "Hi. Any trouble?" she asked, all smiles and with a knowing little twinkle in her eyes that said, "I know a secret."

"Not a bit. She came right out with the first tug." As soon as they were out of sight from the house and hidden by the barn, Heck kissed her full on the lips without even touching her with his muddy hands. "Poor ole Susie looked mighty glad to see me when I got back there," he told Pearl.

"I'll bet she did. We may have to help her stand up in the morning, you know." Pearl had experienced cows in the bog before, as had Heck.

"Yep," he said.

The day had finally come for Marcus to come, and Callie was in a twit. She had cleaned the house until she was blue in the face. She had cooked everything she could think of that she thought he would like, and his room was ready. They had some fine china she was planning to use, also. Pearl looked askance at all the preparations. Must be some kind of dude, was what she was thinking. Then when Callie told her and her father that he was a married man, Pearl really did wonder. Mr. Mac was pretty much past caring about things like that. He never had been too strict about such things, anyway, and his hardened arteries and bum knees were his main concern.

Callie got her mother situated with clean bed linens, a clean gown and chairs along the side of her bed just in case she should move, although she was totally paralyzed. Then she went out to sweep the yards before getting her bath and dressing. She didn't want Marcus to think they were trash. "Pearl," she called to her sister at noon when Pearl came to the house to eat a bite. "Please get something else on besides that old cotton house dress. Marcus will be here any minute."

"Well, my gosh, Callie. What do you want me to put on?" Pearl responded. "Do you want me to sell cow feed and fertilizer in a silk church dress?"

"No, but surely you have *something* a bit more decent that that old thing." Callie was really getting revved up by the time Pearl finished eating and went in to change her clothes. Pearl was amused and thinking if you only knew, sister Callie, that I have been tumbling around in a pile of straw in my clothes, I wonder what you would say then.

Sadness and Joy

It was a very cool night, probably in the 40's, when Pearl discovered that Rose was missing. It was also late, and after she had hunted all over the house, she decided she must wake Callie and Heck. Callie decided to also call Marcus. He had arrived the day before. She knew he would want to help search.

"Did you look all over the house, Pearl?" Callie asked, pulling on her warm shawl and preparing to start looking outside.

"Yes, everywhere," Pearl responded. "I am going to wake Heck and we will search the barn, wash house and all the outside buildings. You and Marcus look through the house again, but try not to wake Dad." She flew out to the bunkhouse and pounded on the door. "Heck!" she screamed. Heck was up and already pulling on his pants. He went to the door to see what was the matter. Pearl told him quickly and asked him to bring his lantern when he came out. It was a very dark night and wouldn't be daylight for another three hours. As she ran on into the barn calling Rose with every breath, she began looking under, on top of and behind everything. She was joined in a few moments by a fully dressed Heck in his boots and ready to start hunting in the woods, if necessary. Marcus and Callie were coming out of the house calling Rose, also.

Homestead

Heck took charge of the situation. Both Callie and Pearl were crying. Marcus looked as if he didn't know where to start, and not knowing the area made it impossible for him to do very much. Heck suggested they split up and be more effective. He sent Pearl to wake the Sewards. He and Matt could start looking in the woods right around the house. Then if they didn't find her by daylight, they would alert the rest of the neighbors. A complete search of the woods would then be conducted.

"Callie, why don't you and Marcus stay here in case she shows up? You could fix us a big pot of coffee, if you want to," Heck told them. With that, he started out into the outlying area with his lantern. Marcus was trying to comfort Callie the best he could. She had a bad case of guilt, because she had virtually ignored the poor little girl ever since she had gotten home. "Oh, Lord, please let us find her," she kept praying. Nobody really had time for the children. They were just there, and she had noticed Rose seemed more withdrawn than usual.

Matt dressed quickly and headed out to help in the search with his lantern in hand. He went down the fence row, thinking she might have started to their house and gotten tired along the way, falling asleep by the fence, but she was not there. He and Martha had talked about the poor little children and wished they could take them. The McDougald girls had about all they could handle with the parents and store to care for, plus the worry of the farm. He was glad Heck had come along, though. He surely did seem like a nice fellow. He was taking a huge amount of strain off Pearl's shoulders. Poor Pearl. The whole community had felt dreadfully sorry for her before Callie finally got herself home from Mobile. He was wondering what was up with that Marcus DeVille fellow, too. He seemed like an all right person for a city fellow.

Nate was in the cow lot just after daylight feeding the stock when Heck rode up in a great hurry. "Hello, Nate," he called as he pulled the horse up quickly and stopped. "Say, we have a big problem and need your help. Little Rose is missing."

Sadness and Joy

"Oh, my word!" Nate said. "How long? Since when? When did you find out?"

"About three this morning. Pearl was up checking on her mother, and as she often does, checked on the children, too. Rose was gone. We have no idea when she left. Can you help in the search? We have already looked in the most obvious places."

"I will be right there," Nate told Heck. "I will let Melissa know." He had finished outside with the chores, so he ran to the cabin. He quickly told her what was going on, and they had a short conversation. As they talked very seriously, Nate grabbed a cold piece of cornbread and a strip of bacon left from the night before to eat on the way. Then he was out the door in a flash. He saddled Dewey as fast as he could and started the trek up the road toward the McDougalds'. He had a good idea what had happened, and he wanted to kill old man Mac. He was of a good mind to walk in that house and get the old man by the throat. He wanted to kill him! And he vowed if anything had happened to Rose, he would kill him. That did it. Something had to be done about the situation, and Nate wasn't shirking his responsibility any longer. He had done that much too long now. He hated the man he had become, and that was going to change.

The whole community soon joined in the search as Pearl alerted all who came to the store. The word spread fast. She opened the store, not to sell merchandise, but to get the word out about the missing child. The fall sky had a hint of rain that would surely bring colder weather. Rose was dressed only in a thin nightgown, as best Pearl could tell. None of her clothes seemed to be missing. She had a rag doll, her very favorite possession, which was in the bed where Rose had left her. She seldom even went out to play without the doll close by.

As the day wore on into afternoon, the searchers gathered back at the store to discuss the situation. Someone asked about the pond, but it was very shallow and certainly not deep enough for even a child to drown. Several of the men had ridden all the way around it anyway. There seemed not to be an inch within miles they had not covered. Some men had ridden as far as five or six miles away, calling Rose as they went. Heck suggested they have a bite to eat, since Pearl had crackers and sausage waiting at the store, rest a little while, water their horses, and then they would search until dark. They were looking in a very systematic pattern which should find her, if she were out there.

Marcus felt perfectly useless, so he helped in the store. Callie had to go in and care for her parents, then make supper, and Mr. Mac withdrew to his wife's bedside and stayed there, saying very little.

It was totally dark before the men gave up the search. Nate was reluctant to stop then knowing Rose must be terrified in the dark and very, very cold. He spoke to Heck, as he was leaving and told him he would be back at first light the next morning to hunt some more. Heck went into the barn to get hay for the animals and while there heard muffled sobbing. At first he thought it was a cat. It was high pitched'— a sort of whine — and then he realized it was a child. He knew Ben was with Callie at the house. Maybe, just maybe, it was Rose! But where was it? Running to the door of the barn, he quickly called to Nate, who was just rounding the corner at the pond. Nate turned Dewey and rushed back fearing something dreadful.

"Come inside and listen," Heck said. They walked into the darkened barn and stopped to listen. The whimpering was coming from behind the huge stack of hay bales that probably weighed two tons if it weighed a pound. "She's back there," Heck announced.

"I wonder if she's hurt?" Nate said. The two men began moving hay bales as fast as they could. Heck got to her first. She was wedged between several bales of hay and the barn wall. But she was alive. When she saw Heck, however, she began to scream. She seemed not to recognize the man at all, so Nate stepped up to comfort her. Pulling her from the spot where she had spent at least the past twenty-four hours, he cradled her in his arms and began comforting her. The screams stopped and just the whimpering remained. Nate took her inside the house to Pearl, who was crying again with relief. Then Nate took Pearl into the kitchen and spoke quietly to her for a few minutes. When they emerged, Pearl started packing clothes for Ben and Rose. Just as she had gotten enough together for a short time, Nate returned from the barn, where he and Heck had hitched the McDougalds' buggy to Dewey. With virtually no explanation, Nate took the children and drove off in the direction of the cabin and Melissa.

On the way, Nate talked to Rose and cuddled her and Ben against the cold and misting rain. Dewey trotted the entire way home with Nate's precious little cargo as though he understood that something magnificent was taking place.

During the day while Nate was gone, Melissa had been making preparations. She suspected her family was suddenly about to increase, and she was very happy over the prospect. The little shed room had been converted from Melissa's private sanctuary to a bedroom for two children. Little pallets for beds was the best she could do in a hurry, but that would be fixed as soon as Nate could get home and build beds. Melissa spent the day praying for Rose to be found and to be safe and sound. She was horrified at what Nate told her before he left to go and search.

A short while after dark, Melissa heard the buggy. Since Nate left on Dewey, she knew he had the children! She flew to the door of the cabin and opened it. With arms flung wide, Melissa greeted the two children who were to become hers. As soon as Nate jumped them to the ground, they ran to Melissa. Rose was quiet at last with the assurance Nate had given her that she would be safe now. Never again would the squeaking of Mr. Mac's chair come toward her room in the night. No longer would the rough hands violate her tiny body, and no longer would she have to endure such horror. Ben seemed a little confused about the situation, but time would fix that. They were home ——*really* home for the first time since their parents had died in the awful fire. And Nate was at peace, partially at peace now. He still had some issues to work through, but one major load was off his shoulders.

When Nate went out to the lot the next morning to feed the stock, he noticed Dewey favoring his right front leg. Wondering what that horse had done to himself, he cornered him and tried to look at his foot. Dewey snorted loudly and broke away immediately.

"Oh, it hurts, huh, boy," Nate said to him, and then gently cajoling him, he tried again. Dewey neighed softly but did allow Nate to look at the foot. It was then that he realized the terrible truth. It was a nail! Dewey had stepped on a nail in the lot. It, no doubt, had fallen when the tin roof was put on the crib during the building process. It was also a rusty nail and deeply embedded in the poor animal's hoof. Nate couldn't imagine by what fluke he had managed to do that.

Patting Dewey as comfortingly as he could, Nate tried to think what on earth to do. The only doctor was Dr. Haygood, the family doctor, twelve miles away and a half-day drive into Creighton. They had a blacksmith at the livery stable, but Dewey wouldn't let that man within a half mile of him. He never even liked going to be shod.

Nate thought about Matt, wondering if between the two of them they could somehow tether him and pull the nail out. He knew that was a long shot, though, because as sore as it was, it would be terribly dangerous to try that. Dewey would kick and buck somehow; so he couldn't ask his best friend to endanger himself like that nor could he take such a chance with Melissa now in the family way. He had to begin thinking like a daddy and taking care not to take chances.

"Oh, God," Nate prayed. "Please give me an answer. You know how I love that horse and how I need him. Please help me." It was time to start the spring plowing. Horses cost a lot, and Nate had very little set aside. With a baby coming, it was going to take money for Dr. Haygood to come out for the delivery, and since Melissa had lost the first baby, he was determined to have the doctor on hand.

Dewey sensed Nate's frantic state and hobbling over to where he stood nuzzled him with his nose; a nose which was supposed to be wet, cool and sloppy, but instead was dry and very warm! It was a nose which had nuzzled his master many times, to his chagrin, often messing up a clean shirt in the process. Now that Nate had discovered Dewey was fevered, despair set in for certain. He could see the handwriting on the wall. Lockjaw! There could be no explanation for the fever other than the rusty nail so deeply and firmly embedded into the fleshy part of the horse's hoof. There was no use to go and get Matt. There was no use to do anything. Nothing. The only thing he could do was stand by and watch his horse suffer and die a horrible death. Or— no that was unthinkable. He could never shoot Dewey or let anyone else do it. He would just have to let nature take its course. He wondered why he hadn't noticed the limp sooner; no doubt because over the weekend he hadn't used him for anything. If only he had noticed sooner. No, he knew realistically that it would have made no difference.

He patted the horse again, turned and walked back to the cabin to tell Melissa. She was in the back, scrubbing clothes on the washboard. The pot for boiling them was steaming away nearby ready with the lye soap already in it. Looking up, she could see the agony in his face without Nate saying a word. "Dear, what on earth is the matter?" she asked, alarmed. Living in an untamed area of nothing but homesteaders, she was accustomed to trouble. It was a harsh country, and anything could happen.

"It's Dewey," Nate said with resignation. "He has a nail in his foot. It must have been left in the lot when we built the barn."

"Well, isn't there anything we can do? Go and get Matthew. Maybe..." but Nate stopped her.

"No. There isn't anything. It's no use. He has fever already, and I *know* it's lockjaw. There can be little doubt." With that,

Nate sank down on the top doorstep, looking as whipped as Melissa had ever seen him look. She knew how he loved Dewey. He had bought him with the first money he was able to save working for Mr. Mac, and she knew Dewey loved him too. There seemed little she could say in the way of comfort.

"I am so sorry, my darling." She dried her hands on her apron, went over to the steps and sat down beside him. Words would not be helpful, so she just sat with her arms around him for a long, long time.

That evening, it looked like rain, so Nate led Dewey into his stall. He could see how sick the horse really was and feared the end was not far away. He offered water, but it was refused.

When Nate went out with his lantern later that night to check, Dewey was lying down and was sweating profusely. Nate knew it was from the fever. He seemed unresponsive, but suddenly he went into a violent convulsion, his whole body shaking. It was a startling sight, but it was over in a few moments, so Nate began to rub his flanks, his head and his back all the while muttering, "There, there, boy. I'm so sorry." Dewey knew he was there and tried to nuzzle him once, but his jaws were tightly locked just as the name "lockjaw" implied.

Grabbing the lantern, Nate ran to the cabin. He yelled for Melissa. "I am staying with Dewey, dear! I will be in later. Go on to bed." With that, he ran back to the lot, grabbing the milk stool as he went, and into Dewey's stall where he lay prostrate on his straw. Another seizure began. This time it lasted a little longer. Nate wished he knew some way to comfort him and make the ordeal easier. He began to pray again, this time for a quick end to the suffering. He could hardly bear this ordeal.

Trouble, who had been barking at what Nate figured was a treed squirrel, had apparently just realized something drastic was wrong. He slinked into the stall, lay down nearby whimpering and stayed the rest of the night.

Sadness and Joy

As the night went on, Dewey's eyes rolled back in his head. Nate had to move away from his spastic feet, which kept kicking out uncontrollably as each convulsion came. Through the night while Nate kept his vigil by his horse, he thought of how he had saved to buy him, how they became such great workers together with Dewey just knowing what Nate wanted him to do instinctively, and the many tight places the horse had gotten him through. He had looked forward to teaching his children to ride on Dewey and to many more years of work together, but about four in the morning, after another severe convulsion, the big animal raised his head just once. He looked into Nate's eyes with his big, dark ones that had once been so devilish, threw his head back and died.

Nate put his head in his big hands and sobbed like a child. He sat for an hour or more with his horse, and finally, as day began to break, he went to the cabin, with Trouble at his side, hoping to turn his mind off and sleep for a little while. Later in the morning, he would go after Matt and his team to pull Dewey's lifeless body way off into the woods.

Franklin Rogers had worked for the Harrison Turpentine Company since he was about eighteen. He was a woods rider, whose job it was to check on the men as they unloaded the turpentine cups into big drums when they took them off the trees. Each tree had a place that was skinned so the turpentine would leak out. A nail was placed in the tree at the bottom. Then a terra cotta cup was placed at the bottom of the tree, on the nail, which would catch the dripping turpentine. The men were paid according to how many cups they emptied in a day.

The turpentine still, houses where the families lived, and Commissary were located about six miles from where Franklin lived and from the Yorks'. He was on his way in to the little office at the still when suddenly he caught sight of something unbelievable. He stopped his horse up on the little rise and peered down at the sight though the trees, thin now from lack of leaves.

It was Callie and that fellow she had visiting her from Mobile in a very compromising position. They had a blanket of some kind spread out on the ground in the branch head, and were making love fiercely. Franklin wasn't one to spy, so he quickly went on his way but with the image still in his mind.

A few days later, when Franklin was talking to another neighbor, the man mentioned Callie's friend who had come to visit from Mobile. He said the community was talking, and that Mozelle Weeks was saying Callie and that man had wallowed out the head of every branch in Catawba Community. Franklin made the mistake of saying, "Yes, I happened along and saw them one afternoon." He immediately wished he hadn't said that. Nate heard it up at the store one day, too, and he was not surprised at all, thinking she must be a lot like her sister. He knew that Marcus had stayed a whole week.

Melissa had noticed a decided difference in Nate since her father's death, particularly as pertained to religious matters. He no longer would talk of going to church and would not say the blessing as they had always had done at mealtime. Finally, she brought it up one night after they got into bed. "Nathan, please tell me what is the matter. We now have the two children, and we should be teaching them about God, and you won't even say the blessing at meals."

After a brief pause, he finally spoke. "I just find it hard to worship a God who takes a fine man like your daddy and fine people like my mother and daddy. There are so many sorry people in the world. Why doesn't He take some of them and leave the good ones?"

"Nathan," Melissa said after thinking for a minute, "If I knew the answer to that, I would be God. It is not up to us to know God's mind or His plans for us in the world. Maybe He took them to save them from something really bad here on earth. Maybe they are the fortunate ones, and we are the ones left here to struggle and have hard times. Maybe if you prayed about that,

He would help you see the answer." Nate didn't commit himself, but he still felt the same way. His religious days were over.

Rose and Ben settled into their new home as if they had been there all their lives. They had to change schools, but that didn't seem to upset either of them. Rose started gaining weight, too. Nate had been shocked, when he picked her up in the barn, at how bony and thin her little body was. She hardly weighed anything. Now in her new home, the only thing they were concerned about was the terrible nightmares she continually had. Melissa would go to her and comfort her so that the screaming would stop, and they were coming less frequently. They both continued to reassure her in every way possible.

They had a fire in the fireplace, because it was a cool day. The children had come from school, and Nate was hanging around very closely, because Melissa was about to term. He wanted her to go in to Creighton to deliver the baby at the infirmary, but they had about reconciled themselves to the fact that it would be impossible to know when to go. Then there wouldn't be time for them to get into town anyway. Suddenly a pain hit. Then another, and Melissa doubled up. She had been peeling potatoes, sitting beside the fire. She told Rose to run get Nate, which the child did in a great hurry. He rushed into the cabin and, realizing what was happening, went for the dinner bell. After three gongs, he rang it three more times. Melissa had made it to the bed and was bleeding profusely. Nate had to get the children out, so he sent them into their room to play telling them to stay.

The pains were coming very regularly. Nate thought about every six to eight minutes. He didn't know how often they were supposed to be when the baby came. He didn't know anything at all, and he was hoping Lily or Grace would have heard the bell and would be there soon. Both knew to hurry when they heard it. Lily was inside and didn't hear a thing, but, as luck would have it, Grace had gone outside for something and heard it. She told her family where she was going, grabbed one of the horses and rode bareback all the way to the Yorks'.

Melissa was in severe pain. The bleeding was heavy which scared Grace. She had no idea what was wrong, but she knew that it had to stop. Nobody could bleed like that for very long and live. The baby was not coming yet, so she applied pressure in a pushing motion to Melissa's upper stomach area. Nate took the children to the barn where they played by lantern light on bales of hay and had a great time. They knew Mama Melissa was having a baby, and Nate wanted them away from the cabin so they couldn't hear her screaming. He then ran back to help Grace in whatever way he could. She motioned for him to go outside with her where she told him that the bleeding had to stop or Melissa couldn't live.

"What can we do? What about the baby?" he asked.

"All we can do is try to get this baby here as fast as we can and pray that the bleeding will stop on its own." She went back inside leaving Nate outside, walking the yard frantically.

Grace kept pushing. A few minutes went by and nothing.

Nate, in the meantime, realizing the gravity of the situation, and knowing he would very likely lose Melissa, fell on his knees in the yard, and with his face up to God, bared his soul and began to pray for the first time in many weeks. This time he prayed aloud, realizing only God could save his wife and child. "Oh Lord, my God. I beg you to forgive me for denying You. I *beg You, Lord,* please let my wife live, and let our baby live. Father, I will serve You the rest of my life, and I will *never again* question anything You do. Thy will be done. Amen." When he stood, he wiped tears from his face, tears he could not control, tears he did not even want to control. He walked around the yard, in his great coat to shield him from the biting cold, and continued to pray. He had gone out to the barn and covered the children, asleep now on bales of hay, with a heavy goose down comforter.

About midnight, the screams stopped. Nate was afraid to go

inside, afraid of what he would hear, but he had been having a feeling of total peace for the past hour or so. He would later describe it as the peace that passes all understanding, which he had heard of from the Bible. Suddenly, the door of the cabin opened, and Grace stuck her head out.

"Nathan, your wife is fine. The bleeding stopped awhile ago, and you have a wonderful little son!" she said to the poor soul standing there as forlorn as anyone she had ever seen. Nate let out a yell and ran to the cabin. Melissa was holding the baby, such a tiny child. He hardly looked real. Nate would be afraid to hold him for weeks, but he looked so perfect. They figured he was about a month early accounting for his tiny size.

"Daddy, meet John Alexander York," his mother said. Nate began to cry again. Melissa looked terribly pale, but she felt much better with the ordeal over.

"Oh, my sweetheart, he is wonderful!" Nate said. "You need to rest, now, though." Grace had come back into the cabin, leading little Rose and Ben by the hands. She had awakened them to come in and see their little brother. Both sleepy children were fascinated with the tiny infant. They had never seen one so new before.

After the children went on to bed and Grace left for home, Nate cradled Melissa in his strong arms and told her how happy he was and what he had talked to God about. "I will never again have the slightest doubt about the existence of God," he said. "Never." Then he took his tiny son and placed him in the cradle John had made, in front of a warm fire, with two wrapped bricks to keep him warm.

The name was one they had decided to use if they had a boy. He was named after his two grandfathers, neither of whom would ever have the joy of holding their little grandson in their arms, thanks to untimely deaths at the hands of some cruel monsters. But he would grow up knowing about them from parents who were determined that he would.

Homestead

Rose, Ben and then "Little John"

Nate went early the next morning to tell Lily and the girls about the baby. It was Saturday, so the girls were home from school. They shrieked with delight at the news about the baby. Lily only smiled through her depression, then seemed to lapse back into her own world of sadness, but as soon as Mary could hitch Dixie to the buggy, they set out to the Yorks' to see the new arrival. Nate had their horse, Sally. He had gone to get her after Dewey died. He was thankful John had the two horses. It saved him from having to buy one right at that time, and Lily surely didn't need two. She and the girls were having a hard time feeding and caring for the stock as it was with Nate helping out as much as he could.

At the cabin, Melissa handed the baby to her mother, who thought she could see a resemblance to John right off. The girls were twittering about, talking to Rose and Ben, and looking at Little John's fingers and toes. They couldn't get over how very tiny he was. Lily seemed to think he was at least a month premature. He had no hair; his fingernails were developed, but barely, and judging by his weight, she thought a month was a pretty good guess.

"How much do you think he weighs, Miss Lily?" Nate asked.

"Oh, not over four or four and a half pounds, I'd say," Lily told him.

"That's about what I thought," Nate agreed. "He cried right off, though. Didn't even have to be spanked." Nate spoke proudly, realizing that was a good thing.

Lily didn't seem to take as much delight in John Alexander as Melissa and Nate wanted or expected her to, but expressed her dismay at not hearing the dinner bell. "I guess the wind blowing and us having the windows and doors all tightly shut kept the sound out. I am sorry I didn't hear." Since John's death, she and the girls kept things locked up tightly at night, although they had spent many nights alone when he was out on the range. Nate supposed it was just the idea that they were totally alone now and John would not be coming back. Nate was having a very difficult time accepting that fact even then, but with Little John's birth, there would be at least one more man in the family — a York to carry on his name. There would not be a son to carry on the Tate name.

Melissa told her as much as she could, with the children standing around, about the tough delivery. But she and Nate assured her that Grace Rogers had done a great job with the birthing process. Lily noticed the deep, dark circles around her daughter's eyes. She silently thanked God Melissa had lived. So many women didn't live through childbirth. Losing her oldest daughter, right after John, would simply be more than she could bear.

Melissa said, "You know Grace has three of her own and has delivered three or four others in the area."

"I know, but I wanted to be here," Lily said. "I will be able to help now, though." She suggested that Nate bring mother, baby and the other two children right on up to her house, but Nate thought it best not to move Melissa for a day or two, because he feared the excessive bleeding might start again. She would spend at least two weeks in the bed. That was the custom after having a baby, so he told Lily he'd take her and the children all up in a couple of days.

Rose, Ben and then "Little John"

"I will get your room ready. You can bring the cradle," Lily decided. She and the girls loved Rose and Ben; so they would get a full measure of attention at Grandma Lily's. Mary and Liz were thrilled when the children came to live with Melissa and Nate. There was so much love in the Tate family. Nate only wished John could be there for all the children. What a grandfather he would have been!

Lily did a number of chores around the cabin for the rapidly increasing York family. My! How it had grown in a few short weeks. The little cabin was bulging at the cracks between its logs. She had offered to have Nate and Melissa move in with her and the girls when John died, but they wanted their privacy, which she could understand. Soon they would need to build on or build a big house, however. Lily had some thoughts along those lines. She knew Nate didn't have the money to build right now, but she did. John left money and a pension, which was more than enough for her and the girls. At least his government job provided for his family at his death.

The Tate ladies stayed quite awhile, because they wanted to see Little John nurse. He awoke after a while and took to nursing with no trouble at all. Everyone had been afraid he might have trouble since he was so tiny, but he sucked with little effort, to their delight. Then Grandma and the girls got all the dirty clothes together and washed them. Nate built a fire under the wash pot so they could be boiled, and they were hanging high in the bright sunshine before they left for the day.

"We will be back late this afternoon with your supper," Lily told them. She had perked up and seemed genuinely interested in her new grandson. Maybe this is just what she needs, Melissa was thinking. She had been quite worried about her mother since her daddy's death, especially after she caught Lily drunk on the elderberry wine. She hadn't mentioned that to Nate, not wanting to add to the burdens he already carried.

Rose and Ben were coming out wonderfully since their move to the Yorks' a few short days before. Melissa was so glad she had a little while to dote on them before the baby came. She was able to make them feel special, cook favorite things for them and make them feel at home. Both were gaining weight, too. Little Ben had begun talking more. He seldom hushed, in fact, and he followed Nate every step. Both children loved the pets. Ben took to Trouble right away, but Rose liked Buttons and the kittens. All was well, except, of course, for the nightmares Rose continued to have. There was seldom a night that Melissa or Nate didn't have to go in and comfort the poor little thing in the night when she would wake them, crying out in her sleep the pitiful whimper or half-cry of a wounded animal. When that happened, Nate had that feeling again of wanting to kill Tom McDougald.

At least, Nate thanked God for having given him a chance to get Rose and Ben away from that situation. He had, to a degree, lessened his burden regarding Rose, but he had a terribly guilty feeling that he had been too weak to do something sooner. He also thanked God that his wife was the kind of person she was and agreed for them to take the children in. In fact, she saw this as a real blessing to their family. They had talked of it many nights. Melissa knew that she would not be able to have more children, so they were happy that Little John would not be an only child. He would have a brother and sister to grow up with.

The night they had found Rose in the barn behind that two tons of hay, and Nate spoke with Pearl in the kitchen, he simply told her what he had seen two or more years before. Somehow, Pearl didn't show any signs of disbelief, causing Nate to wonder.

"Pearl," he said, "I have never told anyone this. Not even Melissa until this morning, but I caught your dad with his hands down in Rose's step-ins, and I believe that is still happening, so I want to take her and Ben to live with Melissa and me. You know I love the children, and I want to raise them."

"Very well," Pearl had said, "I will get some things together. You can come for the rest later on." With resignation, she had packed for them, told them good-bye and Nate rode off with them in Mr. Mac's buggy. On the way, he had a chance to tell them they would be safe now and that they would live with him and Melissa from now on.

"Forever and ever?" Ben asked.

"Forever and ever," Nate responded.

Nate had no idea that Pearl later crumpled on her bed and wept bitter tears; tears for what had been and for what might have been. When Callie was able to pull away from Marcus, she went into Pearl's room to see what was the matter, although she knew perfectly well what the trouble was. It had happened first to her, then to Pearl. Neither girl knew what to do or had the emotional strength to do anything. Telling their mother was out of the question. You just didn't *do that.* If their mother knew, she never let on. In talking about it, Callie and Pearl both spoke of how horrified they were over the same thing happening to little Rose.

"I honestly thought he was too old to do that anymore," Callie said. Pearl agreed that she had thought the same thing.

"I feel so awful that I was not paying better attention. I just had so much on my shoulders," she told her sister. "To think I let him get away with that again! Poor little Rose. It's not as if she hadn't already suffered enough, and we brought her here to give her a better life." Pearl was clinching her fists until her nails cut into her palms. She felt such shame that Nate knew about it, too.

"How did Nate know about this?" Callie asked.

"He walked into the barn, not too long after Rose and Ben came here to live, and caught him with Rose, but he didn't say anything."

Callie could hardly believe her ears. "What! He didn't say *anything?* I can't believe it."

"He said he was just too shocked and didn't know how to handle it. He didn't want to upset mother or you and me. Now he figures mother won't know anyway, and you and I are old enough to handle it. Of course, he doesn't know it happened to us, too, when we were her age," Pearl said.

Callie was infuriated with her father. He had not only tormented her, and then later Pearl, but he had now brought shame to the family by doing it and getting caught with Rose. She wanted to tear into him, and later she did.

News of John Alexander's arrival spread through the community rapidly. Folks started going to see him, especially Martha Seward, Grace and others of Melissa's friends. Martha had saved little clothes belonging to her Matthew that she took to Melissa for John.

Martha had been a wonderful friend. She and Melissa grew closer and closer when Melissa worked at the McDougalds', and one day Martha confided in Melissa.

"Do you remember when those two boys were caught in the unnatural act?" she asked.

"Yes," Melissa answered. "Why? What has happened?"

"Well, the other night, I mentioned to Matthew that I had seen Wilbur Henry at the store. I just said I thought he and Tommy Cox had left the community and what are they doing back here, and he just blew up! He said he didn't want to discuss that and yelled at me. He said why did I need to bring that up again. Then he stormed out and didn't come to bed for hours. In fact, it was nearly daylight. I had started to really worry. I didn't know where he was."

Melissa was stunned. "Why do you think he was so upset about Wilbur Henry being back here?"

"I finally found out. He came back in, got into bed, and said he was sorry, that it wasn't my fault, and that he needed to tell me something."

Melissa was all ears. She and Martha had wondered about all that for a long time.

"He said that when he was a kid, he and another little boy were playing, you know, playing with each other, out in the wash house when his mother caught them. He said she sent the other boy home, took him into the house and beat him with a belt until

he couldn't sit down. He has never forgotten that, because he was very upset about it and very ashamed, so he just didn't want to talk about Wilbur and Tommy."

"But children do things like that, Martha. Did you tell him that? It is just something children do. They experiment. I don't see why his mother got so upset."

The two friends discussed the fact that they wouldn't react that way if they found one of their children doing something like that. They decided they would tell them it was not a proper way to behave and to go and play something else.

"I just hope I can do that," Martha said. "So far, my children haven't done anything like that that I know of."

Homestead

The day was cold and dreary enough the day Miss Mattie died without her death occurring, but then death doesn't wait for a convenient or appropriate time. It would have been a sad time for Callie, Pearl and their father regardless of whether the day was sunny and bright or cloudy and gloomy. It was cool, with clouds that indicated rain was likely. Pearl had come in from the store for some lunch when her father wheeled himself in and told her and Callie, who had fixed them a bite, to come and check their mother. He didn't like the way she was breathing. Pearl took one look and began to cry. Callie quickly checked her pulse, found it very irregular and told Pearl to call Heck and have him alert the Sewards, which she did immediately. Before Heck rode the short distance over to Martha and Matt's and got back, Miss Mattie had begun to breathe in short gasps. It was about one o'clock in the afternoon when Martha and Matt got there. Martha had left the children with Bonnie, who, at ten, was very responsible, but she could only leave them for a few minutes.

Matt got Mr. Mac out on the porch, trying to get his mind off the situation, and they had only talked for a short time when Callie came out and said she was gone. Pearl collapsed into a grief-stricken heap in the sitting room, so Martha tried to comfort her. Mr. Mac was overcome with grief, too. He sat in his chair on the porch, head down, shaking with sobs for hours until the girls took him in to see their mother. They had bathed her, with Martha's help, and gotten her dressed in a burial dress. They would get a coffin from Creighton — a ready-made one that would be pretty with a nice lining, and since they could afford such amenities, they would also have a horse-drawn hearse come from Creighton to take the coffin to the cemetery. It would be done in a classy way. Certainly, if Callie had anything to do with it.

Callie closed her mother's eyes; they bathed her tenderly, and then as Pearl pulled the sheet over her face, she said "Good-bye, Mama."

It was, by far, the saddest day in Pearl's life. Callie had been in attendance when people died, so death was not as strange to her. It was something she had been forced to learn to deal with, but it was the first time Pearl had actually seen someone die.

Callie wanted Heck to go to Creighton and send a message to Marcus, who had gone home several days earlier. She had some hope that he might come for the funeral. What she didn't know was about the cough Marcus had developed and how poorly he was feeling. He had influenza and couldn't seem to get over it, so when the telegram got to him, he had to wire her back that he was unable to go.

Instead of Heck going to Creighton alone, Pearl went with him to help select the coffin. The store was closed, anyway, so she was able to go. They selected a pretty, gray one with a soft, white lining. Then they went outside at the funeral parlor and looked at the hearses. There were two, one white and one black. Pearl decided on using the white one. The funeral would be the following day at one o'clock in the afternoon. That would give the hearse time to get out to Fox Hollow, place the body in the coffin and be ready.

Callie was crushed when she got the return wire that Marcus couldn't come. She thought the flu was not a very good reason for him not to come, unless it was more than that. Perhaps it was pneumonia. She was concerned. He was quite thin, and pale when he had been there to visit. There was so much to think about, however, that Callie had to place Marcus in the back of her mind for awhile. She would check up on him again soon.

It was going to be a problem for Mr. Mac to get into a wagon or buggy for the ride to the cemetery in his wheelchair. Heck had to come up with a way to manage that. He went out to the barn on the morning before the funeral to see what he could do. Nate had come up to help in any way he could, but Melissa had sent her condolences. She would not be able to go, with the baby still so young, so she would stay at Lily's while the rest of the family, except for Liz, would go. Liz was young, and funerals upset her, especially after her father's death still so fresh in her mind.

Nate and Heck decided the thing to do was build a kind of ramp for the wagon, similar to the one at the porch and at the store. Nate had built both of them, so they set about the task and completed it with time to spare before the funeral. The men in the community could easily roll the chair up the ramp and into the wagon.

Neighbors had taken so much food that everyone attending could have lunch easily before the funeral. Pearl and Callie were not hungry, but Martha Seward served everyone else with help from several other ladies from the area.

The beautiful white hearse bore Miss Mattie's body to the church at Catawba in a stately manner. The windows let the gray coffin be seen as the little procession of horse riders, buggies and wagons made its way down the winding, sandy road the six miles to the church. It had brass lanterns on each side and brass door handles. A coachman drove the hearse, wearing a black suit and looking grand. It was mid-afternoon when it arrived. Ordinarily, Miss Mattie would have been buried at the church in Creighton where the family had been attending, but with the new church and cemetery at Catawba it made more sense to bury her there. Reverend Lock was eloquent in his eulogy, so Callie was pleased. Pearl was grieving so that she was hardly aware of anything but Heck literally holding her up as they entered the church and on the way to the cemetery.

Dark overtook the family as they returned home. The others went their separate ways from the cemetery, but Martha and Matt went home with them, and Martha served them supper.

After supper, Callie and Mr. Mac were still at the table when they got into a discussion and began to disagree over some minor thing. They were the only two in the kitchen at the time since Heck had gone with a lantern to tend the stock, and Pearl was lying down. Callie had made the statement that she was going to soon begin thinking about going somewhere, maybe Mobile again, and start looking for a job. Her father made the mistake of saying something about her and Marcus that caused a terrible flareup, something like Callie shouldn't be carrying on with a married man.

"Well, you have plenty of room to talk!" she yelled. "How can you criticize me when you did what you did to Pearl and me all those years? You really have nerve!" The look on her father's face was nothing but one of sheer horror. He had *never* expected to hear one of his daughters talk to him in that manner. It was an age when parents were the absolute in authority, and children were more or less like chattel; they were to be seen, not heard, and they did what they were told without question. The fact that Callie and Pearl had never said anything to a soul about the misery they had endured spoke to that.

Mr. Mac moved his wheelchair away from the table, leaving food uneaten, and started out of the room. Callie was mad by that time, and determined to have it out with him. "Go ahead and run!" she said, again yelling. "It is about time that you sit and face us and apologize for what you have done, but you don't have the guts." Now that she had opened the floodgate, the words came tumbling out unabridged. "How could you do such a thing to us and to our mother?" Her face was red, and her eyes were flashing. Mr. Mac realized she was no longer a child that he could order around but a grown woman who had a mind of her own. He decided to go ahead and retreat. There seemed to be no way he could win in this awful argument. He had been wrong, so terribly wrong, and he knew it. He had no idea what had driven him to perpetrate such acts upon his children and little Rose. It was something far beyond his limited understanding, but he did know one thing: it had nothing to do with the way he felt about his wife and daughters. It went much deeper than that. He *loved* his family. Callie had one parting shot as he started out of the room. "Then you had to start in on Rose and get caught by Nate, so everybody in the community probably knows your dirty little secret by now!" she shouted, completely unrestrained by now.

"I - I hope you can forgive me," was all he said as he wheeled himself to his room, a broken and grieved man, who had very little left to live for. His health was gone. He was in constant pain with rheumatism. He had lost his wife, whom he did dearly love. His daughters didn't respect him — hated him it seemed — and Nate knew about it, so others must surely know, too.

Callie immediately realized she had done something that probably would never lead to anything positive, but she had at least gotten the burden off her shoulders by confronting her father. She wondered if Pearl would ever do the same. The funeral was over, and her thoughts could now turn to Marcus again. She must try to see what was really going on with his health.

Intolerable Guilt

Nate took Melissa, the baby and Rose and Ben up to Lily's when Little John was four days old. He needed to get them settled so that he could get work done about the place. A homestead *always* had work to be done. He was either building or mending fences, feeding animals, cutting trees, setting stumps on fire to clear them out or plowing new ground. He had many acres still to be cleared, but enough already done that he would be able to make enough crops to feed the family, the animals and sell some for cash.

Trouble went along to stay with the family and got shut up in the chicken yard because he followed Nate every step, and Nate didn't want the dog in the way down at the cabin. Since Dewey died, the dog stayed right at his heels. They left Buttons and the kittens in the barn, where they had a job to do ridding the place of rats.

When Nate got up to Miss Lily's, she drew him aside for a short chat.

"Nate, I want to talk to you about building a new house," she said as an opener.

Nate was shocked. He knew he couldn't afford to build, although he and John had a lot of lumber stored in their barns for that purpose. "Gosh, Miss Lily, I can't build! I am barely making it as it is," he told her. He felt almost angry that she would not know that already.

"I know *you* can't afford to build, but suppose I could?" she asked.

"Oh, no. I can't take money from you!" Nate was appalled. He knew John made pretty good money, but he didn't think it would have put him in a position for her to help him build a house. "Why, Miss Lily, you have the girls to think about, and your own house to keep up. You need your money," he told her, but Lily was adamant. She had evidently spent a great deal of time thinking through this.

"I have money in the bank in Milton, and I also have an income from the government — a pension which will more than care for the girls and me, and I want you to get started building. I can supply money for tin for the roof, nails, and any lumber you have to buy. Let's get started. You see, what I have is yours, Melissa's and the childrens' too, and I want to do it." She collected her thoughts for a moment while Nate stood there trying to take in the magnitude of what she had just said. He wanted a house, all right — needed a house — badly, but it had never occurred to him in his wildest dreams that she would do such a thing. What a lady! The quiet, unassuming woman who moved mountains when she wanted to.

"You see, Nate, John and I talked a lot about the house before he died. I think John had a premonition, and he wanted his family taken care of. You are a fine man, and you have already helped the girls and me more than I can ever repay, so it is settled. We will get the house built."

Nate cleared his throat, wiped his eyes, and gave her a big spontaneous hug. He had never hugged Miss Lily before, but she hugged him back.

"Well, I thank you more than I can ever tell you, and I accept. I want you to know, also, that what Melissa and I have is yours and the girls', too. That works both ways. Thank you, Miss Lily," was all he could say. He feared he would cry. Now he could tell Melissa!

All the way back to the cabin, Nate was thinking and trying to digest the news. Lumber was cheap. Labor was cheap, and he could do a great deal himself. He suddenly had awful pangs of sadness, though, as he realized John would not be there to help. It was a sadness he felt would never leave him. He knew Matt would help when he could spare the time, but he would, of course, pay him. It would be wonderful to have a house and more room. Nate began to feel his life was at last really coming together. He had sometimes doubted that he wanted to continue with the homestead. It was a hard life, but it was beginning to look like things would ease up.

Tom McDougald had hardly left his room since the day of Mattie's funeral. He had a downcast appearance, and he cried most of the day as he sat looking out the window at the bare trees and overcast skies. He ate very little, even though Pearl tried her best to get him to eat. Pearl was worried about him, but Callie said he'd be all right. She said old people grieved like that when they lost their mates.

One late afternoon, three weeks after Mattie's funeral, Pearl was at the store when her father wheeled himself off the porch and down the ramp, then came up the ramp at the store. "Hi, Daddy," Pearl said as he came into the store. He hadn't been there in weeks, and she was glad to see him come in. Maybe it would help him to get out of the house and visit with some of the customers, if someone happened in. Business was not good in the bleak winter.

Mr. Mac looked around for a few minutes, wheeling his squeaky chair about to check the stock. He appeared to be in a better frame of mind, almost cheerful, and that made Pearl happy, too. She had grieved about her mother, but she worried about her dad.

"I need to run to the house a few minutes, Dad. Do you want to watch the store for me? I'll only be a few minutes." She was getting her sweater.

"Sure, go ahead. I will watch it," he replied. He really does seem happier, Pearl was thinking as she ran out the door toward the house.

Tom had exactly the chance he had been waiting for so he moved as swiftly as he could. He maneuvered his chair behind the counter in the back of the store enough to get a section of rope he had left back there. Taking the rope, he wheeled out onto the loading dock in the back. Pearl would be back any minute so he had to hurry. He took the rope and, throwing it as best he could toward the rafter on the roof of the dock, he tried but failed to get it over. He tried it again and again, and finally, on the fourth try, it went over and dipped down enough for him to barely reach it. He then made a noose with the rope. When it was fashioned well enough for him to get it around his neck and make it hold, he tightened it. He backed the old chair, which had been his prison long enough, back to the door, where he tied the other end to the brass door handle. Then, he was ready.

The loading dock was not very high — only about five to six feet — but with luck that would be high enough. With as much of a distance as he could get, he made a run at the edge and went off the end of the dock into eternity, to be judged by his God. The chair fell away, his body writhed and contorted for a few seconds, then became still and it was over. A tortured life that had ceased to have any meaning. A life which had brought torture to his daughters, possibly his wife, and to his little adopted daughter, and in so doing, had brought torture to himself. He had prayed that God would have mercy on his soul.

Callie looked out the window of the sitting room just before dark and began to scream. Pearl, who was starting back out to close the store, ran to see what was the matter and began to scream. Heck was just coming to the house for supper when he heard the girls. Running to the window, he saw what had happened. He ran to the dock as fast as he could, but it was too late. There was no pulse. He then lifted the lifeless form to the floor of the dock, covering it with his great coat as the daughters stood frozen to the spot at the window, staring out in absolute horror.

Nate had just gotten to Lily's, from working at the cabin, and was washing up for supper, when Heck came rapidly riding up to the gate. He ran up on to the porch, with Nate meeting him in the hall where Heck gave him the news. "Have you let Matt and Martha know?" Nate asked.

"Yes, I went there first so they could stay with the girls. They are both hysterical," Heck said. Nate didn't ask why Mr. Mac would take his own life. He knew. Expressing his regrets, Nate told Heck he would be right up there.

Nate went up to help Matt and Heck prepare the body for burial. Callie got out Mr. Mac's best suit, a blue serge, for him to be buried in. His shirt and tie would cover the deep purple marks on his neck. After the men had finished the grim task, they carried the body to the house and laid it on his bed. Martha had the girls in the kitchen so they wouldn't have to watch all that taking place.

The whole community was shocked beyond words at Mr. Mac's suicide. Nobody could understand why he had done such a desperate thing. Most thought it was his loss of Miss Mattie and grief over that. Some speculated that it was that and his health combined, but none knew the awful truth except the family and Nate.

The McDougald girls were now informed in planning funerals. Pearl was in deep mourning, but Callie had rallied and seemed able to attend to the business at hand, so Heck drove her to Creighton, where they made the arrangements. It would be very much the same, except that Callie chose the black hearse. That seemed more in keeping for a man than white, as Miss Mattie's was. While there, she sent a telegram to Marcus in hopes that he would be better by then and able to come for the funeral. The funeral was to be the next day at the same hour as her mother's, so she didn't think he could get there in time, but perhaps he could come for a visit.

Once again, neighbors were coming in and bringing food. Since Little John was older now, and Melissa was up doing limited housework, she would be able to go to the funeral. Lily decided to stay at home to keep the baby, but Melissa said no to that. She wanted to show him off to the community, and what better chance? It would be his first outing at six weeks old.

The church at Catawba was packed. The community held Tom McDougald in high regard, but, as Nate was thinking, you never know about people. Things are not always the way they seem. He was one of the first to homestead in that particular area, so Nate figured he deserved some honor.

No matter how badly parents abuse children, the children still seem to love them, for some strange reason, known only to God. It was no different with Callie and Pearl. Callie was of a much less forgiving nature than her sister, who had a more tender heart. Pearl was hurting. Badly. Callie was, too, but she had more guilt than pain. She had not told Pearl of her confrontation with their father a few days before. Somehow, she thought she might never disclose that information. Pearl would not understand.

Just before they left for the funeral the next day, a messenger arrived at the house with a wire from Marcus. He was much improved, but would not be able to get a train in time for the funeral, however, he would be there the following day on the eleven o'clock train. Callie was delighted. She would get Heck to go with her to meet the train.

Melissa dressed Little John in his best baby dress. She was still weak and very tired from being up nights. The baby cried at night, then tried to sleep all day. She was irritable, not feeling like being with people and had no business trying to go, but she was determined. Nate watched the dressing process as he put on his best clothes and got ready. "Are you sure you ought to try this right now?" he asked, casually.

"I am going! "Melissa snapped." I have been at home for six weeks, and I am ready to get out for awhile, even if it is to a funeral." She had been cranky for days, and Nate hoped that would soon stop. He wondered if it was because she had just given birth. He didn't know if that was common for new mothers or not.

They were taking Rose and Ben. They decided it would look strange if the children didn't go. With Rose twelve and Ben eight, it was time they began learning about death and funerals, anyway. Nate and Melissa had explained to everyone that the reason for Rose and Ben coming to live with them was Miss Mattie's illness, Mr. Mac's disability and the fact that Callie and Pearl were not able to give the children all the care they needed. Nobody seemed to think anything about that was odd, or if they did, nobody said anything to Nate and Melissa about it.

The funeral was over, and Thomas Watson McDougald was laid to rest beside his wife of thirty-seven years, Matilda Smith McDougald. Heck again held Pearl up as they walked into the church and then to the cemetery. Again, everyone noticed. They had to postpone getting married because of the deaths, but with the funeral over, that would now be next on the agenda. Pearl was thinking of having a very quiet ceremony at the church, before or after the regular service, and soon. She was well aware of the community talking. Things were being said about her "carrying on" with the hired help and wonder if he really lives in the bunkhouse?" The sooner they were married, the sooner everyone would forget and start talking about someone else.

As the congregation was leaving the church, and as Melissa expected, people stopped to see Little John. She and Nate were proud, smiling parents. All the comments were things like "beautiful baby", "so tiny", "mighty sweet", and "I know you are proud of him" until Mozelle Weeks came along. She took one glance and said, "Huh, looks just like all other little babies. No hair, either."

Melissa, who was sometimes known to be catty, looked at her and said, "Well, Mrs. Weeks, if your daughters ever get married, maybe they will have babies with hair!" She realized, of course, that her remark was lost on Mozelle's back as she disappeared out of the building and into the crowd. Melissa was furious. All the way home, she fumed to Nate. "Old lady Weeks has the ugliest girls I have ever seen. If they ever get married, and I pity the poor man that has to look at them, their children will not stand a chance at being anything but ugly! She is a fine one to talk about Little John not having any hair."

"Sweetheart, don't let that bother you. Aren't most tiny babies bald?" Nate dared to ask. He was thrilled at being a father, but so far, he had been unable to relate in any meaningful way to his son, who cried all night and slept all day. He could neither nurse him nor quiet him when he cried, it seemed, so the father-son relationship was having to wait until John grew a little. The comment Mozelle made had no effect on him at all.

Melissa was in no mood to let it go. She continued to fret about everything she could think of, and Nate hoped that state would soon pass. Women! He did not understand them.

Callie approached Heck after the funeral about meeting Marcus at the train the next morning. "Do you have the time to go?" she asked. Of course, Heck was still a hired hand, and had not forgotten that, so he readily told her he could, although he truly needed to be working on the land. Planting time was just around the corner, and he had lost valuable preparation time with all the illness, deaths and things he had to do at the house.

While Pearl was grieving, Callie was off to get her lover at the train, giving little thought to events of the past month. She couldn't wait to find out if Margaret DeVille had given any ground on the divorce situation. Her last letter from Marcus was three weeks earlier. Something could have come about in that length of time. She still had hope. She got a letter from Sara, her former roommate, several days before in which she said the talk in various circles in Mobile was that nothing had changed and nothing ever would. Margaret's health, as best Sara could learn, was good except her legs were still paralyzed. Of course, they always would be. Their landlady usually heard things at church. Sara heard gossip at the hospital and from patients who knew she had a connection to Callie. She also told Callie Marcus still was not working.

Heck knew Marcus, of course, from his first visit to Fox Hollow. They shook hands when Marcus stepped from the train, and Heck went to get his baggage while he and Callie said "hello" with a long hug. He didn't kiss her right there in front of the people. That would come later. Callie was stricken by the way Marcus looked: thin, gaunt and pale.

Homestead

Callie's Despair

The family was all at Lily's on Saturday afternoon, picking up the last of the pecans that had fallen late in the season. Nate, Melissa and the children were all helping, and they were making great progress. The three trees had produced a bumper crop. Nate would take the rake and gently rake the dry leaves away so that Mary, Liz, Rose and Ben could see the pecans. Lily was watching the baby so that Melissa could be out there also.

The children heard the horse first. A rider was coming from the south toward Milton. They all took a deep breath, because anyone approaching meant some kind of news. People were too busy to do much visiting just for the sake of visiting. It had to be connected with some special function, such as church, a wedding or funeral, and nothing was going on, so that meant news. They all straightened their aching backs and waited.

As the rider got closer, Nate recognized Wilson McLean from the sheriff's office. He laid his rake down and walked over to the wire fence. "Howdy, Mr. McLean," he called, as Wilson got off his horse and threw the reins over a fence post. "What brings you way out here this time? Good news, I hope."

McLean smiled. It was obvious he did have good news and couldn't wait to tell it. "Yep, I sure do."

"Well, wait a minute until we get Miss Lily out here to hear it. In fact, let's all go on in to the porch where we can sit down. Ben, go tell Grandma Lily we have news!" Nate said to the child who was gawking at the stranger. Ben ran as fast as he could to tell Lily. It was late enough to suspend the pecan search, anyway, until later, but they would probably try to finish the next day to keep the squirrels and other rodents from getting them.

The family gathered on the porch, eagerly waiting to hear what had been important enough to bring Mr. McLean so far to tell it. Before he said a word he parked himself comfortably in a rocker, laid his broad-brimmed hat with the sweat ring around the crown carefully on the floor beside him and drank long and hard from the dipper of water Lily had brought for him. The suspense was killing all of them. Then in a slow drawl he began. "We got two men in jail for killing Mr. Tate," he said. There was an audible, collective sucking in of breath on the porch, but nobody spoke. The tension was mounting.

"We don't have enough evidence to convict them in a court of law, but enough to hold them. And we are working on that, but we picked them up after they got drunk and bragged at a poker game about what they did. They wuz playin' down at one of the fish camps. Everbody got drunk but this one feller, and he stayed sober and kept listnin'. As soon as he got enough information, he came straight into the office to tell us. They wuz arrested that very day. That was Saturday'll be a week ago. We get more evidence ever day now that folks have started talking. At first, they wuz afeered to talk. Them two that we got in custody is a mean pair, and folks wuz afeered of what they would do to them if they told."

"Who are they?" Nate finally asked.

"Names are Curtis Mims and a feller they call Snake Peaden. Bad pair. Do anything for a dollar, and we are pretty sure Atlantic Land and Lumber Company put 'em up to it." That was about all Mr. McLean was willing to tell at the time. He didn't want to tell the family anything that would give them false hope if it hadn't been proven. Better not to get them too excited until all the facts were gathered.

Lily wanted to know when there would be a trial, and Melissa wanted to know if they would be allowed to make bail. McLean said they didn't know when a trial would be. It was much too soon to know that, and no, they would not be able to make bail. It was set mighty high.

Nate asked how high, and McLean said it was set at a thousand dollars! "Those two couldn't buy a nickel pack of stick candy," he told his audience. "They are more or less drifters. No jobs even." He picked up his hat and heaved himself up out of the rocker. "Guess I better be gittin' back to the office," he said. "We will keep you informed, though."

Lily, who had been reliving the news of John's death as the man talked, thinking of the day he had ridden up to tell her, and the pain thereafter, finally spoke again. "We all sure want to be at the trial. Will you let us know when that is to be?" she asked.

"I sure will, ma'am. You can count on it." With that he walked down the steps and to his horse without another word.

"Thank you!" Nate called after him, finally remembering to thank the poor man for all his trouble.

Except for Rose and Ben, who didn't know anything about the situation, the family was quiet for several minutes while each one digested this latest information. Finally, it was Melissa who broke the silence.

"Oh, they've got them!" she shouted with glee. "They got 'em. I just knew they would be caught. I hope they hang them in the court house square," she said emphatically. Now the family had hope again. That helped to relieve the pain. They all believed the men who had killed John would now be punished.

There was seldom a night that Rose didn't wake the family screaming. She usually was saying, "Stop the squeaking! Stop the squeaking!" She was, of course, talking about the squeaking of the wheels on Mr. Mac's wheelchair. Nate wondered how the McDougald family could have not heard the child in the night. Or, perhaps she wasn't doing it at their house for fear of Mr. Mac. Somehow, she might have just known, even in her sleep that she couldn't cry out. Then he remembered her room being around a corner and down a rather long hall from the other rooms. Nate was still wrestling with the fact that he had let that go on as long as it did. He would never forgive himself until his dying day for taking the cowardly way out of that situation.

Pearl and Heck had put their marriage on hold, but word was now out that they planned to marry. The wedding would take place at the church immediately following the church service only four weeks after her father's funeral. Of course, nobody thought anything of that except Mozelle. Dear Mozelle, the community critic, had a great deal to say. She thought it showed a lack of respect for her daddy for Pearl to marry so soon after the funeral. Melissa told Nate she was glad poor Pearl finally got someone to marry her. "They shouldn't reproduce, though," Melissa said.

"Why?" Nate asked, puzzled as could be. "Why shouldn't they have children?"

"They are both so homely. Nobody that ugly should have children!" Of course, Melissa was making a cruel joke. She was being catty again. She had a perverse sense of humor at times, anyway.

"Melissa!" Nate said in an admonishing way. "You are terrible!" Of course, he laughed at his prim little bride's bad behavior. It was very unlike her to talk that way. "If the community only knew how bad you are, you'd get kicked out of the church, like Grace and Franklin did for dancing." She cut her blue eyes at him and threw her head back in her defiant little manner, then went on with fixing breakfast for everyone. The older children had begun to eat like pigs, and both were gaining weight. Little John demanded to be picked up every morning just as Melissa was getting breakfast, so it had become his daddy's job to entertain him for awhile, after a dry diaper, of course. Nate was beginning to develop his abilities to care for children. With so many older children and adults in the York-Tate families, Little John was getting a *lot* of attention. He now had hair, thin, blond fuzz — and all the loose skin he originally had was now filled out so that Melissa said he was beginning to look human.

"I want Mozelle Weeks to see you now, my precious," she told her son. "She will see that you don't look like every other baby!" She was still burning over Mozelle's thoughtless little comment at church.

Pearl chose a pale blue street-type dress for the day of the wedding. Heck would wear a regular suit, and when the service was over, the preacher would simply say they were having a wedding, invite the congregation to stay or leave as necessary, and that there would be a reception at the McDougald home after the ceremony. Everyone was invited. The couple had decided to go to Creighton to the hotel for a couple of days, and Callie, to her extreme displeasure, would man the store. She was also standing up with her sister, also to her extreme displeasure. Marcus was invited but wasn't feeling well again, causing Callie great distress. Matt Seward was standing up for Heck. They had become friends in the short time since Heck had come to the McDougalds.

Heck and Pearl decided to live at the house with Callie for awhile and build a house of their own when they could. Pearl hoped that would not be too long in coming, because her sister had a way of being quite high-handed and bossing everyone around. Heck would be out and about the place working, but Pearl would be around Callie more. She hoped it would work out with the three of them living there together. Callie was talking about going somewhere and getting a nursing job. Maybe that would happen. The store actually produced enough income for the three of them to live comfortably, so that she would not have to work, but she wanted to get away from Fox Hollow the worst way. Never had she expected to be living back there in that God-forsaken place!

Homestead

After the wedding, the reception and the trip to the hotel for a couple of days in Creighton, things settled down and got back to normal rapidly. Pearl and Heck seemed to be made for each other and were very happy. That irritated Callie. She was disgusted with their cooing over each other all the time, and she wanted to see Marcus.

Spring was in full swing. Dogwoods bloomed everywhere in the woods, and wild honeysuckle dotted the landscape, especially in the branch heads. There were two kinds, one was a low bush with pink blooms, while the other was a climbing vine, which had yellowish blooms. It was the one that gave the air a sweet fragrance. Nate was plowing from first light until nearly dark. He was tending Lily's small acreage along with his own, and one day he used Dixie to pull the plow; the next day he used Sally. So while the horses got a rest, he never did. Sometimes there seemed to be more than one man could do around the two places. He needed a farm hand. If he could find someone, he would try to get a job as a log man with Southern Lumber Company, a job which would pay actual cash. Farming was a satisfying job. It produced results, unless there was a drought or pestilence such as grasshoppers, and then he could barely make enough to feed the family and the stock. The log men rode booms of logs, timbers that were connected together, as they floated them down creeks and rivers to terminals where they were sent to sawmills or loaded on barges and ships for ports about the world. It took a certain skill to keep the logs from jamming and coming to a stop. The men used what they called a peavey to hook the logs, turn them and get them moving. It was an instrument on a handle, similar to a hoe, but with a hook that would actually hook into a log and turn it.

Log men worked hard, were away from home for several days at the time, and it could be dangerous if a man didn't know what he was doing. When someone fell overboard, for example, in very cold weather, everything halted, and someone yelled, "man overboard!" It was necessary to build a fire immediately and dry him out, because he would die shortly otherwise. A man's clothes would freeze to him almost instantly in very cold weather.

Nate knew Melissa and the rest of the family would not want him to be away from home doing that kind of work, but it was one of the few ways to make money. He had talked to several fellows who worked for awhile to get ahead financially.

Callie was expecting to hear from Marcus telling her he was coming for a visit. Heck went to Mrs. Gay's to get the mail one late afternoon and returned with the expected letter. Callie sat down on the porch to enjoy the cool breeze and read her letter. She was always in a happy mood when it was time for one of Marcus' regular visits. He usually tried to go up every six weeks or so.

The letter began:

My Dearest Callie,

I have dreaded writing this letter because of the bad news I must tell you. I know you will be disappointed, as I am, but I cannot go for the visit we have planned. I am in the Infirmary, and I have been diagnosed with tuberculosis.

The cough I have had for several months, and what we thought was pneumonia, seems to have been TB all along. It has gotten a real hold on me, my love, and I fear it may not be curable. I think you should know the truth, although it saddens me greatly to have to tell you this.

I will be transferred tomorrow to the sanitarium on Magnolia Avenue, where I will be placed on complete bed rest. I will not be allowed to do anything, and I think I shall go mad! I selfishly want you here so very much. I need a wonderful nurse!

Homestead

Please don't worry about me, my darling. I will do everything I am told to do, and hopefully I can beat this thing.

Give my regards to the bride and groom.

Yours always,

Marcus DeVille

Callie began to weep. It should have occurred to her long ago that Marcus had TB. She knew the symptoms so well. Her senior paper had been on TB. How could she have overlooked that!

As the afternoon shadows lengthened, Callie sat in the rocker, crying softly and with complete dejection. Her hopes for a future, married to Marcus, had crumbled when Margaret refused to grant him a divorce. And now this. Oh, she knew about TB, all right. It was a devastating disease and rarely curable. That also explained why Marcus was so thin and pale, especially lately. What should she do? What *could* she do? If she went to Mobile, the doctor probably wouldn't let her see him. He would be in isolation.

Suddenly, her world turned dark, and the lovely spring evening was no longer lovely. She was without hope. But maybe not. She suddenly had a thought!

Gathering up her writing materials, Callie seated herself at the kitchen table to write a reply to Marcus before Pearl and Heck came in from work. She began:

My darling Marcus,

I was devastated to receive your letter, and I refuse to give up! I cannot believe I have been so blind about your condition. I should have realized months ago, when your cough didn't go away after the "flu" that it was TB. Oh, my dearest, I am so sorry.

My first inclination was to rush to your side and care for you, but I know the doctor would not allow me to do that with you in isolation. I have been thinking of a plan, however, and I want you to consider it. I could move you out west; maybe to Arizona or New Mexico. I have known of cases where people went to the west where the climate is very dry and were cured. We could find a place to live, and I could care for you. Will you consider it? I will be awaiting your reply, and I will be ready the minute you say the word. I love you more every day, dearest. Do everything the doctor says, please.

Yours forever,
Callie

Pearl and Heck appeared after work at the house to find it totally dark and no supper cooked. The stove didn't even have a fire in it and no lamps were lit. Pearl realized something was gravely wrong. Seating herself across from Callie at the table, she heard the disturbing news. It was hard to know what to say. There was hardly any use in being cheerful and trying to be optimistic. Everyone knew about TB, so they consoled as best they could, and Pearl cooked supper. Callie ate very little and went on to bed to toss and turn miserably the entire night.

Instead of a reply from Marcus, ten days later a messenger delivered a telegram to Callie early one morning. Her hands trembled violently as she opened the yellow envelope. It was from a doctor she had never heard of at the sanitarium. It read:

Regret to inform you Stop Marcus DeVille expired at 2 A.M. this date Stop
Arrangements pending Stop.

Callie sank to the floor, her body racked with sobs. She couldn't even call to Pearl at the store. Fortunately, Heck had come back into the house for something and found her. He helped her to a rocker and yelled out of the front door for Pearl.

Homestead

The next morning, Heck took Callie to the train which left Creighton for Mobile about one o'clock. It was the one she had taken when she first went to Mobile and had ridden many times since. It was always a happy ride until now. She had hours to think about Marcus, her situation and what it would be now, and what she would do with her future. She was thirty-one and her life was over.

Marcus had listed her as the person to contact in case of an emergency. She went directly to Mrs. Downing's and arranged to stay with her old roommate for a few days. Then she got a rig out on the street and went to the sanitarium. The doctor was not in, but she learned the body had been released to Rogers and Wilson Funeral Home right downtown. The arrangements had been made by the time she got there, so she could only assume Margaret, or perhaps Marcus before he died, had done that.

The grave was right under a huge magnolia, which spread its long limbs out for many feet. The air was heavy with the fragrance of the many blooms covering it, but Callie didn't notice. A minister, whom she had never seen, intoned a short eulogy and prayer, and the service was over, along with Callie's dreams. There were, in all, about thirty people there, all unknown to her. Margaret, thankfully, was not in attendance, nor did Callie expect that she would be. After the service, the people hurried away, leaving Callie with a few moments beside the grave before the funeral home men came to close it. There was one bouquet of flowers, the red carnations she had sent from a florist near Mrs. Downing's. Callie selected the prettiest one, pulled it from the bunch and laid it on the casket, signifying the end of an unequaled love affair.

Knowing how Margaret had poisoned the minds of everyone they knew about Marcus, Callie was not surprised that hardly anyone had dared come to the funeral. While she didn't know a soul at the service, she was sure everyone there knew exactly who she was. That was the reason they hurried away so fast. She was an embarrassment to them — all except one. At the gate as she was walking away, she noticed a lone man who seemed to be waiting for her. She approached, smiled sadly, and he spoke. "Hello, ma'am," he said. "I'm Benny Lane. I worked with Marcus at the bank, and I know you are Callie."

"Yes," she replied, grateful for a word from someone, at least. Then she waited.

"Well, I just wanted to tell you that I liked Marcus a lot. We were friends, and he talked to me about his situation. He told me of his love for you, and when he got sick, I went to see him. I had to wear a mask, and I could only stay five minutes. He knew from the start he wasn't going to make it, but he asked me to tell you he was leaving his house and a little property to you." Callie was stunned, but she suddenly realized Marcus had no children, no relatives, and she would be the only one he would have to leave things.

Benny Lane removed an envelope from his pocket and placed it in her hand. "This will is up-to-date and should cover everything. His attorney will be in touch with you. I have to run, but God bless you." With that he was gone, leaving Callie feeling more empty and forlorn than ever. Dear Marcus. How like him to think of everything. She looked back once more to see the men covering the casket with shovels of fresh, wet dirt.

Heck met the train the next day to drive a crushed and broken-spirited woman home to Fox Hollow, where she would help out with the sick in the community and live out her life in a dejected and defeated manner.

Homestead

Forest Fire!

The year was 1890. Nate and Melissa had moved into the big house in 1885. Little John, now six years old, was in school. He walked the nearly two miles everyday with Ben. Melissa and Nate were pleased that he had his big brother to walk with, because there were still dangers along the way. Sometimes the boys encountered snakes, and there were animals such as bobcats, which could attack if provoked or frightened enough.

John decided, as he entered school, he no longer wanted to be referred to as Little John, so the family, as hard as it was to remember, began to call him John. In the South, children were often called by both their first and middle names, but he vetoed that idea, too. He thought John Alexander was a bit much.

Times were still hard, and nothing was being wasted, but the South had begun to revalue its assets, and factories were being built, towns were growing, and people from the North had discovered the warm, temperate climate of the South. Very little was being said about the Civil War out in public, but inside the four walls of the homesteads, there was still talk of the atrocities committed against the South, and a great deal of hard feelings still abounded. The York-Tate family had a saying, always made in a joking way, that the North didn't win the war. Why, they'd say, it's not over yet! Nevertheless, life went on in the homestead community, and progress was being made. Everyone had food, clothing and shelter. Their children were getting educated, although not highly, and they had hope.

Nate was dressed for church. He was standing in the front room, waiting for Melissa. He had shaved and dressed early, as he usually did. The boys were ready and on the front porch swinging in the big swing and singing hymns to the top of their lungs. Now and then, they'd stop singing, and Ben would pretend to preach, much to John's amusement. He'd rear back, stick his stomach out as far as he could and pretend to be Reverend Lock who was still tending the flock at Catawba Methodist Church. Now and then, John would say, "Amen, brother!"

As Nate listened to the boys, his thoughts turned to Rose. What an appropriate name for such a lovely girl. Melissa had done a wonderful job of teaching her the things young ladies needed to know. Now she and Bonnie Seward were in Normal School in Creighton. Sometimes they came home for a weekend, but usually not, due to the distance and time away from studies.

Rose wanted to be a teacher in the worst way and planned to live in a city after graduation, where jobs were available. Nate thought she would probably get married, or have a hard time escaping, because of her beauty. Her hair was long and very black, and her eyes were very brown. She had features like a doll with a fine bone structure, long slender arms and legs, and a good figure. He thought there must have been Indian blood back in her heritage somewhere. Rose had overcome the trauma of her younger years after coming to live with him and Melissa. Security had made a marvelous difference in her life, freeing her from the nightmares and fear she had suffered so long.

Bonnie Seward was also a pretty girl. She had few remaining scars from the burns she had as a little girl from the wash pot. Nate and Melissa shared with Matt and Martha in the joy of having their daughters attending the school together and being great friends from childhood.

As Nate stood in the front room reflecting over their lives together, Melissa joined him. He watched her stride into the room in a periwinkle blue dress that matched her eyes perfectly. "Hello, my love," he said as he held out his hand to her and pulled her over to the wall where he studied the land grant he had gotten in 1889, one year earlier. It was in a double frame, very ornate, and commanded the center of attention in the room on the biggest wall. "Look at it!" he said. "We did it."

"I never had any doubt we would," Melissa stated emphatically, tilting her defiant little chin upward as she always did.

"Well, there were times I almost decided to leave, you know." She had not known at the time how close he came. Now she realized that losing her father had a profound effect on Nate, much more so than she knew at the time. But he got his faith back and was now a stalwart and strong Christian, unshakable in his beliefs. Together, they read the land grant for the hundredth time in the past year. Nate could read rather well after her years of tutoring, so he began:

THE UNITED STATES OF AMERICA
To all to whom these presents shall come, Greeting:
Homestead Certificate No. 6989

Application 18586

Whereas there has been deposited in the General Land Office of the United States a certificate of the Register of the Land Office at Gainesville, Florida, whereby it appears that, pursuant to the Act of Congress approved 20th of May, 1862, "To secure Homesteads to actual settlers on the Public Domain," and the acts supplemental thereto, the claim of Nathan York has been established and duly consummated, in conformity to law, for the Southeast quarter of section ten in township six, north of range twenty-nine West of Tallahassee Meridian in Florida, containing one hundred and sixty acres and fifty hundredths of an acre according to the official plat of the survey of said land, returned to the General Land Office by the Surveyor general.

Now Know Ye, that there is therefore granted by the United States unto the said Nathan York thereof, and unto the said Nathan York the tract of land above described TO HAVE AND TO HOLD the said tract of land with three appurtenances thereof unto said Nathan York and to his heirs and assigns forever.

In testimony whereof, I Benjamin Harrison, President of the United States of America, have caused these to be made Patent, and the Seal of the General Land Patent Office to be hereunto affixed.

Given under my hand, at the City of Washington, the third day of March in the year of our Lord, One thousand, eight hundred and eighty nine, and of the Independence of the United States the one hundred and thirteenth.
By The President:

and it was signed by Benjamin Harrison. It was also signed by J.M. Townsend, Recorder of the General Land Patent Office.

After they finished reading the document, so precious to both of them, Nate pulled her to him and kissed her soundly on the lips. "My beautiful wife," he said to her, looking into her violet blue eyes, still the most beautiful he'd ever seen. "I could never have done all this without you," and taking one of her hands in his, he looked at the red, rough surface, which had washed so many clothes, and dishes, scrubbed so many floors, and cleaned so many yards. "You know, I want your life to be easier from now on," he told her. "I want these hands to be soft and white like a lady's hands should be."

Melissa threw her head back and laughed her melodious laugh. "They could look like that now if I would remember to put the lard on them regularly," she told him. "Come on, you silly old dreamer. It's time to leave for church." They never missed a Sunday unless someone was really ill. The church was flourishing be-cause of members like Nate and Melissa, who went faithfully and took their children. It was still the center of, not only worship, but most of the community social activities, too. There were frequent functions at the school, also, which served as social gatherings, but the church was dominant. Any occasion, whether a baptism, christening of a baby, wedding or funeral was an excuse for a recep-tion or dinner. The men had built on a reception hall and Sunday School rooms some years earlier.

As they drove into the churchyard in the buggy, Melissa saw Mozelle Weeks making her way slowly across the parking area to the door. She was using a cane now and looked terribly frail. She still had her caustic tongue, but Melissa had long since come to terms with that and no longer allowed the old lady to irritate her. "Morning, Mrs. Weeks," she called, but Mozelle's hearing was so poor that she didn't answer. Lily and Liz were behind Nate and Melissa in their buggy, so she went over to help her mother down, although she was still remarkably well and agile, despite the usual aches of rheumatism.

Mary married Wallace Marshall, a fellow she met in Creighton while in Normal school. They were living in Creighton. Liz, the only daughter remaining at home, was being courted by a local young man everyone thought would soon ask for her hand in marriage. She and Zack might live with Lily, but in case they didn't, Melissa was ever so glad she and Nate lived nearby. Lily would go down and spend nights with them, or John said he would stay with Grandma Lily and keep her safe.

The sermon that day was on faith. It had become Nate's favorite subject in the Bible since his was so magnificently restored that late night in the yard while Melissa was giving birth to John. He had never again doubted God or what He could do for His believers. Nobody knew why Melissa had bled so profusely or why it stopped, but Nate knew Who had stopped it. He was forever grateful to God for not taking her from him, and for giving him a wonderfully healthy son. Neither he nor Melissa had minded not having more children. Rose and Ben filled that void well and were loved the same as John. Ben still adored Nate and was following in his footsteps in many ways. He was a tall boy, now fourteen, and almost ready to finish at Catawba School. He was still deciding what to do next.

After church, the Yorks stopped to have Sunday dinner with Lily and Liz. Zack was due to be there, too. Lily was having her famous fried chicken, turnip greens, cornbread and pecan pie. Melissa had the pie recipe, but declared she couldn't make them as well as Lily. The recipe was simple. It called for a fourth of a pound of butter, one cup of syrup, one cup of sugar, three large eggs beaten, one teaspoon of vanilla, a dash of salt and a large cup of pecans poured into an unbaked pie shell. It was divine!

During dinner, as usual, the conversation turned to John, his death and the trial for Curtis Mims and Snake Peaden. They were found guilty, sentenced to life with no parole and were serving their time in a Florida prison. Although it didn't bring John back, it gave the family a great deal of satisfaction to know they were behind bars. Nate would never know who was responsible for his parents' deaths, but he had been able to visit with his sister Jane and her family regularly. They visited the Yorks in Catawba annually, and Nate, Melissa and the children went to Guntersville a couple of times a year.

While visiting after the meal, Lily brought up the trial and search that was made for John's grave. She had finally reached the point of being able to talk about it without crying. The sheriff had asked for volunteers to search each side of the Yellow River banks, in any area they could reach. Nate went on the search. Some areas had such thick, tangled vines and brush that it would have been impossible to dig a grave there.

The two men who found John's body drifting in the canoe went on the search, also, but they had little idea of where they were when they dug the grave in the long, vast stretch of the river's banks. The river had overflowed its banks many times since, and there were hundreds of wild animals that could have disturbed the grave, so nothing was found. The family had been forced to accept the memorial they had placed in the cemetery as John's grave. Lily said "If only those men had marked the area where they buried him with a notch on a tree or anything!"

"I think they were scared to death, Miss Lily," Nate told her. "They were afraid whoever did it would be after them next." Nate thought hard to come up with some comforting words or words of explanation that would soothe her troubled heart. "I think they were so shocked and frightened they could only think of getting out of there." Truthfully, Nate wondered the same thing. He couldn't think of any real, satisfactory excuse for them not having done that. He had even wondered if they were the murderers, and he had wondered if they had actually buried John's body or maybe just left it to the wild animals. He couldn't, of course, ever say that to John's wife and daughters.

The search parties had gone about twelve miles up the river, through the most untamed area he had ever been into, before they had called off the search. Nate, at least, had the comfort of knowing he had gone along and tried to find the body.

Homestead

When they got home, Nate and Melissa sat on the porch in the big swing. John went squirrel hunting in the branch with Ben. He loved to tag along, and Ben never seemed to mind. Melissa sat studying Nate's profile. He was as handsome as ever; his hair now entirely gray, he had few wrinkles except the little crinkles around his eyes from working outside and squinting in the sun. Nate said his father had been almost gray when he was killed. She thought it must be a trait that ran in the family. How she loved this man! Their life together had been as serene as a life could be considering all the outside influences such as death, illness and hard work. They were true soul mates.

Melissa, now just turning twenty-six, had maintained her youthful appearance, despite hard work and exposure to wind, sun, heat and cold. She enjoyed life and still had her cheerful personality. As they sat in the swing enjoying the lazy afternoon, they heard a rig coming, then another. Soon the first one was in sight. "It's Franklin and Grace!" Melissa exclaimed. "They didn't say a word about coming today at church." She was puzzled by their appearance, and then they heard the next buggy. It came into view shortly and revealed Matt and Martha. "Well, forever more! What on earth brings you all here this afternoon?" she asked. Nate had a smug look on his face as if he already had known what was going on.

"Well, don't you *want* us to visit?" Grace said. "We can turn around and go back." She was teasing, of course.

"No, no. You certainly aren't going back. Do come in." Melissa was suspicious. Grace had a cardboard box, and Martha had a jug of something. They both headed straight for the dining room with her right behind them. The men followed. As they placed their surprises on the table, everyone said "Happy Birthday!" in unison.

"Oh, my goodness. You all should not have bothered to do this," Melissa was saying in her sweet Southern voice. "But, thank you so much."

Forest Fire

"We know your birthday is next week, but we will all be working and busy, so we told Nate we were coming today," Martha explained. She had made lemonade, and Grace had made a cake. "We thought we needed to celebrate your twenty-six years in the world. After all, that is over quarter of a century!" Melissa laughed and was genuinely pleased. She set about getting glasses and plates to serve the refreshments to everyone. Over the years, she and Nate had enjoyed many wonderful times with the two couples. They had been the best of friends, helping each other in times of joy and times of sorrow.

After everyone was served, Melissa said, "Let's go out onto the porch where it is cooler." On the porch, the conversation turned to the weather. It was dreadfully hot and dry. They were expecting and hoping for rain to cool things off. The crops were beginning to show effects of the drought, and Nate had just remarked to Melissa that even the corn stalks were showing their need for rain. Their long slender leaves were curling like ribbons on a package.

Pretty soon, Nate, Franklin and Matt got into a conversation about Harrison Turpentine Company where Nate and Franklin were both working. As the big house was being built, Nate was fortunate to get a young man named Daniel Beckford to work for them and tend the farms, including Lily's. He was young, but under Nate's tutelage, he learned rapidly and soon was able to manage both places. All the land was now under cultivation. It had taken the whole seven years necessary to work and live on the land for homesteading to accomplish the clearing, but there were now about a hundred and sixty acres under cultivation. It was all Dan could handle. He was strong, dependable and very capable, plus he was a little sweet on Liz. He had hinted to Nate that he would like to court her when he became a little more established.

When Nate was building the big house, Dan continued to clear new ground, when he wasn't needed to help with the building process. He proved to be a hard worker, and when Nate and Melissa wanted to go somewhere, they knew they could rely on Dan. He had moved into the cabin when they moved out, and he even kept John and Ben at times if they needed to be away on school days. That particular weekend, he had gone to Milton to visit his family.

After the big house was completed, Nate mentioned to Franklin at church that he was thinking of try-ing to get a job with one of the lumber compa-nies. Franklin immediately said, "Harrison is always looking for workers. I am sure you can get a job as a chipper, and you wouldn't have to be away at night for days at a time like you would with a lumber company. I will put in a word for you." So, Nate had now worked for Harrison Turpentine Company for sev-eral years.

Chippers were the men who cut the bark off the side of the large pine trees, skinning it down four feet or so, and placing a cup on a nail at the bottom to catch the turpentine as it ran from the open gash on the tree. It was backbreak-ing work, but it would be regular pay immediately, not after a crop made, or failed, as the case might be. It was a more surefire thing. Of course, there had been times, especially during the war, when the men were paid in clacker, a kind of "money" Mr. Harrison had made up to use only at the commissary at the still. The tur-pentine still was composed of a number of little shanties, a few storage buildings, which housed the barrels of rosin, terra cotta cups, and tools. Then there was the commissary, a general type of store, where anything necessary for survival was available, — for a price! Many of the workers were uneducated blacks who seldom left the still except for work. After work, the men, and some of the women, usually gathered at the commissary, where they drank moonshine, sang or talked loud, and often got into fights. There had been one of those fights the night before. It ended terribly, with one man dead — cut from one side of his abdomen to the other with a knife. He was literally holding his intestines in his hands when he bled to death. Franklin told Nate the cutting had been over a woman. Funds were needed for the man's family, so a collection would be taken among the workers on Monday. Nate and Franklin would give generously, as always.

The men were trying to talk quietly so their wives couldn't hear, but Melissa got the gist of what had happened. Later she would quiz Nate. She often worried that he might incur the ire of some of those men, but he assured her regularly that he was in no way in danger of doing that. He never admitted to her that some of the men blamed the woods riders, the job he was now doing along with Franklin, when they didn't get paid as much as they thought they were owed. Franklin and Nate kept tabs on the number of trees these men chipped and the amount of rosin each of them emptied into their barrels. They were paid accordingly. Now and then someone thought he had collected more rosin or cut more trees than he had and became disgruntled. They were not drunk on moonshine when Franklin and Nate were dealing with them, however, and they were more reasonable.

Once Melissa got a break from her conversation with Grace and Martha, she sidled over to the men and asked, "Will that man who did the cutting be arrested?" The fellows looked sheepishly at each other, realizing they had not talked quietly enough.

"Probably so," Franklin told her. "But the trouble is that nobody in the community will ever testify against another. They are always afraid they will be next so crimes go unpunished. They more or less have their own brand of law down there at the still." Melissa cast a sideways glance at Nate, who was keeping quiet. She had known all along there really was danger in his job. She was thankful that he hadn't gone to work for a lumber company. At least he was home most nights.

Martha had just said, "Pearl, Heck and their boys are planning to come if nothing comes up," and about that time they heard the buggy coming. It sounded as if they were in a terrible rush. Realizing something was amiss, they all sat forward in their chairs looking in the direction of the hard pounding hooves. Matt realized immediately what the trouble was. There was a wall of black smoke to the northwest, slightly out of view as they sat on the porch. It could mean only one thing, a woods fire! "Quick, everyone!" he shouted. "A fire!" They set their plates and glasses down on the floor where they were sitting and ran for the gate just as Heck, Pearl and their family got there.

"It's a fire!" Heck confirmed. He quickly threw the reins over a fence post, securing the buggy carefully in case the horse became frightened over the fire. Then he ran for the edge of the clearing along with the others. Their children were six, four and six months; so Pearl told the six-year-old in emphatic tones to stay with his brothers and *not* to leave the porch under any circumstances. "Don't even go down into the yard!" she said. Sometimes snakes ran from a fire and took sanctuary in any safe place, like a yard clear of brush and fire. When she left, the boys did finish off everyone's cake left on their plates.

Nate had plowed a fire line at the end of the clearing, but they were often ineffective in the path of a hot fire fueled by a strong wind like the one that day. The wall of fire seemed to reach for fully a quarter of a mile, and as it reached huge pines with the turpentine cups and sap oozing out three of four feet high, they caught immediately. The bark was dry, also making it easy for the fire to climb the tree trunks in a hurry. There was tangled brush everywhere, very dry from the lack of rain, and the entire area was a tinderbox. Everyone had grabbed a small pine sapling, eight to ten feet tall, popped the bushy top out making a sort of broom and begun to beat the wall of rapidly moving fire beating furiously to put out the flames. There was no water except in Melissa's rain barrel where the spout from the roof poured down during a rain, and it was reserved for fighting a fire if the house caught. They would keep their attention on the woods, but if the house caught, everyone would immediately turn their full attention to it.

The wall of fire looked to Nate to be about twelve feet tall in places, and it was very hot. He had never seen more favorable conditions for a fire, which was one of the most dreaded things homesteaders ever faced. There was so much noise from the fire's roar along with crackling and crashing from the huge tree limbs falling, brush burning, and the snapping of twigs that it was almost impossible to hear, but suddenly Nate heard Melissa scream. She was a hundred yards from him nearer the branch. He started that way and could only make out her saying, "Ben! Ben!" Then he realized the problem. There was a huge wall of fire burning hotly and heading straight for the branch. It had turned while he was not looking in that direction. Suddenly, he could just make out Ben's silhouette in the smoke, and John was not with him. Then he could tell Ben had evidently soaked himself in the branch, which was quick thinking. He was wet all over and coming from the direction of the branch head. They must have seen the fire and started for home, but where was John? Ben merely pointed in that direction as he came out.

"John!" Nate began screaming, "John!" Melissa was starting toward the fire between her and the branch, but he caught her in time to stop her.

"John! John!" was all she had breath enough to say, and, breaking away, she again started toward the wall of fire, but Nate managed to stop her again.

"Stay here!" he shouted above the roar. "I am going!" He knew it would be at the risk of his life, but he had to get to John. "You see to Ben." With that, he pulled his coat, which he had never taken off after church, over his head and picking out the spot where the flames were lowest, he dived through them, then fell to the ground and rolled when he reached the other side of the wall. Fortunately, only his pants leg seemed to have caught. The ground was not yet hot enough to burn through his shoes. Screaming "John!" as loud as he could over and over again, he went in the direction Ben had come from. Thank God the head of the branch was not yet burning and, if he could find John, they could soak themselves, hunker down in the branch head and probably survive.

Nate realized he didn't have much time. The fire was within a hundred yards of the branch then. There were dry leaves and pine straw littering the ground like a thick mat, residual ones from two or three seasons, and all very dry. The descent to the head of the branch was quite steep, causing Nate to nearly lose his footing several times, but he managed to catch to vines and branches and get himself down to the small stream's edge. Still calling John, Nate was desperate and frantic. Where, he wondered *could* his son be? He stopped long enough to wet himself down thoroughly and, ignoring the burns on his legs and also his face, he continued looking through the thick brush and vines the best he could calling John's name every breath. The smoke was getting thicker. It was harder and harder to see and breathe. Finally, he thought he heard him. Then, suddenly, above the incessant noise of the large tree limbs crashing to the ground and the vines and trees crackling, he heard a small voice. "Dad!" John was saying, and then Nate saw him crouching downstream in the widest part, soaking wet and scared, but fine.

"My son! My son!" Nate said, and picking him up, hugged him as hard as he could. John wrapped his legs around Nate's waist and hugged back

"Dad, I did just what Ben told me to do. I hunkered down right where he said."

"Good for you, son, and I will get you out of here. Don't you worry. You are going to be just fine." Nate was starting up the hill carrying John, but the heat was too intense from the flames, and the ground was getting hotter and hotter. There were beginning to be coals everywhere — red, live, hot coals that would be hot for hours. Stumps, left where trees were cut for timber, were burning now. They would smolder for days. The dry bark on the tall stately pines was burning in places twenty or thirty feet high. It was a formidable sight to see and hear. Nate retreated and put John down. He was heavy, so taking the frightened child firmly by the hand, he started making his way to the south, hoping to get ahead of the fire and get around it and back to the others who were still working up on the ridge. The dense smoke was blowing right at them, making it harder and harder to see. Stepping back down into the water area, Nate's foot went into the mud causing him to turn his ankle. He gasped from the pain. It hurt severely, but there was no time to stop.

The little branch was no wider than two or three feet in most places, affording little protection from the intense wave of heat coming toward them as the fire progressed. The only thing the water could do was wet them and help their clothes not catch.

Nate had thought he knew every inch of that branch, from the spring box he had built to where it ran into the creek three miles further down, but things looked altogether different in the late afternoon, under the hill covered with thick trees. One could not see the sky for the trees overhead on a bright day, and it was really impossible under the present conditions. Nate knew the stream was big enough to stop the fire, but there was nothing to keep it from circling the head of the branch and meeting them on the other side. The vines and trees overhead could also burn, and had begun to do just that. They had no choice, however, but to try to outrun it. Now his ankle was hurting badly, and John was too little to make a lot of fast time. Nate knew he couldn't carry him very far, either.

"Pray, John," he said. "Pray! We must have God's help."

They seemed to be in a tunnel of fire. The heavy vines, many dead from previous years, were huge and were burning overhead now, along with the trees. Suddenly, as Nate pulled John along, he jerked the child violently to the side by his arm. A water moccasin slithered out of the way. He was running from the fire and in too much of a hurry to care about them. Nevertheless, it was a chilling sight.

Melissa was working as fast as she could to help their friends beat back the fire and keep it from jumping the fire line. It had jumped in a couple of places, but the men were able to beat it out in the new sections with their pine tops. Pearl was running to the house now and then to check on the boys. They were playing sweetly together and watching their little brother. She kept cautioning the oldest, Cal, to stay right on the porch with Joseph, the middle one, and James, the baby. Then she would run back and beat at the flames again as hard as she could.

Grace and Martha were no strangers to fighting woods fires, so they were working steadily with good success. It seemed the fire was slowing down. For one thing, the wind, as it got later, was dying down, and Matt, Franklin and Heck had started a back-burn against the raging flames that were so rapidly moving toward the south. It was, at last, becoming effective. They would burn a short segment at the time, so as to keep that under control, put it out, and then burn another. They continued doing the same thing over and over.

Nobody had heard anything from Nate and John, as far as Melissa knew, and she was becoming frantic with worry. She couldn't scream loud enough to get the attention of the men, so she ran down to Heck, who was nearest her.

"I am worried sick about John and Nate!" she screamed above the noise."Have you seen or heard anything?"

"No, but we are trying to back-burn to the branch so that we can get in to them," he shouted back. "Try not to worry. Nate will take care of John, and they will be all right."

With that, he went back to the task at hand. Melissa did as she was told, grabbed her pine top and continued the fight.

Nate and John were running out of any place to go. They couldn't see the sky, and but for the fact that Nate knew to continue down the stream, he would have been totally disoriented. The smoke was burning their eyes terribly. John was trying not to cry, but tears were running down his face from both smoke and fear. Nate pushed him on until suddenly a large dead limb burned in two and fell right in front of the child. He shrieked and jumped back, but Nate hoisted him high above it and then leaped over it himself. Finally, he felt they could go no farther, so he pushed John down into the bed of the little stream and fell down, covering the child's body with his own. There he prayed and begged God to get them out safely. He could not help but remember another time, among many since then, when he had knelt down in the yard and begged God to save his wife and child during John's birth. God heard that petition, spared Melissa and gave him a healthy son who was looking more like him every day. It was a miracle that Melissa stopped bleeding, and now they needed another miracle! "Please, dear Lord, help me to get my child out of here. I know You hear all prayers, and this time I beg you again to help us. Please, Lord."

Homestead

As they waited for a break in the wall of fire, Nate continued to pray. John, realizing the straits they were in, cried softly, but didn't panic. Nate's ankle was throbbing. He wondered if he might have broken it, but there was no time to look at it now. Shortly, if there were not a break, he would wrap John in his coat and try to run through the flames somewhere at their lowest point. He feared, with the fire on both sides of the branch, they would be hopelessly trapped. Then he heard Matt calling him. "Nate! Oh, Nate!" Matt was saying. At first, he couldn't believe his ears, but then he was sure he heard plainly. John heard him, too.

"Daddy, listen. It's Uncle Matt. I heard him!"

"Matt!" Nate yelled as loud as he could. "We're here. We're coming" He grabbed John's hand and they began to hurry toward Matt's voice as fast as Nate's ankle would permit. Matt kept calling them so they could find him, and then they ran right into him. Matt was dirty, smoky and exhausted, but he was all right. He directed the frazzled pair around the smoldering areas.

"Come on, fellows. We will get you out," he told them. "Hey, what did you do?" he asked as he realized Nate had hurt his ankle. "Here, let me help." He put his arm around his friend's shoulder, and together they walked over the area where the men had burned the backfire. There were still little patches of fire on some of the tufts of grass, but they were nothing compared with what Nate had gone through to get to John, and then Franklin grabbed John and carried him over those spots. The ordeal was over, but Nate had injuries to be treated. His clothes were ruined, and he had burns on his face and one leg.

Telling the others to go on ahead, Nate stopped to get his breath. He was suffering from smoke inhalation and exhaustion, and suddenly, he began to vomit. As soon as that was over, he went on to catch up with the others. Melissa, realizing John and Nate were both safe when they all got to the clearing, ran to them and began hugging both at the same time, crying tears of relief and joy.

"Oh, thank God you are safe!" she kept saying over and over.

"The cabin?" Nate asked.

"Untouched," Heck said. "We got there in time."

"Thank God," Melissa continued to say.

"Yes, it was God who did it and my friends, who helped by starting the backfire. Thank you all. I was beginning to think we might not make it." Nate said. Nate had decided, while in the desperate situation, that if they got out alive, he would leave the homestead area for another life. He had had enough of the hard life, strain and struggle. He wanted to get his family and himself out of that harsh place where there was one crisis after another. He was tired. Bone tired, and he could kick himself for staying so long as it was.

John was unhurt, but Melissa discovered Nate's injuries and insisted he stop and take off his shoe. His ankle was grossly sprained and swollen, but they decided it was not broken, because he could walk on it and wiggle his toes. His eyebrows, eyelashes and hair were singed, and he had a rather large burn on his leg where his pants caught. His face was also scraped by a limb, no doubt, and burned in places, but not seriously. All in all, he had fared quite well, considering what he had been through.

The house was safe, too, and when Nate thought about it a little more on the way to the house, he knew he couldn't leave. After all, they were keepers of the land. They were strong, hearty stock who had their God to see them through. They were *homesteaders,* and they would never leave!